Don't miss the beginning of The New Jedi Order series, which begins with VECTOR PRIME, by R. A. Salvatore!

They had been living on the very edge of disaster for so very long, fighting battles, literally, for decades, running from bounty hunters and assassins. Even the first time Han and Leia had met, on the Death Star, of all places, and in the gallows of the place, to boot! So many times, it seemed, one or more of them should have died.

And yet, in a strange way, that close flirting with death had only made Han think them all the more invulnerable. They could dodge any blaster, or piggy-back on the side of an asteroid, or climb out a garbage chute, or . . .

But not anymore. Not now. The bubble of security was gone.

To Han Solo, the galaxy suddenly seemed a more dangerous place by far . . .
—from *Vector Prime*

Now join veteran Star Wars author Michael A. Stackpole as he continues the adventure in the galaxy that Han Solo calls: a more dangerous place by far . . .

STAR WARS

THE NEW JEDI ORDER

DARK TIDE
ONSLAUGHT

MICHAEL A. STACKPOLE

ARROW

Published in the United Kingdom in 2000 by
Arrow Books

1 3 5 7 9 10 8 6 4 2

First published in the United Kingdom in 2000 by Arrow

Arrow Books
The Random House Group Limited
20 Vauxhall Bridge Road, London, SW1V 2SA

Random House Australia (Pty) Limited
20 Alfred Street, Milsons Point, Sydney, New South Wales 2061, Australia

Random House New Zealand Limited
18 Poland Road, Glenfield
Auckland 10, New Zealand

Random House (Pty) Limited
Endulini, 5a Jubilee Road, Parktown 2193, South Africa

The Random House Group Limited Reg. No. 954009

www.randomhouse.co.uk

A CIP catalogue record for this book is available from the British Library

Papers used by Random House are natural, recyclable products made from wood grown in
sustainable forests. The manufacturing processes conform to the environmental regulations
of the country of origin.

Printed and bound in Australia by Griffin Press Pty Ltd

ISBN 0 09 940993 3

DEDICATION

To Timothy Zahn
For all the obvious reasons, and a few more.
(Next time we're in Tasmania, I want to try driving.)

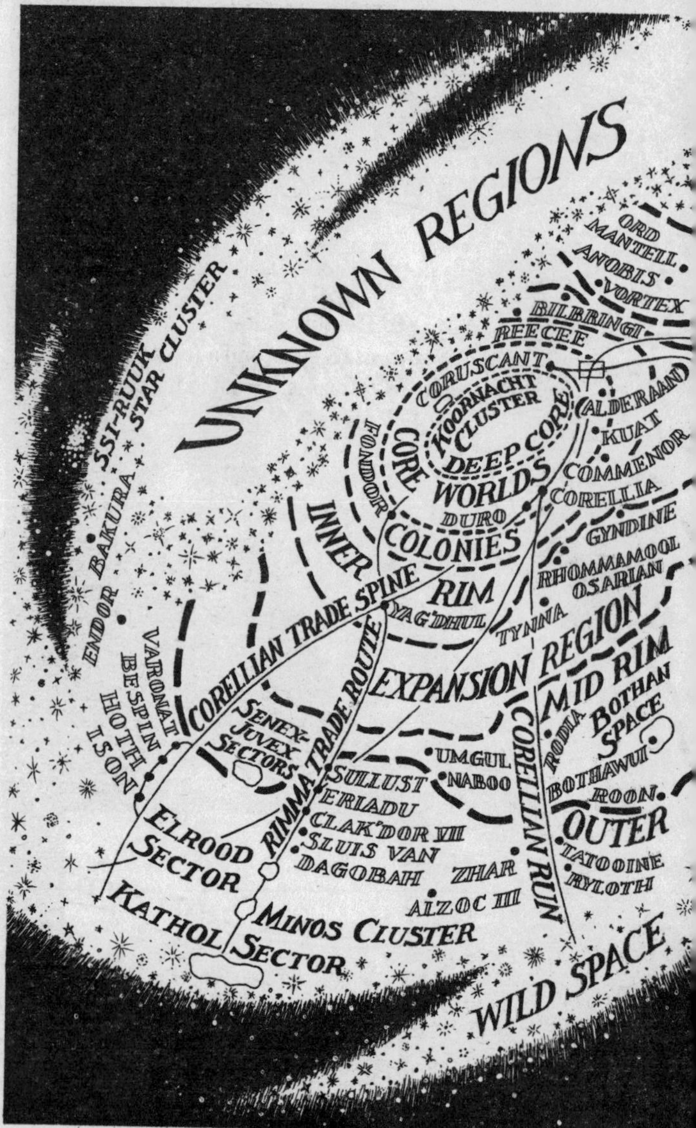
UNKNOWN REGIONS
SSI-RUUK STAR CLUSTER
BAKURA
ENDOR
VARONAT
BESPIN
HOTH
ISON
ORD MANTELL
ANOBIS
VORTEX
BILBRINGI
REECEE
CORUSCANT
KOORNACHT CLUSTER
DEEP CORE
ALDERAAN
KUAT
COMMENOR
CORE WORLDS
FONDOR
CORELLIA
INNER
DURO
COLONIES
GYNDINE
RHOMMAMOOL
OSARIAN
CORELLIAN TRADE SPINE
RIM
YAG'DHUL
TYNNA
EXPANSION REGION
MID RIM
RODIA
BOTHAN SPACE
BOTHAWUI
SENEX-JUVEX SECTORS
RIMMA TRADE ROUTE
UMGUL
NABOO
SULLUST
ERIADU
CLAK'DOR VII
SLUIS VAN
DAGOBAH
ZHAR
AIZOC III
CORELLIAN RUN
ROON
OUTER
TATOOINE
RYLOTH
ELROOD SECTOR
KATHOL SECTOR
MINOS CLUSTER
WILD SPACE

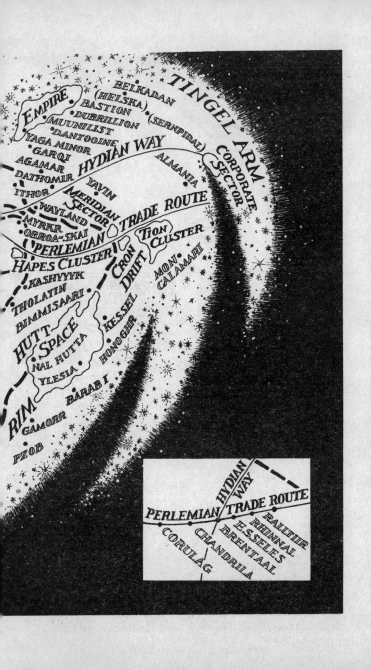

STAR WARS: THE NOVELS

44 YEARS BEFORE	32 YEARS BEFORE	22 YEARS BEFORE	20 YEARS BEFORE
STAR WARS: A New Hope	*STAR WARS: A New Hope*	*STAR WARS: A New Hope*	*STAR WARS: A New Hope*
Jedi Apprentice #1–2	*Star Wars:* Episode I The Phantom Menace	*Star Wars:* Episode II	*Star Wars:* Episode III

3 YEARS AFTER	3.5 YEARS AFTER	4 YEARS AFTER	6.5–7.5 YEARS AFTER
STAR WARS: A New Hope	*STAR WARS: A New Hope*	*STAR WARS: A New Hope*	*STAR WARS: A New Hope*
Star Wars: Episode V The Empire Strikes Back Tales of the Bounty Hunters	Shadows of the Empire	*Star Wars:* Episode VI Return of the Jedi Tales from Jabba's Palace THE BOUNTY HUNTER WARS: The Mandalorian Armor Slave Ship Hard Merchandise The Truce at Bakura	X-Wing: Rogue Squadron X-Wing: Wedge's Gamble X-Wing: The Krytos Trap X-Wing: The Bacta War X-Wing: Wraith Squadron X-Wing: Iron Fist X-Wing: Solo Command

14 YEARS AFTER	16–17 YEARS AFTER	17 YEARS AFTER	18 YEARS AFTER
STAR WARS: A New Hope	*STAR WARS: A New Hope*	*STAR WARS: A New Hope*	*STAR WARS: A New Hope*
The Crystal Star	THE BLACK FLEET CRISIS TRILOGY: Before the Storm Shield of Lies Tyrant's Test	The New Rebellion	THE CORELLIAN TRILOGY: Ambush at Corellia Assault at Selonia Showdown at Centerpoint

— What Happened When?

10–0 YEARS BEFORE
STAR WARS: A New Hope

THE HAN SOLO TRILOGY:
The Paradise Snare
The Hutt Gambit
Rebel Dawn

APPROX. 5–2 YRS. BEFORE
STAR WARS: A New Hope

THE ADVENTURES OF LANDO CALRISSIAN:
Lando Calrissian and the Mindharp of Sharu
Lando Calrissian and the Flamewind of Oseon
Lando Calrissian and the Starcave of ThonBoka

THE HAN SOLO ADVENTURES:
Han Solo at Stars' End
Han Solo's Revenge
Han Solo and the Lost Legacy

STAR WARS: Episode IV A New Hope

0–3 YEARS AFTER
STAR WARS: A New Hope

Tales from the Mos Eisley Cantina
Splinter of the Mind's Eye

8 YEARS AFTER
STAR WARS: A New Hope

The Courtship of Princess Leia

9 YEARS AFTER
STAR WARS: A New Hope

X-Wing Isard's Revenge
THE THRAWN TRILOGY:
Heir to the Empire
Dark Force Rising
The Last Command

11 YEARS AFTER
STAR WARS: A New Hope

THE JEDI ACADEMY TRILOGY:
Jedi Search
Dark Apprentice
Champions of the Force
I, Jedi

12–13 YEARS AFTER
STAR WARS: A New Hope

Children of the Jedi
Darksaber
Planet of Twilight
X-Wing: Starfighters of Adumar

19 YEARS AFTER
STAR WARS: A New Hope

THE HAND OF THRAWN DUOLOGY:
Specter of the Past
Vision of the Future

22 YEARS AFTER
STAR WARS: A New Hope

JUNIOR JEDI KNIGHTS:
The Golden Globe
Lyric's World
Promises
Anakin's Quest
Vader's Fortress
Kenobi's Blade

23–24 YEARS AFTER
STAR WARS: A New Hope

YOUNG JEDI KNIGHTS:
Heirs of the Force
Shadow Academy
The Lost Ones
Lightsabers
The Darkest Knight
Jedi Under Siege
Shards of Alderaan
Diversity Alliance
Delusions of Grandeur
Jedi Bounty
The Emperor's Plague
Return to Ord Mantell
Trouble on Cloud City
Crisis at Crystal Reef

25 YEARS AFTER
STAR WARS: A New Hope

THE NEW JEDI ORDER:
Vector Prime
Dark Tide: Onslaught

ACKNOWLEDGMENTS

This book could not have been completed without the tireless efforts of a host of folks. The author wishes to thank the following people for their contributions: Sue Rostoni, Allan Kausch, and Lucy Autrey Wilson of Lucas Licensing Ltd.; Shelly Shapiro, Jennifer Smith, and Steve Saffel of Del Rey; Ricia Mainhardt, my agent; R. A. Salvatore, Kathy Tyers, and Jim Luceno, my partners in crime; Peet Janes, Timothy Zahn, Tish Pahl, and Jennifer Roberson; and, as always, Liz Danforth for keeping me sane through the whole process.

DRAMATIS PERSONAE

Elegos A'Kla; New Republic senator (male Caamasi)
Lando Calrissian; Dubrillion planetary administrator (male
  human)
Colonel Gavin Darklighter; Rogue Squadron (male human)
Borsk Fey'lya; New Republic chief of state (male Bothan)
Corran Horn; Jedi Knight (male human)
Danni Quee; ExGal Society (female human)
Ganner Rhysode; Jedi Knight (male human)
Shedao Shai; Yuuzhan Vong Commander
Luke Skywalker; Jedi Master (male human)
Mara Jade Skywalker; Jedi Knight (female human)
Anakin Solo; Jedi Knight (male human)
Jacen Solo; Jedi Knight (male human)
Jaina Solo; Jedi Knight (female human)
Leia Organa Solo; New Republic diplomat (female human)

PROLOGUE

Standing there, on the bridge of his Nebulon-B frigate, the pirate Urias Xhaxin clasped his cybernetic left hand to the small of his back with his right hand. He stared straight ahead at the tunnel of light into which his ship, the *Free Lance,* flew. Given the nature of the frigate's design, with the bridge far forward, he felt as if he were flying there alone, making his way deep into the territory of the Outer Rim where no one in his right mind would be found.

He glanced back over his shoulder at the Twi'lek working the navigation station. "Time to reversion, Khwir?"

The Twi'lek's long lekku twitched. "Five minutes."

Xhaxin turned on the comlink clipped to his jacket's collar. "All hands, all hands, this is Xhaxin. Red and Blue Squadrons, prepare for launch. You will be moving to the outbound vectors and disabling the smaller yachts. Gunners, we will aim for the escorts. Everyone look sharp and this may be the last run we ever need make. In and out, clean and easy. You'll all do well, I know. Xhaxin out."

A dark-haired woman stepped up beside Xhaxin. "You really think this haul will earn us enough to retire?"

"It depends upon the quality of retirement you desire, Dr. Karl." The white-haired, white-bearded man turned and smiled at her. "Your skills will earn you a good living almost anywhere in the New Republic, and your share of this raid should be enough to buy you a new identity or two."

Anet Karl frowned. "Ever since the peace between the Imperial Remnant and the New Republic six years ago, we've been forced to go after smaller and smaller targets. The New Republic never condoned what we did, but they turned a blind eye to it while the Imperials were still a threat. Pickings were good as unreconstructed Imperials fled out here to the Remnant, but that trade has been trickling off. Is this raid going to be different?"

Xhaxin pursed his lips for a moment, then lowered his voice. "It's a fair question you ask. The answer is yes, I can feel it in my bones. This raid will be like nothing we've seen in the last five years."

Anet smiled mischievously, her brown eyes sparkling. "You're not going Jedi on me, are you? The Force tells you about this raid?"

"No, I'm far more practical than the Jedi, and more dangerous, too." He spread his arms. "We've nearly nine hundred crew on this ship—nine times the number of Jedi in the whole of the galaxy. And while they have the Force to aid them, I have two powerful allies with me: greed and arrogance."

"Oh, your plan was good."

"Correction, my plan was brilliant." Xhaxin laughed. "We let a couple of ships go free because they're traveling together, then I set up a guy who says he can organize convoys through deep space to the Remnant. We had people demanding positions in our convoy. In fact, they paid well for the privilege of traveling safely."

"But no refunds, correct?" The doctor smiled. "The credits they've spent are just a down payment?"

"Exactly. They gathered at Garqi, have headed out, and the last of them should be hitting the rendezvous point in ten minutes. We'll round up what's already there, then pick off the last one and go." Xhaxin smoothed his mustache with his flesh-and-blood right hand. "It's been a grand run. This last raid—it will be remembered. I would have had history recall me in other ways, but this will be good enough, especially if all of you can be rewarded for your hard work."

Anet Karl looked at the various humans and aliens busy at their duty stations on the bridge. "We had no love lost on the Empire either, Captain. We owe you our thanks for keeping us alive and allowing us to pay them back all these years. We'd keep going, too—"

"I know, but the New Republic has made peace with the Remnant." Xhaxin sighed. "One cannot underestimate the allure of peace. I think, perhaps, we've finally earned some ourselves."

"Ten seconds to reversion, Captain."

"Thank you, Khwir." Xhaxin waved a hand toward the viewport. "Behold, Doctor, our destiny."

The tunnel of light shattered into countless stars of varying hues. They'd come out into the middle of nowhere, literally— a point in space that had been selected only because gravitational forces made it perfect for speeding the way from Garqi to Bastion in the Imperial Remnant. *This place is supposed to be empty.*

Empty it was not. Aside from the burning wreckage of a twisted freighter spinning madly, life pods and yachts darting about, a large object hung there in space. Xhaxin thought at first it had to be an asteroid because of its appearance, uneven surface, and torpid pace. Other smaller asteroids seemed to orbit around it, then streaked out on attack runs on the yachts.

And now they're orienting on us! Xhaxin spun away from the viewport. "Full shields up, now! Deploy the fighters. I don't know how some fool managed to fit a hyperdrive core to an asteroid, but he's not stealing our ships! Gunnery, get a firing solution on that big rock and open it up."

"As ordered, Captain!"

Even as he issued orders and pondered making a planetoid somehow mobile, Xhaxin knew that that line of reasoning did not explain the smaller rocks that moved like starfighters. "Sensors, what's going on out there?"

A Duros looked up through holographic displays of data, his long face wearing an expression that was even more morose than usual. "Gravitic anomalies, sir, everywhere."

"Tractor beams? Gravity-well generators?"

"Different, sir." The Duros frowned as a wash of data filled his holograph with overlapping spheres of color. "Focused, tighter beams, more powerful."

The *Free Lance*'s turbolaser batteries opened up, sending long streams of sizzling red bolts at the asteroid. The shots looked to be on target, then deviated sharply in their flight. The bolts sharpened their angle of attack, coming together nearly half a kilometer before they hit the asteroid. Xhaxin expected the beams to flash through that new focal point and still hit the target, but instead they vanished.

"What happened? Guns, sensors, what happened?"

His gunner, an Iotran named Mirip Pag, shook his head in disbelief. "We had firing solutions, Captain. We were on target."

The Duros, Lun Deverin, stabbed a quivering finger at a small sphere in a holograph. "A gravitic anomaly pulled the shots in. It's as if they're using a black hole to shield themselves."

Xhaxin turned to look at the data and watched as the sphere in question expanded and moved toward the frigate. At the moment of contact, a jolt ran through the ship. Alarms began to sound, announcing that the starboard shield had collapsed.

"Come about to a heading of 57 mark 12, ahead full. Shear off whatever that beam is."

"Another one coming in, Captain. It will take the aft shield . . ."

Pen Grasha, the *Free Lance*'s starfighter control officer, shouted above the warning sirens. "Captain, our fighters are having their shields stripped. Their blasters and lasers are not getting through to the enemy."

The Duros waved a hand, then grabbed his sensor station in a tight grip. "Brace for impact. They've fired upon us."

Impact? Xhaxin turned toward the viewport and saw a sizzling golden ball of something—plasma?—flash past. It caught the frigate in midmaneuver, hitting just port of center. The port shield caught the blast, but collapsed in seconds, sending a shower of sparks through the bridge and skittering one crewman across the floor. A heartbeat later whatever had gotten through the shield slammed into the *Free Lance*'s armored hull.

Thank goodness we have extra armor. Xhaxin had devoted a lot of resources to reinforcing the armor on the frigate. It had stood up to shots from an Imperial Star Destroyer before, and they'd lived to tell about it. *We also ran away so we could tell about it.*

The impact momentarily knocked the ship's artificial gravity generators out of phase, so Xhaxin flew from his feet and into Dr. Karl. Within a second, gravity returned, dropping both of them to the deck, but neither landed too hard. Xhaxin rose to one knee and helped the doctor up into a sitting position as he turned to look at the Duros. "What was that?"

"I don't know, Captain, but it's still eating into the hull." The blue-skinned alien paled. "I project a hull breach on deck seven in twenty seconds."

"Evac the area and close the bulkheads."

"More shots incoming!"

No! This can't be happening! Xhaxin's hands, both flesh and metal, convulsed into fists. He pushed aside the despair and panic raging through him. *Time to be the sort of man that causes a crew to be so loyal.*

"Pen, recall our fighters. Load those without hyperdrives first. Khwir, plot me a jump out of here."

The Twi'lek's lekku palsied. "The gravitic anomalies are constantly shifting. Calculating a jump solution is impossible."

"Are they enough to prevent us from jumping?"

"No, but—"

Xhaxin snarled, then staggered to a knee as another shot from the asteroid shook the frigate. "Then jump blind. Send the coordinates to our fighters, but jump blind."

"Captain, a blind jump could kill us."

"A blind jump *might* kill us." Xhaxin stabbed a finger at the viewport. "They *will* kill us. Do it, Khwir, do it, *now!*"

"As ordered, Captain." The Twi'lek started punching

coordinates into the navicomputer. "Ready to jump in five seconds, Captain. Four, three . . ."

Xhaxin looked at the viewport and saw a glowing golden ball expanding to fill it. He didn't know who his attackers were, why they were there, or how their weapons functioned. As he pondered those things the view of space exploded. In that moment, somehow he knew that while having the answers to his questions might bring him some inner peace, the same would not be said of the New Republic.

CHAPTER ONE

Standing near the head of the senate chamber, waiting to be invited to the dais by Chief of State Borsk Fey'lya, Leia Organa Solo found herself a bit nervous. Years rolled back—decades, in fact—reminding her how she had felt when she first entered the Imperial Senate as the youngest person ever elected to such high office. She'd stood as a candidate to help her father, Bail Organa, continue his opposition of Palpatine and the madness that would permit things like Death Stars to be created.

I was young then, very young, and understandably nervous. She looked around at the massive chamber and across the sea of senators filling it. It didn't have the grandeur of the old chamber, the one in which she had first served, but she felt a rich sense of tradition in it from the New Republic's days. Back in the Imperial era—after Palpatine had seized full power—there were no more than a handful of non-humans in the chamber, and then they were just aides to human senators. Now the humans were in the minority, much as they had been in the Old Republic. She could see Senator Viqi Shesh of Kuat and one of her telbuns, and Senator Cal Omas from Alderaan, but beyond them she had a hard time seeing more humans.

And it's not just age catching up with my eyes. She smiled to herself, not wanting to be reminded of how much of her life had already passed by. Much of it had been spent here on

7

Coruscant, helping form the New Republic into the star-spanning confederation of worlds that had emerged from the Empire's shadow. *Or I was out fighting the Empire, being shot at. In here the attacks were more subtle, but almost as lethal.* She shivered as she recalled the old senate chamber even being bombed once.

Glancing back over her shoulder, she saw Danni Quee, the young woman who barely two months ago had survived an attack and capture by an aggressive alien group that had assaulted several worlds on the galaxy's Outer Rim. Danni had been working at a research site used to monitor space beyond the edge of the galaxy and had collected some evidence to suggest the invaders had actually come from another galaxy. Their ruthless tactics, coupled with the sheer economics of mounting an invasion from a distant galaxy, suggested to Leia that the aliens had to be intent on taking a great portion of this galaxy for their own. She'd come to the senate to apprise the New Republic of this threat and enlist aid for the Rim worlds that would be facing the brunt of the alien onslaught.

Beside the petite, brunette woman stood Bolpuhr, Leia's Noghri bodyguard. The Noghri were devoted to Leia and her brother, Luke, because of their efforts to repair the damage done to the Noghri homeworld of Honoghr by the Empire. In their gratitude, the Noghri warded Leia and her family with a fierce loyalty that was second only to that of a Wookiee with a life debt.

The pitch of Borsk Fey'lya's voice shifted out of a deep drone to something a bit higher. Leia remembered how his voice would rise when he felt stressed. It brought her head up, and she focused her attention on what the Bothan was saying.

". . . And so, it is my distinct pleasure to welcome back to this chamber a woman who has been more at home here than anyone else in the senate's history. I present to you Leia Organa Solo, envoy from Dubrillion."

And about time, too, Leia thought. *You've been giving me the runaround long enough.* She'd been trying to get this audience for weeks.

Fey'lya turned away from the podium and waved her forward. The Bothan had chosen to wear a sand-colored robe that was only a shade or two darker than his cream-colored fur. Violet piping that matched his eyes trimmed it. Leia found the robe reminiscent of the simple garments Mon Mothma used to wear when addressing the senate or the people, but somehow it failed to grant the Bothan the air of simple nobility it had given Mon Mothma.

Leia had chosen to wear black boots and slacks, with a cerulean tunic. She also wore her hair up, letting her entire outfit and demeanor hint at the martial encounters that were the basis for her report. She knew it made her distinctly underdressed for the opulent senate, but she also hoped it would make some of those present harken back to the days when battle dress was the order of the day and decisions had to be made quickly.

"Thank you, Chief Fey'lya. Esteemed senators and honored guests, I bring you the greetings and well wishes of the people of Dubrillion. It is their wish I inform you of a grave crisis in the Outer Rim. A previously unknown species has launched a series of attacks in the Rim. They wiped out the ExGal-4 station on Belkadan, attacked the world of Dubrillion, destroyed the New Republic ship *Rejuvenator* at Helska, and annihilated the world Sernpidal by crashing its moon into it. We managed to locate the alien base at Helska 4 and destroy it, but this does not end the threat."

Leia looked up at her audience and was surprised at how many senators seemed to be bored, as if she were the narrator for some Kuati manners-play. *Well, I've not told them anything they don't already know, but now they have to acknowledge it and deal with it.* She cleared her voice and glanced at the datapad on the podium for her notes.

"On Belkadan, Luke Skywalker found evidence of an ecological disaster that radically altered the atmospheric composition of the world. This disaster has been traced to an alien agent who was present on the world and slain there after he attacked Mara Jade Skywalker and my brother. The evidence seems to suggest that the aliens were preparing the world to be used as a base for invasion."

Before she could continue, a hunchbacked, saurian senator representing the various Baragwin communities stood
slowly. "If it would please the senate, I would ask the speaker
if she is the same Leia Organa Solo who undertook to me-
diate the Rhommamool-Osarian dispute."

Leia's eyes narrowed as she lifted her chin. "Senator Wynl
is well aware that I am the same person who went to try to
broker peace in that conflict."

"And was it not the action of a rash Jedi Knight that forced
the Osarians to launch the attack that embroiled the system in
war, killing Nom Anor, the Rhommamoolian leader, in the
process?"

Leia held her hands up. "With all due respect, Senator, the
Rhommamool-Osarian conflict has little or nothing to do
with the invasion I'm talking about."

Borsk Fey'lya turned toward Leia from his position on the
dais to her right. "Little or nothing? This would suggest there
might be some sort of a connection."

She nodded uneasily. "When the invader attacked Mara,
he first tried to destroy Artoo—the R2 astromech droid my
brother uses. The alien was shouting the same sort of anti-
droid rhetoric that the Red Knights of Life on Rhommamool
used in their crusades."

The Bothan blinked his violet eyes. "So you are suggesting
that these Red Knights are behind the poisoning of Belkadan, the destruction of Sernpidal, and the attack on Dubrillion? And they had weapons sufficient to drag a moon from
orbit, yet were not able to defend their leaders against an attack by the Osarians? Am I understanding you correctly?"

"No, I don't believe you are, Chief Fey'lya." Leia let a hint
of iciness enter her voice. "I don't believe the alien on
Belkadan was influenced by the Red Knights, but it is possible that the Red Knights are part of a covert plot to disrupt
the New Republic."

Another senator, this one a Rodian, stood. "You would
have us believe, Envoy, that your effort failed because of a
conspiracy born from outside the galaxy?"

"That's not what I'm saying."

Niuk Niuv, the senator from Sullust, rose to his feet. "I don't believe it is, either. I believe you are trying to deflect us from the threat the Jedi present to the New Republic. It was a Jedi who raised the tension level of the Osarians, triggering that war. You tell us a Jedi reported to you about this alien, and about what he said. I am not so stupid that I cannot see the effort of a Jedi to turn us away from trouble their order has spawned."

"The Jedi on Belkadan was my brother, Luke Skywalker, Jedi Master!"

"And who would more want to have the errors of his disciples forgotten?"

Leia forced her grip on the podium to slacken. "I am well aware of the controversy surrounding the Jedi, but I ask you, in all good conscience, to focus beyond that debate and concentrate on what I'm telling you. An invasion has been mounted from outside this galaxy, and it will destroy the New Republic if you do not act to stop it now."

A human senator Leia failed to recognize rose to speak. "Forgive me, but it is a well-known and long-established fact that a hyperspace disturbance on the edge of the galaxy makes travel into or out of the galaxy impossible. This supposed invasion could not have taken place."

Leia shook her head. "If that barrier does exist, they found a way around it. They were here, and there is ample evidence of their invasion in the Outer Rim."

The Quarren, Pwoe, rose and brushed fingertips over his pointed chin. "I am confused, then, Envoy. You told us that you had been part of an effort to destroy the invading force. I was led to believe you had been successful."

"We were."

"So there have been no more sightings of these invaders since then?"

"No, but that—"

"And do you have evidence to link them to the Red Knights other than hearsay about comments by a creature that is now dead?"

"No, but—"

"You do have physical evidence of the invaders?"

"Some. A couple of bodies, a couple of their coralskippers."

Fey'lya smiled, flashing sharp teeth. "Coralskippers?"

Leia closed her eyes and sighed. "These aliens appear to rely on genetically engineered biomechanical creatures. Their fighter craft are, well, grown out of something called yorik coral."

The Bothan shook his head. "You're telling us that they used rocks to kill a Star Destroyer?"

"Yes."

Pwoe glanced down at his desk, then looked up with a malevolent glint in his black eyes. "Leia, as one who has looked up to you in the past, I beg you, please, stop now. You cannot know how pathetic you appear to be. You chose to leave public life. For you to come here now, with this story, in such a bald attempt to take back control from our hands, is a pitiful thing."

"What?" Leia blinked her astonishment away. "You think I came here to make a power grab?"

"I am given nothing else to think." Pwoe opened his hands and took in the whole of the chamber. "You want to protect your brother, your children, for they are all Jedi, and I can understand that. It is also clear you do not think we are capable of surviving any catastrophe without you, but the plain fact is that things have gone well since the resolution of the Bothan situation. We all understand the human lust for power, and we have admired you for suppressing it for so long, but now, this—"

"No, no, that's not my intention at all." Leia looked aghast at the senators. "What I am telling you is true, it's real. We may have thrown back a vanguard, but they're coming."

The Sullustan senator covered his ears with his hands. "Please, Leia, no more, no more. Your loyalty to the Jedi is laudable, but this attempt to make us think they might be useful because of some nebulous threat—it is beneath you!"

"But very *human* of her," the Baragwin sniffed.

An invisible fist seemed to close around Leia's heart and

squeeze hard. Her elbows bent and she rested her forearms on the podium. "You *must* listen to me!"

"Leia, please, do what Mon Mothma has done." Pwoe's voice filled with pity. "Fade away quietly. The government is ours now. Let us remember you fondly, as someone who transcended her humanity."

Leia looked out at the senators and wished age had dulled enough of her vision so she couldn't see the looks of contempt being directed at her. *They won't see because they can't allow themselves to see. They need to be in control so badly they will ignore danger instead of admitting there is a crisis. They will lose everything just because they want to prove they are in control.* Their willful ignorance left her drained and speechless, with the weight of their pity and contempt crushing her down.

This can't be happening. Everything we have gained to be thrown away so foolishly. Leia's grip on the podium slackened as she began to back away from it. *To lose everything . . .*

A strong, sharp voice cut through the low murmuring in the senate chamber. "How dare you? How dare any of you speak to her this way?" In the middle of the room, a golden-furred alien, long and lean, with purple striping rising up and back from the corners of his eyes, rose to his full height. "If not for this woman and the sacrifices of her family, none of us would be here, and most of us would be dead."

Elegos A'Kla opened his three-fingered hands. "Your blatant ingratitude lends credence to the Imperial vision of our being mere beasts!"

The Rodian senator stabbed a sucker-tipped finger at the Caamasi. "Don't forget, she was one of them!"

Elegos's eyes narrowed, and Leia felt a wave of pain wash off him. "Can you say that without realizing how feeble-minded it makes you sound? To lump her with Imperials is pure prejudice—prejudice of the sort that the Imperials flaunted when they oppressed us."

Niuk Niuv waved away the Caamasi's comments with a flip of his hand. "Your criticism would bear more weight, Senator A'Kla, were you not known to have collaborated with

Jedi before. Your sympathies for them run deep. Was not your uncle one of them?"

Elegos drew his head back, emphasizing his height and slender form. "My loyalties to friends and relatives who were Jedi do not blind me to what Leia has tried to say here. You may choose to see the Jedi as a threat—and even I would acknowledge that the activities of some leave me cold—but she is reporting a new threat, perhaps a greater one, to the New Republic. To willfully ignore it so you may pursue your own glory is the height of irresponsibility."

Pwoe's tentacles curled up in anger. "This is well and good for you to say, A'Kla, but your people and their survival owes much to Leia and her family. Many of you died on Alderaan, and it has been human guilt and charity that has protected you for decades. Your rising to her defense is not surprising, akin to a nek battle dog licking the hand of the trainer that beats it."

Leia felt that comment sink home and returned to the podium. Her voice remained low and placid, despite the anger spiking inside of her. Though she resented calling upon a Jedi calming technique, she did, allowing her to focus. Her expression sharpened and her gaze swept out over the assembled senators.

"You will choose to project on me all manner of sinister motives. This is your right. I can even understand old resentments being transferred to me, though I would have thought my history would have shown you where my heart is. Now I don't even expect you to listen to me, I guess. You see the New Republic as your own, and I applaud your rising to take responsibility for it. Despite what you might think or want to believe, you make me very proud.

"Where you disappoint me is in turning on yourselves. The New Republic's strength has always come from its union of diverse peoples." She shrugged, then straightened up. "I will leave for you all that we have learned about these invaders. I hope you will find the information useful when you find a time to employ it."

Borsk Fey'lya regarded her closely as she stepped back from the podium. "What will you do now, Leia?"

She huffed quietly and stared at him for a moment. *Afraid I will stage a coup to get my way, Borsk? Do you think I have that much power?* "I'll do what I need to. The New Republic may have abandoned me, but I've not abandoned it. This threat must be stopped."

The fur on the back of the Bothan's neck rose slowly. "You have no official standing. You can't just commandeer equipment, issue orders, and the like."

She slowly shook her head, then smiled as Elegos appeared at her side. "I know the rules, Chief Fey'lya, both those publicly codified and those by which the game is truly played. I have no desire to pit myself against you, so don't make it necessary."

Elegos rested a hand on Leia's shoulder. "*This* senator wishes to learn more about the threat. I trust, Chief Fey'lya, there will be no interference with my investigation."

"Interference, no . . ." The Bothan's violet eyes became slits. "Be careful, however. Curiosity will be permitted, but treason will be punished. Do you understand?"

Elegos nodded and Leia joined him. "Your message is received, Chief Fey'lya. Senator A'Kla and I will be very careful, and so should you be. A judgment of treason in a time like this could haunt you through history, *if* the invaders leave anyone alive to care."

CHAPTER TWO

Snug in the X-wing simulator cockpit, Colonel Gavin Darklighter, Rogue Squadron's commanding officer, flicked his right thumb against the ring he wore on that hand. Apprehension gripped him, but he knew there was no sense in stalling a second longer. He glanced over his shoulder at the R2-Delta astromech droid sitting behind him. "Okay, Catch, run the simulation designated 'skipchaser.' "

The little gold-and-white droid tootled pleasantly, and the simulator cockpit came alive with lights and data scrolling on the primary screen. Despite the years of refits the little droid had undergone in Gavin's service—including requisite memory wipes and programming upgrades—it always greeted him with a brief summary of the weather on Tatooine and Coruscant. Gavin appreciated that little bit of pleasantry, which is why he'd not traded the droid in for a newer model—though the Delta upgrade had been most welcome for speeding up navigational computations.

The biggest change in his relationship with the droid had been its name. In the early days he'd called it Jawaswag, figuring that any Jawa would love to have the droid. Later, after the Thrawn crisis, a group of Jawas had tried to steal Jawaswag, but the droid had fended them off and actually hurt one. From that point forward Gavin had taken to calling the droid Toughcatch, which had just become shortened to Catch.

The simulator's visual field filled with stars and then an asteroid belt, into which Gavin guided the X-wing. It felt much like the old T-65s Rogue Squadron used to fly when he'd first joined the Rebellion, but the T-65A3 model was a couple of generations advanced over the original models. While not as slick as the new XJ model, the A3 had improved shields and lasers that boasted improvements in accuracy and power. The peace reached with the Imperial Remnant meant that there were few competent foes to test the new fighters against— and the fighter had proved quite lethal when unleashed on pirates in the Rimward regions of the New Republic.

Gavin glanced at his primary monitor, but nothing was popping up as a threat. He punched up a supplemental data plug-in that expanded the available target profiles. "Catch, give me biologicals down to the size of mynocks and anything that appears to be moving erratically or on a course that is beyond norm for orbital debris."

The droid whistled an acknowledgment, but still nothing showed on Gavin's screen. He frowned. *What is it I'm supposed to be seeing? It makes no sense for Admiral Kre'fey to have given me access to this simulation if there is nothing out here.*

Gavin hesitated for a moment. He knew that his idea of what made sense and a Bothan admiral's idea of same could be vastly different. Many times he'd had to deal with Bothan manipulation of himself or his command, and most of those times had been a disaster. Yet, despite the Kre'fey clan having a negative association with Rogue Squadron because of events over two decades old, Gavin had found young Traest Kre'fey to be remarkably straightforward in general, and very much more so when dealing with the Rogues.

The primary console beeped, and a small box appeared around a distant object on the X-wing's heads-up display. Gavin selected the object as a target and glanced down at its profile and image on the secondary monitor. At a quick glance it could have been mistaken for an asteroid and dismissed easily, but to Gavin it looked far too symmetrical. It reminded him a great deal of a seed—a bit bulbous in the middle, but tapered at both ends. The rear had a couple of recesses in it that could have hidden propulsion exhaust units, and a couple more up front that could house weapons.

Gavin shivered, then nudged the X-wing's throttle forward. "Catch, start recording this run. I want to be able to study the playback." Applying a little etheric rudder, Gavin pointed the X-wing's nose on a course that would cut behind the seed. Reaching up to his right, he flipped a switch that locked the S-foils in attack position. With a flick of his thumb, he shifted his weapons control to lasers and quadded them up so all four would fire with a single squeeze of the stick's trigger.

The seed shifted itself around so its nose swung into line with his approach vector. Sensors gave him no read on energy weapons powering up, which disturbed him less than getting no power readings for propulsion. *How is that thing moving?*

Before any answers suggested themselves, Gavin quickly kicked the X-wing into a barrel roll to starboard and leveled out with his crosshairs covering the seed. He triggered a quick blast and waited for the seed to explode, but that didn't happen. As the quad burst neared the target, the bolts all whirled into an invisible vortex and vanished into a pinpoint of white light.

Emperor's black bones . . .

The seed jetted forward, swinging around to bring its nose to bear on the X-wing. Gavin started to roll port and dive, but something shook his ship. In a heartbeat Catch started screeching and the X-wing's forward shields collapsed. Something dully red blossomed on the seed's nose, then shot toward the X-wing. It hit hard and splattered a bit, then what appeared to be molten rock started melting through the fighter's metal flesh.

Warning sirens blared, drowning out Catch's panicky tones. Bright red damage flags began to scroll up over the primary monitor, all but one of them moving too fast for Gavin to read. The one he could see reported a premature ignition of a proton torpedo's engine, which lit up the whole port magazine and tore the X-wing apart.

Stunned, Gavin sat back in his seat as the screens went black and the cockpit's hatch cracked open. He glanced at his chronometer and shook his head. "Catch, we lasted twenty-five seconds. What was that thing?"

A human orderly appeared at the edge of the cockpit. "Colonel Darklighter, the admiral sends his compliments."

Gavin blinked and stroked a gloved hand over his brown goatee. "His compliments? I lasted less than half a minute."

"Yes, Colonel, very true." The orderly smiled. "The admiral said he would meet you in your office in an hour and explain why you are to be congratulated on doing so well."

Gavin sat behind his desk, idly punching up holographic images on his holoprojector plate. The first picture showed him and his two sons—orphaned boys who had lived near the Rogue Squadron hangar after the Thrawn crisis—all smiles. The next showed the boys two years older, still smiling despite being all dressed up, standing with Gavin and his bride, Sera Faleur.

She'd been the social worker who had helped him through the adoption process for the boys. Gavin smiled as he remembered squadron mates telling him that their mixed marriage couldn't last. They were both human, but she came from Chandrila, having grown up on the shores of the Silver Sea, and he was from Tatooine, yet despite the differences in their homeworlds, they easily made a life together.

The next image showed Sera and Gavin with their first daughter; after that came shots of them with their new son and then another daughter. An image made as a New Year's greeting card showed all seven of them together. Gavin easily remembered how happy they'd all been together. Prior to meeting Sera he'd pretty much resigned himself to never finding someone to love, but she'd been the balm to heal his broken heart. She'd not made him forget the past and the lover he'd lost, she'd just helped him recapture the joy of life and all its possibilities.

"I hope I'm not interrupting anything, Colonel."

Gavin looked up through the image of his family and

shook his head. "No, Admiral, not at all." He shut off the
holoprojector, relieved that the Bothan admiral's arrival had
stopped the cycle of pictures right there, at the happy times.

Admiral Traest Kre'fey bore a striking resemblance to
the other members of the Kre'fey family Gavin had seen: the
late General Laryn—the admiral's grandfather—and the admiral's brother, Karka. Despite having spent a certain amount
of time in the company of Bothans, Gavin couldn't remember
any outside the Kre'fey family whose fur was pure white.
Traest didn't have the golden eyes the other two had; instead
his were mostly violet with flecks of gold. Gavin assumed the
violet came from Borsk Fey'lya's line, since he knew the two
of them were related through some complicated tangle of
marriages between the two families.

Traest wore a black flight suit that he'd unzipped down to
midchest. He closed the door to Gavin's office, then uncere-
moniously plopped himself down on the couch to the left of
the door. Gavin moved from behind his desk to one of the two
chairs making up the conversation nook in his office.

He sat and rested his elbows on his knees. "It killed me in
twenty-five seconds. What was it?"

The Bothan smiled. "Congratulations. I died in fifteen in
my first engagement. Pulling the biological targeting data on-
line is what gave you some warning."

"If I weren't dead, I'm sure that would make me feel
better." Gavin frowned. "Do we know what it was?"

The Bothan admiral raked claws back through his pale
mane. "Two days ago Leia Organa Solo spoke to the senate
and tried to warn them about an unknown alien force that had
attacked several worlds on the Rim, out beyond Dantooine.
She didn't get a very warm reception. She left data behind,
from which the simulation was created."

Gavin sat back in his chair. "You're telling me that seed,
that 'thing,' is a starfighter being used by folks who attacked
the Outer Rim?"

"Yes. Technically it's called a coralskipper by the species
that created it. They grow them out of something called
yorick coral. I know the name is not terribly inspiring of fear,

but I assume it loses something in the translation from their tongue. I've designated them 'skips' for our purposes."

"And the princess brought this to the senate's attention, and they didn't listen?"

Traest shook his head. "Opposing forces have been gathering power to fight over the whole Jedi question. It's heated up because of the charge that a Jedi's rash action sparked the Rhommamool conflict. A number of powerful senators saw the princess's story as an attempt to divert attention from the Jedi question. It didn't help that Jedi were key to defeating the invaders."

Gavin nodded. He'd never had a problem with Jedi and, in fact, counted one of them, Corran Horn, as a very good friend. There were some high-handed Jedi, but Gavin had seen those sorts of ego cases among fighter pilots, so their existence didn't surprise him at all. The fact was that there were some tasks only Jedi could perform, and he'd been too long in the military to discard a force just because some of the elements were disruptive.

"Is there any evidence that the invaders are still coming in?"

"Actual, no, but logic suggests that the expenditure of resources needed to travel from galaxy to galaxy necessitates gaining a foothold through which those resources can be replenished." The Bothan smiled. "If you spend enough credits to get somewhere, you usually plan to stay for a while."

"Right, and the Rim worlds really aren't the sorts of places you'd drop in for a vacation." Gavin rubbed a hand over his mouth. "These skips—they're fairly formidable. How do they move? How did they take my shields down?"

"We need more research to be certain, but it appears that they have creatures called dovin basals that are part of the fighter itself. They manipulate gravity, which is how they were able to soak off your shots and rip down your shields. We think that boosting the sphere of the inertial compensator can actually prevent shields being taken down. I also think that cycling more, lower-power shots through the lasers will force the skip to expend a lot of energy creating those black-hole shields. As long as it's worried about catching shots, its maneuvering ability is degraded. These strategies are hypothetical, however, and can really only be tested in combat."

"I see." Gavin pressed his hands together. "I can have the squadron simming against these things, then you can point us at them in the Rim and we'll try it."

"I knew you'd be game for that, which I appreciate. We have another problem before that, though."

"And that is?"

The Bothan sighed. "Because of the way Princess Leia was dismissed, any action that even hints that she might have been right is frowned upon. Though my command is out in the Rim right now, I can't order up sweeps of any of the battle sites, I'm not allowed to help others look, nothing. It's political suicide to act as if her report has any credence to it."

"Yeah, but isn't it *real* suicide to assume it doesn't?" The man glanced down at the floor and then back up into Traest's violet eyes. "Given that Borsk Fey'lya now leads the New Republic, this can't be easy for you, but to ignore—"

Traest held a hand up to forestall Gavin's comment. "Colonel, because of my grandfather's failure at Borleias, my family's power waned around the time I entered the Bothan Martial Academy system. I went to one of the smaller satellite schools, and I had an instructor there who pointed out certain flaws in the way Bothan society functions. I would hope you've seen enough of me through the years to know that being of a newer, younger generation, I'm not one to follow exactly what my superiors think I should be doing. For example, if they knew I'd run you through that sim, I'd be busted down to flight officer and have to work myself back up to flag rank again."

"You did it quickly enough the first time, Admiral."

"Having key personnel in the upper echelons of the Bothan military resign as a result of the Caamasi problem sped me on my way. I don't mind using politics when it moves me in a direction I want to go, but I resent it when it prevents me from doing what is right." Traest opened his hands. "I was thinking, Colonel, that I'd like to use Rogue Squadron in the Rim, having you simulate a pirate group in attacks on outlying systems. My forces out there will pursue you, but you'll be free to run and hide and explore anywhere you want to go."

"And if we happen to run across a force of skips while we're out there?"

"I hope, for all of our sakes, you don't." The Bothan smiled grimly. "But if you do, we'll take them apart and give the senate evidence it will never be able to dismiss."

CHAPTER THREE

Luke Skywalker stood at the edge of the grove, allowing Yavin 4's light breeze to tease and snap the corner of the dark cloak that shrouded him. In the circular opening of the grove stood a number of gray plinths, one each serving as memorial for fallen Jedi and students. Gantoris had been the first, then Nichos Marr, Cray Mingla, and Dorsk 81. Others had followed them, and now the latest was Miko Reglia.

Luke felt conflicting emotions tear at him as he studied the memorials. He felt great pride in the sacrifices these Jedi had made. Even half-trained, they had accepted the responsibilities of Jedi and had acquitted themselves admirably. They were welcome examples to the new students about how difficult it could be to be a Jedi.

Regret also gnawed at him. *I would not be human if I did not wonder if I could have done something to prevent their deaths.* The early days of the Jedi academy had been difficult because he was still finding his way as a Jedi and a teacher. His experience of going over to the dark side when the Emperor returned had also blinded him to some of the things his students needed. While he acknowledged that he may have taken on students a bit prematurely, to have failed to do so would have meant there would be even fewer of them to face the Yuuzhan Vong invasion.

"We're *not* going to be putting one of those memorials there for Mara, you know."

Luke raised his head and felt the hint of a smile touch his lips. He glanced back at the dark-haired Jedi Knight in green robes behind him. "That isn't what I was thinking, Corran."

Corran Horn shrugged. "Maybe not at the moment, but it had to be lurking there somewhere. Pops for me every time I look at the place, since I heard . . . But there won't be a marker for her there."

Luke arched an eyebrow at him. "That could be taken two ways, you know. One suggests this disease won't kill her. The other suggests there won't be any Jedi around to plant the marker."

The green-eyed Jedi nodded, then scratched at his beard—which had been brown once, but now was shot through with white. "I'm betting on the former, though I know there are lots of folks in the New Republic that wouldn't shed a tear about the second case."

"Unfortunately true." Luke sighed and glanced at the markers again. "They were all so young."

"Ah, Luke, compared to *us*, *everyone* is young." Corran smiled easily. "Measured by life events, you should be, what, about a thousand years old?"

"Being married to Mara has slowed that process, I think."

"Yeah, but the years she put on you before you two finally got together still count." Corran jerked a thumb back over his shoulder. "Before we get any older, I thought you'd want to know they're all here. The last shuttle came in ten minutes ago or so. Kyp Durron was on it. He made a grand entrance, as always."

Luke shook his head slowly. "I don't doubt he made an entrance, but your 'as always' comment was unwarranted."

Corran raised his hands. "Perhaps it was, but his arrival excited a lot of the younger Jedi Knights and apprentices."

"Including your son?"

The Corellian hesitated, then bowed his head. "Valin was certainly among those who were impressed, but I'm more worried about the cadre of young Jedi Knights who are looking at Miko as a martyr. Too many seem to want to take his place. Ganner Rhysode and Wurth Skidder were right there with Kyp, as were a number of the other bright young Jedi. If not for Jacen, Jaina, and Anakin holding themselves back, I'd have thought everyone would have swarmed Kyp with greetings."

The Jedi Master exhaled his anxiety in a long, slow, calming breath. "I know your concerns, and you're not alone in expressing them. Kam and Tionne have worries about the academy. Teaching the children here as a group has been good. Opening the older apprentices up to mentoring experiences with other Jedi Knights has sharpened their skills immeasurably. Of course, that does mean that some of the Jedi Knights who are taken with Kyp's proactive view of the order do end up instructing our senior apprentices."

"I'm not arguing the methods, Master Skywalker, and I see the risks inherent in them." Corran sighed. "What worries me is that Kyp is clearly aware of the political storms his actions are creating, but he just ignores them. We've discussed this before, all of us, but the problem has really become acute because of Skidder's actions at Rhommamool."

"I know. This is the primary reason I recalled everyone here." Luke noticed a smirk tug at the corner of Corran's mouth. "And, yes, I know that issuing a recall lets everyone know who is in charge. I may not have been raised on Corellia where that sort of stuff comes naturally, but I am aware of it."

"Good. And you know Kyp's choosing to be the last to arrive means he fought you to the last."

"Yes, caught that." Luke turned from the grove and waved a hand toward the Great Temple. "Shall we?"

Corran nodded and started off, with Luke catching up easily enough. He watched Corran for a moment, then smiled. When Corran had first come to the academy, to train as a Jedi to save his wife, Mirax Terrik, he'd been willful and arrogant—all the things Luke expected out of a fighter pilot and law enforcement officer. *And a Corellian.* Through the process of learning what it was to become a Jedi, however, Corran had matured and changed. While it wasn't until the peace with the Empire some six years earlier that Corran resigned from Rogue Squadron to become a full-time Jedi, the

Jedi philosophy and demands had become fully integrated into his life.

Oddly enough, while Corran had let go of his arrogance, Kyp and others were being dangerously misguided by their pride in being Jedi. Luke easily recognized how it could happen. When one was attuned to the Force, life and reality became rendered much more sharply. Options others could not see or fathom became painfully clear. While when solving a problem Luke and other Jedi took care to explain what they were doing and why, Kyp and his followers tended just to act, confident that they knew the best solution for whatever problem it was they were facing.

Luke didn't doubt that the Jedi probably *did* find the best solution available in most situations, but the consequences of that solution might be hard for others to take. Ultimately it would be others who had to live with those results, not the Jedi who caused them, and resentment at high-handed Jedi actions was really inevitable.

The Jedi Master reached out and rested his left hand on Corran's shoulder. "Before we get into the meeting, I do want to thank you for stepping in and helping here since Mara became ill."

"My pleasure. I get to see Valin and Jysella. She's spent more of her life here, at the academy, than with her mother and me. I do want to maintain ties."

Luke gave Corran's shoulder a squeeze. "In the old days, all potential Jedi were taken from their families as children to be trained. I can't imagine it was easy even then, though. There's so much we don't know . . ."

"True, but we can't allow ourselves to think what you've created here is wrong or bad or that the old Council wouldn't approve. After all, Obi-Wan and Yoda still *did* take you on. Training an older Jedi isn't impossible, just more difficult." Corran shot his Master a sidelong glance. "And despite my early differences with you over training, I do think you've done a superb job. We have a hundred Jedi traveling the galaxy, and more ready to serve each year. It's quite an accomplishment."

"It will be if we are allowed to go forward." Luke followed
Corran into the turbolift. "Leia's report on the climate on
Coruscant was not good. I was there only a short time ago,
and the senate has soured decidedly because of Rhommamool. This may not be the best time to propose a new Jedi
council."

"The hand's been dealt. We have to play it and hope the
flux won't get us." The turbolift door opened, and Corran
hung back so Luke could emerge first. "Your students await,
Master."

Luke strode from the turbolift and felt his heart swell in
his chest. The Jedi had been arrayed in ranks in the Great
Temple's Grand Audience Chamber. They were neither as numerous nor as colorful as the Rebel soldiers who had similarly been gathered after the Death Star had been destroyed,
but Luke still felt the return of the same giddy emotions he'd
known then. Just seeing the Jedi there—good mix of humans
and nonhumans, male and female—peeled back the years
and reminded him of the heroic efforts that had been necessary to stave off the Empire.

He paced down the red carpet that split the hall lengthwise
and slowly mounted the steps to the dais at the far end. He
nodded to Kam Solusar and Tionne, the academy's husband
and wife administrators, then turned and caught sight of
Corran slipping into place in the rank behind his son. The
younger students had been positioned closest to the dais, with
Jedi Knights and their apprentices arraying themselves back
through the hall, grouped by their own choice.

*If those on the left side have aligned themselves with Kyp,
then the division is more marked than I thought.* The left side
of the room held nearly two-thirds of the adult Jedi and
half of the nonhumans. On the right side, along with Corran,
Luke recognized Streen and several others who had staunchly
opposed Kyp's stance. The Jedi Master sensed no hatred
flowing between the groups, but the level of tension in the
chamber was slowly increasing.

He noticed that Jacen stood alone, aloof, in the backmost
rank. Though the boy stood on Kyp's side of the room, Luke

felt no connection between his nephew and Kyp's faction. Anakin, on the other hand, stood three places away from Streen and, while subdued, had a fierce loyalty to Luke burning deep inside him.

Luke made himself smile at the younger students. "I am glad to see you all here. Your bright, shining faces are lit with the Force. You all work hard, and someday, you young Jedi will stand here with us as Jedi Knights. I look forward to that day, and I know you do, too."

"We can be out fighting the bad guys," a young Twi'lek piped.

The innocently enthusiastic comment brought smiles to many faces, Luke's included. "Yes, that will be it. However, for now, I would ask Tionne to take you away to continue your studies. There are things I need to discuss with the others that you need not know about at the moment. Thank you for greeting all of us, and may the Force be with you."

The children marched out in even rows, with the eldest helping conduct the youngest out and down the stairs. The adult ranks broke as people closed in on the dais, though the left and right division remained. Kyp worked his way toward the front of the pack, placing him opposite Corran and Streen. Expectations of a confrontation filled the air.

Luke held a hand out, palm down. "We face two very grave problems. Either one of them could destroy the Jedi. Together, they most certainly will unless we put aside any differences and work together. Kyp, perhaps you would share what you know of the Yuuzhan Vong."

The request clearly surprised the dark-haired Jedi. Kyp had come to the Jedi academy as a gangling youth of sixteen. At thirty-two he had grown into a strong, slender man with sharp features and angry eyes. He had been the first among the Jedi to encounter the Yuuzhan Vong, and his escape from their clutches spoke volumes about his skill as a pilot and with the Force.

"As you wish it, my Master." Kyp's low voice filled the hall. "My Avengers and I were ambushed by these Yuuzhan Vong. They fly living ships, made of something like coral.

The ships can collapse the shields on an X-wing, or cause laser shots to be sucked into a small black hole. We can kill them, of course, but it is not easy. They wiped out my Avengers, capturing and later killing Miko. I barely escaped with my life."

"What was the most important thing you learned about the Yuuzhan Vong?"

The younger man frowned. "I don't understand the question."

"You said you were ambushed by the Yuuzhan Vong. How is it that a Jedi Knight is ambushed?"

"They looked like rocks in their fighters—pieces of asteroids, really . . ." Kyp's voice trailed off as his face closed. "I registered no hostile intent from them. I didn't even sense them through the Force."

His admission started conversation buzzing through the room. Luke let it go, permitting the surprise and anxiety to replace the sense of impending confrontation before he spoke. "Yes, exactly. I engaged the Yuuzhan Vong, as well, and could not sense them in the Force. They seem disconnected or shielded from it."

Streen, the old Bespin miner, frowned. "If they are not connected with the Force, how can they be alive?"

"That's an excellent question, Streen. I have no answer for you. I just don't know." Luke folded his arms across his chest. "The New Republic is of the opinion that the Yuuzhan Vong threat has been eliminated, but I believe they have come from outside our galaxy, and therefore, all we've dealt with so far is a strong probe. They will continue to come."

Kyp snorted. "Once again the New Republic remains blind to a threat, leaving us to deal with it."

Corran narrowed his eyes. "But this is a threat we may not be able to handle without help from the New Republic. If we say we can handle the problem and they're right, that none exists, then we look to be fools. If it *does* exist, and we *fail,* that could be the end of the order."

"We won't fail." Kyp looked around, and numerous heads bobbed in agreement with his statement. "With the Force as our ally and lightsabers as our tools, we'll destroy the Yuuzhan Vong."

Jacen Solo stepped forward, coming down along the carpet. "Listen to yourself, Kyp, and think about what you're saying. The Yuuzhan Vong are camouflaged against the senses we rely on. They've got armor and weapons that a lightsaber can't cut instantly, and they're trained warriors. More importantly, if Master Skywalker's thinking is correct, they will be coming in numbers suitable for conquering a *galaxy*. Even if each of us stands against a thousand of them, we will be too few."

Kyp's head came up. "Then what do you suggest, Jacen?"

Before his nephew could answer, Luke raised a hand to stop the discussion. "Our situation is this: We've got a foe who is able to blindside us coming forward in unknown numbers, at unknown sites, for reasons unknown, and a galactic government that has decided to do nothing about it. That government also does not trust us. I think, no matter which way this turns out, we will be in for a lot of blame."

"All the more reason we shouldn't care what the government thinks." Wurth Skidder tucked his thumbs in his belt. "They're clearly not interested in what's best for the galaxy."

"Meaning we are?" Streen fixed the younger Jedi with a hard stare. "That's what you're saying, isn't it?"

"What he is saying, Streen, is that disaster has struck the galaxy whenever the Jedi order has been weakened." Kyp pointed a hand toward Luke. "If we will be blamed for what happens, I would rather be blamed for being zealous in attacking this problem, than timid in waiting for developments."

Luke closed his eyes for a moment and studied the danger in Kyp's comment. The Jedi Knights were always meant to be defenders of peace, but Kyp encouraged offensive action, proactive and preemptive strikes. He'd called his squadron the Dozen-and-Two Avengers, instead of something more suitable like the Defenders. Now he spoke of *attacking* the problem. *To some it might be word games, but the words he uses to express his ideas and communicate them to others show me how close to the edge he is.*

The closeness to the edge did not surprise Luke, for he'd seen it develop in Kyp over the years. While still an apprentice, Kyp had been influenced by the spirit of a dead Sith Lord. He'd stolen a superweapon and destroyed the planet Carida, killing billions. Kyp had worked tirelessly to atone for what he had done, but had chosen more difficult and visible campaigns as time went on, so more people could see that he *was* making amends. *This invasion must seem to Kyp as a grand crusade through which he can win the acceptance of even his most harsh critics.*

Luke opened his eyes again, then took a step down toward the crowd of Jedi before him. "It is premature to speak of any attacking of the Yuuzhan Vong. Jacen is right—we cannot stand against them alone. Our job, right now, is to prepare for the worst and to learn as much about the Yuuzhan Vong as we can. We have to have good and useful data the New Republic can use to plan a defense or an offense. Our role here is as guardians, and our skills can allow us to scout out this threat. Once we have good intelligence about the Yuuzhan Vong, then we can plan what we will do."

He looked around at the Jedi Knights arrayed there: male, female, human, and nonhuman. "Over the next week or so I will give you assignments. I will be sending you into dangers I cannot even guess at knowing. I hope all of you will return unhurt, but I know that will not happen. While the outside world may be divided about us, we cannot afford to be divided against ourselves. If we do not stand together, we will be torn apart, and with us will fall our galaxy."

CHAPTER FOUR

Leia turned from her packed luggage and glanced at the suite's doorway as C-3PO opened the door and admitted Elegos A'Kla. The Caamasi wore a gold cloak over his shoulders, and subtle weaving of purple threads into it mimicked the striping on his face and shoulders. The Caamasi gave her a quick smile, then waved off C-3PO's invitation to take his cloak.

She sighed. "I thought I'd be ready by now, but I'm just finishing my packing. Don't know when I'll be back here, and I wanted to take a few things with me."

"Please, take your time." Elegos shrugged simply. "If not for my senatorial duties, we would have been away from here a week ago."

Leia waved him into the two-level suite's central chamber, and the Caamasi settled himself into one of the nerf-hide chairs angled toward the big viewport that looked out over Coruscant's cityscape. A hallway heading back to the south led to her study—which had once been the boys' room—and a smaller bedroom they'd given to Jaina and then, during her time at the academy, had turned into a guest room. The master bedroom lay in the second level, accessed by a curving stairway built against the far wall. The kitchen had been installed to the north of the living room, with a small dining area between it and the living room.

Leia stuffed a small holocube into a bag and started

closing the fasteners. "The senate didn't want to let you head out immediately?"

"I doubt they wanted me to head out at all, but they had no choice. Instead I was given committee assignments and work to clear. My daughter is dealing with most of it for me. Releqy will serve as my liaison with the senate in my absence. This is why I've not been in closer communication with you."

"But your daughter has, so I've been apprised of your delays." Leia straightened up and looked at the three red fabric bags she had stuffed to bursting with clothes and other things she couldn't bear to leave behind. *I left Alderaan with even less than this. Here I am, a quarter of a century later, a refugee once more—this time of my conscience rather than any external act.* "I should have been ready before this, but things keep cropping up."

Before she could even attempt to explain, she saw Elegos's nostrils flare and his gaze flick past her to the upper landing for the stairs. She turned and found her husband, Han, hanging there in the doorway, his hands on either side of the jamb. She shivered because the haggard look on his face and the position of his hands reminded her far too much of when he had been frozen in carbonite. She wanted to believe the darkness under his eyes was just shadow, but she couldn't deceive herself that way.

She heard Elegos rise from his chair. "Captain Solo."

Han's head came up slowly, and his eyes narrowed as he faced the voice. "A Caamasi? Elegos, isn't it? A senator?"

"Yes."

Han staggered forward and almost fell down the stairs. He caught himself on the banister, made it down a couple more steps, then slid his way around the curve. He got his feet under him again, leapt the last few steps to the floor, and strode past Leia. With a grunt, he flopped down almost boneless into one of the chairs opposite Elegos. In the viewport's light, the rainbow of stains on Han's once-white tunic was evident, as was the grime at cuffs, collar, and elbows. His boots were badly scuffed, his trousers wrinkled, and his hair utterly unkempt. He ran a hand over beard stubble, flashing dirty fingernails as he did so.

"I have a question for you, Elegos."

"If I can be of service."

Han nodded as if his head were balanced on his spine instead of connected by muscle. "I understand you Caamasi have memories, strong memories."

Leia extended a hand toward Elegos. "Forgive me, Elegos. I learned about that from Luke, and I thought, my husband . . ."

The Caamasi shook his head. "I have no doubt you all are to be trusted with the information about our memnii. Momentous events in our lives create memories. We are able, among our kind, and with certain Jedi, to transfer these memories. They have to be strong memories, powerful ones, to become memnii."

"Yeah, the strong ones do stick around." Han focused somewhere between the wall and the edge of the viewport. He fell silent for a moment, then fixed Elegos with a hard stare. "So what I want to know is this: How do you get rid of them? How do you get them out of your head?"

The tortured tone of Han's voice drove a vibroblade through Leia's heart. "Oh, Han . . ."

He held up a hand to keep her back. His expression sharpened. "How do you do it, Elegos?"

The Caamasi lifted his chin. "We cannot get rid of them, Captain Solo. By sharing them we share the burden of them, but we can never be rid of them."

Han snarled, then curled forward in the chair, grinding the heels of his hands against his eyes. "I'd tear them out if that would stop me from seeing, you know, I would, I really would. I can't stop seeing it, seeing him, seeing him die . . ."

The man's voice sank to a bass rumble; rough, raw, and ragged as broken ferrocrete. "There he was, standing there. He'd saved my son. He'd saved Anakin. He tossed him up into my arms. Then, when I saw him again, a gust of wind knocked him down and collapsed a building on top of him. But he got up. He was bloody and torn up, but he got up again. On his feet, he got up and he raised his arms toward me. He raised his arms toward me, so I could save him, the way he'd saved Anakin."

Han's voice squeaked to silence. His larynx bobbed up and down.

"I saw him, don't you get it? I saw him standing there as the moon hit Sernpidal. The air just combusted. He was standing there, roaring, screaming. The light turned him black. Just a silhouette. Then it ate into him. I saw his bones. They turned black, too, then white, so white I couldn't watch. Then nothing." Han swiped at his nose with a hand. "My best friend, my only true friend, and I let him die. How am I supposed to live with that? How do I get that out of my head? Tell me."

Elegos's voice came softly, but with a strength that belied its gentle tone. "What you remember is partly what you saw and partly your fears. You see yourself as having failed him, and you think that's how he saw you at the last, but can't be sure. Memories are not always that clear."

"You don't know, you weren't there."

"No, but I have been in similar situations." The Caamasi sank into a crouch, with his cloak pooling to the floor around him. "The first time I used a blaster, I shot three men. I watched them dance and collapse. I watched them die, and I knew I would carry that memory with me forever, the memory of me killing them. Then it was explained to me: the blaster had only been set to stun them. My belief was wrong, as, perhaps, is yours."

Han shook his head defiantly. "Chewie was my *friend*. He counted on me, and I failed him."

"I do not believe he would see it that way."

Han snarled. "You didn't know him. How would you know?"

Elegos laid a hand on the man's knee. "I didn't know him, but I have known of him for decades. Even what you just told me now, that he saved your son, tells me how much he loved you."

"He couldn't love me. Chewie died hating me. I abandoned

him, I left him there to die. His last thoughts were filled with hatred for me."

"No, Han, no." Leia dropped to her knees beside Han's chair and clutched his left forearm. "You can't believe that."

"I was there, Leia. I was close to saving Chewie, and I failed. I left him there to die."

"Regardless of what you believe, Captain Solo, Chewbacca did not share that view."

"What? How can you know what he was thinking?"

"The same way you will." The Caamasi blinked his violet eyes. "He saved your son. In Chewbacca's eyes, Anakin saved you by piloting the *Millennium Falcon* to safety. Yet one more time Chewbacca saved you, this time through your son. You don't know that now, but you will come to see that is the truth. When you relive this memory, think about that. As noble a hero as Chewbacca was, he could not have had anything but joy at knowing you survived. To think anything less demeans him."

Han shot to his feet, pitching the chair over backward. "How dare you? How dare you come into my home and tell me I'm demeaning my friend? What gives you the right?"

Elegos slowly rose and spread open hands before him. "I apologize for any offense, Captain Solo. I have intruded on your grief. It was unthinkable."

He bowed to Leia. "My apologies to you, as well. I shall leave you."

"Don't bother." Han stalked forward between them, then headed toward the door. "Threepio, find out from Coruscant's constabulary which tapcafs lead the list for incident reports. Comlink me the list."

Leia got up. "Han, don't go. I'm going to be leaving soon."

"I know. Off to save the galaxy again, that's my Leia." He didn't turn to face her, just hunched his shoulders. "I hope you have better luck. I failed to save even one person."

The suite's closing door eclipsed Han Solo's back.

C-3PO, his head cocked at an angle, looked at Leia. "Mistress? What do I do?"

Leia closed her eyes and sighed. "Get the list, give it to

him. Maybe call Wedge or any of the other retired Rogues. Hobbie or Janson or someone ought to be at loose ends and could keep an eye on him. And when he comes back, take good care of him."

She felt a hand on her shoulder. "Leia, I can head out to the Rim on my own. You can stay here to care for your husband. I can report to you."

She opened her eyes, then covered Elegos's hand with her own. "No, Elegos, I need to go. Even that deep in grief, Han's right. I want to stay, all of me wants to stay, but I have to go. Others can't, so it is up to us to rescue them. Han can take care of himself—he'll have to."

CHAPTER FIVE

Luke looked up and smiled as Corran escorted his two nephews into the briefing room.

"Did you see your sister off on the shuttle?"

"She's on her way." Jacen, the older one, glanced around the room, always looking to see if anything had changed since the last time he'd been there. "She wishes she had a better assignment."

"I'm sure she does." Luke watched Jacen for a moment. *Always checking the world, verifying what he could assume, not trusting until he is certain.* "Right now, I need her picking up Danni at Commenor, then meeting with your mother and Senator A'Kla."

Anakin, the younger nephew, toyed with an ancient piece of equipment left in the corner since the time when the Rebels fought the Empire in the skies above Yavin 4. "If Danni had just stayed with our mother on Coruscant, she could have come out with her and not needed Jaina."

Jacen frowned. "Jaina's going to help Danni work on her Force skills, that's why she's going. They'll be traveling for a few days with nothing else to do, and Jaina's a good teacher."

Luke nodded. "And, after her ordeal, Danni did need time to meet with her family and assure them she was unharmed." He didn't know if "unharmed" was accurate; the trauma of capture by the Yuuzhan Vong had to have been severe. Still,

Danni Quee had been intelligent and resilient, so Luke felt she'd recover from her ordeal if given the proper support.

Anakin popped the panel off the old transceiver and peered inside. "What is it you have for us to do? Pretty much everyone else has their assignments already. I bet it's something good."

Jacen snorted in his brother's direction, narrowing his brown eyes. "He let the others go first because our assignments are going to be no better than Jaina's."

Corran frowned. "How did you get a target lock on that idea?"

Jacen half turned to face the Corellian Jedi. "He won't play favorites because of his relationship to us, and realistically, we are young. At least, by saving us for last, he saves us some embarrassment."

Jacen's words didn't seem as full of disappointment as they should have, which reinforced a decision Luke had already made concerning assignments. "Anakin."

The younger boy, blue eyes bright, glanced over at his uncle. "What?"

"I'm going to have you accompany Mara to Dantooine."

"Huh? What?" Anakin straightened up. His brows furrowed, and just for a second, Luke caught an angry expression that meant trouble whenever he'd seen it on Han Solo's face. "But I thought I'd be out doing something . . . I thought . . ." The anger that had flashed over his face drained away with his words. "I understand."

Luke arched an eyebrow at him. "And what is it you understand?"

"You don't trust me." Anakin looked down at his dust-smeared fingertips and whispered hoarsely, "You don't trust me because I killed Chewbacca."

The mournful tone of the boy's voice sent a shiver down Luke's spine. Regret and hurt poured off Anakin, underscoring the turmoil he felt over the Wookiee's death. *Anakin has always wanted to be a hero, has always wanted to redeem his name, and suddenly finds himself drowning in a tragedy.*

"There is something you must understand, Anakin, first

and foremost: You did not kill Chewbacca." Luke walked over to his nephew and rested his hands on the boy's shoulders. Using his thumbs, he tipped the boy's face up until their gazes met. "The Yuuzhan Vong caused Sernpidal's moon to come crashing down into the planet, not you. For you to accept blame for Chewbacca's death absolves them of his murder and the murder of all those you couldn't save. You can't do that."

Anakin swallowed hard. "It sounds logical when you say it, but, in my heart, what I feel . . . What I see in my father's eyes."

Luke lowered his face to a level with Anakin's. "Don't be reading something into your father's eyes that isn't there. He's a good man, with a good heart. He'd never blame you for Chewie's death."

The Jedi Master straightened up again. "Regardless of misunderstanding, I don't know how you can think I don't trust you. I am very specifically entrusting to you my wife, the person I hold most dear."

The boy frowned. "Are you sure it's not the other way around?"

"Ah, Anakin, do you think Mara would like an assignment baby-sitting an untrustworthy apprentice?"

"Um, no."

"And do you think she'd give me an earful about it?"

Corran laughed. "An earful would be getting off lightly."

Anakin smiled a little. "I guess she would, Uncle Luke."

"I may be adept in the ways of the Force, but there's no Jedi ability that'll take the sting out of the sharp side of her tongue." Luke stepped back and gave Anakin a brave smile. "Mara needs some time to get her illness under control. Dantooine is a world teeming with life, so it's full of the Force. I want her there to be able to recover, and I want you with her to help her out. If you'll accept this mission, I'll be very grateful."

Anakin hesitated for a moment then nodded. "Thanks for trusting me."

"I've never had any doubts about you, Anakin." Luke

winked at him. "You should go get your things together, then see to gathering the provisions you'll need on Dantooine."

"Blasters and lightsabers included?"

Luke nodded. "Lightsabers, of course. Blasters because I think you can use the work concentrating and focusing the Force. Target practice demands that sort of concentration."

Anakin's smile broadened. "Besides, Aunt Mara wouldn't be caught dead without a blaster."

"Only one?" Corran laughed. "Run heavy on the power packs, Anakin."

The youth clapped his hands together. "I'll take good care of her, Uncle Luke, I really will. We'll come back ready to do whatever we need to beat the Yuuzhan Vong."

"I'm sure of it." Luke nodded to his nephew and watched the boy leave the room. He waited until he could sense Anakin's presence descending in the turbolift, then turned his attention to Jacen. "Do you really think I've got some embarrassing duty planned for you?"

"No, Uncle Luke, I'm just afraid I might embarrass you."

Luke turned and walked toward the table that had been behind him. He gave himself a moment to ponder Jacen's words. He turned and leaned back against the table. "I suppose this conversation has been coming for a while, hasn't it?"

"Probably." Jacen shrugged. "I've been thinking since the Yuuzhan Vong arrived, and since all the Jedi were here and talking."

"Sounds like this is a family talk." Corran levered himself away from the room's back wall. "I'll return later."

Jacen held a hand up. "No, wait. It *is* a family matter, but one for the entire Jedi family, not just us."

Corran looked at Luke. "Luke?"

"Do stay. I suspect more than two perspectives will be useful here." Luke looked over at his nephew. "What have you been thinking?"

The youth sighed, and a certain amount of relief pulsed off him. "If this sounds harsh, I don't mean it to be, but I've come to realize something pretty fundamental about the Jedi order.

We're all trained to use the Force to allow us to do things to keep the peace and stave off disaster. We do that because we're following your teaching. You're following the teaching of your masters, Uncle Luke, but they had to instruct you in those things you needed to defeat the Empire. They did a great job forging you into a weapon, and you even went beyond their training to do things they probably didn't think you could."

The Jedi Master nodded. "I can accept that."

"Okay, the thing of it is that you were shaped as a weapon by Jedi Masters who were part of a tradition that had developed into peacekeepers. I get the feeling, though, that's not how the Jedi began. I think the Jedi philosophy started as something that strengthened people within. The *powers* we manifest—I think those are all outgrowths of the internal strengthening, but a lot of *those* teachings were lost along the way. I mean, I feel the need for something inside."

With anguish on his face, Jacen looked at his uncle. "I'm not sure being a Jedi Knight is my calling in life. I'd really prefer it if you gave me no assignment at all."

Luke shifted his shoulders involuntarily as a twitch shot up his spine. "Wow, I'd not expected that."

Jacen glanced at the floor. "I'm sorry I disappointed you."

"No, it's not that." Luke frowned. "I was going to tell you that what you wanted didn't matter right now because I need you. And as I was getting ready to say that, I heard Uncle Owen telling me the same thing, right before he died."

Jacen's head came up. "Then you understand?"

"Oh, very well."

"Then you'll let me seek the answers I need?"

"No." Luke held his hands up quickly. "I mean, yes, you'll be able to seek for your answers, but not as a replacement for an assignment. You have to remember that absolutely key to the Jedi philosophy is a respect for all life. For you to go off now means you'd be putting your life ahead of that of others, and that's not good."

"But, Uncle Luke, you've always put yourself last. You—and Mom and Dad and everyone else—are always being pulled every which way." He balled his fists and pounded them against his hips. "You don't have the time to figure out what it is you need to do to develop yourself further in the Force. You're always distracted."

Corran scratched at his throat. "You've got a point there, Jacen, but you're assuming that only by going off like a hermit to contemplate the Force and your integration with it are you going to be able to get anywhere. That's just not true."

"How do you know, Corran?" Jacen crossed his arms over his chest. "None of the Jedi alive today have had that chance. For all we know, Yoda spent the first three centuries of his life as a hermit. Maybe that's what we need to do."

"Or, maybe, Jacen, that's just one path to get where you want to go." Corran pointed a finger at Luke. "Your uncle and I differed over paths to becoming a Jedi Knight, but we're both here. And, sure, there might be distractions out there, but there are lessons learned from doing things and succeeding or failing that aren't easy to learn from tranquil consideration. You're right, having time to consider them and their consequences is useful, but I find it hard to concentrate on introspection when folks out there are in trouble."

Luke nodded in agreement. "Corran's point is well taken, Jacen. I do understand what you are saying, and I promise you that if you decide that your path is one of introspection, I won't stand in your way."

The youth's eyes narrowed with suspicion. "There's a catch."

"There is. I really *do* need you. I've saved the most dangerous mission in all this for myself, and I want you with me. Because you've dealt with the Yuuzhan Vong before, you have the experience I need. We're taking Artoo and going back to Belkadan, to see what that Yuuzhan Vong agent was trying to create there. This is a very important mission, and I really do need you with me."

Corran snorted. "Great, I guess that leaves the aforementioned embarrassing mission for me."

Jacen glanced at him. "Trade you."

"No, you won't." Luke reached down and clutched the

edge of the table. "You wouldn't like the assignment I'm giving him, and given what you've told me, you're really not suited to it. The Belkadan mission, however, is one you're perfect for."

Jacen's face closed for a second, then he nodded, but stiffly. "I'll go along with you for now, but I have such mixed feelings. I'm afraid I'll be no help to anyone."

"Fair enough."

The youth bowed his head. "If you will permit me, Uncle Luke, I'll leave you two to discuss Corran's mission."

"No, wait, listen to what you almost asked to do."

Corran rolled his eyes. "This is going to be worse than I thought."

Luke laughed. "Okay, so yours is the second most dangerous mission. Out on the Rim there's a system designated MZX33291 by Imperial surveyors. It has a pulsar in the area that disrupts communications from the only habitable world in the system. The Empire had made the planet off-limits to everyone for reasons that are unclear. There is some evidence that they had xenoarchaeological teams out there, but no trace of what they might have discovered."

"Okay. You think the Yuuzhan Vong are there?"

"I don't know." Luke shrugged. "The University of Agamar uncovered the records concerning the fifth world there, which they've named Bimmiel after the Imperial survey team leader. About three months ago they sent a xenoarch survey team out as part of a for-credit course. No one has heard from them, which isn't wholly unexpected. We were sent word by the university administrators, who thought, if we had Jedi in the area, we could swing by and make sure everything was okay."

The Corellian smiled. "They think our budget for interstellar travel is bigger than theirs?"

"Something like that. I also think they believe Jedi will be better in the rescuing department than students they might send out." Luke sighed. "Initial reports from the team indicated the climate had changed from that seen by the Imperial surveyors. The students arrived during the stormy season there. It's pretty severe."

Corran nodded. "Bad weather doesn't sound that dangerous."

"I want you to take Ganner Rhysode with you. He'll be your partner."

The Corellian hissed. "That trade offer still good, Jacen?"

"If it's any consolation, Corran, Ganner was no more in favor of this pairing than you were when I told him what he'd be doing." Luke gave his friend a simple smile. "Look, if there is nothing going on out there, then the mission should be simple. You get in, you locate the university's people and evacuate them."

"Ganner could do that by himself."

"He *could,* but if the Yuuzhan Vong *are* there, I think he'd be likely to launch into them, and that would leave the folks he came to save in a very bad position. You're in charge, and he will obey you, albeit rather reluctantly."

Jacen smiled at Corran. "Besides, Corran, you have to admit that your lacking telekinetic abilities does put you at a bit of a disadvantage."

"Sure. I can't move a rock with my mind, but, boy, can I make that rock think it's been moved." He sighed. "Ganner is pretty good with TK. Makes sense to include him. And things could have been worse. You could have paired me with Kyp."

"I'd not be so cruel to either of you."

"Hey, I'm not that bad." Corran arched an eyebrow at Luke. "Or are you thinking this is one of those from-a-certain-point-of-view things?"

"See, all that training did pay off." The Jedi Master nodded. "This is also a chance, Corran, to show Ganner that Kyp's approach to the Force isn't the only way to do things."

"Got it." Corran smiled. "Well, may the Force be with all of us, I guess."

"Yes, please." Luke nodded solemnly. "You know, I like the fact that the Jedi are the galaxy's first line of defense, but what I'm dreading here is that the Yuuzhan Vong will show us how very weak a line that is."

CHAPTER SIX

Corran Horn found Valin in a small clearing in the Yavin 4 jungle. The boy sat on the ground cross-legged, with his hands on his knees. He stared intently forward, concentrating on a small rock a meter in front of him. Sweat beaded up on his brow and threatened to trickle down into his hazel eyes.

Immeasurable pride and anguish roiled around in Corran's heart as he watched his son. The Horn-Halcyon line of Jedi Knights was notorious for its lack of telekinetic abilities. Corran still recalled his complete frustration with trying to move objects through the Force. Except under extreme circumstances, when he'd used the Force to contain energy that would have hurt others, he couldn't so much as tickle drool from a Hutt's lips, much less move a rock.

That Valin would try so hard to move the rock impressed Corran. Valin already had surpassed his father's expectations. Though only eleven years old, he already stood shoulder-height to Corran and clearly was going to take after his grandfathers in terms of size. His dark hair and hazel eyes were a compromise between his parents' coloration, while his features were more Mirax, with hints of Corran's own mother in there, too. *It's good he doesn't take after Booster Terrik in that aspect.*

Like every father everywhere, Corran's chest tightened as he watched his son try a task he knew the boy would fail. He wanted to step in, to save Valin from the disappointment, but held himself back. Learning the lesson might hurt his son, but learning how to handle disappointment was more valuable than being able to move all the rocks in the galaxy.

And, to Corran's surprise, the small, ovoid rock began to move. It tottered on its base, then slowly flopped over on its side.

Corran whooped out loud. "Valin, that's great! You moved it."

"Dad?" The boy's head whipped around, his long brown hair flicking sweat away. One lock pasted itself under his right eye. "I didn't see you there."

"No, you were concentrating. That was great." Corran advanced into the clearing and helped his son up to his feet. "I mean, what you did, I could never—"

"Dad, it wasn't what you think."

"I know what I saw."

Valin smiled and fingered the hair off his cheek. "Remember how you've talked about points of view?"

"Yes?"

"It's a point-of-view thing." Valin squatted down and waved his father down with him. "Look again."

Corran studied the rock. The ground at its base was alive with small, purple insects. They were swarming up through the dirt and around the base of the stone. "I don't get it. You set the rock on the entrance to one of their colonies?"

"No. I have been studying the garnants. They communicate through vibration and scent. I used the Force. I reached down and made them think there was a trail up. I made them think the rock was food. The first one marked it with food scent." Valin shrugged sheepishly and pulled a small morsel of food from a pocket. "I have a reward for them, so it's not like I'm forcing them to do anything."

Corran frowned for a moment. Compelling the behavior of a sapient individual, especially if it was against the individual's will and for the selfish benefit of the Jedi, undoubtedly would be of the dark side. Luring nonsapients into doing something natural didn't fall into that class at all, especially when the task was harmless and they were paid back for their actions by something that would replace the energy they'd expended.

"It's probably closer to the borderline with the dark side than you want to be playing with, but I'm very impressed." Corran reached out and stroked his son's head. "Communicating with another species isn't easy."

"Not really communicating, Dad." Valin rolled his eyes. "They're just bugs. I make them think a rock is food."

"More than I could do at your age."

"But you weren't trained."

"True enough." Corran stood. "That notwithstanding, I'm very proud of you."

"I'd like to make you prouder." Valin stood and sighed heavily. "I'd been trying to move the rock with my mind for a while first. Then I decided to try that other way. I guess I'll never be a powerful Jedi."

Corran rested his hands on his son's shoulders and touched his forehead to Valin's. "There are those among the Jedi that view strength as how far you can move something, or how easily you can break something. The real strength of a Jedi comes from within, from his heart and mind. Some Jedi move rocks just to prove they can move them, but the strongest Jedi don't see any reason to move rocks when that isn't going to solve the immediate problem."

His son sighed again and smiled. "So, what are you telling me, Dad?"

"He's telling you, boy, that being weak is something you'll learn to get used to, perhaps a handicap you'll even get over."

Corran's head came up as he turned toward the voice. "Ganner!"

The other Jedi nodded solemnly. The man stood a full head taller than Corran. His broad shoulders tapered down to a narrow waist and hips, but the man's body fairly rippled with muscle. Jet-black hair had been combed back to emphasize a widow's peak. The mustache and goatee he wore combined with his handsome features and piercing blue eyes to give him the sort of rakish good looks that easily made the man the object of admiring glances. The midnight blue and black Jedi robes he wore set him apart from the jungle and gave him the bearing of a government official.

Corran could feel the Force gathering in his son. He gave Valin's shoulder a squeeze. "Don't do it."

The taller man opened his arms easily and let the hint of a smile twist his lips. "Please, Valin, show me what you can do. Project whatever vision you wish. I promise to be afraid."

The boy lifted his chin as the Force drained out of him. "Scariest thing I can think of is you standing there."

Ganner clapped slowly. "He has a lot of spirit, this is good." He looked at Corran. "Our ship is ready to go."

"I was just going to say good-bye to my son."

"We have some time. Not much, but a little yet."

Corran turned to Valin. "Go back to the Great Temple. Your mother and sister are there. Tell them I'll be along presently to say farewell."

The boy arched an eyebrow at him. "Are you sure?"

Ganner laughed. "I won't hurt him."

Valin turned his head and spitted Ganner on a hard stare. "As if you could . . ."

"Go, Valin. Your mother will get impatient, and you don't want that any more than I do." Corran ruffled the boy's hair. "Your mother will be worried, so ease her fears, okay?"

The boy nodded, then started sprinting off toward the temple.

Corran watched him go, then slowly looked back at Ganner. "Okay, and now the *real* reason you wanted to meet me here, away from the others."

"Perceptive, good." Ganner's arctic eyes narrowed. "You're nominally in charge of our expedition—"

"Correction, I'm in charge of it." Corran folded his arms across his chest. "You are my aide on this run."

"In the data files, yes, that's it. In reality . . ."

"Meaning?"

"Meaning you're an old-style Jedi, you and your dual-phase lightsaber. Meaning I'm a much more powerful Jedi than you are. Meaning I know that you don't care for Kyp Durron's philosophy—a philosophy that I think must be em-

CHAPTER SEVEN

braced if the Jedi order is to fulfill its destiny in the galaxy." Ganner gestured easily, and the rock rose in the air as if lodged in some invisible turbolift. "I will do what must be done for us to complete our mission, but I will not brook interference from *you*."

The rock shot straight at Corran. He dodged to the right. The rock veered wide to the left, then tumbled and crashed back through the underbrush.

Ganner smirked at him. "Do you understand what I am saying?"

"Sure." Corran let his hands fall to his sides easily. "You're saying that your philosophy is more important than the job we're being sent to do."

"That's not it at all."

"Sure it is, but I don't expect you to understand that." Corran shook his head. "You and Kyp and the others that believe the way you do—you're working very hard to establish what the Jedi mean to this galaxy. You're doing that by wearing sharp uniforms and taking strong stands. Much of the time you're probably right in the stands you take—I can't disagree with them. What I don't like is how you make the stands, and how you work. You're all saying, 'Hey, we are Jedi. We deserve your respect.' I happen to think we need to earn it."

Ganner's expression darkened. "We *have* earned it. The Jedi made order out of the chaos of the Empire."

"No, *a* Jedi did that, *the* only Jedi there was at the time who was willing to stand up and fight the Empire. Luke Skywalker earned the galaxy's respect, not the rest of us. Our fight has to be waged each and every day out there, and here's a hologram you'd best study from all sides: People end up being inherently suspicious and resentful of anyone who sets himself up to sort right from wrong." Corran gave him a half smile. "I saw it when I worked for CorSec, and I've seen it as a Jedi."

The taller man threw his head back and laughed. "You, of all people, have the least call to criticize us for trying to establish an image that makes our jobs easier."

"How do you plot that course?"

Through the doorway to the bedroom they shared, Luke Skywalker caught a glimpse of his wife reclining on the bed. She lay there very comfortably, her red-gold hair spread around her head like a halo. Her chest rose and fell regularly and gently—peacefully, really—prompting him to realize how little peace they had known in their life together.

Beside her, on the bed, lay a few folded garments that needed to be stuffed into the traveling bags at the foot of the bed. Hers were mostly full, and two bags had been set out for him. Luke smiled, appreciating her thoughtfulness, and admiring her for taking the extra effort to get his bags out, despite the draining fatigue that was part of her illness.

He entered the room quietly, hoping not to disturb her, but her eyes flickered open. "Luke. Good, it's you."

"Who else would you have expected?"

She smiled, a bit haltingly, but with enough strength to send a thrill through him. "Anakin. I don't want to be late for our departure."

"Don't worry about that. Anakin is a very understanding boy." Luke set aside the folded garments and seated himself at Mara's feet. "How are you?"

One corner of her mouth tucked itself into a smirk. "You're the Jedi Master, you tell me."

Luke reached out through the Force toward her and quickly encountered the defenses she'd set up. It felt as if she'd

"What you did on Courkrus. You terrorized people. Made them see frightening things that weren't there." A triumphant smirk played over Ganner's features. "You might have been going by the name Keiran Halcyon then, but you used the methods we use. You know how effective they can be."

"No, no, no." Corran shook his head. "You're not going to use what I did at Courkrus to justify your actions. Courkrus was an outlaw planet, ruled by pirates. I used their fear against them to break down their confederation. I made those who deserved to fear someone bringing justice, actually fear justice having arrived. You all come into a situation and hold yourselves back, aloof, judging always. No one can feel safe around you—they always have to wonder when you will come to judge them."

"We deter them from turning to the dark side that way."

"Yeah, I've heard that argument before, from guys at CorSec and in every security service on any planet I've ever visited. Fear, regardless of what good it might accomplish, is a stepping-stone on the path to the dark side." Corran held his hands up. "None of that matters, though. You don't want me interfering with you on this mission of ours, fine. Don't give me cause to interfere with you. We're to go, find some academics, and bring them home. It's very simple."

Ganner Rhysode snorted at his description of the mission, and Corran felt just a glimmer of respect for the man's rejection of that description. *Perhaps you are a little bit sharper than I am willing to grant.*

"I do hope it will be simple, but these things never are." Ganner waved a hand back toward the Great Temple. "Though some are taking refuge in the idea that the hyperspace disturbance around the galaxy will keep out all but the few Yuuzhan Vong who squirted through, I think the analogy that it's like a storm, a storm that may be abating, is more likely true. If so, we will likely find Yuuzhan Vong on that world and many others. I'll be ready."

Ganner dropped a hand to his lightsaber. "I'll do whatever it takes to show these invaders why they never should have come here."

"Aren't you forgetting something?"

"What?" Ganner snarled a bit as he slapped his neck. "The Yuuzhan Vong are invaders. W them back."

"Our mission is to save the academics." carefully as the larger man slapped at more i little detail, but you can see how painful miss things can be."

Ganner growled again and brushed garnan clothes. "You did this to me."

"Not me. Perhaps you stepped on a colony's m Corran kept his mirth in check. *I* will *have to spe about this.* He admired his son's sense of family, bu wasn't a tool for playing practical jokes. *I think he k I just have to remind him of it and make sure he doe that mistake again.*

Ganner angrily scratched at his clothes and slappe nants. "They're everywhere."

A shiver ran down Corran's spine as he caught a mental image of the Yuuzhan Vong swarming over Ganner the way the insects were. "Head back to the temple and hit a refresher station. They've painted you with a scent that will draw more to you. We'll go as soon as you are rid of them."

"You may think this is funny, Horn, but I'm serious about what I've said. Don't get in my way." The taller man tore his tunic off and started running toward the Great Temple.

Corran watched him go until he could no longer see the re bite bumps all over Ganner's back. "I have no intention being in your way, Ganner, unless you force me to be there he muttered at the retreating figure. "If you do, I guess w find out just who really *is* the stronger Jedi."

wrapped herself in thorns, then cobbled together body armor from starship hull plates. Beyond that were kilometers of wrappings holding her in all tight. Each line of defense brought his probe up short, then a little, tiny gap opened, allowing him to move deeper and deeper.

Finally, beyond the wrappings and past an ocean of images, hopes, and fears, he reached Mara's core. When he experienced her through the Force this way she always appeared to him to be white-hot, flaring brilliantly. She was the most vibrant and alive person he'd ever known—something made all that much more remarkable since the Emperor would have tried to dampen down her vitality while she was in his service.

The illness she had contracted had sapped some of her strength, but her resilience kept it at bay. He could feel the Force flowing through her, constantly rebuilding the damage done and keeping the disease beaten back. While the initial encounters with the Yuuzhan Vong had distracted her and allowed the disease to advance, she had made a major effort toward recovery.

She is not yet whole again, but she is gaining in strength. Luke gave her a smile. "I'd say you are doing very well, my love."

Mara sat forward and reached out to stroke Luke's cheek. "I'm doing better, but not well enough."

"Give it time, Mara." He kissed her on the wrist. "Impatience is handmaiden to despair."

"And despair is of the dark side." Mara nodded slightly. "I understand, Master Skywalker."

Luke shook his head. "You know what I mean."

"I do, Luke, and I know why you warn me that way. Your empathy and caution are two of your more endearing qualities." She lay back down, drawing her knees up to give Luke more room.

Luke rested his chin on her right knee. "You don't mind having Anakin accompany you to Dantooine?"

She shook her head. "I *can* go it alone, if you need him elsewhere."

"If you don't want him with you, I can find another assignment for him." The Jedi Master kissed her kneecap. "I don't want you burdened with something that's really my problem."

"Luke!" Mara's voice gained in volume and developed a little of an edge. "When we married, your problems became my problems."

"Yes, but Anakin is part of my family, and the way you grew up, you didn't have a chance to—"

Mara spitted him with a green-eyed stare. "Want to consider again what you're saying there, Raised-as-an-only-child Skywalker?"

Luke laughed silently for a moment. "Point taken."

"Take this one, too. When I agreed to marry you, I knew what I was getting into. We agreed to share our lives, which means we agreed to share all of the problems as well as the joys." Mara closed her eyes for a moment. "I like Anakin. I can sympathize with what he is going through." She opened her eyes again. "He feels responsible for Chewbacca's death. At one time I felt responsible for the Emperor's death. Both of us have lost someone who was part of the foundation of our lives. If I can help him through that, well, he won't have to go through the things I did to find his way back out again."

She glanced up at Luke. "Of course, I imagine he's not thrilled at being saddled with a sick old lady heading to a backwater world for a rest cure."

"Actually, he accepted the assignment very willingly. I told him I was entrusting you to his care. He shouldered that responsibility very positively. He's done a good job requisitioning all the things you'll need on Dantooine."

Mara's eyes flashed. "I caught that burst of caution from you, Luke. What is it?"

"I clearly need to work on control more." He sighed. "You know the star charts. Dantooine is fairly well Rimward. It could be in the Yuuzhan Vong invasion corridor—if there is one. Sending you and Anakin out there all alone—"

"Is probably the best shot you have at getting some scouting done so you can assess the scope of the invasion." Mara scooted back, sitting up and piling pillows behind her back.

braced if the Jedi order is to fulfill its destiny in the galaxy."
Ganner gestured easily, and the rock rose in the air as if
lodged in some invisible turbolift. "I will do what must be
done for us to complete our mission, but I will not brook interference from *you*."

The rock shot straight at Corran. He dodged to the right.
The rock veered wide to the left, then tumbled and crashed
back through the underbrush.

Ganner smirked at him. "Do you understand what I am
saying?"

"Sure." Corran let his hands fall to his sides easily. "You're
saying that your philosophy is more important than the job
we're being sent to do."

"That's not it at all."

"Sure it is, but I don't expect you to understand that."
Corran shook his head. "You and Kyp and the others that believe the way you do—you're working very hard to establish
what the Jedi mean to this galaxy. You're doing that by
wearing sharp uniforms and taking strong stands. Much of
the time you're probably right in the stands you take—I can't
disagree with them. What I don't like is how you make the
stands, and how you work. You're all saying, 'Hey, we are
Jedi. We deserve your respect.' I happen to think we need to
earn it."

Ganner's expression darkened. "We *have* earned it. The
Jedi made order out of the chaos of the Empire."

"No, *a* Jedi did that, *the* only Jedi there was at the time who
was willing to stand up and fight the Empire. Luke Skywalker
earned the galaxy's respect, not the rest of us. Our fight has to
be waged each and every day out there, and here's a hologram
you'd best study from all sides: People end up being inherently suspicious and resentful of anyone who sets himself up
to sort right from wrong." Corran gave him a half smile. "I
saw it when I worked for CorSec, and I've seen it as a Jedi."

The taller man threw his head back and laughed. "You, of
all people, have the least call to criticize us for trying to establish an image that makes our jobs easier."

"How do you plot that course?"

"What you did on Courkrus. You terrorized people. Made them see frightening things that weren't there." A triumphant smirk played over Ganner's features. "You might have been going by the name Keiran Halcyon then, but you used the methods we use. You know how effective they can be."

"No, no, no." Corran shook his head. "You're not going to use what I did at Courkrus to justify your actions. Courkrus was an outlaw planet, ruled by pirates. I used their fear against them to break down their confederation. I made those who deserved to fear someone bringing justice, actually fear justice having arrived. You all come into a situation and hold yourselves back, aloof, judging always. No one can feel safe around you—they always have to wonder when you will come to judge them."

"We deter them from turning to the dark side that way."

"Yeah, I've heard that argument before, from guys at CorSec and in every security service on any planet I've ever visited. Fear, regardless of what good it might accomplish, is a stepping-stone on the path to the dark side." Corran held his hands up. "None of that matters, though. You don't want me interfering with you on this mission of ours, fine. Don't give me cause to interfere with you. We're to go, find some academics, and bring them home. It's very simple."

Ganner Rhysode snorted at his description of the mission, and Corran felt just a glimmer of respect for the man's rejection of that description. *Perhaps you are a little bit sharper than I am willing to grant.*

"I do hope it will be simple, but these things never are." Ganner waved a hand back toward the Great Temple. "Though some are taking refuge in the idea that the hyperspace disturbance around the galaxy will keep out all but the few Yuuzhan Vong who squirted through, I think the analogy that it's like a storm, a storm that may be abating, is more likely true. If so, we will likely find Yuuzhan Vong on that world and many others. I'll be ready."

Ganner dropped a hand to his lightsaber. "I'll do whatever it takes to show these invaders why they never should have come here."

"Aren't you forgetting something?"

"What?" Ganner snarled a bit as he slapped at a garnant on his neck. "The Yuuzhan Vong are invaders. We need to drive them back."

"Our mission is to save the academics." Corran smiled carefully as the larger man slapped at more insects. "It's a little detail, but you can see how painful missing the little things can be."

Ganner growled again and brushed garnants from his clothes. "You did this to me."

"Not me. Perhaps you stepped on a colony's main tunnel." Corran kept his mirth in check. *I* will *have to speak to Valin about this.* He admired his son's sense of family, but the Force wasn't a tool for playing practical jokes. *I think he knows that. I just have to remind him of it and make sure he doesn't make that mistake again.*

Ganner angrily scratched at his clothes and slapped at garnants. "They're everywhere."

A shiver ran down Corran's spine as he caught a mental image of the Yuuzhan Vong swarming over Ganner the way the insects were. "Head back to the temple and hit a refresher station. They've painted you with a scent that will draw more to you. We'll go as soon as you are rid of them."

"You may think this is funny, Horn, but I'm serious about what I've said. Don't get in my way." The taller man tore his tunic off and started running toward the Great Temple.

Corran watched him go until he could no longer see the red bite bumps all over Ganner's back. "I have no intention of being in your way, Ganner, unless you force me to be there," he muttered at the retreating figure. "If you do, I guess we'll find out just who really *is* the stronger Jedi."

CHAPTER SEVEN

Through the doorway to the bedroom they shared, Luke Skywalker caught a glimpse of his wife reclining on the bed. She lay there very comfortably, her red-gold hair spread around her head like a halo. Her chest rose and fell regularly and gently—peacefully, really—prompting him to realize how little peace they had known in their life together.

Beside her, on the bed, lay a few folded garments that needed to be stuffed into the traveling bags at the foot of the bed. Hers were mostly full, and two bags had been set out for him. Luke smiled, appreciating her thoughtfulness, and admiring her for taking the extra effort to get his bags out, despite the draining fatigue that was part of her illness.

He entered the room quietly, hoping not to disturb her, but her eyes flickered open. "Luke. Good, it's you."

"Who else would you have expected?"

She smiled, a bit haltingly, but with enough strength to send a thrill through him. "Anakin. I don't want to be late for our departure."

"Don't worry about that. Anakin is a very understanding boy." Luke set aside the folded garments and seated himself at Mara's feet. "How are you?"

One corner of her mouth tucked itself into a smirk. "You're the Jedi Master, you tell me."

Luke reached out through the Force toward her and quickly encountered the defenses she'd set up. It felt as if she'd wrapped herself in thorns, then cobbled together body armor from starship hull plates. Beyond that were kilometers of wrappings holding her in all tight. Each line of defense brought his probe up short, then a little, tiny gap opened, allowing him to move deeper and deeper.

Finally, beyond the wrappings and past an ocean of images, hopes, and fears, he reached Mara's core. When he experienced her through the Force this way she always appeared to him to be white-hot, flaring brilliantly. She was the most vibrant and alive person he'd ever known—something made all that much more remarkable since the Emperor would have tried to dampen down her vitality while she was in his service.

The illness she had contracted had sapped some of her strength, but her resilience kept it at bay. He could feel the Force flowing through her, constantly rebuilding the damage done and keeping the disease beaten back. While the initial encounters with the Yuuzhan Vong had distracted her and allowed the disease to advance, she had made a major effort toward recovery.

She is not yet whole again, but she is gaining in strength. Luke gave her a smile. "I'd say you are doing very well, my love."

Mara sat forward and reached out to stroke Luke's cheek. "I'm doing better, but not well enough."

"Give it time, Mara." He kissed her on the wrist. "Impatience is handmaiden to despair."

"And despair is of the dark side." Mara nodded slightly. "I understand, Master Skywalker."

Luke shook his head. "You know what I mean."

"I do, Luke, and I know why you warn me that way. Your empathy and caution are two of your more endearing qualities." She lay back down, drawing her knees up to give Luke more room.

Luke rested his chin on her right knee. "You don't mind having Anakin accompany you to Dantooine?"

She shook her head. "I *can* go it alone, if you need him elsewhere."

"If you don't want him with you, I can find another assignment for him." The Jedi Master kissed her kneecap. "I don't want you burdened with something that's really my problem."

"Luke!" Mara's voice gained in volume and developed a little of an edge. "When we married, your problems became my problems."

"Yes, but Anakin is part of my family, and the way you grew up, you didn't have a chance to—"

Mara spitted him with a green-eyed stare. "Want to consider again what you're saying there, Raised-as-an-only-child Skywalker?"

Luke laughed silently for a moment. "Point taken."

"Take this one, too. When I agreed to marry you, I knew what I was getting into. We agreed to share our lives, which means we agreed to share all of the problems as well as the joys." Mara closed her eyes for a moment. "I like Anakin. I can sympathize with what he is going through." She opened her eyes again. "He feels responsible for Chewbacca's death. At one time I felt responsible for the Emperor's death. Both of us have lost someone who was part of the foundation of our lives. If I can help him through that, well, he won't have to go through the things I did to find his way back out again."

She glanced up at Luke. "Of course, I imagine he's not thrilled at being saddled with a sick old lady heading to a backwater world for a rest cure."

"Actually, he accepted the assignment very willingly. I told him I was entrusting you to his care. He shouldered that responsibility very positively. He's done a good job requisitioning all the things you'll need on Dantooine."

Mara's eyes flashed. "I caught that burst of caution from you, Luke. What is it?"

"I clearly need to work on control more." He sighed. "You know the star charts. Dantooine is fairly well Rimward. It could be in the Yuuzhan Vong invasion corridor—if there is one. Sending you and Anakin out there all alone—"

"Is probably the best shot you have at getting some scouting done so you can assess the scope of the invasion." Mara scooted back, sitting up and piling pillows behind her back.

"As we've discussed, the attacks we've already dealt with were decidedly unmilitary. There was no reconnaissance in force, no establishment of forward bases that could be supported, none of the things we'd expect from an invasion. Whatever is going to be following this up will now have to work more cautiously because they know we're alerted."

"I can't fault your logic, but I don't like the idea of having you on the front line."

"But Dantooine isn't a serious military target. That's why the Rebels chose it as a base, only to abandon it later. And that's why Tarkin didn't destroy it with the Death Star."

Luke shrugged uneasily. "That's assuming *their* sense of targets is the same as ours. You remember what they did on Belkadan. Maybe their selection criteria are different from ours."

"All the more reason we need to have people scouting far and wide, to figure them out."

The Jedi Master shook his head. "There's basically no way that you won't be able to twist my concerns around into proof that you and Anakin *should* be sent to Dantooine, is there?"

"It is only because I know you so well, my love." Mara crooked a finger, beckoning him closer.

Luke stretched out on the bed, resting his upper body on his elbows. "You do know me, Mara, better than I know myself."

"But not as well as I will know you when we're old and gray together." She leaned forward and kissed him on the forehead. "And I know your concern for me, and for all the other Jedi heading out, is simply a mechanism you use to avoid thinking about the dangers you will face. After all, we are going to worlds where the Yuuzhan Vong *might* appear. *You* are going to a world where we already know they've been, and we have no clue as to what you will find on Belkadan."

"All I want to find there is something to help cure you. You said you felt a connection between the plague there and your illness. If I can track down something that will be more helpful—"

She pressed a finger against his lips. "You will, Luke. Facing all we've faced, there is no way I'm letting some ague kill me. If the cure comes from Belkadan, great. If we have to find it elsewhere, that's fine, too. The key thing is to find out for certain if my illness is connected to the Yuuzhan Vong. If it is, when I get healthy, the Yuuzhan Vong will pay."

Luke raised his face and kissed her on the lips. "When, ah, you and I were on the opposite side of things, that sort of spirit made me a bit fearful of our finally having to face each other in combat. Now I almost feel sorry for the Yuuzhan Vong."

"They brought it on themselves. No one invited them here." Mara returned his kiss, long and fiercely. "Don't you worry about me, Luke. Take care of yourself and Jacen. Anakin and I will do just fine."

He nodded. "I know you will." He kissed her again. "I will miss you terribly, you know."

Mara ran her fingers back through his hair. "And I will miss you, too, husband. But, our being apart from time to time is something I also accepted when I became your wife. We part now so we can be together forever. Not the best bargain in life, but not the worst, either. And, for now, husband mine, it is a bargain I am more than happy to accept."

CHAPTER EIGHT

As his X-wing cleared the dorsal launch bay on the Bothan Assault Cruiser *Ralroost,* Gavin Darklighter tugged back on the stick and rolled to starboard to watch the rest of the squadron emerge. The Bothan Assault Cruiser was one of the latest additions to the New Republic fleet. While slightly smaller than a *Victory*-class Star Destroyer, and possessed of leaner and less angular lines, the *Ralroost* boasted 20 percent more firepower than a Vic and almost half again as much in terms of shielding and armor. The ship had been designed to take a severe pounding and still hammer an enemy.

Gavin recalled the discussion he'd had with his wife and his sister when the Bothans announced plans to build the Assault Cruisers. Peace had been declared with the Imperial Remnant, so the ships were seen as either a foolish allocation of resources, hints at future Bothan aggression, or, as far as Sera and Rasca were concerned, a gross waste of money. Given that peace reigned in the galaxy, both of them thought the money needed to build one of the ships could be better spent on healing the scars of decades-long war.

Their arguments had been persuasive, but Gavin had reserved judgment, and as he looked down at the ship, he was glad the Bothans had built it. The fighter hangars were amidships and had launch apertures that would let the fighters head up or down, as needed, to get into battle. The dual launch paths also meant recovering fighters after a battle was faster, and Gavin very much appreciated that detail.

He keyed his comm unit. "One flight on me. Five, you have two, and, Nine, you have three."

His two subordinate commanders, Major Inyri Forge and Major Alinn Varth, acknowledged his command, and not for the first time did the incongruity of having female voices linked to those flight designators strike him. For almost the whole of Gavin's time in the squadron, Nine had been Corran Horn, and Five had been Hobbie or Janson or Tycho Celchu. *Then again, Lead was almost always Wedge, but now I'm the leader.*

The flights spread out and turned toward the center of the star system. It wasn't much to look at, with an asteroid belt separating two small, very hot planets from three larger gas giants. None of the planets themselves supported life, though the largest gas giant did have some moons that were almost hospitable—if one could tolerate a low-oxygen, high-nitrogen mix for breathing. *If not for some mining done in the asteroids, and the fact that traffic from Bastion uses this as a nav point to the Corporate Sector, this would be another dull spot on star charts.*

The system didn't even have a name, which struck Gavin as appropriate, for it had been largely without any notoriety for as long as folks had visited it. That had changed within a week, when a freighter stopped to scout the asteroids for any salvage. Fighters of unknown origin had jumped the ship, but the freighter got away and reported the incident. Admiral Kre'fey had taken his *Ralroost* out to investigate. Rogue Squadron shifted from playing pirates to becoming pirate hunters and shipped along.

Gavin punched up an analysis program and loaded it into his targeting computer. "Catch, push sensors. We know there were snubfighters out here, but I need to find their base."

The droid warbled his understanding quickly.

Inyri's voice crackled through the comm speakers in his helmet. "Lead, we have transient contacts in the asteroid belt, 247 mark 30. They're shadowing us."

"I copy. Got enough to identify them?"

"Matches aren't coming up easily, so I'm guessing uglies."

"Keep an eye on them." Gavin thought for a second, then nodded to himself. "On my mark, all Rogues will break onto course 270 mark 27. We're aiming for the big asteroid there, the one that's slowly rolling."

Confirmations of the orders came back to him over the comm unit.

Gavin reached up and flicked a switch that locked the fighter's S-foils in attack position. He studied his sensor scopes but got nothing. *Well, if they won't show themselves easily, we'll just have to root them out ourselves.* "Rogues, on my mark, three, two, one, *mark*." He kicked his X-wing up on its port stabilizers and eased the stick back, then leveled out and saw the rest of his flight cruise in behind him.

He switched his comm unit over to the command frequency he shared with the *Ralroost*. "Rogue Leader here. We have contacts and are investigating."

"Understood, Rogue Leader. Good hunting."

Gavin forced himself to take a deep breath, then to exhale slowly. While he trusted Inyri's judgment about the ships they'd be flushing from the asteroids, he couldn't shake the sense of dread that came with the memory of his first sim encounter with the coralskippers. *Even though we've run sims against skips, coming up against them for real will be very dangerous.*

From behind the big asteroid burned opposition. Catch painted contact after contact on Gavin's secondary monitor. All of the ships were, in fact, uglies, cobbled together from parts of older fighters. They included TIE-wings, which were TIE fighter cockpits married to Y-wing engine nacelles; X-ceptors, which were X-wing bodies with TIE interceptor wings; and triple-finned tri-fighters, nicknamed clutches because the ball cockpit was held in the grip of the three fins' forward edges. All the ships were as common in pirate fleets as hydrogen was in the galaxy, and all of them could be very deadly.

Gavin dropped his targeting reticle on the lead clutch and

flicked his weapons over to lasers. He linked them for dual fire, then glanced at his targeting monitor. The range to target scrolled down quickly, but that concerned him less than another detail the sensor scan provided him.

The clutch had no shields. There was no reason any pilot going into combat wouldn't bring his shields up to full power. The tri-fighter was known to possess shields—which was one of the reasons it had become a successful pirate-ship design. Without shields the pirates would never stand a chance against the Rogues.

"Catch, get me their tactical frequency." Gavin nudged his stick to the right and triggered a burst that burned red past the clutch's nose. "Five, you show any shields on these guys?"

"Negative, Lead. Hulls are weak, too."

What's happening here? Gavin lined up another shot at the clutch and waited for it to fire first. The clutch kept coming, closing well within optimal range, then finally shot a green laser bolt at Gavin's X-wing. The energy sent a static hiss through the comm unit's speakers as it dissipated against the shields. It had done less damage to them than it should have, and only one of the two lasers on the clutch had fired.

And the only reason a pilot has to get that close is if he's shooting with visual data—his sensors must be out.

The clutch flashed past, and Gavin rolled to starboard, then hauled back on the stick and started chasing the clutch. He inverted, then dived and goosed his throttle to follow the tri-fighter through its evasive maneuvers. He switched his lasers over to quad fire, then settled his middle finger on the stick's secondary trigger button. *This modification was meant to use against the skips, but could be of use here, I think.*

He lined up his shot, then pulled the secondary trigger. The lasers cycled quickly, producing a hail of down-powered laser darts that stippled little burn marks all over the clutch's fins. The fire gnawed away at the pirate ship, burning off black-and-white droid-fist insignia emblazoned there.

The clutch rolled to port, then climbed sharply. Gavin chopped his throttle back, inverted, and started to climb after the clutch. He let the pirate fighter climb into his sights, then sprayed more laserfire over the ship. These bolts struck on the forward canopy and clearly surprised the pilot. The clutch jerked to starboard, then one of the ion engines belched a long jet of flaming exhaust. The other engine flared for a moment, then both shut down.

Gavin started to cruise in for a closer look at the fighter when a heavy turbolaser bolt slashed through the void between him and it. Catch shrilled a warning, so Gavin rolled to port and dove toward the large asteroid that had been his goal.

The climb after the clutch had taken him above the asteroid's horizon, exposing him to the ship that lay hidden behind it. He vaguely recognized it as a Nebulon-B escort frigate, but that was only from the general profile. The ship had been hammered badly, with gaping holes opened in the hull. His sensors showed some flickerings of shields, but they remained weak enough that Gavin knew a strafing run by his X-wing would punch through and do serious damage.

"Catch, put their tactical frequency on comm channel four." The requisite button on his comm unit began to glow, so Gavin punched it, intensifying the light. "This is Colonel Gavin Darklighter of the New Republic. Identify yourselves and stand down, or you *will* be destroyed."

"This is . . ." The voice coming through the speakers started bold and defiant, but faltered quickly, weakening sharply. "This is Urias Xhaxin of the *Free Lance*."

"Lead, break port."

Without thinking, Gavin juked his fighter left, then saw green laser bolts blaze through the space he'd just left. A TIE-wing dived through, followed closely by Rogue Two. Kral Nevil's quad burst burned one of the Y-wing nacelles from the ugly, leaving the pirate fighter to spiral down and explode against the asteroid's craggy surface.

"Thanks, Two."

"Just my job, Lead, watching your back."

"Captain Xhaxin, order your forces to stand down. They can't fight us. Your ships are all damaged. You don't want a slaughter any more than we do."

Weariness weighed heavily in the man's reply. "You're right, of course. There comes a time when you have to stop fighting. I'll give the order, Colonel."

Gavin punched up the squadron's tactical frequency. "The pirates will be standing down. Fire only if fired upon."

Kral's X-wing came up on Gavin's port side. The Quarren pilot got a look at the frigate, then glanced in Gavin's direction. "It looks reef-raked in high seas, Colonel. What could have done it?"

"I don't know, Two, but I don't think we'll like the answer when we get it."

Gavin saw to the recovery of the pirates to the *Ralroost,* then joined Admiral Kre'fey in his ready room. Aside from the two guards standing inside the door, the Bothan admiral was alone with the pirate leader. "Ah, Colonel Darklighter, thank you for joining us. You've spoken with Captain Xhaxin."

"I have." Gavin turned to the seated human and offered him his hand. "Thank you for ending the fight so quickly."

The pirate glanced up, his dark eyes filled with exhaustion and something else. The man looked haggard. His long hair and neatly trimmed beard were white. It and his pale flesh contrasted sharply with his black uniform, and save for the red of bloodshot eyes, the man could have been a simple black-and-white holograph. "I should thank you for letting me permit my people to live."

Traest Kre'fey waved Gavin to a chair. "You may not know this, but Urias Xhaxin has quite a history with the *Free Lance*. He operated as a privateer raiding Imperial shipping, then continued to prey on Imps during the warlord period. Since the peace he's been out here, on the Rim, taking off the occasional unreconstructed Imperial making a run for the Remnant. Pickings have been slim, and his choice of targets has made him a low-priority issue for the New Republic."

Gavin nodded slowly. "I remember seeing a holodrama about him once."

Xhaxin snorted. "Purest fiction. A holojournalist came out

to report on my activities. She had some romantic idea of what we were doing. She was disappointed, so she created her fantasy and someone committed it to holo."

Traest's head came up. "I take it what happened to you recently on the Rim wasn't a fantasy."

"Not mine." The man hugged his arms to his chest. "I set up an operation to lure in people wanting to travel in a convoy to the Remnant. They met on Garqi and departed on a schedule I'd devised, to a point of my choosing. I intended to capture them all. We arrived just before the last ship was supposed to get in, and found the ships already under attack. The things hitting them—I guess they were ships . . . I'd never seen their like before. Gravitic anomalies all over. They shot plasma that ate into ships. They oriented on us almost immediately."

The man's eyes focused distantly and his voice shrank. "I did what we could, but there were too many of them. We plotted a blind jump out, then another, which landed us here. My hyperdrive motivators blew, and the structural damage— well, I don't know if the *Free Lance* could ever hit lightspeed again. I know I don't have the resources to salvage her."

Xhaxin looked up at Traest. "So, Admiral, you've caught me. I don't think the old Imperial bounty is still good, but I'm certain someone will pay for my carcass. Other than that, I'm useless. If I weren't, I'd not have lost my command."

"Oh, no, Captain Xhaxin, not at all." Traest nodded at Gavin. "Colonel, if you would see Captain Xhaxin to guest quarters, I would be obliged."

Xhaxin raised an eyebrow. "I don't understand."

"You met and fought with an enemy we're going to be seeing a lot more of—much more than we want. Your understanding of their tactics and nature is worth far more than any bounty." The Bothan smiled carefully. "I need to know what you know. I need to understand what you understand. If we can't learn how to deal with this threat, you'll find that, all too quickly, your *Free Lance* could be left the most powerful ship in the whole of the New Republic."

CHAPTER NINE

Leia Organa Solo smiled cautiously at Danni Quee and Jaina. The two of them had arrived at the temporary office she'd been given by the Agamarian Council with enough time to spare so she could inspect their clothes. Leia circled a finger, prompting a sigh from Jaina, but both young women turned around to show off their attire.

Jaina wore a dark brown pilot jumpsuit, but had pulled a lighter tan Jedi cloak over it. She wore no gun or gunbelt, but did have her lightsaber dangling from her side. Her dark hair had been pulled back into a single braid and fastened with a silver ribbon.

Danni, on the other hand, wore a simple dress, functional and somberly colored. The dark green of the vest she wore over the top matched her eyes, while the darker brown of the dress itself contrasted well with her pale skin and blond hair, which Danni wore unbound. She carried no weapons, and while she did not look helpless, she clearly was not a warrior by birth or training.

Leia glanced over at Elegos. "I think they will do."

The Caamasi glanced back over his shoulder at the two women. "Quite presentable, indeed."

Leia frowned. "You don't think this will work, do you?"

Elegos shrugged, gathering his hands at the small of his back. He stared out through the balcony doors at the ocean north of Calna Muun, the Agamarian capital. "I think your reading of these people, of their respect for tradition and family, is accurate. We know they contributed much to the effort against the Imperials, and they suffered for it. Keyan Farlander was but one of their sons and daughters that flew from here to wage war against the Empire."

"But?"

Elegos turned away from the balcony. "Some are capable of shouldering burdens for light-years, and others just kilometers."

An Agamarian appeared in the doorway to the office. "If you are ready, the council will hear you now."

"Danni?"

The young woman started for a moment, then looked at Leia. "Yes, I guess I am ready."

Elegos crossed to her and settled his hands on her shoulders. "Just remember, Danni, what the ExGal Society set out to do, it did. You are a witness to that fact. You are reporting to them what you know. That you can do, easily."

"Thank you. I know."

Leia let Elegos lead, with Danni in his wake. She slipped in beside her daughter. Keeping her voice low, she glanced at Jaina. "Something the matter?"

Jaina's head came up a bit. "I've got better control than that."

"Of the Force, yes, but not the expression on your face." Leia composed her own expression into one of serene confidence and nodded to various Agamarians lining the high-ceilinged hallways of the Council Center. The open, airy architecture that the Agamarians affected worked well for the warm, dry climate, keeping things cooler than might otherwise have been expected on such a bright, sunny day. Pillars and archways broke the corridor into segments, each featuring its own holographic tableaux of Agamarian history and culture.

Jaina sighed, clearly irritated. "I'm not a diplomat. I'm a pilot and a Jedi Knight. I don't mind teaching Danni some things while we fly, but my talents are being wasted here."

"I see." Leia smiled at her daughter, and then looked sharply at Jaina. "Jaina, tell me what's really going on."

Jaina's voice sank into a whisper. "Mother, you are good at this sort of thing, but if you'd completed your Jedi training, you'd be more effective."

"I worked hard at developing my skills."

"Mother . . ." Jaina faltered for a second. "Mother, you don't even wear your lightsaber."

The disappointment in Jaina's voice drilled through Leia. For years she had wanted to work more at becoming a Jedi. She saw it as a way to get to know her brother, Luke, and to help him with his dream of reversing the evil their father had done by destroying the Jedi. She'd practiced as much as she could, but other demands on her, demands born of her training as a politician and diplomat, always pulled her away.

I told myself I was doing my best by helping to create the government, then to run it. I let Luke train my children so they could reach their full potential, or so I thought. Did I also let them become Jedi to ease my guilt over having failed to realize my potential with the Force?

Jaina reached out with her left hand and settled it on her mother's shoulder. "I didn't mean it to sound the way it did. I . . . I know you didn't get to make some choices . . ."

"The choices I made, Jaina, were choices made to help others. They came first. Your father. You. Your brothers. The New Republic."

"I know that, and I'm proud of you, Mom, for being who you are." Jaina shrugged. "It's just that you're not a Jedi, not really, and, you know, it's just, well, weird when you play around with the Force."

"I see." Leia caught a flash of horror in her daughter's eyes, and that gratified her. *At least she knows there are boundaries she shouldn't overstep yet.* Then Leia sighed and raised her hand to hug Jaina's hand to her shoulder.

"You may be right, Jaina, that I never completed Jedi training, but I don't play with the Force. I use it, perhaps not as well or fully as you do, but I use it to get done the things I need to do."

"I know. I'm sorry."

"We'll discuss this more later, Jaina. Right now I need you with me in this chamber, being silent but strong, projecting confidence and benign power."

"Being everything that Kyp and the others aren't."

"Pretty much." She gave her daughter a wink, then stepped through the doorway into the Agamarian council chamber.

Though Leia had seen holographs of the chamber, they had failed to convey its breathtaking majesty. Wood had been used to finish the floor, panel the walls, and furnish the room; and incredible craftsmanship had gone into the project. An oceanic motif dominated everything—with the rows at which council delegates sat being arrayed like waves. Their desks flowed up and out of the flooring like cresting swells, in fact. At various points wooden streams of water linked leaping fish to the floor, and birds were bound by wing tip to the ceiling or walls.

At the podium, which appeared to be a stone being washed at the base by clashing waves, a tall, slender woman stood and turned toward Leia and her party. She beckoned Leia forward. "I have briefed the council on those things we have discussed over the past couple of days, so they are prepared for your presentation."

"Thank you, Madam Speaker." Leia, herself wearing a dark flowing robe whose only decoration was a wave motif embroidered at hem, collar, and cuffs, approached the podium. She nodded solemnly to the men and women seated before her.

"I thank you all for allowing me to address you. Before I begin, I want to identify those people I've brought with me. Elegos A'Kla is a Republic senator conducting a fact-finding mission here in the Outer Rim. Next to him is my daughter, Jaina, who has firsthand knowledge of the problem we face. And last is Danni Quee. She was stationed at ExGal-4, based on Belkadan, when the Yuuzhan Vong invaded and held her captive."

Leia rested her hands on the podium. "The Agamarian history of service to the New Republic is well known. I have no doubt that if not for the courage of Keyan Farlander, I certainly would not be standing here before you. I know that what I will present to you here, what you will have downloaded into your datapads, will be rather astounding, and yet, because it has been reduced to clinical analysis and data, it will be easy to dismiss. To do that would be the sort of error that will hurt Agamar and the New Republic. Please, hear what Danni has to say, read over the information, and listen to what I would like you to do. I hate to say that, once again, the New Republic is relying upon you, but it is."

She waved Danni forward, and the scientist coughed into her hand before beginning. "Please forgive me, I don't often address important people. I think that if I took to this sort of thing, I would not have become a scientist. In my work at ExGal, I was involved in looking outside the galaxy, where it was supposed nothing existed. Maybe I looked outside because looking back in meant I would face crowds, and that scares me more than a little."

A mild bit of good-natured chuckling greeted Danni's overture and seemed to put her more at ease. "What scares me more, now, is a combination of two things. One is the fact that there *is* something from beyond the galaxy. I know the stories you've all heard, the theories that have been taught, that a disturbance in hyperspace makes travel outside the galaxy impossible. That's a wonderful theory, but those who advanced it didn't think scientifically about it. A storm that lasts an hour for us would have been a lifetime of storm for an insect. Just because that disturbance has existed for as long as we've been able to measure it doesn't mean that it always did, or always will.

"And it doesn't mean someone else couldn't find a way through it or past it or around it. And they have." Danni's chin came up. "They are the Yuuzhan Vong. They are humanoid and capable of mimicking humans well enough that I never penetrated the disguise of Yomin Carr, the Yuuzhan Vong agent who infiltrated our team on Belkadan. I see some of you looking around at your fellows, wondering, perhaps, if they are Yuuzhan Vong. I don't think so. I hope not, but I do know the Yuuzhan Vong will be coming, and when they arrive, you will not like it at all."

Danni took in a deep breath, then let it go out slowly. "I was taken prisoner by the Yuuzhan Vong. I watched them torture another captive, a Jedi Knight. They sought to break his spirit and mind. I know that if they had subjected me to the same tortures, I would have just . . . fallen apart. Miko Reglia resisted and sacrificed his life so I could escape."

She pressed her hand to her mouth for a second, then blinked and continued. "The Yuuzhan Vong are a cruel people who employ biological devices the way we use machines. The reports you have will fill you in on the details. Some of it may seem silly, like having starfighters grown out of coral, but the fact remains that these ships had capabilities we've not faced before and have no easy way to counter.

"Perhaps worst of all, we are unclear as to the Yuuzhan Vong motive for invading our galaxy. We don't know if they will listen to reason, if they will negotiate some sort of peace. They showed no evidence of that when I was in their power. They told me I wouldn't be sacrificed, which tells me others were and will be, if they are not stopped."

Danni looked over at Leia and nodded. Leia approached and ran her hand down Danni's back. Leia glanced at her daughter, and Jaina came forward to direct Danni back to her place next to her. Danni's retreat took place to the accompaniment of murmurs from the council members, though that hubbub tailed off as Leia returned to the podium.

"As you already know, I am not here as a speaker for the New Republic government. In fact, I am certain that you will all find waiting for you messages from the local Republic envoy reminding you of this fact. I have no official standing with the New Republic. I went to Coruscant to ask for help for Dubrillion and other Rim worlds that will bear the brunt of this onslaught. I was sent away, so I have come here, with my daughter and friends, to alert you to the threat and to ask your help in dealing with it."

Leia frowned. "As I said before, I am well aware of all Agamar has done in the past for causes I espouse. You have always been friends of the New Republic, and now, I am afraid, the New Republic will abrogate its responsibilities to you. The worlds of the Rim must look to themselves to deal with this threat. In being driven away from Coruscant, I am now, like you, a citizen of the Rim. Please remember that as you consider what I am going to say.

"The Rim worlds need to band together and muster their military might to fight against the Yuuzhan Vong. We don't know where they will strike next, but we must all be ready to devote forces to that battle. Every victory we allow them will make them stronger. I know that asking you to do this will cost you greatly, both in money and, potentially, in the blood of your men and women. These are not sacrifices I ask you to make lightly."

As Leia looked out over the assembly she began to sense growing resistance to her words. This did not surprise her, but it did cut at her spirit. She had hoped that if she could get Agamar to take the lead against the Yuuzhan Vong, other worlds could be convinced to follow their example. *Perhaps Elegos is right—they've carried their burden as far as they can.*

She shifted her approach. "Regardless of your ability to contribute forces to any military effort, as a neighbor, I urge you to prepare for what the Yuuzhan Vong invasion will cause. Refugees will likely be coming this way, fleeing in small ships and large. I know the Agamarian people will not turn them away, but the burden of caring for people who have been driven from their homes is not one to be undertaken without preparation. Gather resources, establish plans, do whatever you must to help those who will be helpless."

Leia hesitated for a moment, then nodded slowly. "I know I am asking a lot of you. I know you will do what you can, and even more than that. In the name of the countless people who share the Rim with you, I thank you. We will be heading deeper into the Rim, back toward Dubrillion, to face the Yuuzhan Vong. Knowing that you, the people of Agamar, are here, supporting us, will brighten the darkest hour and lighten the heaviest load."

She took a single step back from the podium, then lifted her chin and clasped her hands behind her back. She waited for questions or comments, steeling herself for the sort of snide accusations she'd faced on Coruscant, but none came. Here and there, starting at the back of the room, but quickly moving to the front, council members stood and began to applaud. Currents of sympathy and pride flowed through the chamber, swirling around her, and sweeping past to embrace Danni, as well.

The council speaker stepped over to Leia and shook her hand. "You have made an honest presentation to us, and we will give it all due consideration—more consideration than Coruscant offered. I cannot tell you what the outcome of our debate will be. I do not know what we can offer you, since there are those who do want to rebuild Agamar, and those individuals do hold a considerable amount of power."

Leia nodded. "I understand."

"Well, understand this, too. We, the people of Agamar, have prospered by helping each other. Your refugees will find safe passage through our system, and assistance. More than that I cannot say, but less than that would be unthinkable."

Leia shook the older woman's hand solemnly. "Well, then, the fight to stop the Yuuzhan Vong begins here. If other worlds are as brave as Agamar, perhaps the fight will stop out there, beyond the Rim, and the peace we've all earned will never again be threatened."

CHAPTER TEN

The freighter *Dalliance* reverted from hyperspace smoothly and began a long arc in toward Bimmiel. Corran Horn liked how easily the freighter handled. It was nothing like an X-wing, but it didn't feel as if he was driving a planetoid either. "Estimated time of arrival is thirty minutes."

Ganner barely grunted an acknowledgment of Corran's comment. He stared intently at a trio of overlapping holographically projected data windows. One showed Bimmiel as a khaki ball with slender stripes of blue radiating out from a large ocean in the southern hemisphere. Ice caps covered either pole, with the one in the south extending out into the ocean. Atmospheric readings and other data filled the space around the world. A second window showed a group of images of flora and fauna native to the world. Third and final—and the window Ganner was studying hardest—was the image of a communications relay satellite that appeared, to Corran, to have lost its antenna array.

"The satellite is damaged. The pulsar would make communications difficult under the best of circumstances. Without the satellite, though, messages aren't going to get out."

Corran nodded. "Do we have the codes needed to interrogate the satellite and dump its message cache to us?"

The other Jedi punched a button on the communications console, then shook his head. "Either the codes don't work, or without the antenna the satellite can't hear us. We could recover it. I can use the Force to load it into a cargo bay. From there we can run a wire in and make direct contact."

"Not that important at the moment." Corran glanced at his navigational data. "The satellite was placed in a geosynchronous orbit over their base camp, wasn't it?"

"Right. They're down there, below it, on the northern continent."

"What does the weather look like down there?"

Ganner frowned. "Tail end of sandgales. The air will be full of dust, but definitely breathable, provided we use filtration."

"Not like Belkadan?"

"No indication of any atmospheric changes that are out of the ordinary. Bimmiel has an elliptical orbit, and we're on the outward leg now. The Imp survey came on the inbound leg, so we're not sure what to expect. The Imps reported very little in the way of life down there, but I can feel a fair amount, can't you?"

"I can, yes."

"I get no evidence that the Yuuzhan Vong are down there." Ganner peered at him ice-eyed through the satellite image. "And, before you ask, no indications if the damage to the satellite was caused by some coralskipper's plasma blast or just a micrometeorite hitting the antenna."

Corran took Ganner's cautionary comment in stride. "I know, not all trouble can be or should be attributed to the Yuuzhan Vong. We don't know if they are here or not." *Of course, since we can't feel them through the Force, the only way we'll know if they are is when we see them. I'm not looking forward to any such encounter.* "Our mission is to find the academics and get them out."

"Simple."

"Unless we make it complicated." Corran glanced at the forward viewport. "I'll take the ship in and try to land as close to their camp as is prudent."

The freighter, which was a modified Corellian YT-1210, had a flat disk shape that enabled Corran to slide it into the Bimmiel atmosphere without a lot of difficulty. The freighter's mass meant the dying storms didn't bounce it around too much. Corran had dialed the inertial compensator down to 90 percent, just to give him a better feel for how the *Dalliance* flew. The storm did manage to bump and drop the freighter a little, but Corran didn't mind.

The fact that the turbulence made Ganner a bit gray also worked for Corran. The trip out from Yavin 4 had taken a few days, and his relationship with Ganner had become more cordial as the garnant bites faded from the larger man's flesh. Even so, it was readily apparent to Corran that Ganner wasn't going to back away from what he saw as the right method for projecting a powerful Jedi image, and Corran, on the other hand, wasn't going to embrace using fear as a tool to coerce cooperation from people.

As they got closer to reversion and landing, Ganner had begun to tighten up again. He'd donned his blue and black robes, polished his lightsaber, and been very precise in combing his hair and trimming his beard. Corran did have to admit that the man looked every millimeter a recruiter's dream and that, physically, the man was very impressive. *He's overconfident, overbearing, and abrasive, but he looks the perfect example of a Jedi.*

Corran flicked a switch, lowering the freighter's landing gear. He glanced at the altimeter and cut in the repulsorlift coils to settle the ship down easily. He got a bump four meters above where he felt the ship should have touched down, then the *Dalliance* continued to descend. It sank until the bottom hull pressed against the ground.

Wind-whipped sand hissed a tan curtain over the viewport. The sand slid away, providing a brief glimpse of a distant horizon, then another layer coated the transparisteel. Darker shadows loomed nearby, but the shifting sand gave Corran no chance to see what they were.

"Looks like we've sunk into the sand, so we're not going out through the landing ramp." Corran pointed a finger up toward the ceiling. "Topside hatch."

Ganner nodded and handed Corran a pair of goggles and a rebreather that had a comlink built into it. "There are sensor readings to the west, about a hundred meters off. Probably their camp."

"No life?"

"Life, yes. Human, no." Ganner closed his eyes for a moment, then nodded. "Fairly small life-forms. Nothing to worry about."

"Thanks." Corran rolled his eyes as he stepped past Ganner and into the companionway that gave him access to the top hatch tube. He mounted the ladder, disengaged the interlocks, and shoved up on the round hatch.

A brown curtain of sand poured down over him. Corran reflexively ducked his face away and felt a kilo of dirt stream down the back of his tunic, to be trapped at his waist by his belt. Because the rebreather filtered only the airborne sand, he could still smell the dry scent in the air. What surprised him about the wind was how cool it was. *Moving away from the sun has this world cooling off, so it won't be hot like Tatooine, just dirty. So much for Ganner's wardrobe.*

Corran glanced down to see what sort of a mess the sand had made of Ganner, but all he saw was sand around his feet, as if he was standing in a rapidly filling hole. He reached out with the Force and discovered the shield Ganner had erected with the Force to trap the sand in the tube. *Oh, very cute.*

He scrambled up the ladder, then watched the sand rise behind him and slide off the Force dome that rose to cap the tube. Ganner expanded it as he came up, but did not extend it to cover Corran. As he emerged, the bubble shrank, covering Ganner like a cloak. While Corran admired Ganner's control with the Force, he found employing it like an umbrella to be almost as bad as what Valin had done to Ganner with the garnants.

Corran walked to the edge of the freighter and looked down at the sand piling up against the craft's port hull. Beyond it, barely visible, he caught a hint of color—a small reddish pyramid—which he assumed marked the university camp. He crouched and let a handful of sand dribble out through his fingers.

Ganner stood above him. "Not that far down."

"Be my guest." Corran tugged his tunic from his trouser waistband and let sand pour out. "Show me how it's done."

The younger Jedi leapt from the ship's hull and immediately sank to his waist in the sand. His fists clenched for a moment, then he leapt up and rose serenely from the sand and returned to the freighter's hull. His boots and trousers were coated with dust.

"Little further down than it looks, isn't it?"

Ganner snorted. "Shall we break out the speeder bikes?"

"Nope. Dust is too fine for the engine filters to pull out of the air, so they'll just stall."

"Then how do we get over there?"

"We walk."

"But . . ."

Corran leapt out from the freighter and landed in a crouch. He sank to ankles and wrists in a trough between two little sand dunes. Rising up a bit, he started walking toward the university camp.

"How did you . . . You don't have enough ability in the Force to . . ."

Corran looked back at Ganner and waved him forward. "Move through the troughs. The lighter particles blow around, the heavier ones sink and are more compact. Still slow going, but it's going."

He heard Ganner crunch down behind him, but a gust of wind raised a cloud that obscured the younger man. Corran spread his senses into the Force and found Ganner easily. All around them he found other hot spots of life, ranging from small insects to more complex creatures. Fist-size mammals were most numerous, and something larger lurked at the fringes of his awareness.

He pushed on toward the camp and reached it with relative ease after a several-minute trek. A couple of rocky outcroppings defined the western edge of the camp. Long, dark-gray plinths thrust up through the sand like the fingers on a drowning man's hand. Below them were scraps of fabric that had once been part of tents. They flapped, red, blue, and green, from tent structural supports that were almost entirely buried in shifting sand.

Reaching out through the Force, Corran searched for life beneath the sand. Again he found insects and the small mammals—with many of the latter huddled together deep in a crevasse in the rocks. Others were moving through the sand, into one of the tents and back out again. Their course was so regular that Corran assumed they were moving along a tunnel and raiding a food store of some sort.

He looked at Ganner. "Aside from you, I get nothing very big."

"Same here. The small creatures are shwpi. The Imp survey team found them fairly common. The report says they're herbivores and indicates they grazed on the abundant vegetation."

"They've overgrazed it, then, very badly." Corran looked around, then climbed up on one of the rocks. "There is a much larger rock formation to the northwest, maybe half a kilometer off. The openings in it could lead to caves. Fly or walk?"

Ganner frowned. "Even I would tire if I had to float the two of us over there."

"Not with the Force, with the ship."

"Oh." He shrugged. "Walk, I guess. I've seen enough of that ship for a while."

"Me, too." Corran climbed down and started off toward the northwest. Because the wind was coming from the west, he was able to cut along a trough for a bit, then had to go over a dune crest and move along another trough. It was easier than trying to wade through an ocean, since the sand waves didn't pound into him. Still, sand managed to get everywhere and was decidedly more abrasive than water. The exertion also made him sweat, and the dry, cool air sucked as much moisture as it could from him.

As he made his way toward the rocks, he relied on the Force to tell him about his surroundings. He didn't sense many of the shwpi, and those he did encounter seemed paralyzed with fear. They trembled in deep burrows. And, still, at the very edge of his awareness, other life-forms moved and gathered.

Corran pushed on, then dropped to one knee about a hundred meters from their goal. He swiped a hand across his brow, then wiped his muddy palm off on his trouser leg. "At least it's not hot like Tatooine."

Ganner came over the low dune and crouched beside him. "True, that would just compound our misery."

"I should have thought to bring water, though." Corran frowned, then his head came up as something tickled his awareness. *Something is moving out there.* He glanced at Ganner. "Feel it?"

"Yes, coming in along this dune line, coming fast." Ganner pointed directly north. "The sand is shifting a bit there."

Corran turned and fingered his lightsaber. Sand moved, ever so slightly, falling from the crest of dunes and down. He sensed a life-form speeding within the lighter, dusty layer of sand near the surface. It burned brightly in the Force, almost blinding in intensity as it raced closer. Corran took a half step back by reflex and tapered down his sense of the Force.

The thing burst from the dune. Nothing more than a gray and white blur, it shot past Corran and dived into the next dune. Its powerful flat tail snapped back and forth, then disappeared within the sand. The beast shot off to the south, and both men watched the sand shift in its wake.

It wasn't until Ganner turned to look at him that Corran felt the stinging across his left thigh. His dusty black trousers had a neat gash slashed in them, and the pale flesh below was smeared with blood. The wound wasn't deep and didn't hurt that much, but if he'd not recoiled, it would have taken a huge chunk from his thigh.

Ganner's eyes grew wide, and he pointed to Corran's leg. "Is it bad?"

"No, but it could be." Corran turned and pointed to the south. "It's coming back."

"Two of them, and another starting from the north." Ganner pulled his lightsaber from his belt and ignited a sulfurous-yellow blade. "We can stop them."

"Yeah, maybe those three, but there are more out there." Corran could feel the shwpi burrowing deeper. He rejected that as a plan that he and Ganner could follow, which meant there was only one thing they could do. "Run for the rocks! Now!"

The *things*—and that was about the best Corran could do in making up any sort of name for the gray blur that had slashed him—came on fast and oriented on the two Jedi as they made their dash for the rocks. Corran threw himself up over a dune and did a shoulder roll down the other side. He saw the sand rippling in a line toward him, so he dropped into a crouch.

The thing burst from the dune and dove straight at him. Corran ignited his lightsaber and brought it up and around in a parry. The sizzling silver blade caught the creature behind the jaw and right in front of its shoulders, at what should have been a neck. Gray fur combusted into acrid smoke, and black blood splashed over the sand. The creature's head snapped at Corran's leg, once, then kept snapping and rolling across the ground until life drained from it. The body, stuck halfway into a dune, whipped the tail back in slackening slashes.

The creature's snout was long and tapered back into a wedge-shaped skull that was entirely covered in chitin or keratin, like fingernails, but much thicker and polished smooth by moving through the sand. Short but powerful limbs sprouted long claws, clearly designed for digging. The creature's gray fur was little more than down except for a fringe at the back of the skull, and the long flat tail was covered with keratin scales. Its side-to-side undulation obviously helped propel the supple body through the sand.

As striking as the creature's physical presence was the horrid stink it gave off. It smelled to Corran like vapor from rotting ronto meat mixed with the sourest ale and harshest cigarra he'd ever tasted. He choked back a desire to vomit and didn't terribly mind the scent of his gorge burning the creature's odor from his nostrils.

Corran leapt past the thrashing body and sprinted as fast as he could along the dune trough. He could feel two of the things pacing him. *They'll catch me, unless . . .*

He skidded to a stop, then lunged back at one dune. As he did so, he twisted the grip of his lightsaber, cutting in the dual-phase function. His lightsaber blade doubled in length and went from silver to purple. It sparked as he plunged it deep into the sand to skewer one of the things. The sand immediately boiled as the creature writhed out the last of its life.

Old-style Jedi, indeed!

The Corellian Jedi flattened as the second creature burst from the dune to his right and dived at him. Its attack tore a strip of cloth from his tunic, but missed scoring flesh. The creature's flight took it into the dune where its fellow was dying, and the second creature attacked the wounded one. Its jaws closed hard, cracking bones and making wet popping sounds that inspired Corran to get up and run again without looking back.

He went over another dune, and another, with Ganner pacing him slightly to the south, leaping dunes in prodigious bounds. Some of the creatures seemed to still be following them, but a growing number broke off and oriented toward the rolling bloody balls that were corpses being worried and devoured. The beasts arced from dune crest to dune crest, like fish leaping from the waves, and let loose with undulating little cries that made them sound like feral R2 units on a rampage.

Two men appeared on the rocky outcropping toward which the Jedi ran. Each of them bore a blaster carbine and started triggering off random shots, scattering them across the most direct route to the caves. More of the creatures moved away from the shots, letting Corran and Ganner come in fast.

Chests heaving, they reached the rocks. Corran extinguished his lightsaber and bent over to catch his breath. He glanced sidelong at one of his saviors. "Thanks for the help."

The young man nodded, then raised the carbine's muzzle as an older woman emerged from the mouth of a cave. Thickly built, and with dark gray hair pulled back in a tight bun, the woman had a hard look in her cobalt eyes that indicated she brooked no nonsense by those associated with her. For a half second she reminded him of his father-in-law, Booster Terrik, then she scowled and he realized he probably wasn't going to get along with her even that well.

Posting her fists on her hips, she shook her head. "Jedi. I should have known."

Ganner gave her a hard stare. "What do you mean?"

She lifted her chin to indicate the dunes. "Only fools or Jedi would cross a slashrat killing field. You've got light-sabers. That makes you Jedi." Her eyes narrowed. "Of course, that doesn't mean you're not also fools."

CHAPTER ELEVEN

Jacen Solo felt turmoil gathering in him like the roiling clouds down on Belkadan. He knew part of it was simply impatience. He and Luke Skywalker had entered the star system out toward the fringe and R2-D2 had plotted a simple course to Belkadan. It was designed to make them look like a piece of debris being drawn into Belkadan's atmosphere by gravity. To augment the deception, they shut down the engines and most sources of power, leaving the small ship a bit cold and decidedly dark.

He sat alone on the bridge, watching the stars slide past as Belkadan grew ever closer. Studying the planetary profile from Luke and Mara's previous visit, and supplementing it from the ExGal-4 survey of the planet, had prepared Jacen for a yellow-green ball with an atmosphere made mostly of carbon dioxide and methane, but new readings indicated the atmosphere had returned to near normal for Belkadan. The carbon dioxide level remained a bit elevated, and that contributed to it being warmer than archival data indicated it should have been, but not unpleasantly so.

So says Uncle Luke, but he grew up on Tatooine.

Part of Jacen understood exactly what had happened to Belkadan. The Yuuzhan Vong had released some sort of biological agent that had radically altered the planet's ecology, and apparently had something else in place to restore it again to near normal. Jacen was well aware of other examples of a population managing to alter a world's climate and ecology to suit them, so the Yuuzhan Vong's action wasn't unprecedented.

What *was* stunning was the speed with which they accomplished the changes. Just over two months had passed since Yomin Carr had destroyed the ExGal facility here, and already Belkadan was back to normal. Jacen allowed that the readings his uncle and aunt had taken from before might have been artificially high because of local concentrations of gases, but he knew that to be a rationalization and didn't believe it. He wanted to, however.

The reason for wanting to believe it touched on his turmoil. He was a Jedi Knight, schooled and skilled in the ways of the Force, yet when he reached out and touched Belkadan, he didn't sense anything that was terribly wrong. The world fairly pulsed with life, and none of it was malignant.

That latter fact bothered him because he'd seen the Yuuzhan Vong. He'd listened to Danni's stories of what they'd done to her and Miko. There was no doubt in his mind, no doubt whatsoever, that the Yuuzhan Vong were evil. *Such evil should be radiating off that planet like light from a glow panel.*

The fact that the Yuuzhan Vong's evil didn't register through the Force shook Jacen deeply. His life had been built on a foundation of good and evil, of light and dark. While he had never known the Emperor or Darth Vader, he *had* been touched by evil. Recognizing that sensation—the feeling of fiery needles being scraped over flesh—had been a mechanism by which he had steered himself. Now, all of a sudden, just like the blastboat, he was adrift and had no way of avoiding trouble.

The second that thought occurred to him, Jacen knew it wasn't true, but the Yuuzhan Vong's Force invisibility fed into the greater question of whether or not his uncle had found the correct path for the development of Jedi Knights. Luke's training had been predicated on good and evil, yet here was a clear threat and the Jedi Knights were at a disadvantage fighting it. Everything that they had been taught would not help them confront and defeat the Yuuzhan Vong.

He wondered if *his* approach—the idea of moving off into solitary contemplation of the Force—would provide him the means of recognizing and dealing with the Yuuzhan Vong. He couldn't bring himself to believe they were not part of the Force in some way. Jacen assumed that at whatever levels he had become attuned to the Force, the Yuuzhan Vong's presence did not somehow register. Animals could hear sounds he could not; alien species could see in spectrums he could not. *Is it possible that the Yuuzhan Vong can be spotted in the Force if one's awareness of it is expanded?*

He had no answer for that question, but he felt equally certain that his uncle's approach was going to be useless in handling the Yuuzhan Vong. He had no doubt that the Jedi Knights would fight long and hard, and he even counted on them being able to win some battles. Mara had succeeded in killing a Yuuzhan Vong warrior on Belkadan in a duel, but even she admitted that being unable to sense him through the Force put her at a severe disadvantage.

Yet, as much as Jacen wanted to withdraw, he felt guilty and selfish when he contemplated doing so. Danni's pained descriptions of how the Yuuzhan Vong had treated her tugged at his heartstrings. It also reminded him of how much his parents had done to help those who were helpless. He'd grown up in a family where taking responsibility for others was as much a part of life as breathing, and rejecting that ethic was something that just felt wrong to him.

By the same token, he'd seen what it had done to his parents and his uncle. Luke had fought the Empire for twenty years, and his mother had fought even longer than that. They constantly put their lives on the line, never having a moment that could be considered normal in their lives. If it wasn't kidnappers and assassins trying to snatch or kill them, it was some planet's population trying to wipe some other species out. His parents and his uncle never had time for themselves.

Jacen frowned and avoided descending to self-pity. Despite having to deal with the problems of others, his parents had always done their best to nurture their children. There might have been times when official business kept his mother away, but she always managed to make up for it—not by bringing some gift from a faraway world, but by sharing time with him and his siblings. And his father had gone from being protector to good friend and confidant. Luke had been friend and mentor, and all of them meant more to Jacen than he knew he would ever be able to express.

Which is why rejecting them and the way of the Jedi seemed wrong, and yet so necessary. His hands flexed into fists, then he forced them open again. Having grown up with an awareness of the Force, he understood it in ways that Luke never could. He had insights he could share with his uncle or mother, but they would never come upon those insights by themselves. *They see things in large chunks, and I see the details on those chunks.*

"It's almost time, isn't it?"

Jacen started, then looked over and saw his uncle hanging in the cockpit hatchway. "Yes. We're being pulled in by Belkadan's gravity. We have two minutes to atmosphere. I can take it in, you know."

Luke nodded, then slipped into the cockpit and dropped into the copilot's chair. R2-D2 rolled into the cockpit behind him and locked himself into a landing bracket built into the bulkhead. Luke smiled at the droid, then looked at Jacen. "Just remember, we want as little nudging as possible. We want everything to look natural."

Jacen nodded. His uncle had advanced the theory that if the Yuuzhan Vong used living creatures the way others used machines, then the patterns those creatures would be most adept at noticing would be the sort that were unnatural or panicked—prey behavior patterns. A smooth insertion with minimal course changes would seem unremarkable, or so he hoped. Jacen agreed that his idea made sense, but that was from a human point of view. *I just hope the Yuuzhan Vong concur.*

He settled his hands on the control wheel and restarted the engines. He kept thrust at zero, but fed a little power into the

repulsorlift coils. A little rudder and a gentle easing of the
yoke forward brought the Skipray blastboat, *Courage,* into
the atmosphere. It bucked at first, but Jacen kept his hands
steady on the controls. He glanced at Luke to see if his
handling of the ship suited his uncle.

Luke gave him a little nod, then glanced at a monitor containing navigational data. "We're ten thousand kilometers
from the ExGal site. Heading 33 mark 30 at the moment,
dropping as we go."

"Got it. I wanted to be over the mountains before I turn us
to port."

"Good plan." Luke closed his eyes and started breathing
very slowly. "Nothing amiss at the moment."

"Thanks." Jacen flipped a switch to reverse thrust and then
nudged the throttle forward. Airspeed began to drop, and the
blastboat with it. It didn't fall so sharply as to be under control, but just enough to suggest the ship was about as aero-
dynamic as a meteorite burning into the atmosphere.

He brought the ship lower and lower until, over the heart of
the northern continent, he dropped beneath the level of a
mountain ridge to the east. Once it hid him, he pumped power
to the engines, killing his airspeed quickly. He dropped the
blastboat down low and killed thrust. He flipped the switch
again, setting the engines to propel him forward, then he
stretched out with the Force and scouted ahead for signs
of life.

He found plenty, and most all of it was within normal
limits for what he expected to find. There was some that
seemed harsh, almost like clashing colors, and he steered
away from these areas. He took the ship north, then darted
through a mountain gap and piloted the ship in toward the
ExGal site. He brought the ship down to the north and east,
well away from the antenna arrays attached to the facility's
communications tower, then shut the engines down and un-
buckled himself from the restraining straps.

"We're here."

Luke opened his eyes slowly, then nodded. "We are. You
recognized the sources of the Force out there, yes?"

"I caught something. It didn't feel right to me. What do you think it was?"

"I don't know. Sentient life-forms, definitely under stress, perhaps diseased. They seem worn away, frayed somehow. What I do know is that I didn't find them here weeks ago."

Jacen's head came up. "Does Mara ever feel like that to you?"

Luke's quick intake of breath suggested the question stung a bit. "Not that, no, but Mara is strong. If it's the same disease, it might be that they're in the end phase of whatever she has, but we have no way of knowing that."

The younger Jedi led the way from the cockpit. He pulled on a belt from which hung his lightsaber, a pouch with a rebreather, a canteen of water, and a blaster. His uncle joined him, taking a similar belt from the equipment locker, then handed Jacen a pair of goggles.

Jacen frowned. "What are these for?"

"You remember Mara's description of her fight with Carr? I don't know if the Yuuzhan Vong amphistaff can spit venom to blind you, or if they have some other sort of weapon that will accomplish the same end. Since we can't sense them through the Force, sight is going to be our most powerful ally, and one we shouldn't lose by chance." Luke pulled on his own goggles, then loosened his blaster in its holster. "Mara said their armor turned blaster bolts and even slowed down lightsabers, so shoot well and cut even better."

Jacen smiled. "Wow. For a second there you sounded like Dad."

R2-D2 hooted a quick comment.

Luke cocked his head for a moment, then nodded. "It seems that whenever I'm in a situation where the odds against success are pretty substantial, I think about what your father would say or do. Doesn't mean I do *that,* but his example is one it's tough to forget."

Luke punched a big red button on the bulkhead, and the landing ramp on the blastboat slid open. He led the way down and crouched at the foot of the ramp. He pressed his hand to the ground, rolled some of the dirt around between his fingers, then sniffed.

"What?"

"When I was here last, there was a lot of sulfur in the air, but I don't smell much at all right now. Something managed to drag it out of the air." He pointed at some creeping green ground cover that had spread over much of the facility and its walls. "None of that was here, either. Perhaps it was what cleaned the air."

Jacen shrugged. "You were the one raised on a farm."

"That was a moisture farm on a desert planet." His uncle looked up at him. "Anything like this in the data files you reviewed?"

"Nothing I recall."

Luke stood and started walking toward the gate in the ExGal facility wall. The gate itself stood open, but the leafy green plant had grown all over it. Luke pushed the vines apart and ducked his head to get through. Jacen followed closely and quickly found himself in a green tunnel.

He was watching his feet, making certain he didn't trip, which is why he bumped into his uncle's back. "Sorry."

"No matter. Look at this."

Luke stepped clear of the vines and into a small courtyard. Jacen followed him, and R2-D2 rolled up between them. The little droid started bouncing from foot to foot and issued a low, mournful moan.

Luke rested a hand on the droid's dome. "I know, Artoo, I know."

The green plant overgrew everything save in a wide oval, the end of which included the door to the ExGal facility. Equipment had been placed in the oval, only two meters from the door, and it took Jacen a couple of seconds to identify everything gathered there. He knew what it all was, of course, but he'd never seen it arranged the way it was.

The centerpiece of the display was an R5 unit that had been decapitated. Where its truncated-cone head should have been sat a fleshless human skull. Rainbow-colored wires came up and out through the eye sockets and mouth, the latter having a wire ribbon roll out like a tongue. Scattered around it like toys spilled from a broken bin lay computer consoles, holo-projector plates, food synthesizers, and a hair dryer from a re-fresher station. These items had been smashed to the point of uselessness, and the dents in their metal flesh looked as if something had kicked or stomped them.

Jacen looked at his uncle. "What is it?"

Luke's expression sharpened. "A warning, clearly. What I wonder, though, is who it's directed at."

"Whoever it was that you felt out there?"

The Jedi Master sighed. "That would be my guess, but guesses aren't what we came here for. Learning the answer—that will be tough. I just hope it's not too tough, or the answers we get will remain here, on Belkadan, and you and I could spend eternity like this poor fellow: warning others to stay away."

CHAPTER TWELVE

Anakin Solo looked around the Dantooine camp site and slowly nodded. He stood there with his back to the dying sun, watching his shadow stretch out before him. He planted his hands firmly on his hips and felt pleased with his effort. He'd hauled all their equipment up from the *Jade Sabre* while Mara rested after bringing the ship down in a narrow mountain canyon. He'd located the flat area at the top of a bluff, which made it very defensible and gave them a wonderful view of the lavender plains stretching out before a distant, sparkling sea.

He'd set up their tents, orienting Mara's larger one on a north-south axis that would make sure that the dawning sun would warm it, as would the setting sun. His own smaller tent he set up across the clearing from hers. He'd gathered stones and set them around a depression he'd excavated, creating a fire pit. He planned to head north, to a forest of thorny blba trees to harvest dead wood for their fires. While the ship had all the facilities needed to prepare food, Anakin looked forward to eating food cooked over an open fire.

He knew that desire was kind of silly, but he thought it was fun and hoped Mara would, as well. The purpose of their trip to Dantooine was to let her recover her strength on a world where technology and civilization had not overwhelmed nature. The native Dantari were a simple people, traveling along the coasts in nomadic tribes with little more than primitive tools. Anakin felt fairly certain that if any of the Dantari had seen Admiral Daala's attack on a colony established when Anakin was barely a year old, they'd have put it down to a war between gods.

Given that the Imperials sent AT-AT walkers against unarmed colonists, whom the Dantari probably saw as intruders, it wouldn't surprise me to find the Dantari wearing emblems that remind them of the walkers or the Imperial crests emblazoned on the machines. That thought sent a shiver down his spine. The New Republic's battle with the Empire had reached its final conclusion six years earlier, but Anakin knew there were people who still harbored some positive feelings for the Empire. *And some, like the Dantari, who might do so innocently.*

He took one last look at the campsite and frowned. Back beyond his tent he'd stacked the various equipment crates and cases. He'd lined them all up straight, but one had slipped out of alignment. Anakin reached out with the Force and nudged it back into place, then smiled.

"Anakin, don't do that."

He whirled and saw Mara, looking pale, leaning heavily against a rock that stood near the path back to the ship. The jacket she wore was buttoned all the way up to the throat, despite the day's warmth. He steadied her using the Force, then slid a camp chair toward her. "You should have told me you wanted to come up here. I would have gotten you."

Her brows furrowed, and he felt resistance to the Force. The camp chair tipped and tumbled toward her, then bounced away as if it had hit an invisible wall. Mara staggered toward it, bent down slowly, and turned it upright again. She rested her hands on the rear posts. Her red-gold hair slid down over her shoulders to curtain the sides of her face.

Her green eyes blazed with a strength that the weakness in her body mocked. "If I had wanted help, Anakin, I would have asked for it."

His head came up at the chilly tone in her voice, then he swallowed hard and glanced down at the ground. "I'm sorry.

I should have remembered that from when we were landing. You didn't need my help."

Mara sighed, then slowly lowered herself into the chair. Her head lolled back for a moment, then she looked at him. "Don't compound things that have nothing to do with each other. I didn't want you landing the *Jade Sabre* because I wanted to do it."

The youth's blue eyes narrowed. "It was a tricky landing. You didn't trust me to do it. You didn't want me to destroy your ship."

Mara pursed her lips for a moment. "Given that *our* ship is the only way off this rock, I didn't want it damaged, no." Her expression softened a bit. "And the ship is special to me. Your uncle Luke gave me the *Jade Sabre* to replace *Jade's Fire*."

"But you crashed *Jade's Fire* on purpose. You meant to."

"I did, and had good reason to do that, but that doesn't mean . . ." Mara paused for a moment as her voice sank to a dry whisper. She swallowed, then glanced down at the ground. "Your uncle Luke understood how much the ship meant to me. He knew *what* it meant to me. He respected what I had done in sacrificing the *Fire*. He had the *Sabre* made for me to thank me."

Anakin felt his stomach tighten. "I'm sorry. I didn't know."

Mara shrugged her shoulders. "I tend to hold tightly to painful experiences and not to share them, so you couldn't have known. I've grown attached to the *Sabre* because of what it means. It's not that I don't trust you, Anakin . . ."

"You trust yourself more?"

Mara actually smiled for a heartbeat. "Pretty perceptive."

"Even a blind hawk-bat finds a granite slug now and again." He glanced at her. "I do want you to know you can trust me. I'm here to do whatever you want or need. I won't fail you."

"I know." She sat forward, resting her elbows on her knees. "I apologize for being weak, for forcing you to be here with me instead of off doing more important stuff."

Anakin blinked with surprise. "There's nothing more important that I could be doing. Uncle Luke has entrusted you to me. There *isn't* a more important job out there."

"Don't lie to me, Anakin. The desire to be out there saving the galaxy is in your blood so thick I can hear it screaming from here."

"No, really, that's not true." Anakin glanced over his shoulder and used the Force to bring him the other camp chair he'd set up. "I am here to help you, Mara. What's wrong?"

Mara had frowned as he sat. "Stop doing that."

"Doing what?"

"Trivializing the Force."

"I don't get it. What do you mean?"

She heaved her torso erect and sat back in her chair. "Even down in the *Sabre* I could feel it. I admire your desire to make everything perfect for me, but the Force isn't something you use to pitch tents or stack crates."

"But the Force is the Jedi's ally. It's something we use." Anakin shifted his shoulders uneasily. "Size matters not, you know. I mean, if I'd not used it, I would have had to—"

"Break a sweat?"

Anakin's mouth gaped open. "Um, I guess so. I mean, the ship is half a kilometer back in that canyon, and hauling the stuff up here—"

"Would have been hard work." Mara's steady gaze bored into him. "You quote Master Yoda's aphorism that 'Size matters not,' but that was used to tell Luke that he had to banish self-doubt. You're using it as an excuse, or a challenge."

Anakin winced. "But Luke said that Yoda lifted his X-wing out of the swamp at Dagobah."

"To make a point, to show Luke how strong the Force could be, if mastered."

"And I've mastered it."

Her head came up and her gaze sharpened. "Have you, now?"

Anakin immediately flushed crimson. "Well, I mean, I've been trained to it. I know how to use it."

"But knowing *how* to use it is entirely different from

knowing *when* to use it. Think, Anakin, how often do you see your uncle use the Force in raw displays of strength?"

He frowned. "Well, not so much these days. Not since the war ended, I guess."

"Correct, not since he realized that using the Force so directly cut him off from the more subtle aspects of it." Mara looked up, her gaze searching his face. "You can't hear a whisper if you're constantly shouting, and using the Force the way you do is the same as always shouting. Do you see that?"

Anakin's brows furrowed. "I guess so. I mean, it makes sense, but I'm still learning. I need that control. I need to be able to make things work."

"I agree." She glanced down at the ground. "But using the Force isn't the only answer, you know. Chewbacca didn't use it, and he saved your life, your father's life, and countless other lives."

His expression soured. "Don't be trying to tell me Chewie's death isn't my fault."

"I suspect you've heard that a lot, haven't you?"

"Yes, and don't try reversing things around and talking me into defending myself, either. I may still be young, but I'm not stupid."

"I know that. You're not stupid, but you *are* naive." Mara looked at him and let out a quick chuckle. "That expression of outrage, very becoming."

Anakin scowled. "I'm not naive. I've been in the thick of things since I was born. I've grown up on Coruscant and then at the academy. I've been around, you know."

"Not my point, Anakin." Mara gave him the hint of a smile that he found a little bit intriguing and very frustrating. "You've spent your whole life involved with the Force. It's made you weak."

"But Yoda said—"

Mara held a hand up. "You don't know what *you,* Anakin Solo, are capable of without the Force. You don't know if you could have humped all those crates up here. You don't know how much you would ache or sweat in doing it. You don't know how long it would take for you to pitch the tents. The fire pit, did you scoop that out with a shovel? Did you place the rocks by hand?"

"No, but—"

"You know, I was taught a long time ago that whenever someone uses the word *but* it means he's stopped listening. It also means those he's speaking with tend to stop listening. I know what I'm telling you isn't easy to hear. There's probably a reason for that, don't you think?"

Anakin squirmed in his chair a bit. "I 'spose."

"And why do you think that is?"

"I don't know. Maybe . . ." He fell silent as he thought. "I guess part of it is that you're making it sound like I'm not a good Jedi Knight, that I'm doing things wrong. It means I'm a failure." *And that maybe Chewie would be alive if I'd not failed.*

"You may not realize that my early training consisted of much more than learning to harness the Force." Mara clasped her hands together and pressed them flat against her belly. "Running, climbing, fighting, learning to move silently, swimming, zero-g fighting and movement; everything could have been made easier by using the Force. I didn't allow that, though. Why not? What value was there in my learning to rely upon myself?"

"You learn your limits."

"Yes, *and*?"

Anakin closed his eyes and thought hard. The answer to her question blossomed full-blown in his mind and dropped his jaw with its simplicity. "You also learn what others are capable of, others who don't have the Force."

"Right, which means you can gauge how much you need to help them." Mara nodded at him, and Anakin smiled proudly. "Too many Jedi Knights become wrapped up in the fact that they can use the Force, and they employ it as if it were the solution to every single problem there is. This is why Kyp and his followers are so stiff and cold. They come into situations without having an appreciation of what the people can do. They come in and impose a solution. It might be quick, it might work very well, but is it the best solution?"

She eased herself up out of her chair and turned to face the dying sun. "Do you remember the Taanab exercise: the problem about the flood that you were asked to attack as part of your training?"

Anakin nodded. "Sure, I got high marks on that simulation. I looked over the data we were given and realized that it was possible to trigger a rock slide that would dump metric tons of rocks in position to shore up a levee. It stopped the flooding from wiping out a village. I just used the Force to loosen some rocks and start the slide, and everyone was saved."

Mara's eyes had closed, and her face was expressionless. She opened her arms to the sun as if seeking to pull as much of its warmth into her as she could. "So, tell me, Anakin, in that example, why was the Taanabian village in jeopardy of being flooded?"

He frowned. "Well, you know, it was built in a low place."

"Had it ever been flooded before?"

"I don't know."

"You didn't check the history?" She glanced over at him. "I know the local history was part of the files."

Anakin shrugged. "I guess I didn't think it was important, because the flood was the main problem."

"That's where you're wrong. The main problem was people building homes in a floodplain. They were doing that because off-world land speculators had bought up their ancestral lands in the hopes of luring Alderaanians there to establish a colony. Greed was forcing those people to build in undesirable places. You might have been able to stop the flood this time, but what about the next, or the one after that?"

"I didn't think—"

"No, you didn't." Mara turned toward him and folded her arms across her chest. "And your solution, dumping the rocks, worked, but it left the people in that village without any commitment to your solution. You saved them, and they would have been grateful—at least until the next time a disaster loomed, and then they'd wonder why you weren't there to save them again."

Anakin stood. "Well, then, what was your solution?"

Mara laughed sharply. "Not one I think your uncle would consider suitably Jedi, but *after* I'd convinced the speculators that I was going to cut deeply into their profit margin, I'd have helped evacuate the village. Then I would have been there and helped the people who wanted to fight the flood to shore up the levees. I wouldn't have done it for them, but I would have helped them help themselves."

"But if you have access to the Force, and you can save them, don't you have a responsibility to do so?"

"Good question. Follow it, though, to its logical conclusion. These are sentient beings. They know they've built their homes in a floodplain. They know they will be flooded out. Are you responsible for protecting them from their own decisions?"

"I can't just let them die."

"So you know what is better for them than they do?"

"In this case, yes." He stared off at the distant ocean. The dying sun stained it the color of blood. "Don't I?"

"If you start thinking that you know the best for people and denying them the chance to make their own errors . . ."

Breath hissed in between Anakin's teeth. "Using the Force becomes easy, and if you are confident you know what is right, you're making yourself the center of reality. That's just selfish, and selfishness is the core of evil, of the dark side."

Mara walked to him and threw an arm over his shoulders. "That's very good, Anakin. We have to be responsible for ourselves, our actions, and responsible to society. Usurping someone else's personal responsibility, though, denies them their sentience. It's right and good to help someone who cannot help himself, but forcefully shielding them from the consequences of their actions, no matter *how* foolish, is wrong."

"But if someone is drunk and pulls a blaster—" Anakin stopped. "Wait, I know! No matter what, he's still going to have to be responsible for his action, but stopping him would be helping those who are helpless: his potential targets."

"That would be my read on it, yes."

Anakin sighed. "It's not easy to see that fine line there."

"No, it isn't, but the fact that you're willing to look is a very good sign." She pointed off to the north. "Now, I've decided I'm strong enough to go help you lug back firewood. We'll actually be carrying it, right?"

"Right." *If you think you're strong enough, Mara, I'll go with you. If I need to help you, though . . .*

She smiled down at him. "I think the idea of coming here to Dantooine is good, for the both of us. I'll learn my limitations, you'll learn yours, and when we're done, we'll both come out of this stronger than anyone could have expected."

CHAPTER THIRTEEN

Corran straightened up, then brushed dust from the shoulders of his green Jedi overrobe. "I'm Corran Horn. My aide here is Ganner Rhysode. We've come to—"

The woman cut him off, and the two young men with her leveled their blaster carbines at the Jedi. "I know why you're here, and I'm not going to let you get away with it."

Ganner laughed. "You think they could stop us?" Illustrating his point, he flicked a finger upward, and the two young men suddenly pointed their blasters at the sky. They struggled to bring them back down on target, then clung to the weapons as Ganner lifted the youths off the ground and left them with their feet dangling in the air.

Corran flicked a sharp glance in his direction. "Put them down, *now*, and gently." He turned to the woman, noting that her expression had gone from sour to incendiary. "I apologize for his enthusiasm, but I have to tell you that I don't have any clue as to why you think we're here."

The woman laughed. "I may have been here for three months with my students, but I'm not entirely off the net. I hear things." She narrowed her eyes behind her goggles. "You said your name was Horn, right? You were with Rogue Squadron?"

Corran nodded. "Only became a Jedi Knight after peace with the Empire."

"You weren't at Mrlsst, were you?"

"Before my time. I served with a lot of the people who were: Wedge Antilles, Hobbie Klivian, Wes Janson, Tycho Celchu . . . They're retired now." Corran got mixed signals coming off her as he recited the names. She certainly recognized some of them, but pretty much anyone in the New Republic could be expected to know some names from Rogue Squadron. "You were there, at the university?"

"I was. I was working on my doctorate." The trace of a smile softened her expression. "I didn't know the Rogues, but I had friends who met them. One went on to work for the squadron."

"Koyi Komad? I've met her." Corran kept his voice even. Annoyance and frustration were boiling off Ganner, but the woman was letting her anger settle down. "She got married, must be fourteen or fifteen years ago. She married a Quarren from the squadron, as a matter of fact."

"I know, I was there at the wedding."

Corran smiled. "Really? I was an usher. Didn't have a beard then."

"I remember a lot of men in uniform." She offered him her hand. "I'm Anki Pace. I'm running this archaeological survey of Bimmiel for the University of Agamar."

Corran noted stiffness in her grip and tension in her voice. "Why is it you think we're here, Dr. Pace?"

"Various sites, archaeologically significant sites, have suffered thefts. The items, though they've not been studied enough for us to be certain, have been suggested to be related to the Jedi Knights, before the purge. They're priceless, of course, since the Empire tried to destroy as much of that material as they could. More importantly, though, they can tell us much of how the Jedi used to be."

"And you think Jedi Knights have been coming to these sites and taking these things?"

One of the young men snarled. "I have a friend who was on a dig. They left another student at the site to watch over it at night. When they came back, stuff was gone, and she couldn't remember anything."

Corran's head came up. "The thief had induced amnesia so

she couldn't remember who had taken the items that were missing?"

"No," the man spat, "she couldn't remember *anything*. All she'd learned that year and the year before was all gone. It was as if she'd missed two years of life. The Jedi can do that. They can blank your memories or make you remember things you didn't see."

Corran shivered. He had no talent for telekinesis, but he was adept at projecting thoughts and images into the minds of others. He'd even used that ability to dump people's short-term memories—the last ten seconds of what they had seen—to blind them to covert entries and escapes. *And I know Kyp used that ability to wipe the memory of Qwi Xux, the architect of the Death Star and the Sun Crusher. He broke her, left her shattered. It was years before she was able to put her life back together and move on after that tragedy.*

He glanced over at Ganner. "What do you know of this sort of thing?"

Ganner reacted as if Corran had spit in his face. "Nothing. I've no knowledge of thefts, and I would not stoop to same."

"Still, you are aware that certain artifacts have shown up on Yavin 4 that are being studied for their significance concerning the old order." Corran looked back at Dr. Pace. "Some of these items, I know, have come from collectors. My wife has brokered the deals for many of them, and if the provenance was at all suspicious, I would know."

Pace snorted. "All well and good for you to say. Just the sort of thing a Jedi would plant in my mind so I couldn't suspect you of stealing what we've found."

"That's ridiculous." Ganner folded his arms across his chest. "How dare you accuse us of being thieves?"

The other young man barked a quick laugh. "My parents came from Carida. There are other things I could call Jedi Knights."

Corran held his hands up. "Stop. This isn't going to get us anywhere. Now me, I'm getting cold and I'd like to get inside your cave there, but you aren't going to let us in until I can convince you that we're not here to poach your find. I think I can assure you that we aren't, if you'll answer one question."

Dr. Pace cocked her head to the side. "And that is?"

"Have you sent out any messages about this find?"

She frowned for a moment, then shook her head. "No. We drafted the messages, but couldn't raise the satellite. No way you could have known what we found."

The first youth shook his head. "That's not right, Dr. Pace. The Jedi have visions. They can see into the future. That's how they knew we'd found it."

Corran glanced at Ganner. "You want to take it?"

"If I must." The taller Jedi shrugged, spilling dust from his shoulders. "That ability is rare, and one we have little control over. Logically, if we could peer into the future, don't you think we would have come here before you found whatever you found and would have removed it?"

The young man frowned. "Well, I don't know."

Corran winked at the kid. "Don't think too long on it, or you'll figure we've planted the memory of this conversation. You'll end up going around and around in your mind and drive yourself to distraction."

Dr. Pace patted the youth on the shoulder. "Vil, you and Denna go back to your posts. I think the slashrats are all tied up in a killball, but they might come for us, so you'll discourage them."

"Yes, Dr. Pace."

Pace looked at Corran. "So, why *are* you here?"

"We've had reports of some raiding along the Rim. The university hadn't heard from you and asked if we could check in on you. We were afraid you'd been raided, so we came out."

Dr. Pace frowned. "What sort of raiding? Humans?"

Ganner shifted his shoulders. "Nonhuman, we think."

"Interesting." She turned toward the cave, then waved Corran and Ganner in her wake. "Come with me."

They followed and passed between tarps that had been hung to seal the mouth of the cave. Beyond the first set Corran saw another about five meters deeper into the cave. The area between them had been set with a number of buckets filled with a dark, frothy liquid that reminded Corran of engine coolant. It stank horribly. The cloying scent wafted easily through the rebreather's dust filters and coated the back of his throat.

Pace unsealed the second tarp wall, then closed it behind them. She pulled off her rebreather and took a deep breath. Corran did the same, and even though he could still smell some of the liquid, the air tasted much sweeter.

He jerked a thumb at the tarps. "What *is* that stuff in the buckets?"

Pace looked over at a knot of students deeper in the caves. "Trista, come here, please."

A slender, black-haired woman that Corran judged to be half his age came walking over. She had a pert nose and just a touch of dirt on her face that somehow enhanced her beauty rather than detracted from it. "Yes, Dr. Pace?"

"These . . . Jedi are interested in your theories about the ecology of Bimmiel." Pace waved her forward. "This is Trista Orlanis, one of my graduate students."

"Pleased to meet you." The young woman smiled, letting her smile linger more in Ganner's direction than Corran's, which Corran found a minor annoyance. "Are you familiar with the Imperial survey?"

Ganner nodded. "I read it and briefed Corran."

Trista's smile broadened. "Well, then, you know that the Imperial team came here as Bimmiel was inbound in its elliptical orbit. As the planet nears the sun, it warms up, naturally, and the ice caps begin to melt. The resulting moisture triggers an abundance of plant growth. The heat also brings the shwpi out of hibernation. They are herbivores, so they eat, multiply, and eat more. They don't digest most of the seeds, so they excrete them, sheathing the seeds with organic fertilizer.

"Certain other animals cannot tolerate the heat, so they retreat toward the polar regions while the shwpi population explodes. Then, as the planet begins to move away from the sun, the planet cools, which frees these creatures from their ranges to sweep into the equatorial areas. The shwpi have overgrazed the world, allowing the storms to pick up and redistribute a lot of soil through wind erosion. Moisture collects in ice caps at the poles as the world cools, which is why it is so dry now. The predators, most notably the slashrats, are adept at moving through the resulting dunes. They hunt the shwpi that have not found burrows in which to hibernate."

Ganner nodded sagely. "The Imperial survey never saw the slashrats since they were not in the survey area."

"True. They postulated the existence of such creatures, but didn't have enough time here to confirm that theory." Trista pointed toward the tarps. "What we have back there is the essence of rendered slashrats. That's what they smell like after being several days dead. The slashrats move through the sand, tracing the scent that shwpi leave behind as they move through or over the sand. The death scent keeps slashrats back; most creatures consider the rotting scent of their own kind to be a sign of danger. We're safe enough in here because they can't come up through the bedrock that makes up these caves."

Corran slipped his goggles up on his forehead and let his rebreather hang at his throat. "I'm glad to know you're safe, but you didn't bring us in here for a lesson in Bimmiellian ecology, Dr. Pace. You reacted to the fact that the raiders weren't human."

"Perhaps you're not a total fool, Jedi." Dr. Pace waved Corran deeper into the cave. Ganner started to follow, but she held a hand up. "No, you wait here. Him, I trust. You, I'm not sure."

Ganner snorted, but said nothing.

Corran tossed him a wink, then headed deeper into the cave. The passage began to shrink, so Corran stooped as he descended into the planet's flesh. The passageway also began to narrow, then broadened out abruptly and provided access to a large, round chamber. Lights had been set up in it, and a half-dozen students were working with brushes and small trowels to shift sand around. Two other students were at a table running a digitizer over artifacts and monitoring the data coming up on their datapads.

Dr. Pace stopped beside Corran. "Until the storm trapped us in these caverns, we'd not looked much into them. We cleared sand from the passage and discovered this chamber. The sand in here was washed in with the rains, so it was laid down in even layers over the years at a fairly constant rate. We don't have a solid chronology, but as we began poking around we discovered something that we think has been here for forty years, maybe fifty."

She led him over to the computer table. "Jens, call up scan AR-312."

As the young woman punched up a request for that data, Dr. Pace faced Corran. "We've recovered a body, the mummified remains of some creature. As nearly as we can make out, it retreated here and was felled by slashrats. The teeth marks on the long bones and ragged edges of dried flesh were consistent with . . ."

Corran stopped listening as the holographic image of a skull appeared above a holoprojector plate. It had a low cranial ridge, but was longer than a human skull. The features appeared sharper, and the computer enhanced the fracture lines and deformities on the face. The cheekbones had been broken and set oddly, so the face had a slope from right to left, and the nose bones had clearly been shattered.

"Emperor's black bones!"

Dr. Pace nodded. "Not very pretty. Bony, with hooks and claws on the hands, elbows, shoulders, toes, heels, and knees. It killed at least two slashrats. It also had some artifacts that we recovered—armor, some weapons. It's a major find. I've never seen anything like it."

"That's the problem, Doc, I have." Corran shuddered, remembering the images of the Yuuzhan Vong corpses he'd seen in Luke Skywalker's report. "I think you've got one of the raiders there, and if they've been here once, there's little reason to think they won't be back."

CHAPTER FOURTEEN

A quick examination of the ExGal facility proved the efficacy of the Yuuzhan Vong warning at the door. Luke found no signs of life in there, but there was a lot of evidence of the sheer virulence with which the Yuuzhan Vong hated technology. Machinery had been smashed into bits, and enough dark fluid formed footprints or was sprayed over the walls to suggest that the Yuuzhan Vong had been heedless of personal injuries during their orgy of destruction.

That realization, which crystallized itself in his mind as he bent to trace a bloody footprint with a finger, sent a shiver down his spine. His inability to detect the Yuuzhan Vong through the Force had disturbed him, but he'd counted on their invisibility to be the only odd thing about them. Their apparent fanaticism, as evidenced by the willingness to hurt themselves while pursuing their beliefs, took them well outside the ranges for normal behavior as he knew it. Luke did know of species that valued stoicism in the face of pain, but the Yuuzhan Vong seemed to go beyond even that.

He also knew that his impression of their fury had probably grown beyond all reasonable measure because it was devoid of the input he normally found through the Force. In the past, at other sites of such destruction, he had been able to pick up background traces of the anger. It allowed him to gauge the depth of the perpetrator's emotions, reinforcing or discounting the destruction he saw. Corran had once pointed out how the difference between that sort of impression and the physical evidence of violence could indicate if a crime scene had been dressed up to make a simple murder look like a botched robbery.

This was more than dressing up a site, though. The Jedi Master slowly stood, then glanced over at Jacen. "Find anything useful?"

His nephew held up a headless doll. "This is one of those toys that has circuitry inside it to make it respond to phrases and things. It's harmless, but they smashed it just as bad as any of the computers."

R2-D2, rooting through a pile of smashed circuit boards, played a nervous twitter softly.

"The Yuuzhan Vong clearly didn't see the toy as harmless." Luke shook his head. "From their point of view, it might be more of an abomination than any of the other equipment here."

Jacen's brows arrowed together for a second, then his expression eased and he nodded. "If they think of machines as evil, then this would be something designed to corrupt the very young. Instead, now, it's just a broken toy meant for a child who will never enjoy it." The doll's crushed body fell from his fingers and landed amid a pile of debris.

Luke stroked a hand over his jaw. "What I don't see here is anything in the way of changes resulting from the environmental holocaust the Yuuzhan Vong triggered. That green plant hasn't made it inside here . . ."

"May not have had enough time." Jacen toed more broken debris. "There seemed to be an enclave of the diseased, frayed life-forms to the south and west. It would put this facility between them and our ship."

Luke thought for a moment and suppressed a smile as he did so. The nonchalant way Jacen had referred to the blast-boat as "our ship" casually included him in on any scouting mission. Luke would have preferred to leave him behind with R2-D2, but, he realized, he had no way of knowing if the Yuuzhan Vong were close and, therefore, couldn't guarantee

Jacen would be any safer at the station than he would be on the mission.

"Okay, but we take a precaution first. We'll check the communications tower and see if it can transmit data. If it can, we'll link it to the ship and use our comlinks to be able to make a running report on what we see. The ship will cache the data. Artoo will transmit everything if we're cut off or we utter some code words."

Jacen smiled cautiously. "I wouldn't have thought of that precaution."

"We're here to learn what we can to safeguard the rest of the New Republic."

His nephew's head came up. "And to see if we can find anything that will help cure Mara, right?"

Luke nodded. "That, too. Our mission is more important than we are. We take no stupid chances, but we don't shrink from duty, understand?"

The young man nodded. "I do, Master Skywalker."

After arranging the communications relay setup with R2-D2, the two of them changed from their Jedi robes into A/KT combat jumpsuits. The close-fitting, single-piece garment reminded Luke a lot of his pilot jumpsuit, though this one was colored a green dark enough to be almost black. The elbows and knees were well padded, and stiff trauma pads were inserted breast, back, and along the arms and legs to provide added protection. Having heard from Mara just how savagely the Yuuzhan Vong fought, Luke wanted to take no chances.

If they're going to be armored, so are we. He tugged on some straps, tightening the suit up, then pulled on a helmet and gloves. He also donned his goggles. Lastly he fastened a blaster around his waist and hung his lightsaber from a clip on the suit. "I'm ready."

Jacen nodded. "I'm good to go."

Jacen's suit appeared to be identical to Luke's, save for the color. It was a deep dark red, much darker than the color of dried blood. Luke realized that the suit's color would hide any blood that might leak out of Jacen, sending a jolt through him. He allowed calm to flow in to the wake of that thought, though, knowing that he'd be aware through the Force if Jacen were hurt, and taking comfort in the fact that his nephew wasn't stupid.

"We're just out to gather some facts, Jacen. Nothing heroic on this trip."

"I got it."

The two of them slipped from the ExGal compound and headed southwest, through a region of low hills. The green ground cover had spread fairly far and wreathed many a tree that had died under the Yuuzhan Vong environmental assault. There were some signs of native plants trying to make a comeback, but what they had decided was alien foliage seemed poised to move in and smother them. Through the Force Luke gained an impression that was perfectly normal and healthy concerning the Yuuzhan Vong plant; yet everywhere was evidence that its spread was anything but benign.

The other plants here aren't prepared to deal with this invader, so it just spreads and spreads, doing what it does naturally. The implications of that idea tightened his shoulders. The Yuuzhan Vong were certainly analogous to the plant they'd brought to Belkadan. If the New Republic wasn't ready to repulse them, the Yuuzhan Vong would spread throughout the galaxy. *Doing what they do naturally.*

What the Yuuzhan Vong did naturally became more clear as Luke's sense of the frayed ones grew. He and Jacen moved through what had once been a forest. The toppled trees had been carpeted with the green vines, creating more than enough shadow to hide the two of them. They crept up a hill, to the crest line, then carefully slipped over and hid behind the bulk of a fallen log.

They looked down into a broad, shallow valley that had a decently sized stream running through it. The green vines grew throughout, though they did leave circular openings of black sand at various points. In the center of these circles were small plinths, all pointing needle-sharp noses toward the sky.

In the center of the valley lay a small cluster of buildings. The green plants grew around the perimeter of them and took on a shrublike quality at the edges. Aside from where bare paths would allow people to move from the shacks to the plinths, the plants would make it tough for passage. Anyone running from the village would undoubtedly get their feet tangled and would go down.

Not that the folks in the village look as if they are capable of doing much running. Luke slipped a pair of macrobinoculars from a pocket on his left thigh and focused them on the heart of the village. He saw what looked to be a pair of Trandoshans, a Rodian, a half-dozen humans, and a Twi'lek shambling listlessly along. All were barefooted and walking awkwardly, as if their knees had been broken and then only partially repaired.

He looked closer for signs of trauma and saw nothing as obvious as scars, but there were odd calcifications on the legs, exposed areas of the arms, and even the skulls of these creatures. Concentrating, Luke got a sense of them through the Force and could see the life energy flowing in them in a muted fashion; these people were the stressed life-forms he'd sensed before. The energy seemed to eddy around these odd formations, revealing that, at least on some of them, the bony protrusions also extended deeply into their skulls and body cavities.

He passed the macrobinoculars to Jacen. "Tell me what you see."

Jacen focused and watched. Force energy gathered as he concentrated. "Those things, those growths . . . they work like restraining bolts on a droid?"

"That would be my guess." Luke's blue eyes narrowed. "And the people—any idea where they came from?"

Jacen looked again. "The clothing is pretty bad, but some of it has pirate insignia on it. Rim raiders that the Yuuzhan Vong ran into and made into slaves?"

"I think so, too."

His nephew shivered. "The way they feel in the Force is just not right."

"I know. It feels almost as if they're dying by degrees."

"What is the sense of killing your labor force?"

Luke shrugged. "If they were able to pick them up so easily on the Rim, perhaps they think the supply is infinite. It might also be that they're adapting their slave control technology to the inhabitants of this galaxy. Maybe they don't mean to kill them, but they need more work on their control devices. I don't know."

"It's definitely creepy, no matter what is happening." Jacen stretched out on his belly, lowered the macrobinoculars, and looked at his uncle. "What are they doing here?"

Luke pointed at the plinths. "Anything familiar about them?"

"Not really."

"Okay, use the Force. Concentrate on the flow of life within the valley."

Jacen closed his eyes, drew in a deep breath, then let it out slowly. "Everything is moving in, toward the plinths, along the vines." His jaw hung open for a second, then he looked at his uncle. "These plants are like a big solar collector. They're channeling energy and the nutrients they're sucking up back into the valley, toward the things. That sand is black because of a nectar the plants are flooding into it."

"That's what I sensed." Luke pointed a finger at the plinths. "Unless I miss my guess, I'd say those plinths are coral-skippers in their infancy. We're looking at a shipyard. They're growing a squadron right down there, and they're using slave labor to help do it."

The youth studied the valley again, then shook his head. "Growing fighters? How efficient can that be?"

Luke accepted the macrobinoculars back from him and opened a small compartment on the device. He snaked out a small cable and connected it to his comlink, then focused on the plinths. "The ships look fairly well along, and Belka-dan has been under Yuuzhan Vong control for less than a month. That output would rival an Incom factory turning out X-wings, and since these ships are living and can heal, the wastage rate is lower than we get with our machines. What's stunning here is the speed with which they're able to grow these ships. This is serious trouble."

He turned off the macrobinoculars, unhitched them from the comlink, and returned them to his pocket. "We got some good visuals. Come on."

Jacen looked puzzled. "Shouldn't we wait until dark to free the slaves?"

"We have other things we have to do first." Luke pointed toward the west. "There are more slaves over there. Either they're growing more coralskippers, or they might be growing other components for the ships. We need to see what is going on."

Jacen followed him as they worked their way west. They came across one valley that resembled the one they'd just vacated, save that what had been plinths were simply small rocks in the ground. The village was completely overgrown, and Luke caught no evidence of slaves in the area.

One difference he did discover was a dozen-meter-long bit of stone that appeared to be lifeless obsidian. It had the outline of a coralskipper, but where there had been a cockpit opening on the one he'd examined on Dubrillion, this one remained sealed in stone. Luke ran his hand over the fighter, letting his fingers play over the irregularities in its surface.

Jacen frowned. "I don't get it. Why did they leave one behind?"

"Birth defect?" Luke raced a finger along the line of the cockpit canopy. "It grew without a separation here. Could have been a local microbial infection, or just lousy genetics. Perhaps the xenoforming of the planet was intended to sterilize the nurseries, then free up the sort of nutrients that the plants need to feed the ships. Something went wrong with this one, so they dumped it. Still, this indicates they must be growing other components elsewhere, because the propulsion creatures aren't here."

Jacen squatted in the coralskipper's shadow and parted the alien ground cover's leaves to expose the soil. "Look at this. The dirt isn't black anymore." He took some up in his left hand and smoothed it against his palm with his thumb. "It's completely sterile."

Luke dropped to his knee beside Jacen. "I wonder . . ."

"What?"

"An Ithorian once explained to me that there are some crops that exhaust the soil in which they are raised. Perhaps the Yuuzhan Vong have done that here, raising a crop of coral-skippers too fast." He nodded to his nephew. "Take a sample of the soil, and we can have Artoo check it later."

Once Jacen got the sample, they continued their reconnaissance mission and discovered a small lake with water thickened by the presence of brown algae. On the water, which lapped weakly at the shores, floated plants with three large blue triangular leaves. From the center grew a stalk, and from it hung two round berries, about the size of a human's head. Some plants did have more than just two, and by the far shore, Luke spotted a different species with slightly smaller berries growing in bunches.

Jacen frowned. "Villips? Their communications devices?"

"I think so. Different sizes for different needs, I suppose." Luke sighed quietly. "So much to learn about them."

From the cover of large rocks, they watched as slaves waded through the turgid water, using ladles to pour water over the villip plants. One, an older man whose spine sprouted horny growths, could barely lift a dripping ladle to bathe a villip. The ladle slipped from his fingers, and he tried to catch it. He lunged forward to grab it, but lost his footing and went down in the water.

The man started splashing in a panicked manner, churning the water into a yellow-brown froth. Several of the other slaves started shouting. They vocalized in a high range that rose above Luke's ability to hear, though the anxiety pouring off them slammed into him in waves. Several started for the drowning man, high-stepping through the gelatinous fluid as fast as they could.

A harsh whip crack froze them in their places. Appearing at the western edge of the lake, backlit in the dying sun, stood a tall and lean figure. His right hand snapped out and forward again, cracking the whiplike weapon in his hand. After the second snap, the whip became a staff, and the figure brandished it over his head, pumping it upward the way one of the Sand People would triumphantly pump a gaffi stick.

The Yuuzhan Vong—Luke knew it was one because the figure didn't exist within the Force framework—dashed forward, splashing his way into the lake. He artfully cut between villip stalks and reached the row where the man was striking for the surface. The man reached out as the Yuuzhan Vong extended the amphistaff toward him. The man grabbed at it, then recoiled, with his hand sliced open. He started to scream, but fluid boiling up out of his throat sank it into a gurgle.

The Yuuzhan Vong lunged with the amphistaff, driving the sharp, flattened end through the man's chest. As he pulled the amphistaff back, the man came halfway up out of the water, then slipped from the staff. The Yuuzhan Vong stabbed him twice more, then stepped back away as the man flopped into the water one last time. The body bobbed there for a second, then, leaking air from lungs and mouth, slowly sank from sight.

The Yuuzhan Vong raised the amphistaff and shouted something. The slaves understood enough of it to cower. The amphistaff then slacked for a moment before coiling itself around its owner's arm. The Yuuzhan Vong strode from the water, then beckoned over two slaves, a man and a woman. They pulled off the rags they wore and dried the Yuuzhan Vong's legs.

A siren of sorts echoed through the hills. The Yuuzhan Vong shouted another order, and the slaves formed themselves into a rough line. They began to trudge off to the south. The Yuuzhan Vong took one last look at the villip paddy, then strode off along the path his slaves had taken.

Luke felt an emotional chill coming from his nephew. "I'm sorry you witnessed that."

"I'm sorry for the man who died there." Jacen shook his head. "The Yuuzhan Vong I faced when rescuing Danni— they were formidable, but nothing like that one. He had no mercy at all in him."

"No, just a cold, efficient killer. He was bigger than the one Mara fought, longer and leaner. I wish I had seen more than just a silhouette."

Jacen smiled. "We'll get to see them up close soon enough."

Luke shook his head. "I certainly hope not."

The younger Jedi blinked. "But we have to do something for the slaves."

"Do we?" Luke's expression sharpened as disbelief rolled out from Jacen. "Remember why we're here."

"To save the New Republic, and those people are part of the New Republic." Jacen pointed to the south. "You can feel how much pain they're in, how much damage the Yuuzhan Vong have done to them. How can you not think of moving to free them?"

"I do think of it, but I also know it's not practical, not at this stage. We have a lot to learn here. It's not a satisfactory choice, but a necessary one."

Jacen's head came up. "Freeing them will doom the New Republic? Or will it merely make your mission to save your wife that much tougher?"

Luke stiffened, but choked down the outrage his nephew's question had sparked in him. It helped that he could read the horror in Jacen's eyes, but the question had still stung bitterly. "Is that what you think the real reason for our being here is? You think I would come here just to save Mara?"

"I think, Uncle Luke, that you love her so much that you'd do *anything* to save her." The youth glanced down. "I'm sorry for saying what I did. I didn't mean it."

"Actually, Jacen, you did mean it. It is a paradox. We have to allow some people to be in pain so others can avoid it. It's an easy choice when you're the one who will be hurting, but tougher when others have to suffer. You have to agree, though, that we can do nothing right now. We don't know enough about the Yuuzhan Vong presence here; we don't know enough about the slaves; we don't even know if they *can* be saved. For all we know, they've agreed to this treatment."

Jacen glanced out at where the man's body had returned to

the surface and floated there placidly. "I can't imagine his death was part of any bargain."

"You're probably right, but we are not in a position to do anything for the slaves."

"But, to do nothing, that's not . . . not being a Jedi."

The flesh around Luke's eyes tightened. "I thought you were the one who didn't want any part of these missions. I thought you were the one who decided the essence of being a Jedi was to go off and study your relationship with the Force."

"I . . . I did, but—"

The Jedi Master cut him off. "Jacen, you have to understand something, something very important. As smart as you are, as much training as you have, as much of the galaxy as you've seen, you still are only sixteen years old. You only have sixteen years of experience."

Luke sighed. "Having more experience doesn't mean making difficult decisions are easier, but it does let you know that sometimes the tough decisions must be made."

Jacen's expression hardened into an impassive mask. "I understand, Master."

You use the word Master *with the same tone a slave might use to address his owner.* Luke shook his head. "We need to get back to the ExGal facility before darkness falls completely. Without being able to sense the Yuuzhan Vong through the Force, we're more vulnerable at night. Besides, going back there will give both of us time to process what we've learned today, and think about what we need to find out in the future."

Jacen shrugged. "It's a plan, Uncle Luke. A plan."

A ripple of dread ran through Luke at the tone of his nephew's voice, but the Force brought to him no vision of what might yet happen on Belkadan. He reached out and settled a hand on Jacen's shoulder. "Just remember, some problems have no easy or elegant solution. The Yuuzhan Vong are clearly one of *those* problems."

CHAPTER FIFTEEN

Trapped in the cockpit of his X-wing as it hurtled through hyperspace, Gavin Darklighter had nothing to do but sit and wait. For as long as he could remember, he'd never liked having to wait for his fighter to revert to realspace. That dislike had increased when he became Rogue Squadron's commander. *Prior to assuming command I only had myself to worry about. Now I have a lot more to concern me.*

Unconsciously he twisted the silver ring on his right ring finger, even though it and the fingers that moved it around were sheathed in heavy flight gloves. The ring had the Rogue Squadron crest on it—a crest he'd designed when he first joined the squadron. It also sported the quadruple-dot rank insignia of a colonel on either side.

Tycho Celchu and Wedge Antilles had given it to him upon his assumption of command. They had chosen to retire after peace had been won with the Imperial Remnant, and both had evidenced great pride in welcoming Gavin into a position that only they and Luke Skywalker had held in Rogue Squadron. They'd had the ring made up specifically for him, and presented it to him on a special "commander's night out."

Gavin smiled as he remembered the quiet, elegant dinner in one of Coruscant's better restaurants. The three of them comported themselves as would gentlemen, not at all living up to the reputation of fighter pilots everywhere. The calm dignity with which Tycho and Wedge spoke to him and discussed various issues told him that they had accepted him as a peer and had full confidence in his abilities to lead the Rogues.

Wedge had looked at him over the rim of a snifter of Corellian brandy. "Biggs was with us at the start, and you were with us when we restarted Rogue Squadron. In many ways the Darklighters and their victories and sacrifices are more emblematic of Rogue Squadron than anything Tycho and I have done. It's certainly the right thing to have you in charge."

Wedge's pride and faith in him had seen Gavin through some early rough spots. With peace came the retirement of many of the pilots. In addition to Wedge and Tycho, Corran Horn, Wes Janson, and Hobbie Klivian had all opted to retire. Peace also brought with it an economic boom that lured pilots away with offers of lucrative pay for interstellar goods transport. Still, a lot of new young pilots vied for positions in the squadron, and weeding them out made for a very difficult job.

And let me know what Wedge faced when he rebuilt the squadron back when I joined. Luckily for Gavin he had a good command staff to help him out. Major Inyri Forge had been with the Rogues almost as long as he had. Major Alinn Varth came from a military family and had been flying most of her life. With each of them in command of one of the flights, the new pilots were quickly molded into a superior fighting team. Gavin wasn't certain if his Rogues could have defeated the old Rogues in a head-to-head simulation, but he knew they'd give them a run for their money.

But will that be good enough?

A cold lump sat in Gavin's stomach. Based on Xhaxin's information, Admiral Kre'fey took the *Ralroost* out toward the rendezvous point where the pirate said his people were ambushed. They launched a probe droid toward that point, but the data it sent back was inconclusive. Gavin pointed out, and Kre'fey had agreed, that the droid really didn't have the programming or database necessary to be able to analyze the area for the presence of the Yuuzhan Vong. "If there isn't something big and anomalous there, it isn't going to see anything to report."

That fact really left them with no choice but to send in a T-65R reconnaissance X-wing. While it would collect data in all of the ranges that the probe droid did, the living pilot would be able to direct it toward anything that felt suspicious. Rogue Squadron was flying along to provide cover; they had spent most of the time outbound in the *Ralroost* running through simulations of battles with the coralskippers.

When it came down to it, Gavin was of two minds concerning the mission. Returning to an empty point in space where some pirates and fleeing Imperials had been ambushed weeks ago was probably an exercise in futility. There was no logical reason for the Yuuzhan Vong to maintain a presence in that area since it had no resources, no planets—nothing to see, nothing to conquer, nothing to hide behind. All of that had argued against the mission. The fact that the point in space from which the task force was traveling provided access to a number of inhabited worlds both in the New Republic and the Remnant—where the Rogues would be far more valuable in helping evacuate people—also diminished the mission profile. *Why go somewhere that is out of the way when we might be needed to respond to trouble quickly?*

A vague argument for the mission could be made on the slender chances that some people had somehow survived the attack and remained trapped in drifting hulks. More likely was the idea that by collecting data on any ship hulks in the area the New Republic would be able to assess the capabilities of Yuuzhan Vong weaponry. What little they knew already trickled some dread into Gavin's guts, but the strategies they'd come up with to work around the Yuuzhan Vong defenses worked well in simulation.

Catch whistled and started a ten-second countdown to reversion. Gavin settled his right hand on the stick and positioned his left on the throttle lever. He watched the white tunnel of light that extended beyond his fighter's nose suddenly develop cracks, then disintegrate into a black field with stars studding it.

"Rogues, report."

All the pilots reported in and formed up in their three

flights. The recon X-wing, which had the designation Snoop, climbed above the squadron's flight plane and slowly deployed the twin sensor pods from the rear of the fighter. The T-65R had no weapons because sensors filled all the available space in the craft, but in a fight the pilot could jettison the pods and end up with a very fast and maneuverable ship that could keep him out of trouble.

"Pods deployed. Sensor run commencing now."

"I copy, Snoop."

Without a word being said the rest of Rogue Squadron fanned out, leaving One flight trailing behind and below the recon ship. Two flight, under Inyri's command, moved to starboard and up, while Major Varth's Three flight moved ahead and down to port. The Rogues kept the comm chatter to a minimum so the computers on Snoop wouldn't have to filter their calls out. *Unless there is an emergency, this run should be silent.*

Gavin looked ahead and dialed up the gain on his sensors to see if he could spot any debris from the ambush. Because there was no large mass—star or planet—in the area to pull the debris toward it, he expected to see plenty of wreckage. In the distance, nearly ten kilometers away, he did catch sensor blips, but nothing his targeting computer could recognize as being a ship.

Catch gave out with a low moan, and new targets started to scroll up on Gavin's secondary monitor. The half-dozen targets were spilling like droplets of water from a cracked cup, appearing from the blips that were all that remained of the ships that had been ambushed. Gavin shivered, thinking of times he'd seen insects crawling from within corpses.

"Heads up, Rogues, we have contacts at 354 mark 20. S-foils in attack position." Gavin checked his sensors. "Snoop, come about and orbit here, pull in all the data you can on the fight, then hyper out if we can't stop them from coming after you."

"As ordered, Lead."

The new sensor database package on the X-wings allowed them to target the coralskippers, but not very easily. Since each ship was grown in a different environment, it had different characteristics. Not all of them had the same chemical composition in the hull, nor the same shape exactly. The computers had to account for a wide range of variables, and Gavin couldn't be certain that his computer might not lock onto some chunk of rock and designate it a target.

Which means we have to move in close. Gavin nudged his throttle forward and saw his wingman, Captain Kral Nevil, come up on his port wing, then they both nosed their ships down and cruised in at the coralskippers. Gavin brought his aiming reticle over one of the coralskippers heading toward him, but the computer refused to give him a proton torpedo lock until they hit the one-kilometer range. It went from red to green instantly, accompanied by Catch's shriek, so Gavin hit the trigger, then pulled up and inverted the craft.

The proton torpedo rode an azure flame to the target, and the coralskipper made no attempt to evade it. Instead, nearly ten meters away from the target, the torpedo shrank from a dot of light to something smaller, like a distant star, and the supernova of light Gavin had expected to see never showed up.

A quick glance at his secondary monitor did show a gravitic anomaly, which confirmed that the coralskipper had somehow created a small black hole, which it used to swallow the missile. The energy from the explosion couldn't escape the void; hence the coralskipper remained undamaged. Being able to generate black holes wasn't the same as having shields, but in some cases could be even more effective.

"Lead, the black-hole idea seems to be right. Do we tip our hand?"

"Yes, Deuce. Rogues, new combat programming now." Gavin hit a switch on his combat console. "Catch, start allocating the power."

The droid dutifully tootled as Gavin rolled out to the right, then came around for another run at the coralskippers. He flicked his weapons over to laser fire and quadded them up, so all four would fire at once. As he came in at one of the rocky pods, he hit the trigger once and pulsed a red-gold burst of energy at the fighter, but another black hole blossomed and swallowed the laserlight.

Smiling, Gavin tightened down on the auxiliary trigger button beneath his middle finger on the stick. The X-wing's lasers began cycling very fast—faster than they would have in single-fire mode. Each bolt burned with a scarlet intensity, yet was shorter and decidedly less powerful that those in the first burst he'd fired. As long as he held the auxiliary trigger down in quad mode, the lasers would produce a cloud of shots that wouldn't do much damage, but were next to impossible to distinguish from the heavier bolts.

His target positioned a void to pick off the scattered shots from his fighter, then another to absorb the damage Nevil was pumping out. The coralskipper began some evasive maneuvers, rolling to port and climbing back against the angle of their attack, but it didn't fly as gracefully as the coralskippers had in simulation. Gavin let his own fighter flash past, then pulled back on the stick and came over in a loop, before he rolled out to port and came back around on that same ship.

He came in on its tail and triggered off a long burst of flickers. The coralskipper positioned a black hole above its tail, but Gavin noticed that, this time, the hole was closer to the coralskipper and had a smaller focal point. Some of the splinter shots that were headed long, past the craft's nose, were bent down by the force of the black hole, but not trapped by it. They struck the coralskipper's nose, burning tiny pits in it.

The coralskipper shifted to port and started to roll as more flickers scored it. Gavin rolled to port, as well, and chopped back his throttle, matching his speed to that of the coralskipper. He dropped his crosshairs on its tail, then hit his main trigger and delivered a full-powered quad volley at point-blank range.

The quartet of bolts converged on the coralskipper, and only one of them got sucked into the diminishing black hole. The other three burned into the cockpit assembly. They reduced the crystalline canopy to molten stone that melted through the pilot. Their energy unabated, the bolts superheated the coralskipper's mineral flesh, producing a geyser of rock vapor that jetted back out of the cockpit and propelled the dead fighter deeper into space.

Gavin rolled to starboard and away from the dying ship, then felt a jolt run through his fighter. Another gravitic anomaly had hit him and tugged at his shields. *That's how they strip shields off ships.* He punched a button on the life-maintenance system controls. "Boost it to 100 percent and expand the field to thirteen meters, Catch."

The droid did as commanded, and the shiver that had gone through the X-wing quit. Gavin smiled broadly. To avoid the wear and tear of gravity and inertia on the pilots and fighters, each X-wing came with an inertial compensator built in. It allowed the X-wings to perform very high-speed, high-inertial maneuvers without structural damage to the ship and physical damage to the pilot. By expanding the area covered by this field to thirteen meters—putting it out beyond the shields—the compensator treated the Yuuzhan Vong gravity beams like anything else stressing the fighter.

If enough ships locked onto the fighter, they would eventually demand more energy output than its engines could manage, causing the field to implode and the ship to be ripped apart. Gavin goosed the throttle forward and broke to port, pulling away from the coralskipper that had tried to lock onto him. Suddenly a bright light flashed and the coralskipper disappeared from his rear screen.

"Who got it?"

Nevil answered. "Locking onto you and having you slip away must have tired it or confused it. I dropped a proton torpedo in. Coralduster."

"Good, on me." Gavin brought his X-wing around and back up to the main body of the dogfight. A glance at his secondary monitor showed two Rogues failing to respond on the comm frequency. A flash of orange confirmed at least one pilot was outside his ship. Elsewhere he saw a coralskipper tight on an X-wing's tail, lacing the shrinking aft shield with plasma blasts.

"Snoop, report."

"Good here, Lead. I'm clear. Got it all, including the one that took Eleven and Twelve."

"Which one?"

A pulse of data from the T-65R brought a specific coral-skipper up on his targeting monitor. It didn't look that different from the others, but as he flew toward it, he could tell by the way it moved and maneuvered, it had a hot hand on the stick.

"With me, Deuce?"

A double click coming back through the comm channel confirmed Nevil's understanding of his role. Gavin came up on the port S-foil and pulled back on the stick to run his X-wing in at the killer coralskipper. He plotted a course that would pass behind it and kept adjusting it to tighten the distance between them without arrowing straight in at it.

The coralskipper was intent on tracking one of the X-wings. Gavin identified the ship as belonging to Lieutenant Ligg Panat, a Krish female who had just joined the squadron. The Krish were well known for their love of games, and the way she was flying made Gavin think she was taking the Yuuzhan Vong on her tail a bit too lightly. She was managing to juke her ship around, making it hard to hit, but she still couldn't break away cleanly.

"Seven, this is Lead. On my mark, reverse throttle, break port."

"Lead, I can handle—"

"This is an order, Seven. On my mark. Mark."

Ligg reversed her thrust and rolled to the left, making it look as if she'd just nudged her ship out of the Yuuzhan Vong pilot's way. The coralskipper shot past her, then rolled out right and came up. The Yuuzhan Vong ship's nose came around, and the coralskipper lined up for a head-to-head run on Gavin's fighter.

That sent a jolt through Gavin. *Why would it do that? If it uses its black holes to shield itself, it can't take down my shields, so its plasma shots won't get through. If it takes down my shields, I can dump a torp down its throat. Makes no sense.*

Realizing that if he couldn't tell what the enemy was planning, going along with the enemy's plan was stupid, Gavin triggered a burst of flickers at the incoming target. The cloud of red energy needles flew out and, as he expected, curved in together into the black hole the coralskipper had erected to protect itself. What he hadn't expected is that the void would intercept them that far forward.

Gavin kicked his fighter into a snap roll to starboard, then jammed the throttle full. Sparks shot from the inertial compensator panel as the X-wing grazed the edge of the black hole. Catch screamed, and Gavin hugged the stick back to his chest. The X-wing shuddered and engines whined, but his speed started dropping. *I'm getting sucked into that thing!*

Gavin reversed thrust on his fighter, then ruddered the nose around to point at the black hole. The screaming engines fought the black hole's pull, but surrendered precious centimeter after centimeter to it. He flicked the weapons control over to proton torpedoes and emptied his magazine of six into the black hole. One after one the torps dived into the gravitic anomaly, and somehow the black hole managed to contain the vast energy their explosions released.

But, Gavin noticed, his rate of descent into the black hole slowed.

He flicked his thrust forward. The fighter picked up speed, attracted by the black hole and pushed by the engines. Then he pulled back on the stick and used the velocity he'd acquired to shoot past the black hole's edge.

More sparks shot through the cockpit, and his shields collapsed. His sensor screens blinked for a moment, then came back on full, but he couldn't see the coralskipper. "Catch, where is it?"

Nevil's voice came through the comm speakers in his helmet. "Thanks for distracting it, Lead. Seven and I angled in and got it. Not a pretty kill, but a kill."

"Thanks, Deuce. Flight leaders, report."

"Five here, Lead. Eight lost an engine and will have to be picked up, otherwise we're fine."

"Good, Five. Nine, what about Three flight?"

Alinn Varth's voice came through heavy with emotion. "Lost two, Lead. The one that almost got you dropped that big black hole on his tail as Eleven was closing. Dinger flew into it and never knew what hit him. Twelve got ripped up by it. Tik is extravehicular, negative life signs."

"Do a tight flyby to check. We'll have the *Ralroost* recover him." Gavin glanced at his sensors again. "Snoop, got any more skips in the area?"

"Negative, Lead, but those hulks could be full of them."

"I copy that, Snoop. Reel in the pods and go back to the admiral. Give him the data, have him send someone back for us."

"As ordered, Lead. May the Force be with you."

"Thanks, Snoop." Gavin watched the X-wing recover the sensor pods, then accelerate and vanish into a bright flash in the sky. "Listen up, the rest of you. Keep your eyes open and sensors scanning. We don't know why there were only a half-dozen skips here, or if there are more in hiding. I don't want to be surprised. We did okay for our first engagement with them, and I don't want Admiral Kre'fey to show up here to discover we somehow managed to turn a victory into a defeat."

CHAPTER SIXTEEN

Leia intended to be the first person to disembark from the *Lambda*-class shuttle, *Fond Memory,* when it touched down on Dubrillion, but her Noghri bodyguard, Bolpuhr, beat her to it. He growled at the two men in body armor who came running at the freighter along the narrow causeway that led to the main landing tower. Ignoring him, the two of them turned and set up a position on the causeway to hold people back, then they parted and let a harried Lando Calrissian slip past.

Leia ran down the landing ramp and hugged Lando fiercely. "I'm so happy to see you're not hurt."

"I'm not, but my world is." Lando freed himself from her arms, tossed his cape back over his shoulder, and waved a hand out over the cityscape. "It's all over, Leia."

The pure anguish in his voice arced pain through her heart. She followed his gaze and looked out over a city that she remembered as being pristine during her first visit, with high towers that made this portion of Dubrillion look as if it had been transplanted from Coruscant. The gentle sweep of archways and the elegantly worked decorations on the buildings had reminded her of images from Coruscant while her father was yet a child.

Now it is Coruscant after Thrawn and the Emperor's return. The proud towers had been shattered, with fires guttering from the tops of some. Buildings had holes melted and blasted into them. Faint breezes teased draperies that hung out through broken transparisteel viewports, and down below, on the various causeways and streets, people moved listlessly along carrying their most precious possessions on their backs or in their arms.

Lando sighed. "The Yuuzhan Vong returned a week and a half after you left. They took up a position near the asteroid belt and watched us. Every so often a squadron of their coralskippers descends and hits a particular location. We fight back, of course, and get some of them, but less and less with each strike. It feels like they're using us to cull the weak and stupid from their ranks, leaving only the best and smartest and bravest behind to fight again."

He slammed his right fist into his left palm. "I don't like their attacking us, but I like even less being mocked."

Elegos appeared beside Leia. "Administrator Calrissian, what you see as mocking you could be a healthy respect for your defenses here. Your people *did* stop an earlier assault."

Lando nodded grimly. "We did, but *these* Yuuzhan Vong fight differently. It was the difference between dealing with crack Imperial troops and some local Imp-wanna-be militia. These fighters are much better and, yes, more cautious, but they're just putting the polish on the force pike before they drive it into our guts."

Leia put a hand on Lando's shoulder. "They didn't harry us as we came in."

"They don't. They pick off a few of the outbound ships, but mostly let them run, too. At least, they do now. I think they expected a New Republic response by now." Lando gave Leia a sidelong glance. "You've got nothing from Coruscant to offer us, right?"

She jerked a thumb toward Elegos. "Meet Senator Elegos A'Kla. He's here on an official fact-finding mission."

"Better find your facts fast, Senator, before the Yuuzhan Vong melt them down with plasma blasts."

Leia shivered. In all the time she'd spent with Lando, even when Darth Vader had usurped his command of Bespin, she'd never heard him so frustrated. She was willing to put part of it down to his not wanting to have to start over yet again, but she knew that was only a tiny piece of what was going on inside him. *Lando always looks for ways to work around the system, whatever* system *that is, but with so little data on the Yuuzhan Vong, he can't find an opening to defeat them.*

Leia glanced around at the other spaceport towers. "Things look pretty empty. Everyone fleeing?"

"Those who can, have." Lando shook his head impotently. "I had guards come up on the causeway here because your arrival will draw a lot of folks who want to get away."

"How are your defenses holding up?" Elegos craned his neck and looked around. "I don't see much in the way of turbolaser batteries or concussion missile launchers."

Lando's face brightened a little. "Nor will you. The Yuuzhan Vong hit the fixed sites pretty early on. Everything else is mobile and in hiding. When they come in we try to harass them with fighters and steer them into areas where our mobile guns can engage them. They're learning, so they're making it tough, but we can shuffle things when they're not looking down on us and set up new ambushes."

"That's good as a stall tactic, but it won't win a war against them." Leia's eyes narrowed. "We can do better."

"Really? That mean you have a spare Death Star lurking around that will pulverize the asteroid belt and their command ship?"

"Command ship?" Elegos's head came up. "You've seen a big ship from them?"

"Yes, lurking near the asteroid belt." Lando waved them on to follow him. "Come on down to my central defense facility. I can show you as much holo on that ship as you want. We *did* make an attempt at taking it out, but our fighters never got close enough."

Leia dropped into step with Lando, leaving Elegos to trail behind them and Bolpuhr leaping ahead to lead the way. "It's got to have a weakness. We can find it and exploit it."

"I hope so."

"We will, Lando. We must." Leia sighed. "It's the only chance Dubrillion has."

Jaina pulled a comlink from the bulkhead recharger station on the *Fond Memory*. She handed another to Danni. "My mother has headed off with Lando. We can explore a bit, if you want, stretch our legs."

The blond woman accepted the device and clipped it to the lapel of the blue jacket she wore. "Sorry to take so long to find my jacket. You should have gone with her."

"That's okay. Being cooped up with her for the trip out here was enough for now. I don't need to be there while she's being 'Princess Leia.' "

Danni blinked with surprise. "But, your mother, she . . ."

Jaina nodded and led the way down the landing ramp. "I know, she defeated the Empire and kept the New Republic safe. Oh, don't look at me that way. I know what she did, and I love her dearly."

"Sounds as if there is a *but* coming in there somewhere."

Jaina sighed as they stepped past the guards on the causeway and cut toward a set of stairs that would take them lower in the city. "Didn't you want to move out of your mother's shadow?"

"My mother cast a very small shadow, I guess." The woman's green eyes sparkled. "She is an astrophysicist who got me to be looking out toward the stars. She kept a low profile, trying to pass beneath the sensors of the local government or the Empire or whichever warlord claimed our world in any given week. From her I learned to marvel at distant worlds and systems. That's a big chunk of the reason I joined the ExGal Society."

"Your mother must be proud."

"She is. I think she's pleased I chose to follow in her footsteps."

"Taking after your father didn't interest you?"

"They split up when I was young. He was a bureaucrat, very much into rules and regulations that seemed pointless."

Danni shrugged. "At least, with science, the rules you have to follow have reason behind them and produce results. I don't much care for bureaucracy, which was part of the fun of being with ExGal: the edge of the galaxy was about twenty times closer than the nearest bureaucrat."

Jaina exited the stairs and stepped over a small pile of debris that had spilled into the street from a nearby building. She could have shifted it out of the way with the Force, but she didn't. In fact, she found herself pulling the Force back in because the pure misery of the people of Dubrillion clawed at her spirit. She understood their fear and pain, but the sharpness of it threatened to rend her.

"At least you had some sort of choice, Danni. With my parents I could be a smuggler who saved the galaxy or a diplomat who saved the galaxy."

"And you chose to become a Jedi."

Jaina shifted her shoulders uneasily. "That choice was pretty much made for me. My brothers and I are very strong in the Force."

Danni arched an eyebrow as she pulled abreast of Jaina. "You regret being a Jedi?"

"No, not at all." Jaina hesitated, then sighed. "It's something neither of my parents became, so it let me have something to myself. That's part of being a twin too, I guess; everyone expects we'll be alike even though we're fraternal, not identical."

"I think I begin to see what you're saying." Danni offered her hand. "Pleased to meet you, Jaina Solo. So, tell me, just who are you?"

Laughter erupted from Jaina. "I don't know who I am. I'm only sixteen. I know parts of it. I know I'm a really good pilot, and I'm not bad as a Jedi. I know I'm getting tired of being my mother's daughter and my father's daughter; and part of me even knows that it will take time for me to emerge from their shadows. I also know that there are folks out there who think I'm going to be the salvation of the galaxy because I'm a Jedi, and others who think I'm doom on two feet for the same reason."

The older woman hooked an arm through Jaina's right elbow. "I remember when I was sixteen. I was all elbows and knees and pretty sure I knew all there was to know about anything worth knowing."

"Uh-huh. And now, at the ripe old age of, what, twenty-one, you know how foolish you were back then?"

"Twenty-one, yes. And, yes, I do think I was not as wise then as I am now. Jaina, I remember not wanting advice."

The younger woman smiled. "So you'll give it to me anyway."

"My point is, Jaina, that people have a choice when they start to look at who they are. Some people decide they want to be like others. They use them as examples, try to do the things they do, and do their best to follow in their footsteps." Danni smiled. "I was like that with my mother."

"And the other type of people, they try to be the opposite of someone?"

"Right, and the problem with that strategy is simple: There are a million ways to be unlike someone, and the potential for disaster is unlimited because instead of choosing a path and adjusting it to make it right for you and the circumstances, you push all that away." Danni gave Jaina's arm a squeeze. "You may not want to be your mother, you may ache for the day when you won't be seen as her daughter, but that doesn't mean your mother doesn't have a lot of admirable qualities that you might want to embrace."

Jaina nodded, letting Danni's words bounce around inside her mind for a bit. She knew she was both disappointed and relieved by her mother's failure to learn more about the Force. Being a Jedi already gave her a piece of identity that her mother didn't have. And, in being a pilot, she did seem to have picked up one of her father's better traits. *And Mom's commitment to the causes that catch her up is certainly admirable. Her relentlessness and willfulness, while annoying to me, are good traits, too.*

Jaina shot Danni a sidelong glance. "So, this wisdom thing, that kicks in when, about seventeen or eighteen?"

"Maybe, with a good role model."

"Good. I guess I can take my pick from some of the best." Jaina smiled. "I may not know who I am, but I think you've pointed me to a good path for finding out."

"It's the least I can do for half the team that saved me from the Yuuzhan Vong."

The two of them stopped as they rounded a corner and came upon a crowd of people gathered before a government food storehouse. Armed security troops stood at the doorway. A couple of frantic clerks beseeched the people to disperse. They announced they were waiting for a shipment of supplies and would be setting up local relief centers in neighborhoods. They said no one would be getting food directly from the storehouse, but the sentiment voiced by some in the crowd supported the idea that the troops and bureaucrats wanted to keep the food only for themselves.

Danni shivered. "These people—there's such need."

Jaina slowly opened herself to the Force and felt the desire and urgency pouring off the crowd. She abruptly turned Danni around and headed back toward the spaceport. "I know you're Force-sensitive. I should have steered you clear of here."

"Did you feel it, Jaina?"

"I did, when I opened myself to it. I'd shut some of it out just because it hurt so much, which is why I didn't skirt this place."

"You can do that? You can shut things out?" Danni frowned. "I mean, I thought the Force was vital for the Jedi."

"The Force is vital for everyone, but negative emotions are the bane of the Jedi Knight. Too much of that can frustrate you, lead you to despair and rash acts that are of the dark side." Jaina stretched her senses out and located the distant spark that was her mother. "I can show you how to screen a lot of the negative stuff and teach you a few more of the simple telekinesis exercises, but first I want to find my mother. She ought to have a clue as to how desperate things are getting here."

"You're right. Thanks for getting me out of there."

"No problem." Jaina gave her a quick nod. "That's for calibrating my compass. Now that I've got a better idea where I'm going, perhaps I can actually get there."

CHAPTER SEVENTEEN

The University of Agamar students had been very resourceful in dealing with the conditions they discovered on Bimmiel, Corran decided. Once the sand started to fly, they developed broad, flat footgear that could be buckled to the bottom of boots, expanding the size of a walker's footprint. It distributed enough of the walker's weight that he didn't sink into the sand. A second iteration of the design included a compartment beneath the heel that could be filled with the dead-slashrat scent—referred to, rather accurately, as *stink*—so slashrats wouldn't track folks out scouting around.

The sandgales picked up again shortly after the Jedi's arrival, trapping them in the cavern with the field team. Corran quickly established that he and Ganner would take watches at the cave mouth, especially at night, when their Force senses could make picking out the approach of slashrats much easier. The fact that these watches also tended to be cold meant none of the students lamented giving them up. Because the students had infrared monitoring equipment that allowed them to spot the heat that slashrats gave off—thereby rendering them technologically visible at night—an undercurrent of comments started about how stupid the Jedi were to rely on archaic practices and the Force when technology worked just as well and allowed a full division of labor.

The criticism annoyed Ganner, but Corran didn't mind it. As he explained to Ganner in the dead of the night, "If they think we're a bit slow, they'll believe themselves superior. This makes us much less of a threat in their eyes. Since we'll be living with them for a while, having them think us more buffoon than brute won't be bad."

Ganner had his own ideas about how to improve relations with the students, which resulted in Trista spending part of the watches talking with him in hushed tones that were punctuated by far too many giggles. Ganner's getting along with Trista did have a curious effect on the rest of the company. Males in the group who found her desirable didn't pick on the Jedi too much, lest they risk offending her. Her female friends remained neutral toward the Jedi, or at least toward Corran. The others, including Dr. Pace, seemed to take the budding romance as a sign that Ganner was human—or manipulable—and that eased some tension.

The week of storms did allow Corran to learn more about the Yuuzhan Vong body and artifacts the team had discovered. At his suggestion they looked at the artifacts and confirmed that the weapons and armor were, or once had been, living creatures.

The fact that the Yuuzhan Vong had been on Bimmiel before and, perhaps significantly, during the exit half of the orbit, suggested to Corran that *if* they returned, they would be very well suited to local conditions since they knew what to expect. He felt certain they *had* returned and were in the area: as martial a people as they seemed to be, he could easily imagine them coming to recover the remains of their fallen comrade. Corran had no idea why it took the Yuuzhan Vong fifty years before returning to recover the body. Perhaps this one was an early scout. However, if his hunch was true, everyone in the university field team was in serious jeopardy.

As the gales died down, Corran made plans for himself and Ganner to recon the area. They waited until nightfall, strapped on sandshoes, and headed out to the east, toward the shores of what, during the time of the Imperial survey, had been a lake. Their progress was not fast, but the sandshoes did allow them to keep moving without having to dig themselves out of deep sand.

Corran and Ganner crouched downwind of a discovery. Two dunes over, painted in silver and gray by the moon's light, there boiled a ball of slashrats savaging some other creature. The predators made angry little growls as they shot up through the sand and dived back down into it, or slithered back and forth, wagging their heads in fights over scraps of carrion. Watching them feed, Corran almost felt sorry for the Yuuzhan Vong they'd attacked.

More curious than the battling was a sharp, sour scent that wafted to them on the wind. Corran wrinkled his nose. "That's worse than stink."

Ganner nodded. "That's killscent. Trista says the slashrats exude it when they're making a kill. It lets others know food is in the area. They'll close in, herding the shwpi back toward the main kill site. Some experiments showed that the slash-rats will ignore stink to get at killscent. While the students could synthesize it, they don't for fear of inviting a feeding frenzy."

"Wise idea." Corran got up and started moving around to the south. "We skirt the killball and keep going. I'm getting faint glimmerings of stuff farther on."

"As am I. Strange things."

The two Jedi continued on in silence—at least, audio silence. When one is attuned to the Force, the emotions playing through another can feel as sweet as music sounds, or as harsh as breaking transparisteel looks. Excitement tinged with resentment trailed off Ganner, so Corran decided to give fewer orders and invite Ganner's input on little choices, like how to work around a rising line of stony outcroppings that capped the hills overlooking the lake. Ganner gladly took the lead, and once they had removed their sandshoes, they made good progress through the rocks.

At the pinnacle they paused, then slipped into shadows and descended toward the sand-strewn lake bed. They kept behind cover as much as possible, assuming that if the Yuuzhan Vong were there, they would have had the equivalent of infrared monitors available to them. At the base of the rocks they stopped and studied the flat expanse before them.

A village of sorts had been laid out on the lake bed, but clearly the designer had been working with some logic that Corran couldn't understand. Closest to their position were small rounded buildings, bowl-like and inverted, with any opening in them pointing farther east, away from the Jedi. Corran counted two dozen of the stone huts, gathered in four rough ranks of six each. Beyond them came a trio of larger buildings, on the same design, and closest to the rising sun was a single, very large building—easily large enough to house a freighter and have room left over for storing cargo between trips.

Two things struck Corran about the buildings. The first was that they reminded him of mollusk shells. He knew of sea life that appropriated the castoff shells of other creatures, and found it easy to imagine that the Yuuzhan Vong had just come down and grown domiciles for themselves. He had no idea what they did with the creatures that actually grew the shells, but assumed they either moved on to grow the larger ones, or likely were a prime source of food.

The second thing that he noticed was that he got a Force sense of inhabitants only in the smallest of the shells. He glanced over at Ganner. "Something is wrong with the people."

The other Jedi's eyes narrowed. "It is as if there is static coming through the Force from them. Their link to the Force is weakening. I think they're dying."

"Good insight. And you get nothing from the larger shells?"

"Shells? Of course, that's what they are. No, I don't."

"So, if there are Yuuzhan Vong around, they're likely in those bigger ones."

"That would be my assumption." Ganner pointed a finger at the village and circled it around. "Notice anything about the slashrats?"

Corran stretched out with the Force. He found slashrats easily enough, but they were all twenty meters from the Yuuzhan Vong village. They were active and would move toward it, directly or at an angle, then turn back. Some would even tunnel deep under it but never come up through the heart of it. "Do you think they're able to repel the slashrats?"

"I don't know." Ganner pulled his sandshoes from where he'd fastened them over his back to climb, and started to buckle them to his boots. "A quick look might tell us something."

The older Jedi frowned. "We're not very agile in these things. Going down there could be suicidal."

Ganner smiled coldly. "I have an assist that makes me more agile."

"You're not going down there alone."

"You will be too slow. If we get into trouble, you'll be—"

"I'll be waiting for you to use your assist to get me out." Corran pulled on his sandshoes. "Trista should have you all knowledgeable about what is normal on this rock, so keep your eyes open for anything *un*usual down there. Let's get samples of the sand and figure out what keeps the slashrats back."

"I'm not stupid, you know."

Corran arched an eyebrow at him. "You say that, but *you're* the one who suggested going down there."

"How smart are you for going with me?"

Corran rolled his eyes. "Just move it."

Ganner led the way, and the slashrats gave them a wide berth. The two Jedi slipped into the Yuuzhan Vong village at the western end, and each of them crouched in the shadow of one of the shell huts. From inside the hut Corran expected to sense the peaceful flow of the Force he related to sleeping creatures, but jagged breaks in it disrupted the pattern.

He shuffled his way forward and discovered an opening on the eastern side of the shell. The creature that had originally grown the shell must have coiled about a central axis as it grew its armor home. The shell had been set in the sand so the lip of the opening dug into the sand a little. It appeared to Corran, given his sense of where the inhabitant lay, that the person crawled into the shell, then pulled himself deeper into it, sleeping in the small section that lay above the opening itself.

Paralleling Ganner, he moved deeper into the village. His sense of things remained the same. He stopped and pulled from a belt pouch a small duraplast cylinder, then dug it into the ground to take a sample of the sand. He stoppered it, then noticed movement in the sand. A beetle climbed to the top of the sample and started circling around the glassy wall, looking for a way out.

Corran slipped that cylinder back into his pouch and pulled out another empty one. He dug down a little bit into the sand and noticed a beetle emerge into the hole and inspect it. He scooped that beetle up in a cylinder and discovered, by dint of the twin horns on its head, that it was different from the first beetle he'd captured. He dug around some more and found a third type of beetle, much smaller than the first two, and caught it up. He wasn't certain if it was just young or an entirely different species.

More test holes produced nothing, so Corran started to move on. Ganner had gotten ahead of him and was huddled behind a shell hut in the first rank. Corran immediately cut over to his left, putting him directly on Ganner's track. *He shouldn't have gone that far ahead.* The fact that Ganner appeared to be fingering his lightsaber and had a rising sense of anxiety about him began to alarm Corran.

All of a sudden something shrieked from within one of the shells. A desperate creature crawled from a shell between the two Jedi and stumbled to his feet. He looked vaguely human, but was knock-kneed and had growths on his arms and legs and spine that looked like coral outcroppings. He clawed at a big coral spike growing from his right cheek and shrieked in a hoarse voice that was more animal than man, and more pain than anything else.

The creature ran past Ganner, then fell in the sand and struggled to get up again. The sand itself around the creature began to vibrate, with a dusty mist rising from it as if it were steam boiling off water. Corran couldn't figure out what was causing the sand to shiver, but he felt a curious vibration from his own belt. He pulled out the beetles he'd captured, and one, the horned one, was beating wings furiously.

Two long and lean Yuuzhan Vong warriors emerged from the first two medium-size shells—which had openings large enough so the tall aliens did not have to stoop as they came out. Neither of them seemed surprised or concerned about the slave. With a fluid grace that would have seemed almost sensual, were they not cadaverously slender, the Yuuzhan Vong split up and approached the slave from either side. One, then the other, taunted him with harsh and sharp comments, causing the slave to cower for a moment, and dart away from one, then back toward the other.

All the while the sand around his feet danced as the beetles flapped their wings in alarm.

Corran felt the slave's fear spike through the Force, then a severe burst of static rattled through Corran. The slave's fear vanished to be replaced by fury. With fingers hooked into claws and a feral scream falling from his lips, the slave charged headlong at one of the Yuuzhan Vong.

The alien warrior barked abruptly in what Corran took to be a cruel laugh. The warrior dodged to the right, then brought his left fist up in a punch that caught the slave over his heart. The slave arced up into the air and flew back a meter or so, then landed on his heels and flopped onto his back. Corran felt certain he'd heard ribs crack, but the slave rolled to the left and stood again, then charged the other Yuuzhan Vong.

The second warrior stopped the charge with a straight right hand to the slave's face. The sharp pop of bones breaking overrode the slave's muted whimper. The Yuuzhan Vong took a step back, then dropped another right hand onto the same cheek. The bony knobs on his knuckles came away dark and glistening. Then he swept his left leg up and around in a kick that slammed into the slave's ribs and pitched him back toward the first Yuuzhan Vong.

The first Yuuzhan Vong warrior opened his arms, almost in a welcoming gesture. He said something to the battered slave. It seemed like a question, and the reaction from the slave was one of disbelief. The slave spat, hugging arms to his ribs, then snarled and dashed at his interrogator.

The first Yuuzhan Vong warrior hammered the slave with a left hook that snapped off the coral spike on the man's right cheek. The blow spun him around. The Yuuzhan Vong then drove his right fist into the slave's back, precisely over the kidneys. Corran winced in sympathy as the slave went to his knees.

A quick burst of fury alerted Corran to a new problem. Ganner had brought his lightsaber to hand but had not yet ignited it. Knowing what Ganner wanted to do, but also knowing it would get them and the students killed, Corran acted. He used the Force to drill through Ganner's sense of outrage and pumped the acrid scent of stink straight into his brain.

Ganner immediately dropped to his knees and doubled over. He covered his mouth with his gloved hands as his chest convulsed. What little was left of his supper leaked out through his fingers and puddled in the sand. He shot Corran an incendiary glance, then his body heaved again.

Beyond him, in the space between the huts, the two Yuuzhan Vong towered over their slave. Both of them barked questions at him. Confusion rolled off the slave, then outrage. He coughed out an incoherent comment and composed his face into a mask of defiance. He pushed off the ground with one hand and tried to rise and run, but his captors never gave him the chance to escape.

A kick to the stomach jetted dark fluid from the slave's mouth. Blood rolled down from his cheeks like a flood of black tears. The Yuuzhan Vong circled the slave, their punches and kicks knocking him back and forth between them. If not for the sheer violence of their assault, he would have fallen to the sand. They kept him upright despite the fact that their blows shattered his skeleton and made it impossible for him to keep himself on his feet.

Finally the slave sagged to the ground. He was so far gone that a few more kicks couldn't even send a spark of pain from him to Corran through the Force. The Yuuzhan Vong looked at one another, traded laughter and comments. They mimed blows they had struck and used their hands to mimic the way the slave had bounced between them. Then they stooped and grabbed the slave, wrist and ankle, and carried him to the edge of the village. Swinging him back and forth four times, they lofted him out into the sand, and very quickly a slashrat killball marked the place he landed.

The Yuuzhan Vong picked up handfuls of sand and used it to scrub blood from their bodies, then wandered back to their huts and disappeared back inside.

Corran projected the image of the hills into Ganner's mind, then began his own retreat from the village. He took it slowly and monitored Ganner's progress. He waited close by until the younger Jedi actually got out on the sand outside of the village. He hoped the tang of killscent would remind Ganner how close death lay to them.

Again nestled in the rocks of the hills, the two Jedi removed their sandshoes to begin their ascent. Ganner sullenly strapped the shoes across his back, then turned on Corran.

"If you ever do anything like that again, I will kill you."

"At least then death will be deferred, not immediate, as it would have been here."

"That man, you watched them beat him to death, and you did nothing."

"That's right, I did nothing because our tracks could be followed back to the students. We saw only two of the Yuuzhan Vong, but there could be dozens more, maybe hundreds in the big shell. Cutting those two down, right there, *if* you could have done it, would have doomed Dr. Pace and Trista and the others."

Ganner snorted angrily. "Not if they were the only two Yuuzhan Vong here."

"And what do you think the chances of that are?"

The younger man arched a dark eyebrow. "There are only two Jedi here."

"Unassailable logic, that, Ganner." Corran settled the sandshoes across his back, then tugged on the cuffs of his gloves. "Maybe there are two, maybe there are two thousand. I don't doubt that before we get off this rock, we're going to have to kill some of them, but the longer we can delay that confrontation, the better."

"So more people can die?"

"No, so we have a good chance of stopping the Agamarians from being captured. What we saw here is a data point, and one I want to study. That wasn't just a beating."

"It was sport, cruel sport."

"Maybe, at the end, yes, but there was something else." Corran frowned. "The way they spoke to him, they expected something from him. Their contempt, their anger, as shown by the frenzy at the end—something else was going on there."

"Fine, you think about the motives of our murderers. I don't think that data point will do you any good."

"Maybe not, but it's not all we've got. Our soil samples are more data points—"

"Killing Yuuzhan Vong will generate precious data points for you."

"Maybe. Dead Jedi would make for even more data points." Corran tapped two fingers against his right temple. "The vital thing right now is that we get back to the students, see if they can help us figure out what's going on here, then see if we can get away safely with what we know."

"And, if we can't?"

Corran shrugged. "The first few times the Yuuzhan Vong fought Jedi, we won. We'll just have to see how far we can extend that streak."

CHAPTER EIGHTEEN

Jacen Solo's eyes snapped open, and for a moment, he wondered where he was. He knew he was on Belkadan, but he found himself surprised to be back at the ExGal facility. Why that surprised him he couldn't immediately identify. He kicked off the light blanket covering him, then swung his legs over the edge of the cot and sat up.

Jacen raked fingers back through long brown hair, then pressed the heels of his hands against his eyes. Before he had awakened, he'd been in a Yuuzhan Vong village, the one where the villips were being grown. He'd gone there to free the slaves. He'd waded into the water and called them to him. They'd come, and their master had come after them. As the slave master had done with the old man, Jacen had left the Yuuzhan Vong warrior slowly sinking in the murky, still water.

It feels so real. Jacen pulled his hands away from his eyes, then focused until his hands emerged as ghostly shadows in the dim light. His hands still tingled with the sense of having held his lightsaber in a duel with the Yuuzhan Vong warrior. He shifted his shoulders and stretched his back, searching for any trace of pain to somehow validate the reality of what he'd seen.

He knew it probably had just been a dream. In the week since they watched the murder of the old man, they had done quite a bit of scouting. The Yuuzhan Vong had indeed turned

Belkadan—or at least this section of it—into a shipyard.
They were growing villips, coralskippers, and dovin basals
all over the place. The laborers were slaves all, by the look of
it, though some of the overseers had aides who appeared, to
Jacen, to be human and cooperating. They all had the growths
on them, too, but the Force was not filled with static from the
collaborators, just greatly diminished.

The vision's being just a dream made sense. It was clearly a
fantasy being fulfilled to let him drain away his frustration.
He was almost willing to accept what he had seen as a dream,
then to drop back off to sleep.

Two things prevented him from doing that, however. One
was a sense of urgency wrapped around the vision. While he
was willing to accept that his frustration was enough to give
birth to the dream, his frustration had been strongest the night
after watching the murder. Since then, they had not returned
to that place.

The second thing was the sheer reality of the vision. It
wasn't something he was remembering, per se, but felt as if it
was a glimpse at something he had to do. He knew, very well,
that if a Jedi was open to the Force, bits and pieces of the future might be revealed to him. His uncle's Master, Yoda, was
known for his wisdom and ability to see pieces of the future.
Jacen had never really felt he'd been gifted a vision by the
Force, but it did seem to him as if this was just the sort of
thing a vision like that would entail.

He got up from his cot and staggered out of the room that
had once been Danni's. Pretty much everything in it had been
smashed, but he'd been able to recover a few static holographs and a couple of other little mementos he'd carry back
to her. He shuffled his feet to move aside the detritus in the
hallway, then leaned against the door jamb to the room his
uncle had taken.

A small glow lamp filled the far corner of the room with
warm, golden light. His uncle sat on the floor facing the
doorway, all but reduced to a silhouette by the light. Jacen
started to say something, but then the sense of peace and concentration he got from his uncle stilled his tongue.

This was not the first time Jacen had seen his uncle enter a Jedi trance to tighten his bonds with the Force. After the peace with the Remnant, when Luke had made changes in the structure of the academy, other apprentices had joked that the Master had become old and needed his Force naps. Jacen had laughed at that, but he envied his uncle's connection to the Force. He wanted that intimacy himself, and he knew what sort of a price his uncle had paid to earn it. While he knew that such a bond could not be won easily, he fervently hoped his course to attaining it would be neither as long nor as twisted as his uncle's.

He turned away from the door and stood there with his back pressed flat against the wall. His uncle had said that experience allowed one to know that hard decisions needed to be made, and deciding if what he had seen was real or not certainly qualified as a hard decision. While his head told him to doubt what he had seen, his heart urged him to go.

That choice feels *right, and the Force is more about feeling than thinking.* Jacen slowly exhaled, then returned to Danni's room and slowly pulled on his combat suit. He clipped a comlink to the lapel, so he could record the data about his mission. *That way, Uncle Luke's goal will be served even if I can't attain mine.* He didn't warn R2-D2 that he was heading out, however, since he knew the droid would wake his uncle, and the mission would be ended before it ever began.

As he walked past Luke's door, he bowed once to his Master, and then, with a long Jedi robe shrouding him, he emerged from the ExGal facility and strode into the night.

With every step Jacen took, he found himself becoming further and further enmeshed in the vision he'd had. Every leaf, every wisp of cloud, the buzz of insects, the rattle of gravel coursing down a hillside in his wake—all of it matched what he remembered. He stopped thinking and instead concentrated on feeling, choosing his steps almost at random, yet knowing each time that he had made the right choice.

He stalked through the night, taking great care certainly, but with a growing sense of invulnerability because of what he knew he was heading out to do. His vision was coming true. He was drawing closer and closer to a confrontation that would free the slaves and begin to turn back the Yuuzhan Vong. He knew Luke might not understand, and probably would not approve, but Jacen felt bound to fulfill the destiny the Force had presented to him.

Quickly enough he found himself descending to the shore of the shallow lake. Moonlight filled the troughs between ripples with silver, and more of it pooled in the water on top of the villip leaves. Slaves moved through the stalks, anointing the villips with ladle after ladle of the dark water. The only sounds in the basin came from the splashing of water and the villips' haunting whispers.

Jacen stopped at the water's edge and threw back his cloak. He took a deep breath and let calm flow through him. He smiled, just a little, then composed his face in a benign expression. He opened his arms and spread them wide.

"Come to me, people. I will save you."

The slaves, almost as one, brought their heads up and looked over at him. A series of high whistles coursed back and forth, to be echoed by some of the villips. Jacen recognized the sound as the sort of thing R2-D2 did when the droid was puzzled, so he broadened his smile and waved the slaves toward him.

"Come to me. Your time as slaves is over."

The slaves began to move, but out of sync with his vision. *They're moving away from me!* The slaves slunk away, crouching as if expecting a punishing blow. Those in the front rank watched him while reaching out for someone behind them. The others in the more distant ranks turned and ran as fast as they could, splashing water up over themselves.

Then, toward the center of the slave formation, a part formed. A Yuuzhan Vong warrior clad in armor and bearing an amphistaff stepped down into the water and faced him. He spun the amphistaff in a circle, first between them, then up over his head and finally around his back. He stopped in an eye blink, with the staff trapped between his right forearm and ribs, then lowered himself into a crouch.

Jacen waded out to midcalf and produced his lightsaber. He thumbed the blade to life and let the hiss-crack drown out the frightened mewing of the slaves. His green lightsaber cast a ghastly light over the villips. Jacen whipped the humming blade around in a lazy infinity arc, first slicing through the villip stalk, then slashing in half both falling villips.

The warrior bellowed loudly and started to sprint at Jacen. Water splashed high, but hardly seemed to slow him at all. His amphistaff had begun spinning again, with the point dipping down to nip at the water with each circuit.

Jacen started to rush at his foe, but because he was smaller, the water slowed him. The young Jedi set himself, drawing the blade up high and back by his right shoulder. Then, as the warrior closed, Jacen cocked his wrists so the blade pointed forward, then lunged.

Just as I did in my vision!

The Yuuzhan Vong warrior, however, did not share in that vision. He twisted back to the right, sliding past the green energy blade, and cracked his amphistaff across Jacen's back. One of the armor's trauma pads absorbed much of the damage, but the force of the blow still sent Jacen stumbling forward. He went to one knee, then spun, bringing his lightsaber up to parry the next slashing attack.

The lightsaber's blade *did* fend off the strike, but didn't have quite the effect Jacen had expected. *My parry should have sheared thirty centimeters off that staff!* The young man came to his feet, parried another attack low and to the left, then twisted his wrists and brought the lightsaber up in a slash that should have opened the Yuuzhan Vong from right hip to left shoulder.

Sparks exploded and smoke rose from the alien armor. The warrior stumbled back a step or two, then lunged with his amphistaff. Jacen batted that attack wide, then cut down at the Yuuzhan Vong's right wrist. More sparks and smoke, and even a sizzling sound to go with it, but the hand didn't come off.

Surprised, Jacen cranked the green blade up and around for another attack on that arm, but the Yuuzhan Vong had already pulled it back wide. Before Jacen could shift his attack to a slash across the warrior's belly, the Yuuzhan Vong's left fist came around and caught the youth in the neck.

The heavy blow staggered Jacen and drove him back. He'd have fallen into the water except that he bumped up against a villip plant and it steadied him. He shook his head to clear it, then ducked as the Yuuzhan Vong arced a roundhouse kick at him. The kick missed Jacen, but exploded one of the villips, drenching him in chunky, viscous fluid that burned his eyes, nose, and mouth.

Choking still, Jacen ducked behind the villip plant, then cut behind another. He splashed a handful of water up to wash his face off, then dodged left and slashed twice quickly at the Yuuzhan Vong. The slashes backed his foe off for a moment, but in the blade's light Jacen noticed that the furrow he'd cut in the Yuuzhan Vong's armor had become little more than a discolored scar.

They don't just grow the armor; it's living still!

The Yuuzhan Vong held his amphistaff high and brought it down in a crushing blow aimed at Jacen's head. The Jedi brought his lightsaber up to block, but the amphistaff went from rigid to fluid and, whiplike, wrapped itself around his right wrist. A quick yank pulled Jacen forward, off balance, and into the Yuuzhan Vong's right knee. The knee caught him in the gut, doubling him over.

Jacen felt the warrior's viselike grip close on the back of his neck, then he had his face plunged into the turgid water. Water boiled around his lightsaber, but the whip controlled the movement of that arm enough that he couldn't strike.

The young man shunted away the panic rising in him and immediately summoned the Force. He reached out to pluck the Yuuzhan Vong off him—exactly as he had done countless times with his siblings or comrades when goofing around at the academy. He discovered the flaw with his strategy about the same time his lungs started to burn for lack of oxygen.

I can't sense the Yuuzhan Vong through the Force. And now I can't affect him.

It occurred to Jacen, as he sucked in the first mouthful of

water, that he could use the Force to lift himself out of the water. The concentration necessary for that act died as his body gagged and coughed. The stale air in his lungs bubbled out, then his body reflexively tried to inhale and breathed in more water, which started him coughing and gagging yet again.

Oh, no, Jacen thought, as the world began to go black, *it wasn't a vision. Or a dream. Just a nightmare . . .*

CHAPTER NINETEEN

Anakin crouched in the lavender grasses and peered through them at a small group of Dantari. The native nomads did not appear all that unusual. Humanoid in form, they used a limited vocabulary of spoken words supplemented with hand signals and facial expressions to communicate. They made tools, but had not yet found the secret of working metal. A couple of them did have knives formed from shards of AT-AT armor, but Anakin had never seen the knives being used for anything. He gathered they were a sign of power, since both were owned by large males whose hair was streaked with gray.

For a half second the boy wished C-3PO was there so he could translate the Dantari speech, but the image of the gold droid hiding in the grass was ridiculous enough that he almost laughed aloud.

The Dantari had made camp in a small clearing near a stand of blba trees. One of the elder males had drawn a charcoal design—the Imperial crest—on the upper left side of a younger male's chest. Using a blba thorn and a stick with which to strike it, the elder began to drive the coal-black ash into the younger male's chest, tattooing the design there forever.

The young Dantari was not the only one to be sporting that crest. Others had crude AT-ATs tattooed on them, or images of blasters, or the outlines and seams of stormtrooper armor marking their legs and arms. Small children sat and watched in fascination as the tattooing took place. Elders looked on pridefully as the youth said nothing during the tattooing process.

Anakin looked away and tried to shut the *tick-tick-tick* of stick hitting needle out of his mind. He glanced over at where Mara sat and caught her in an unguarded moment looking very tired. He glanced down immediately, then looked up again. By that time she had composed her face into an expression less haggard and much warmer.

That I could see her looking tired indicates how tired she must truly be. She'd never have let me see her like that if there was any other way around it. Anakin gave her a smile and crawled quietly over to her side. "I would never want to get a tattoo," he whispered.

"Best to avoid identifying marks, I think." She glanced slyly at him. "Never can tell when any of those Jedi will be after you and you want to slip away."

"You don't have a tattoo, do you?"

"I don't know, Anakin." Mara shrugged playfully. "A Jedi caught me, after all, so maybe I do."

He started to ask a question, but thought better of it and closed his mouth for a moment. "More than that answer I don't want to know."

Mara laughed, once, sharply, then covered her mouth with her hand. Anakin reached out through the Force, not sure what he could do, and immediately saw the damage had been done. Several of the Dantari were moving toward them, with three young boys in the lead, and an elder male charging up to get between them and whatever had made that sound.

Without thinking, Anakin shot to his feet and interposed himself between the Dantari and Mara. The male coming toward them towered above Anakin, easily half a meter taller than he was, almost broader across the shoulders than Anakin was tall, and outmassing him by nearly sixty kilos. Shock widened Anakin's blue eyes for a moment, then he lowered himself into a crouch and bared his teeth.

The charging Dantari male came up short. He raised

massive fists above his head and bellowed, but Anakin stood his ground. He didn't ape the motion; he'd learned enough from watching the Dantari to know that would have been a challenge to a dominance fight. Most Dantari confrontations involved the largest male frightening his foe off, and never had Anakin seen a Dantari as small as he was stand his ground before an elder male.

Still keeping his eyes locked on those of the male, Anakin dropped down on his haunches and rested his elbows on his knees. He knew he could have gathered the Force to himself and compelled the Dantari male to do the same thing, but he left the Force alone. In the week they'd been on the planet, he'd been relying less and less on the Force, and while his body ached and blisters had formed and popped, he did feel good doing things for himself. *The Force is an ally, not a crutch. If I learn nothing else from this experience, that will be enough.*

The Dantari male bellowed again, but Anakin did not react. He just sat and stared, keeping his body between Mara and the male. The male leaned forward on his fists for a bit, then sank to his haunches, too. Behind him the younger Dantari did the same thing.

Anakin kept his voice a low whisper. "Okay, I have him seated and quiet. Now what do I do?"

"Take this."

Anakin reached his left hand up to his left shoulder and accepted a small metal disk from Mara. He noticed her fingers were cold as he did so. Then he got a look at the button she'd given him, and a smile blossomed on his face. "I hope this works."

"Pity it only has the New Republic crest on it, not the Imperial one."

"It's shiny, so worth a try." Still watching the elder, Anakin leaned forward and got on his hands and knees. He crawled forward, stretching out to halve the distance between them. On a bare patch of ground he placed the button from Mara, then retreated and resumed his crouch.

The elder moved forward slowly, cautiously, and reached

out a hand toward the silver button. He extended a finger and slowly poked it. He recoiled instantly after touching it once, with the little ones leaping back and screaming as he did so. He crept forward again and sniffed, then touched it a second time. After a half-dozen touches, each lasting longer than the first, he picked up the button and stared at it, utterly enraptured.

Anakin glanced back over his shoulder at Mara. "Might need more buttons if we have to bribe a bunch of them."

Anakin's aunt smiled and tugged at the wrist of her right sleeve. "A couple more on the cuffs. If we have to go more than that, I'll get cold."

"Let's hope we don't get there."

Anakin looked back at the Dantari elder and found him trying to fix the button to a side-lock braid. The Jedi smiled at the Dantari, and the elder returned the smile. The Dantari then turned and galloped back to the encampment, scattering squealing children and earning some sharp-tongued rebukes from the females in the group. He grabbed something from a fabool-hide pouch, then scampered back to where Anakin sat. He opened his hand above the spot where the button had lain and dropped five white tubers, not much longer than Anakin's thumb.

The young Jedi knew they were vincha roots. He didn't know what the Dantari used them for, but he'd seen the Dantari get very excited when they found the plant and were able to dig up the roots. Anakin hadn't seen many of the plants around, so he took the offering to be very valuable as far as the Dantari were concerned.

Anakin smiled and held his hands up, with palms facing the Dantari. "Thank you, but I can't take these."

The elder looked at him, puzzled for a moment, then ran off and returned with another handful. He dropped them one by one on the pile, doubling its size. He hung on to each one longer than the last, and Anakin could sense the pain of his giving them up.

"Help here, Mara?"

"You got yourself into this, you figure it out."

"It was your laugh."

"It was *your* joke."

"Point taken." Anakin scratched at the back of his head with his left hand. "Okay, the button is more valuable to him than ten of the vincha roots, and I bet he'd go five more."

"That could be why some of the females are over there hiding the rest of the inventory."

"Right. He wants a fair exchange. Matter of pride and honor, I'd guess."

Mara patted him on the back. "Right course plotted, I think."

"Then I need to barter vincha roots back for something else, right?"

"Could be, that will work."

Anakin nodded. He waddled forward and gathered up the vincha, then brought them back to where he had been sitting. He got up and jogged off to the side to gather up some dead-fall limbs from a blba tree. He returned and made a small pile of them. He pointed at the elder Dantari, the pile of sticks, and then back to the bluff where he and Mara had their camp. Finally he tossed one of the vincha roots back to the elder.

The elder grabbed the root, then pointed at the pile of sticks and up at their camp. Anakin nodded. The Dantari smiled, then turned on his heel and ran back to the small band he traveled with. He jabbered at them quickly and gesticulated wildly, brandishing the vincha root proudly. The Dantari band all started shouting and leaping about, getting carried away in a joyous frenzy.

Anakin scooped up the rest of the roots and put them in his pocket. He stood and helped Mara to her feet. "I don't think we want to be here if they decide we should join in on the fun, you know?"

"I concur." Mara draped an arm over his shoulders and leaned on him for support. "You did well there."

"And didn't use the Force once."

"Right, though you *did* manage to get out of having to gather firewood."

The two of them chuckled lightly as they walked along.

Anakin made certain to keep his pace slow so Mara wouldn't tire. They lapsed into silence for a bit. Anakin stopped by some rocks that marked the beginning of the steep ascent to their camp and let Mara lean against one of them.

He swiped a hand across his brow. "I don't know about you, but I'm tired."

Mara gave him a quick smile. "You're very kind to say that, but you know I'm—"

"Aunt Mara, it's okay."

"I'm the tired one here . . ." The effort of saying those words seemed to take a lot out of her. "Tell me if I get to be a burden for you."

Anakin adamantly shook his head and swallowed hard against the lump rising in his throat. "Never, Aunt Mara, you'll never be a burden."

"If your mother was here, she'd be proud of how polite and mannerly you are."

"If my mother was here, she'd have negotiated a treaty for this planet to join the New Republic, getting it all for a handful of vincha roots." Anakin sighed, then looked up into Mara's green eyes. "I know you're not feeling well. I know it's a fight for you, but you keep fighting. I can't tell you how much that impresses me."

He flashed for a moment on the fact that his father, in his grief, had scarcely drawn a sober breath. *Why can't you be more like Aunt Mara, Father?*

Mara stared at him and through him. "There are times, Anakin, when things overwhelm us. There are times when you can't fight."

"But you are still fighting. You're being brave."

"It's because I know what I'm fighting. Others may not be able to identify their enemy, so they can't fight."

My father's enemy is me. That thought sent a shiver through Anakin, but another thought followed on its heels. *Or, perhaps, his enemy is the guilt that he's assumed. If only things had happened another way.*

Mara eased herself off the rock and leaned into him again. "Ready to make it up the hill?"

"After you, Mara."

"Together, Anakin, together."

That evening the elder Dantari brought a big pile of blba branches. He returned with a second armload, and Anakin gave him a second vincha root. The Dantari retreated into the darkness, then a frenzied round of hooting and hollering began from the distant Dantari camp.

Snapping a branch in half, Anakin fed it into the fire. "Well, they're happy."

"Indeed, it sounds as if they are." Mara nodded, the shifting shadows cast by firelight hiding the weariness on her face. "You did well."

"Thanks. I think so, too."

And Anakin continued to think so until the next morning when he found the elder Dantari waiting for him in the camp as he awoke. The Dantari sat perched in the middle of a ten-meter-long blba log. The elder wore a grin like that of a Hutt that had a fix in on a Podrace, and extended an empty hand in Anakin's direction.

CHAPTER TWENTY

Gavin didn't pause in the doorway of the office that Admiral Traest Kre'fey had been given on Dubrillion. He rapped on the jamb with his knuckles and swept into the room. He was a couple of steps in when he glanced up from his datapad and actually saw two other people in the office with the admiral.

"I'm sorry, Admiral, I didn't realize you were busy." Gavin pulled himself to attention and saluted.

The Bothan returned the salute. "It is not a problem, Colonel Darklighter. I believe you know Lando Calrissian and Leia Organa Solo."

Gavin felt himself blushing. "We have met, yes, but I don't know them . . ." Lando and Leia had been heroes of the Rebellion along with his cousin Biggs. He had been a child when he'd first heard of them and had even developed a crush on Princess Leia. While he was well past that feeling, meeting them again reduced him to a little boy who felt like an impostor just being in the room with them. "I can come back, sir."

Kre'fey shook his head. "No, no need for that." The Bothan pointed to the holographic display of data and tables. "The Agamarian ships that arrived when we did have been moving people off planet with their shuttles. The Yuuzhan Vong are doing nothing to stop them, so we assume they will strike as the refugee convoys start to move out. Rogue Squadron is going to have to keep them off us."

"I've been working on that, Admiral." Gavin glanced at his datapad. "I've got a full squadron of X-wings ready to go, and Dubrillion's population has a large number of uglies that they've modified for running the asteroid belt and then armed. They should give us as much as a wing of fighters."

Lando smiled confidently. "The pilots here are good. They'll keep the Yuuzhan Vong off the convoy."

"I'm sure they will. What concerns me, though, is that only a handful of those uglies have hyperdrives. We'll need to have a ship capable of recovering the pilots and their ships heading out last. Rogue Squadron can keep the Vong off while the fighters are being recovered, then we can jump out ourselves."

Kre'fey stroked the snowy fur of his chin. "I had assumed the *Ralroost* would be the last ship out. We will recover the fighters."

Leia frowned. "We're loading refugees on the *Ralroost*. If it is the last ship out, the Yuuzhan Vong will concentrate on it. Do you want to take that risk?"

The Bothan snorted quickly. "*Want* to take the risk? No. Do I think we have no choice? Yes." He leaned forward on the table upon which the holoprojector had been set. "We already know, even despite the generosity of the Agamarians in sending all the ships they have, that we can't save everyone here."

Gavin looked past the admiral to the ravaged cityscape. After the squadron had been recovered, Kre'fey had acceded to an Agamarian request that the *Ralroost* escort a convoy of ships to Dubrillion. Gavin actually believed that Kre'fey had engineered that request, which brought his ship into a theater where contact with the Yuuzhan Vong could not possibly be denied by Coruscant. When the convoy arrived, the Yuuzhan Vong did send a half-dozen fighters to harry some of the ships, but the X-wings had beaten them back without getting blooded themselves.

In the four days since the convoy's arrival, the Yuuzhan

Vong had done little beyond staging raids that seemed designed to test the response time of the X-wings and other fighters the *Ralroost* had brought along. Gavin felt certain his every move was being watched and cataloged. He'd not felt this vulnerable since before Grand Admiral Thrawn had died at Bilbringi.

The people of Dubrillion had faced the impending invasion with a stoicism that stunned Gavin. In light of the fact that everyone couldn't be saved, families were being asked to make hideous choices about who would be allowed to live and who would be left behind. The best and brightest of Dubrillion's children, along with historians, artists, and cultural leaders were being culled and processed for transport to Agamar. Children from the same family were split up to prevent the loss of a line in the event a particular ship did not make it. Mothers let children go, lovers were parted, grandchildren said tearful good-byes to relatives they knew they would never see again.

Kre'fey continued. "The people of Dubrillion have made their hard decisions. For me to avoid one that is just as difficult would mock their heroism. I won't do that."

Leia nodded silently, imbuing that silent acknowledgment of Kre'fey's words with nobility and pain. "I'll be on the *Ralroost*, then."

The admiral shook his head. "With all due respect, I think you should travel with Senator A'Kla in his ship."

Leia smiled. "I would have, but I think you'll find the senator has demanded room on the *Ralroost* for himself and his traveling companions. He's given the *Fond Memory* to pilots who have already made a run to Agamar and are back for another group."

"Then it will be my pleasure to have you on board." The admiral straightened up and glanced at Gavin. "Is there anything else, Colonel?"

Gavin extended the datapad toward him. "I've found the pilots I need to fill out Rogue Squadron. I took the liberty of looking over the records of the fliers who've made asteroid runs here. I'm taking the best of them—of those who are still available."

Leia held her hand out. "May I see the list?"

The admiral nodded, so Gavin handed her the datapad. Leia studied it for a moment, then glanced up. "My daughter isn't on the list."

"No, Princess, she isn't."

"Why not? She was the best pilot to run the asteroids." Leia knew that Jaina was restless, annoyed with her recent assignments, and eager to contribute. Jaina would be outraged if she were not chosen as a Rogue Squadron pilot because she was Leia's daughter. And they were all in danger now, whatever their assignments.

"I know that, but she's too young."

The princess's chin came up and her eyes narrowed. "Correct me if I am wrong," she said in a tone that made it obvious that she knew she wasn't, "but my daughter is the same age you were when you joined Rogue Squadron, Colonel Darklighter."

A wave of heat passed over Gavin as his face flushed red. "That's true, yes, but those were desperate times—"

"And these aren't?"

"They are, but—"

Leia let some of the edge drain from her voice. "Let me ask you, Gavin, if one of your sons was one of the best pilots, would you deny him a spot in the squadron?"

"Don't ask me that." Gavin's stomach began to twist itself into knots. "I've flown against the Vong. I know how nasty they can be. I'm not sure if *I'll* survive getting out of here. I don't want to have to subject anyone's *child* to getting killed out there. And especially *your* child, Princess. You've already done more than your share of sacrificing for the New Republic."

Leia took a step toward him and laid a hand on his shoulder. She looked up into his eyes and gave him a brave smile. "Gavin, you and I both know that the people who are capable of dealing with trouble never really get a chance to pass, to rest, to live a normal life. People like us assume responsibilities so other people don't have their lives ruined. We can wish it was otherwise, but it won't happen."

She handed him the datapad. "I cannot tell you how grateful I am that you wanted to safeguard Jaina; but by letting her fly, we can safeguard someone else. She's a wonderful pilot, she can fly an X-wing like no one else, *and* she's a Jedi. The Force might be less effective against the Yuuzhan Vong, but if she picks up that one of your other people is in trouble, she can be there to help."

Gavin swallowed past the lump choking him. "Two of the top pilots in the squadron's past were from Corellia and Alderaan, so having someone whose blood comes from both will probably be good. Do you want to tell her, or shall I?"

"You should tell her, Colonel." Leia smiled proudly. "I think being told of this assignment by her mother would tarnish it somewhat."

"You have my word, Princess, that she will be well taken care of."

"I know, Gavin. May the Force be with you."

"Rogue Eleven, check in, please."

Jaina blinked and kind of jumped in her cockpit seat when she realized the comm call was for her. *I'm in Rogue Squadron!* The realization had a surreal aspect to it because, as she grew up, the part of her uncle's life that had gone before his becoming a Jedi Knight had receded into the dim past. While Luke was acknowledged as the founder of Rogue Squadron, Wedge Antilles and the other pilots in it had really defined the squadron and made it a legend.

Even though she knew she was a good pilot, she didn't think she was good enough to join the squadron, especially not at her age. *Still, desperate times require desperate measures.*

"Rogue Eleven, check in. If your comm unit is giving you trouble, raise a hand."

Jaina keyed her microphone. "Sorry, Nine, I'm all green here. Good to go."

"Have to be alert out there, Sticks. No spacing."

"As ordered, Nine." Jaina grinned, enjoying the fact that

she'd already been given a call sign. She knew it came from the fact that her X-wing had a control stick, and she carried a lightsaber, which the pilots derided as another stick.

Gavin's voice crackled through the comm channel. "All Rogues, head out. We rendezvous at point Angel-One. Orient 342 mark 55 and go to station keeping."

Jaina double-clicked her comm unit to acknowledge the command, then fed power to the repulsorlift coils. The X-wing came up smoothly and hovered very still while she retracted the landing gear. She glanced over at the observation deck windows and thought she saw her mother flanked either side by Elegos and Lando. She gave them a big thumbs-up, then as Rogue Ten moved out of the hangar, she nudged the throttle forward and trailed after her squadron mate. Once out of the hangar, she pulled back on the stick and boosted her throttle full forward, rocketing the X-wing toward the asteroid belt waiting above.

Jaina still felt the way her flesh had puckered when Colonel Darklighter came to her and offered her a position in Rogue Squadron. Rogue Squadron had been the people who liberated Coruscant from the Empire. They'd helped break up the Bacta Cartel. They'd been part of Grand Admiral Thrawn's defeat and played a key role in ending the long struggle with the Empire. As much as her uncle, mother, and father might have been heroes of the Rebellion, the Rogues became a symbol, a collection of heroes that most people could identify with. While she loved her family and cherished being a Jedi Knight, being asked to join the squadron was something that she'd earned, not something granted to her by her ability with the Force or the reputations of her parents.

As she reached the rendezvous point, Jaina glanced at her primary sensor screen. The Rogues were set up midway between the asteroid belt and the Agamarian convoy. Other squadrons of fighters, made up of old TIE designs and a plethora of uglies, formed up behind Rogue Squadron. At the very end of the convoy sat the *Ralroost*. A couple of last shuttles were coming up from the planet to board the Bothan

Assault Cruiser. By stretching out with the Force, Jaina could feel her mother and Danni on board one of them.

They left the planet safely. Now we have to get them out of the system safely.

"Rogue Lead, I have movement on my scanners." Rogue Four's voice dominated the channel for a moment. "At 271 mark 30."

Jaina ruddered her fighter around in that direction and felt a chill run down her spine. "By all that makes a Hutt ugly . . ."

A Yuuzhan Vong warship drifted slowly down from the asteroid belt, with little coralskippers buzzing around it like flies on carrion. The ship itself would have matched an Imperial Star Destroyer in length, but, being something of an ovoid shape, certainly massed a great deal more. The ship's flesh alternated in strips of smooth, glassy, black rock and rougher, craggier patches that housed pits, which she assumed were weapons emplacements and homes for the dovin basals that propelled the ship.

Near the nose, along the spine, and at the aft of the ship grew huge, long coral arms of deep red and dark blue. Coralskippers dotted these arms like buds on a plant. Jaina assumed that some of the larger, unoccupied holes in the arms housed plasma projectors, and judging from their size compared to the coralskippers, a blast from one of them could easily burn a snubfighter from the sky.

The lead ships in the convoy started to move out. They used Dubrillion's gravity well to let them build up some speed, then came about on a course that would let them make the first jump in the journey to Agamar. They weren't going directly, since they had no desire to lead the Yuuzhan Vong to that world. More importantly, by stopping at a way point and shifting to a new course, they'd cut days off the single-jump trip.

The coralskippers that had been orbiting around the big ship formed into squadrons and began their runs at the convoy. Combat traffic controllers on the *Ralroost* started designating squadrons as targets and fed attack orders to the various Dubrillion squadrons nearest them. Jaina studied her sensor monitors intently, watching as little lights representing fighters moved forward, split apart, and in the midst of fierce dogfights, suddenly winked out of existence.

After what seemed like an eternity, but really was all too soon, Gavin's voice broke through the low-level chatter on the comm channels. "Rogues, we have been given the target designated Rock-One. Keep moving fast, do as much damage as you can. Everyone look out for everyone else."

Jaina's R5 droid, a maroon and white model, uttered a low moan.

"What's the matter, Sparky?"

The droid tootled and splashed the target on her primary monitor.

Emperor's black bones, we're going after the warship. In an odd way, ordering an attack by a group of snubfighters against a capital ship made sense. The Empire's big ships had always been vulnerable to close-in actions by small fighters. The New Republic's tactical commanders knew that and employed snubfighters very effectively against their enemies.

Jaina wondered, however, if the Yuuzhan Vong were aware of how afraid they should be of snubfighters.

"As ordered, Lead." Jaina smiled and jammed the throttle forward. "Sparky, hold on tight back there."

"Has your wing, Twelve does, Sticks."

"Thanks, Twelve." Jaina looked at her weapons board. "Nine, do we use our proton torps, or just the lasers?"

"Got something else you're going to be saving the torps for, Sticks?"

"I copy, Nine." Jaina quadded up her lasers and settled a finger over the stutter trigger. She figured she'd use the lasers to scope out the ship's defenses, then drop some torps in if she found a likely target.

The Yuuzhan Vong warship just kept growing bigger and bigger as the X-wings sped toward it. The big ship's aft end came up, allowing it to point its dorsal spines forward, along its line of travel. Golden light blossomed at their tips, then boiling gold balls of plasma shot out, arcing out toward the ships in the convoy.

The shots, taken at ranges of over five kilometers, were not terribly accurate for hitting small freighters. Even so, each of the ships in the convoy had a set flight path if it was going to escape the system. With the Yuuzhan Vong fire cutting across that flight path, a collision was inevitable.

The first freighter hit was one that reminded Jaina very much of the *Millennium Falcon*. The plasma blast caught it on the starboard side, burning clean through the cockpit and eating a crescent deep into it. The ship started tumbling like a chip in a sabacc game, with people and debris spilling out of it. It whirled away toward the brown bulk of Destrillion, destined to burn up in that bleak world's atmosphere.

Jaina watched it die, and she suddenly felt cold—not physically, but emotionally. People who were fleeing, people who had not asked for their world to be attacked, had just been murdered, and more would be murdered along with them if she did nothing. Without conscious thought, just feeling her way through the maneuvers, she inverted her X-wing and dived in toward the Yuuzhan Vong ship. She rolled the fighter up on its port stabilizers, then leveled out and cruised along the ship's hull.

She kept a light hand on the stick, juking left and right, bouncing up and down as she went. The coralskippers mounted in the spines shot small plasma bolts at her in golden streams, but her maneuvering kept her free of their fire. More importantly, she noted, the rough patches on the ship had dovin basals that were projecting black holes to absorb stutter shots from her lasers, and those voids also warped the plasma trajectories.

As her ship streaked over the warship's surface she started firing through plasma streams, letting her bolts cross the plasma paths the way the plasma was cutting the flight path for the convoy. The dovin basals were forced to project voids into those streams to pick off her shots. They absorbed laser bolts as well as plasma shots. This not only tired the dovin basals, but put them in the odd position of providing cover for Jaina's fighter.

Hauling back on the stick, she came up and made a run at

one of the spines. Assuming that whatever mechanism the ship used to direct the plasma bolts was located in the tip, she clipped off a few shots at one. Dovin basals around the tip absorbed all the shots save one. That single shot burned past the tip a second before a plasma bolt raced out at the convoy.

Makes sense. The dovin basals shield the tip until just before a shot comes out. Jaina keyed her comm unit. "Lead, the tips are vulnerable. We have a window before they shoot. I'm taking one out."

"Careful, Sticks."

"As anyone, Lead."

Jaina felt a curious peace settle over her as she brought her X-wing up and around in a spiral that rose along one of the spines. Golden plasma bolts flashed up past her. A couple nicked her shields, but she reinforced the power there very quickly. At the tip of the shaft the bolts curved in toward the gravity wells the dovin basals were creating. She shot past that area, then hit hard port rudder and reversed her ship's thrust. The X-wing swapped itself end for end, then, when she cut her throttle to zero, the fighter hovered there in space, five hundred meters from the end of the shaft.

Jaina looked right down into it. The spine's tip had a triskele valve at the tip. It reminded her of heart valves. It would open up for a second or two, just long enough to eject the plasma, then close again, sealing up the firing tube. It had an elegance about it, yet seemed so primitive when compared to the fighter in which she sat.

She triggered the flicker shots and poured a steady rain of energy darts down at the valve. The plasma shots coming up at her curved in and missed because of the void shielding the tip. "Sparky, let me know when the gravitic anomaly starts to collapse."

The droid tooted an acknowledgement, then quickly keened a sharp whistle.

Jaina thumbed her weapons control over to proton torpedoes and triggered a pair. The pink missiles jetted blue flame and shot straight at their target. A heartbeat before they reached it, the valve snapped open, revealing a golden glow coming from deep down in the shaft. The torpedoes flew on, and Jaina pumped the throttle full forward and inverted as her X-wing dove back toward the Yuuzhan Vong ship.

Somewhere in the middle of the spine, the torpedoes hit the plasma bolt. Cracks immediately appeared in the midnight blue shaft. They leaked silver-gold fire, then the shaft started to come apart. The center of it vaporized into an incandescent cloud of molten yorik coral. A great gout of fire clipped the end of the shaft's upper half at an odd angle, starting it to spin and wobble. It slammed into another spine, shattering both of them.

Another pair of proton torpedoes streaked in at the shaft she'd hit. They came in at a sharp angle, and one skipped off the glowing, molten edge, then impacted the hull. Its explosion gouged a deep scar in the ship and scattered yorik coral into space. The second one made it inside the shaft, and when it exploded, the base of the shaft crumbled from the inside out.

"Nice shot, Twelve."

"Following your lead, Sticks."

Jaina laughed as she leveled out for a moment, then pulled up and shot away from the ship. "We showed them!"

"We did."

"Can the chatter!" Gavin's order coursed through the comm channel, but didn't bring with it any anger.

"As ordered, Lead." Jaina's grin grew larger as she watched the *Ralroost* get closer and closer to the point where it would begin its run to hyperspace. *We're doing okay.*

Then something shook her ship. She glanced about, fearing a dovin basal had somehow locked onto her shields, but there were no fighters anywhere near her. Her secondary monitor did show a gravitic anomaly in the system, but the readings were well beyond that which any of the coralskippers could have generated. *In fact, the only time I've seen readings like this was when I've simmed against an Interdictor cruiser!*

Her heart immediately sank into her belly. The Yuuzhan Vong warship had shifted its dovin basals away from driving the ship and instead had them create a narrow gravity well that blocked the *Ralroost* and a half-dozen other ships from entering hyperspace along the route to Agamar. *We'll just have to find another route out.*

Just as that thought materialized, Sparks whistled to acknowledge receipt of new navigational data. She glanced at it as Gavin's voice came through the comm channel. "Rogues, our exit vector to Agamar is blocked. You now have our new destination. The *Ralroost* has recovered fighters, so head out. We'll rendezvous there in twelve hours. Good fighting."

Jaina double-clicked her comm unit. She looked again at her destination, then pointed the fighter toward a distant star and began the run. *Dantooine, eh? It'll be good to see Mara again. I hope she's gotten her rest because, if we're followed, I know she's going to need it.*

CHAPTER
TWENTY-ONE

Jacen Solo awoke as a great, wracking cough lifted his body, then left him limp. Burning pain from his shoulders and hips formed a backdrop into which the pain from the cough faded. He opened his eyes and saw a pearlescent floor beneath him. While nowhere near as reflective as a mirror, it did provide him with a distorted image of himself, where he was blobby at some points and pinched at others. *Which is pretty much how I feel.*

He determined he was hanging from some sort of rack mounted above him in the ceiling. He could feel the restraint bands on his ankles, thighs, and wrists. The wristbands were the worst, since they twisted his arms enough to lock his elbows. His ankles were higher than his shoulders, and his position made it difficult to get a good look at the device to which he'd been fastened.

He'd have been able to see nothing at all, but the sun had begun to rise on Belkadan, turning deep black night into a misty gray morning that mimicked the foggy sensation in his brain. He estimated he'd been in Yuuzhan Vong control for at least four hours. *More than enough time for them to backtrack me to the ExGal facility, the ship, Artoo, and Uncle Luke. What was I thinking?*

The vision had seemed so real to him, with all the bits and pieces feeling right as they fell together. He didn't want to think he'd deceived himself, using a dream as a pretext to do something his uncle didn't want him to do. The fact that doing just that would be the sort of thing expected of someone his age gnawed at him. *That makes me just like everyone else, but I'm not. I'm special, I'm more responsible.*

Another cough shook him, sharpening the pain that had dulled in his shoulders. Jacen allowed himself a little smile. *Of course, every sixteen-year-old who's been convinced he's not like his peers probably thinks this same thing after he's proved he isn't so unlike his peers as he thinks he is.* He sighed. Even being trained in the Force couldn't insulate him from making mistakes. *You can put powerful engines on a sloop racer, but if the chassis doesn't have structural integrity, the whole thing falls apart.*

And that's what Uncle Luke tried to tell me by reminding me I've not had enough experience. He shifted his shoulders to pull at the bonds on his wrists. *Lesson one from this experience: Realize just how much you don't know. Lesson two: Make sure to learn from lesson one.*

Jacen reached inside to touch the Force and call it to himself, but the pain in his shoulders and hips nibbled away at his concentration. A third cough didn't help the situation. Jacen did his best to try to let the pain bleed away with Jedi pain-suppression techniques, but as he calmed frayed nerves, the bonds on his wrists tightened. They twisted his arms more, grinding his shoulder sockets, making the pain spike.

Jacen gasped and hung there for a second. A cold chill sent a shudder through him, pulsing more pain from his joints. In response the bonds on his arms eased a bit, but Jacen hardly took comfort in that fact.

The device to which he had been attached clearly could sense how much pain he was in. Intellectually he knew this was actually very easy. Sensors could monitor the amount of activity going on in the parts of his brain dealing with pain. Electronics could even measure the output of the pain receptors in his shoulders—much in the same way they read neural signals and allowed Luke's artificial hand to function normally. He was even aware of machines that inflicted pain, like those used on his parents by Darth Vader on Bespin.

What surprised him was that there seemed no active purpose for keeping him in pain. No one was interrogating him. The pain wasn't sufficient to break him down, just to keep him in a distracted state. While that *was* preventing him from accessing the Force, somehow he didn't think the Yuuzhan Vong knew enough about the Jedi to realize how useful this would be.

A raspy clicking entered the chamber, causing Jacen to raise his head. In through the building's threshold came a small gray creature. It walked on six legs and sidled left and then right. It had four other appendages, all raised like flags at a parade. Two of these limbs were stout and two very fine. The creature also seemed to have compound eyes, three of them, hanging in a cluster from a single central stalk, which was segmented and capable of movement. Because it was just coming in through the doorway, which faced east, the rising sun backlit the creature, making it difficult for Jacen to see much more in the way of detail, but what he'd seen already did not please him.

He felt panic rising in him, but he forced it away. On a shelf next to the door he saw his lightsaber and tried to reach out for it. He knew he couldn't ignite it, but if he could pull it toward him and smash the dark end into this creeper, he'd feel much better. He sought to reach out to grasp it with the Force, but couldn't focus his mind enough. The realization of just how defenseless he was ripped through him, leaving him exhausted and drifting toward despair.

The creature scuttled forward, and Jacen felt his guts begin to knot up. Tiny white bumps, looking like gravel and scattered like pimples, dotted the creeper's dorsal carapace. The slender arms doubled back on themselves, with little pincers and feathery fronds brushing over them, touching them. It seemed to Jacen that the creature was taking inventory of its cargo.

The creeper came to a stop below his face. The two stout appendages reached up, pincers held wide. Jacen pulled his head back, preventing the pincers from grabbing his ears or cheeks. With the creeper so close, he got a good look at the white stones and knew, without a shadow of a doubt, that they were the seeds of the calcifications he'd seen on the slaves. *They plant those in me and I'm done for.*

One of the slender appendages swept upward, slapping the delicate frond across Jacen's exposed throat. Lightninglike agony slashed across his neck. He would have screamed, but the pain paralyzed his vocal chords and drained his neck muscles of all feeling and strength. His head bounced down and hung there. Muscles in his face twitched, and a little blood dripped from his mouth from where he'd accidentally bitten the interior of his cheek.

The stout claws caught his earlobes and clamped down tightly. The only good thing about the pain the frond had caused is that he barely noticed the pressure on his ears. With the pain-frond pulled back, one of the slender appendages reached up and pinched the flesh below his right eye, exactly over the curve of his cheekbone. He heard a click and knew the little claws had sliced through his flesh. Blood dripped, splashing scarlet dots over the creeper's pale gray shell.

While one slender stalk opened the wound, the other brought up one of the little bits of gravel and tucked it beneath his flesh. More pinching and the bleeding stopped, but Jacen could feel the foreign body inside of him. He narrowed his right eye and could feel the thing grate against his cheekbone.

A shudder shook him. He knew of countless creatures, insects mostly, that found suitable hosts for their broods. They would implant eggs into these hosts, allowing a crop of creatures to grow inside the victims. The little creatures would mature and eat and eat, devouring their host from the inside out until they were prepared to burst forth and seek new prey. The host that had sustained them was left a withered husk, with its own life sucked out and spent on raising a clutch of its own murderers.

No, I can't let this happen to me! He redoubled his efforts to summon the Force, pushing past the pain, but he never quite felt himself connect. Snarling, he tried harder and harder, refusing to give up. He pushed for all he was worth, seeking that spark that would lead him to the Force, refill him and sustain him.

On the shelf by the door, his lightsaber rattled against its resting place.

The creeper released his ears and scuttled toward the doorway. Jacen stared intently at his lightsaber, willing it to twitch and dance. He wanted it to rise up from the shelf, climb toward the ceiling, then he would drive it down with such force that it would crush the creeper. He didn't know what he could do after that to effect an escape, but that was enough for the moment, and joy surged through him as the lightsaber drifted up off the shelf.

Then it spun away, out toward the east, becoming a black dot against the sun's ball. Jacen watched it vanish, his victory dissolving into astonishment. He tried and tried to recall it, tried to make it return and smash the creeper, but it vanished. He could not feel it, and great sadness slammed into him. Jacen felt as if the Force itself had whisked away his lightsaber, taking away from him the symbol of the Jedi Knight because it no longer felt him worthy of any place in the order.

Then, distantly, he heard the snap-hiss of a lightsaber being ignited. Almost as if an echo, the sound repeated itself. The youth raised his head and looked out the doorway, past the creeper. Half the rising sun burned in the east, pouring molten gold light out over the horizon, and in the center of it came a dark form. It broadened slightly as it approached, and two green blades flanked it. Closer it came and closer, resolving itself into a Jedi Master, dark cloak flowing behind him, twin blades held more like warning torches than weapons.

While his uncle was distant enough to seem no taller than a toy figure, a Yuuzhan Vong warrior darted at him from the left. The Yuuzhan Vong smashed his amphistaff down at Luke's head. The Jedi Master raised his right lightsaber to block the blow and could have easily stroked the other blade across the Yuuzhan Vong's unprotected stomach. Instead he pivoted on his left foot, scything his right leg through the

Yuuzhan Vong's legs, dumping the alien hard to the rock-strewn ground. Luke then brought his right hand down and smashed the pommel of his lightsaber into the Yuuzhan Vong's face, leaving the warrior limp in the dust.

Another Yuuzhan Vong came in from the right and slashed his amphistaff at Luke's middle. Luke leapt back from the tip, then caught the return cut on both lightsaber blades. He raised the amphistaff high in a parry, then spun beneath it. As the Yuuzhan Vong warrior whirled to face the Jedi Master again, a fist-size stone shot from the ground and clipped the warrior in the side of the head. It shattered his helmet, spraying pieces of it into the air, then another slammed into his shoulder. More stones stormed through the air as if trapped in a cyclone, battering the alien warrior relentlessly. Finally one arced in at his forehead, skipped off the shallow dome of his head, and dropped him cleanly to the dirt.

A third warrior came at Luke, but he displayed more caution than his enthusiastic companions had. He twirled his amphistaff around like a propeller, arcing cuts in at Luke's feet or head. The Jedi Master dodged back, then leapt above a slash. He used the Force to push himself high in the air, then he twisted through a somersault and landed behind his foe.

The Yuuzhan Vong whipped around and snapped a kick through Luke's legs. The blow caught Luke in the ankles, dumping him on his back. The Yuuzhan Vong continued his spin, then came up and brought his amphistaff around in an overhand blow at Luke's head.

In the time it took for his foe to complete a revolution, the Jedi Master rolled through a backward somersault and came up on one knee. He raised the lightsabers and crossed them, catching the amphistaff above his head at the green blades' nexus. Furious at being caught, the Yuuzhan Vong flexed his amphistaff, which opened a fang-filled mouth. It reared back, ready to strike at Luke's face. The amphistaff's hiss and the Yuuzhan Vong's triumphant snarl filled the air.

Then Luke slashed both lightsabers outward, drawing their glowing lengths over the amphistaff's throat. While its flesh might have been dense enough to prevent a lightsaber from immediately shearing through it, the double assault snipped the first twenty-five centimeters from the amphistaff with no problem. The rest of the amphistaff recoiled in pain, and the Yuuzhan Vong warrior, who had been leaning heavily on the amphistaff to keep Luke down, stumbled forward. Without rising, Luke brought his right lightsaber up to stroke the Yuuzhan Vong's belly, then spun and slashed the other against the back of the warrior's thighs.

The warrior collapsed to the ground. The remains of its amphistaff writhed in the dust beside him, gradually subsiding.

Luke rose to his feet and stalked forward. Several stones, as if little rodents fleeing from his advance, rolled on ahead of him. They bowled over the creeper and crushed it. The Jedi Master stepped over the oozing mess the stones left in the doorway, then strode past Jacen without a word. Lightsabers hissed and popped, then went silent. Jacen slowly floated to the ground.

He breathed heavily for a moment, then rolled over onto his back. Luke sank to one knee beside him, then touched the youth's face with his mechanical right hand. Jacen felt some pain as Luke pressed the coral seed against his bone, then his uncle pinched flesh between thumb and forefinger. With a flick of his artificial thumb, the Jedi Master popped the bloody seed free of his nephew's face, letting blood streak Jacen's cheek.

Jacen stood and kicked his legs free of the bonds. "Uncle Luke, I'm so sorry."

"No time for that." Luke handed him his lightsaber, then took hold of Jacen's right arm and hauled himself to his feet. "The ship is over there, in a depression, to the southeast. Artoo is waiting for us, sending out the data we've acquired. We have to go, now."

"What about the slaves?"

Luke shook his head. "What slaves?"

Jacen pushed past the aches in his body and reached out to catch a sense of the frayed ones. "I don't understand. There were slaves when I went to the villip paddy."

"They don't exist anymore. They are dead, or, I don't know, somehow they have gone completely over to the Yuuzhan Vong camp. Perhaps they accepted what they are becoming." Luke leaned heavily on his nephew. "We have to get to the ship."

Jacen hugged his right arm around Luke's waist. "What's wrong? Did they hurt you?"

"No, Jacen, it's just that . . ." Luke's chest heaved with exertion. "It's just that using that much of the Force, using it that directly, is exhausting. A Jedi may be able to control and use a great deal of the Force, but there is a price, a fearful price. Hurry, we have to go, quickly."

Jacen hustled his uncle along. "Where are we going?"

"We're going to where others need us, and we can't be late." Luke stroked his right hand across his face, painting it with traces of Jacen's blood. "We're going to Dantooine."

CHAPTER
TWENTY-TWO

Dr. Pace shook Corran gently awake. He blinked his eyes. "Yes, what is it, Doctor?"

She straightened up and pointed a finger back toward the excavation chamber. "Jens has got something on those beetles you brought back."

"Really? So soon?"

"She's good. What can I tell you?"

"I guess. Thanks. Give me a moment." Corran slowly sat upright and pulled the soles of his feet together. Snugging his heels in as close as he could to his groin, he leaned forward, stretching out aching muscles. Using Jedi techniques to get rid of the pain was nothing, but that wouldn't give him back the flexibility tight muscles stole away. The hike back from the lake-bed village they'd seen had been uneventful, and Corran hadn't minded Ganner's silent brooding. It gave him time alone with his thoughts, and what he was thinking demanded lots of brain sweat.

In his years with the Corellian Security Force, he'd seen plenty of cruelty. Among the criminal classes, the strong tended to prey upon the weak, which really came as no surprise. In a world where the only rule was that the most lethal individual was at the top of the food chain, cruelty became a survival trait. Corran had seen the result of hideous tortures and casual cruelty. While all of it had been horrible, none of it quite equaled what he saw with the Yuuzhan Vong beating that prisoner to death.

What got to Corran about the death was that the poor slave had clearly gone mad because of the growths on him—and the growths were something the Yuuzhan Vong had caused to become part of him. It struck Corran that *if* the growths were meant to be used as a means of control, one wouldn't want those means of control to be something that eventually drove the slave beyond control. It would be akin to fastening a restraining bolt to a droid that, eventually, started issuing random commands that required the droid to be destroyed.

From what he had witnessed, Corran began to get a sense of something else going on with the Yuuzhan Vong and their slaves. The abandon and apparent glee with which the two had killed the slave suggested to Corran that this was something they looked forward to. It almost seemed as if the small shells were presents that would unwrap themselves and give the Yuuzhan Vong a chance to indulge themselves in something they found pleasurable. It also seemed to be something beyond recreation for them, which disturbed Corran. While the growths were useful as a means of control, they were also meant to do more.

It is as if the Yuuzhan Vong want to inflict pain and suffering just to see how long it takes for their slaves to break and run. The problem this idea gave Corran was that he primarily understood slavery in terms of greed. With a slave, one got work with minimal compensation to the worker—very economical for the owner of the slaves, especially if the slaves could be controlled enough that revolt was impossible. Using the slaves as agony engines just made no sense unless the pain in some way sustained the Yuuzhan Vong or had some other significance for them. *If* that *is true, this invasion is going to be worse than any war of political or economic gain. Victory for the Yuuzhan Vong demands that every sentient creature live in pain.*

He shivered, then rolled to his feet. He pulled on his blaster belt. His lightsaber dangled at his right hip, just in front of the holstered blaster. He adjusted the belt until it rode snugly on his hips, then descended through the passage to the excavation chamber.

In addition to Jens and Dr. Pace, Corran found Ganner and Trista waiting for him. Ganner just glared at him, whereas Dr. Pace turned to Jens and nodded.

The blond archaeogeneticist waved a hand at a holograph that showed images of all three beetles. "Despite having only a couple of specimens of each beetle to work with, I've been able to figure a number of things out. Mostly I've been analyzing their excreta—"

Corran arched an eyebrow. "Bug dust?"

Jens rolled her blue eyes. "More than that. The sentinel beetle, the one that raised the alarm about the slave, is fairly unremarkable. The other two, though, are interesting. The littlest ones are excreting a compound that is being laced into the soil. Chemically it's a lot less complex than stink, but its molecular makeup is such that it bonds to the olfactory neuroreceptor sites in the slashrats. It's what is keeping them away from that camp, since all the dirt there, as far as the slashrats are concerned, is permeated with stink."

"The beetles are making synthetic stink?" Corran frowned. "That's some fairly advanced genetic engineering, isn't it?"

Jens shook her head. "Not really. These beetles, along with a lot of other life-forms—ourselves included—have a symbiotic relationship with microscopic organisms in their bodies. We might chew food and produce acid that breaks it down further, but it's the bacteria in our guts that takes complex molecules and chops them up into things our bodies can absorb. They nourish themselves on the food we provide, too, and give off waste products. In this case, some of the bacteria in the beetle's gut produces this stinklike substance. Engineering a bacteria is much easier than engineering the beetle; they're just the packaging for the bacteria."

Ganner nodded and pointed to the image of the middle beetle. "What does it do?"

"I've been analyzing the gases it gives off, and it is producing a lot of carbon dioxide. The content of carbon dioxide in the valley, based on the air in the sample bottles that you filled there, is elevated beyond that of the rest of Bimmiel. If I had to guess, since you've reported the growths on the slaves are hard and rocklike, the elevated carbon dioxide content might be promoting growth of the things on the slaves."

Trista bit at her lower lip for a moment. "If enough of those beetles were let loose, could they raise the carbon dioxide content enough to help the world retain heat during its outward orbit?"

The blond geneticist thought for a moment, then shrugged. "It's possible. I don't have the sort of planetary data needed to figure out how long it would take, but if these beetles are prolific in their reproduction, it could happen. Staving off the winter would utterly destroy the ecosystem here, since we'd have moisture, but too little solar energy to let the plants grow. The shwpi come out of hibernation early, the slashrats nab them, then the slashrats die of starvation."

Corran tugged at his goatee for a moment. "Jens, you've managed to use the equipment here to manufacture stink, and you know how to manufacture killscent, right?"

She nodded.

"Could you, with the equipment you have here, create a bacteria that would, instead of manufacturing that artificial stink, create an artificial killscent?"

Jens shook her head. "We don't have the right stuff for making such a bacteria. That would take a lot more specialized gear than I have here."

Corran slammed his right fist into his left palm. "Sithspawn! If we could get the slashrats to overrun the Yuuzhan Vong camp . . ." He pointed over at the corner where the mummified Yuuzhan Vong remains had been recovered. "We already know the little beasts have a taste for them."

Jens's face brightened. "Oh, if *that's* what you want, no problem. The equipment I have here would let me create a virus that would infect the bacteria that produces the stink, inserting new genetic coding that will make it produce killscent instead. For that matter, I can make another that will stop the carbon dioxide concentrators, too."

Corran smiled. "And could you produce a virus that would make the Yuuzhan Vong themselves exude killscent?"

"Killer sweat? Possible. I can check the bones here for viral traces and work from them." Jens positively beamed. "Which one do I start on?"

Corran was about to answer, then Dr. Pace slammed her fist down on the table with the holoprojector on it. "None of them."

The older Jedi Knight blinked. "What?"

"She'll do none of them." Pace stared hard and unblinking at Corran. "Unleashing such viruses could trigger a world-wide calamity that would alter Bimmiel forever."

"Unleashing them will counter the Yuuzhan Vong attempt to do exactly that sort of thing." Corran pointed back toward the surface. "If the Yuuzhan Vong succeed in making changes to the ecology of the planet, they will use it as a base to continue their conquest in our galaxy. We have to stop them, and given the resources we have, using this sort of virus is our best bet. Jens can probably tinker with it so extreme cold will kill it, destroying the viruses when the planet gets to the apex of its orbit."

"Not tough at all."

Pace turned and pointed at Jens. "You'll do nothing of the sort."

Trista weighed into the fray. "You seem to think, Horn, that we're somehow involved in your fight with the Yuuzhan Vong here."

Corran's jaw shot open. "You're up to your neck in it. Best case here is that they're just scouting. Worst case is that they've come to recover the body of a lost explorer and you're sitting right on top of it. You dug it up, have measured and analyzed it. They might consider that some sort of desecration, and they might be looking to destroy anyone who would do such a thing."

She shook her head. "You don't understand. We're just here to study this world. We are just observers."

"Oh, *I* understand that attitude perfectly. I question

whether or not the Vong will understand it or will see the distinction as significant." Corran looked past her to Ganner. "Your thoughts?"

"Dr. Pace and Trista are correct. Your plan could lead to a planetary holocaust that could render it sterile." Ganner's comment brought an adoring smile to Trista's face. "There *is* another alternative."

Trista nodded. "There, you don't need the virus."

Corran's eyes narrowed. "And that choice is?"

"We go back and do what we should have done last night when you stopped me." Ganner's hand dropped to his lightsaber. "We stop the Yuuzhan Vong very directly."

Pace got a sour look on her face, and Trista's face drained of color. "Ganner, you can't take that risk."

"It is what I do, Trista. You're right. You and the others here are not combatants. Enlisting you in this struggle would compromise you and your beliefs. Corran and I will protect you as you make your escape."

Corran turned back to Dr. Pace. "You've seen the flaw with his plan."

She nodded. "You can't kill all the beetles because you don't know how widely they've been spread. Even destroying the Yuuzhan Vong won't counter their work. Still, I can't authorize this sort of action."

"I understand what you're saying." Corran sighed. "I'd also point out that, like it or not, combatants or not, you're all right in the middle of a war zone. While I respect your position, we might do well to bring everyone in here, tell them what's going on, and let them vote on what we should do."

Dr. Pace fell silent as she considered his proposal. Corran purposely shut himself to the mixed emotions pouring off her and instead stretched his senses out to encompass the whole of the cave complex. *If she goes for the vote, gathering up the twenty people here and polling them won't take long.*

Corran suddenly frowned. "Ganner, counting us, how many people are here in the cave complex?"

"Twenty." The quick sneer on his face dissolved. "But there should be twenty-two here. Two people are missing."

Trista shook her head. "No one is missing. Vil and Denna just went out to their meteorological station to fix the antenna. They stopped getting data last night and headed out before you two returned."

Ganner blinked at her. "You let people go outside, let them head away from the base?"

Her head came up defiantly. "Oh, so only you Jedi are brave enough to escape slashrats and do your duty? We've been here dealing with this world's perils for longer than you have."

Dr. Pace dug for a comlink. She switched it over to a particular frequency. "Vil, this is Dr. Pace. Report."

Only static came back through the open channel.

"Sithspawn!" Corran spun on the ball of his right foot and started pacing. "If the Vong have found the remote reporting station, they might have disabled it, given their hatred of technology. They could have left something in its place, something that those two disturbed. The Vong come out and get them—"

Trista shook her head. "There is no evidence to suggest—"

Ganner reached out and took Trista's shoulders in his hands. He turned her to face him. "I find you intelligent, passionate, and fascinating, but you know, as well as we do, that the chances are excellent that your companions are now Yuuzhan Vong captives."

"No, no." She shook her head, lashing her shoulders with black hair. "I never would have let them go if I thought—"

Corran held a hand up. "Doesn't matter. You let them go before we had proof the Yuuzhan Vong were here in the present, not just in the past. We have a problem, and we have to deal with it. Could be that Vil and Denna will come wandering back in with a comlink that had a bad power cell."

Dr. Pace swallowed hard. "And if they don't?"

"Someone will have to find them." Corran forced a weak smile onto his lips. "And I think I know where our search will begin."

CHAPTER
TWENTY-THREE

Mara's deteriorating condition had Anakin worried. She was being very brave and very strong, but she was tiring more easily and had begun to withdraw. He could feel her drawing on the Force more and more to sustain herself. It clearly fortified her, but demanded so much of her attention and concentration that he was pretty sure she had no idea where she was or who he was a chunk of the time.

He did his best to see that she did not want for anything. He kept the camp clean and fixed all of the meals. By observing the Dantari, he was able to find edible plants and spices, which he used to make their bland rations into something *different,* if not always appetizing. Mara seemed to take the failed experiments in stride along with the good and livened up a bit at mealtimes.

Tuber—which was the name Anakin had given the elder Dantari root trader—clearly had some concerns about Mara. He kept bringing firewood but wouldn't accept the last couple of roots Anakin had. Instead they traded for other things—most of them being trinkets, which Tuber braided into his hair to frame the button Mara had provided.

Anakin set out from the camp just after a supper that Mara had eaten listlessly. She wandered back to her cot and started sleeping again. He cleaned up, then saw his supply of firewood wouldn't last through the night. It struck him as odd

that Tuber had not yet appeared, so he headed down the trail
to the Dantari encampment.

He was still a good five hundred meters off when a spike of
pain reached him through the Force. He thought immediately
of Mara, but it didn't have the feel he would have expected
from her. He next thought of Tuber, then caught an undercurrent of fear rolling out from the Dantari camp.

Anakin crouched in the lavender grasses and slowly made
his way forward. He smiled, putting into practice all the
things Mara had taught him about moving stealthily through
the grasses. He could have reached out with the Force to
move branches that might crack underfoot or to smooth out
grasses so they wouldn't rustle. *I would have done just that,
but I don't need to. I can save the Force for later.*

He worked his way in toward the camp, and twenty meters
away he paused in the shadow of a rock. Looking past the
boulder, he saw Tuber on his knees, bleeding from cuts over
one eye and across his chest. The Imperial crest there had
been taken off in strips. It looked as if his captors had decided
to flay him. The Dantari's hands had been bound behind his
back. The other Dantari likewise were on their knees, all
looking drawn and terribly frightened.

And they had good cause to be. Standing before Tuber
were two tall and lean Yuuzhan Vong warriors, both wearing
chitinous armor. One bore a staff that had a flattened end like
a spear point. The other had a weapon that looked the same,
but was flexible and clearly functioned like a whip. The whip
wielder held the jacket button in his left hand, waved it under
Tuber's nose, then snarled a question at him.

Tuber grunted a response.

The Yuuzhan Vong's whip cracked, and another wound
blossomed on the Dantari's broad chest.

A coldness settled in Anakin's stomach. Without a doubt
he knew the Yuuzhan Vong was asking where Tuber had gotten the button. Clearly the Dantari couldn't have produced
it, and it was far newer than any of the Imperial artifacts,
suggesting to the Yuuzhan Vong that other people had been
here recently. Tuber was refusing to give the Yuuzhan Vong

the information they wanted. *He's in trouble because we are here, because we befriended him.* There was no question in Anakin's mind that he had to do something to save the Dantari.

For a heartbeat he almost despaired. Here he was, a fifteen-year-old Jedi apprentice. He didn't have the experience a full Jedi Knight would have. Mara had experienced trouble killing one of the Yuuzhan Vong on Belkadan. Saving the Dantari seemed impossible. It was a task that would overwhelm him.

Size matters not. Despite Mara's having chided him for overusing Yoda's aphorism, Anakin knew it applied now. His job, as a Jedi Knight, was to protect those who could not protect themselves. He took a deep breath, opened himself to the Force, and felt it flood through him in a way it never had before. It was water to a being dying of thirst; it was sunshine after days of rain; it was warmth after bitter cold. It was all that and more.

Anakin touched the stone behind which he crouched, and nudged it with a fraction of the Force flowing through him. The five-hundred-kilogram stone ripped itself free of the ground and hurled itself at the Yuuzhan Vong. Dirt flew off it in clumps as it spun through the air. It hit the ground again, five meters from its targets, then bounced up and caught the staff wielder in his flank. A crunching, crackling sound came from beneath the stone, then the Yuuzhan Vong's arms and legs beat out a furious but slackening death tattoo.

Sprinting forward from behind the boulder, Anakin drew his lightsaber and settled his right thumb on the trigger button. He leapt up, then kicked off the boulder. He sailed through a high somersault that landed him behind the other Yuuzhan Vong. He ignited his violet lightsaber and lunged, driving the point into a circular depression on the armor, catching the Yuuzhan Vong just below the left armpit.

The glowing purple blade sank in deep. The Yuuzhan Vong's pivot threatened to pull the blade from Anakin's hand because the edges of the armor resisted cutting. The whip came about and cracked him on the left shoulder, shredding his tunic and cutting him. He knew that the blow should have taken his head off, and would have, save that the armor suddenly convulsed and constricted. The joints stiffened, restricting the Yuuzhan Vong's movement. When the armor slackened, the warrior collapsed.

His amphistaff hissed and slithered away.

Anakin looked at the fallen Yuuzhan Vong warriors and began to tremble. He sank to his knees and killed his lightsaber's blade. Somehow he'd managed to kill two trained warriors—warriors that had given Mara trouble. *Granted, I got one with a trick, but the other* . . . He knew his victory should have been impossible, but with the Force as his ally, he had succeeded.

Anakin felt hands on him. He looked up and saw Tuber standing over him. Somehow the Dantari's hands had been freed. Tuber handed him a vincha root, then popped one into his own mouth and began chewing it. After a considerable amount of crunching, the Dantari spat a thick paste of vincha and saliva into his hand and started to smear it on his own wounds.

Anakin nodded and chewed the root himself. It tasted bitter and puckered his mouth immediately. He almost gagged as he swallowed some of it, but he could feel the pain beginning to ease in his shoulder. He dabbed the paste into the wound, and the pain stopped almost immediately.

No wonder they value this root so highly. Anakin slapped a hand against his forehead. *And he wouldn't take my last ones because he expected me to use them on Mara. It wasn't a coincidence that we came to Dantooine. This stuff might not cure her disease, but it might be able to help her fight against it.*

Tuber pulled Anakin to his feet. The Dantari began to bellow orders to the others in his band. They began to gather their belongings and head for the trail up to Anakin's camp. Tuber wore a big smile on his face and shouldered the bag of vincha roots.

Anakin shook his head. He knew these primitive people had decided, somehow, that he and Mara were godlike beings who would protect them. Anakin wanted to believe that he could protect them, but he knew that allowing them to travel with him and Mara would not work. "It would be like me allowing you to build your houses in a floodplain. You'd always be in danger."

Tuber looked down at him, puzzled.

Anakin knew what he had to do. He concentrated and gathered the Force to himself, then projected into Tuber's mind the image of a mountain valley with long grasses and vincha plants by the dozens. It would be a place of easy living, a paradise for the Dantari. And, even though Anakin thought he was constructing this place in his mind—creating an illusion to fool Tuber—part of him knew the place was very real, and that he was seeing it as it appeared right that moment.

Anakin took quick stock of the sun's position in the image, the length of shadows, the position of Dantooine's larger moon, then pointed off to the northwest. "Go, there, in that direction. That will be your new home. Follow the coast and you will find it."

Tuber blinked, then reached out with a hand as if he were trying to touch the vision he'd been given. Anakin took his hand and pointed to the northwest. "Go." He gave the Dantari a gentle shove, then managed to keep himself upright until they crested a small hill and disappeared from sight.

Anakin sank to one knee beside the Yuuzhan Vong he'd slain with the lightsaber. The armor had another similar depression beneath the right armpit. Thin, feathery membranes filled it, and Anakin decided that the twin depressions must have been roughly akin to gills. The lightsaber had punched through the vulnerable points in the armor and killed the Yuuzhan Vong. The armor's own death convulsion had saved Anakin's life by hindering the warrior's attack.

It had been a lucky shot, but he knew Luke would never accept that explanation. *There is no luck, only the Force.*

Weary beyond what he thought the effort should have taken out of him, Anakin stumbled off along the trail back to his camp. He smiled because, had Mara not insisted he work without the Force, he wouldn't have had the physical strength to make it back up the incline. The little aches and pains from his exercises told him just how much farther he could go on, and he knew he'd make it back to Mara.

Darkness had fallen completely by his return, and his fire had been reduced to a glowing mound of ash-strewn coals. He grabbed the remaining vincha roots and entered Mara's tent. She came awake instantly, then slumped back on the cot. "What is it?"

"The Yuuzhan Vong. They're here." He handed her a vincha root. "Here, chew this and let the juice run back down your throat. Local medicine, really good."

Mara swiped her hands across her eyes, then looked at him. "You're hurt."

"It's nothing, but we have to get out of here." Anakin frowned. "I think the Yuuzhan Vong have been here since the start, scouting around. Maybe they're the source of your weakness, I don't know. Maybe their presence enhances things under their control, and your disease could be one of those things. You felt a link on Belkadan. Here, it is more subtle since you aren't in direct contact with the Yuuzhan Vong or their things."

Mara nodded. "That's a trend I'd like to continue."

"Me, too." He sighed. "I killed two of them, but I took them by surprise. It was almost too easy, and that has me worried."

Mara threw back her blanket and swung her legs off the cot. "That's good. You *should* be worried. I have a feeling that dealing with the Yuuzhan Vong will never be that easy again."

CHAPTER TWENTY-FOUR

Leia Organa Solo looked over at the organized chaos going on around her and wished for more organization and less chaos. The *Ralroost* and a handful of freighters had arrived at Dantooine and detected no Yuuzhan Vong ships in the system or having followed them. The freighters and the *Ralroost*'s shuttles began taking refugees down to an equatorial continent that had slender land bridges to the larger northern continent and the southern polar one. Lavender grasses stretched out as far as the eye could see, though the signs of human habitation were beginning to hide them.

The freighters had all picked up more people than they had supplies to sustain on a long run in toward the Core. Dantooine had been a good jump for getting them free of Dubrillion, but the routes back out of Dantooine were few and far between.

Leia sighed. *If Tarkin had taken the bait, this world would have been destroyed, and then we'd not have had this haven to run to right now.*

Her comlink trilled. "Organa Solo here. Go ahead."

"Highness, the last group of refugees is coming down from the *Ralroost*. Now would be the time for you to return to the ship so we can make our run to the Core." Admiral Kre'fey kept his voice low and even, with just the hint of a purr to it. "I know you thought this discussion closed, but I will have Masters to answer to on Coruscant."

"And you think they'll want me there telling them that I'd warned them?" Leia shook her head. "No thanks, Admiral. I'll remain here with the others. You send us out help, and we'll do just fine."

"And if the Vong do follow us here?"

"Abandoning the refugees in that case will be worse." She recalled that a previous group of refugees had been transplanted here, then wiped out by the Empire. *Not a good omen.* "Have a good trip. I'm sure Senator A'Kla will be of help to you."

"He would if he were coming. He's piloting down my command shuttle with the last group. I'm leaving you two companies of infantry and enough weapons to arm a number of the refugees."

"I hope we won't need it."

"No more than I do, I think."

"Speed to you, Admiral. May the Force be with you."

"I'll be back with help, soon."

Leia switched off her comlink, then smiled as Gavin Darklighter came walking over, with Jaina trailing behind him. "Good afternoon, Colonel."

"Highness. I've taken the liberty of appointing my newest flight officer as a liaison between the three squadrons we've got here and the civilian authorities, which I assume will be you." Gavin pointed off north, southwest, and southeast of the camp. "I've arrayed my squadrons to establish something of a perimeter. Our weapons are not meant for suppression of ground troops, but they do a good job of it. Rogues have the north; two squadrons of uglies are splitting the south side of things."

Leia nodded and looked around. The main camp had been set up in a slight depression at the heart of a wide valley. "Doesn't seem particularly defensible here, does it?"

"No, but sensor sweeps showed we can get water from fairly shallow wells. Folks will be needing to build shelters— nasty weather is rolling in from the north—so we can get them to dig some trenches, prepare some redoubts for defense, too. If the Vong are here, having the defenses will be good."

"And if they aren't, people will grumble about having to dig."

"Mother, these people are terrified. Having them dig will give them something to do." Jaina sighed. "Having the freighters here in the middle of the camp will provide temporary shelter, and their guns can cover people if we have to go up and vape some skips."

Jaina's casual use of the phrase *vape some skips* sent a shiver through Leia and made her regard her daughter differently. It felt to Leia almost as if she'd been looking at one holograph of her daughter, all pretty and prim and young, and then someone had switched it for this new image.

Jaina had a touch of dirt on her face, and salt rings from sweat marked her flight suit's armpits. Her hair had been pulled back into a braid and lacked the sheen of clean hair. Leia could tell her daughter was tired, but there was an energy in her eyes that Leia recognized all too well. Her own father—her adopted father—had remarked on it in her eyes, when Leia became involved with the Rebellion.

She's more grown than any parent wants to admit. Leia reached out to stroke her daughter's cheek, but caught a flash of wariness in Jaina's eyes. She shifted her hand to land on Jaina's shoulder and gave it a squeeze. "That's a good point, Jaina."

Gavin nodded in agreement. "We might have to move them around a bit to provide the best in overlapping fields of fire, but they should be pretty effective in holding hostiles off."

"Admiral Kre'fey is sending troopers down, and lots of weapons." Leia shook her head slowly. "We probably won't have any time to train the refugees."

Her daughter raised a finger. "There have to be veterans of the Rebellion and even Imp service among them. We sort them out, have them help organize the camp, and we'll make it more defensible."

"That will work, too. The grasses here aren't very tasty, but they will suffice for most folks." Leia sighed. "That leaves only one other worry."

Gavin frowned. "And that is?"

"Mara and Anakin are supposed to be here on Dantooine. A sweep of comm frequencies is negative for any activity."

The pilot shrugged. "If she is here for rest, they might not have their comlinks on."

"That occurred to me." Leia shivered. "I can't feel them with the Force, either. If they were dead, I'm sure I'd have felt that. Their being cut off like this, I don't know. It's not good, not good at all."

Jaina covered Leia's hand with her own. "Don't worry, Mom. Mara's pretty smart, and Anakin isn't stupid. I'm sure they're just fine."

Leia looked at her closely. "Can you feel them with the Force?"

A pained expression passed over her face. "A little, yes, in fits and starts. Not enough to give me a direction, or I'd be out looking. It feels like Anakin, when he was a kid, playing hide-and-seek. When I get him, he's strong."

Leia sighed. "Let's hope he remains strong, then." *And well hidden, especially if it's the Yuuzhan Vong seeking him.*

The thunder crack from above had faded just enough for Anakin to catch the whirring buzz of the Yuuzhan Vong weapon arcing in at him. He pulled his right shoulder back and twisted his face to the left. He felt the fist-size disk whirl past him, barely missing his cheek. It make a solid thud as it slammed into the bole of a tree.

A flash of lightning burnished a silver edge on the thing. Legs sprouted from the body and began to push the right edge of its carapace out of the divot it had chopped into the wood. As Anakin had learned through experience in his flight from Yuuzhan Vong hunters, the bug would free itself, then fly off, returning to the hand of the warrior that had thrown it at him.

Not this time. Anakin darted forward and smashed the butt end of his lightsaber into the bug's body. The fragile wings shattered, and the body snapped in half. Dark fluid oozed from the bug and began to steam as raindrops hit it.

Repressing a shudder, Anakin turned back and started

along the torturous mountain trail. The track he was following was really just a rivulet that had washed away dirt, leaving wet stones and roots to catch at his feet. Reaching forward, he grabbed a thick root and hauled himself up, then found Mara lying there, in the muddy runoff, her chest heaving.

Without saying anything he pulled a piece of vincha root from his pocket, bit off half, and stuffed the rest into her mouth. "C'mon, Mara, they're right behind us."

"They're always right behind us, 'cept when they're ahead of us." She started to get up, then stumbled, pulling him down, too.

Two more of the razorbugs sailed past to stick in the ground. Anakin squashed one, then tugged Mara to her feet. "Go, go."

She scrambled up the next three meters, then perched on a stone for a second before darting forward. He headed up after her. By the time he got to the top of the incline, he saw her legging it around a leftward bend in the trail. He pulled himself up onto that next section of trail and started running after her, but something thumped heavily on the trail behind him.

Anakin spun, igniting his purple blade as he turned. He parried a slash from an amphistaff and half ducked under it. He lunged at the Yuuzhan Vong warrior's belly, but the armor held despite smoke and water vapor erupting from the lightsaber's touch. The warrior leapt back, then whipped his amphistaff forward. The weapon caught Anakin with a stinging slash to the left forearm, further tattering the sleeve on that arm and the flesh beneath it.

Anakin hugged his arm to his chest, and the Yuuzhan Vong warrior laughed. His amphistaff became rigid, and the warrior rose to his full height, standing there all glorious and terrible at the end of the path. He looked down at Anakin and said something that dripped with condescension.

The young Jedi's eyes narrowed, and the big rock on which the Yuuzhan Vong stood rolled back from beneath the warrior's feet. The warrior leaned heavily on his amphistaff, but the muddy ground gave way, spilling the warrior forward. He

landed hard on his chest and face, splashing mud in all directions. As he pulled his head back and up, Anakin caught him
with a snap kick that pitched him into the darkness.

The young Jedi doused his lightsaber and darted off along
after his aunt. He tried to feel her with the Force, but she'd so
effectively drawn it around her, using it to fend off the disease, that he could barely detect her. He knew he had to register just as faintly to her. He'd been hoarding his own strength
and minimizing his presence in the Force just in case the
Yuuzhan Vong were somehow using the Force to track them.
For three days they had been running through the mountains
and had been pursued from almost the first moment of their
flight. They cut across Yuuzhan Vong tracks before they
reached their ship, so they knew the *Jade Sabre* had been
found and, if the Yuuzhan Vong hatred for technology remained true, had been reduced to scrap.

Throughout the run they had been miserable. The rain had
come on so quickly and poured so hard that Anakin had wondered if somehow the Yuuzhan Vong controlled it or if he was
just growing more and more paranoid. The Yuuzhan Vong
who hunted them seemed to take great delight in coursing
them and chasing them. The razorbugs constantly flew from
shadows, inflicting little nicks and slices. His arms and legs
burned from cuts and fatigue. His robes, which were leaden
with so much rain and mud, seemed more holes than they
were cloth. *I'm pretty much reduced to my body and my
lightsaber.*

Around the turn the trail broadened out. Tall stones, set
like teeth along the edges of the trail, channeled him toward
an overshadowed pathway. Tall trees eclipsed the night sky—
though really only blocked his ability to see the lightning-
spitting thunderheads. Mara sagged against one of the plinths,
then gave him a quick smile and fingered a wet strand of red
hair away from her cheek. Tattered and torn as badly as he
was, and sick and exhausted, she still managed to have defiance play in her eyes.

Her head came up, and her eyes focused beyond him. He
spun, barely a dozen meters into the clearing. Behind him

were three Yuuzhan Vong warriors. Two moved right and left, leaving the third to come straight on. They came slowly, cautiously, and he wondered why. *Any one of them could break me in half.*

Something in their wariness as they approached brought it all home to him. *They are here because of me. I slew two of them in my first encounter. All the single warriors who've come to face me have gone down. I haven't killed any more since then, but perhaps I disgraced them.*

Anakin didn't spare a glance over his shoulder. "Mara, they want me. It's a matter of honor for them, I think."

"They may want you, Anakin, but they'll deal with the both of us." He heard her lightsaber hiss behind him, pouring blue highlights onto the Yuuzhan Vong and their wet armor. "Light your blade. I've got left."

"No, Mara, run." He felt a cold calm coming over him as he brought his hands together on the hilt of his lightsaber. He knew, without any doubt at all, that he would not survive a fight with three of the Yuuzhan Vong. The Force had been with him in his first encounter, and all along the way. *Just be with me one more time, so Mara can escape. One more time.*

He thumbed his blade alive. The energy rod glowed with a violet intensity. He held it forward, with the hilt near his belly and the blade pointing down at the ground. He brought his right leg forward, knee bent; and he planted his left foot. He could see all three of them and nodded to each in succession. Nodding again to the central figure, Anakin impatiently flicked his blade up a centimeter or two, inviting the Yuuzhan Vong onward.

The centermost warrior began to whirl his amphistaff over his head. Lightning seared white-hot edges on his armor and along the amphistaff. The Yuuzhan Vong started forward, and Anakin feinted toward him, kicking a lump of wet sand in his direction. The warrior retreated a step, then his companions hooted at him.

All of a sudden Anakin knew exactly what he had to do. He knew the proper series of steps he had to move through to save Mara. Without giving it any conscious thought, he allowed his body to flow through the choreography that came to him through the Force.

Pivoting on his right foot, he lunged at the Yuuzhan Vong on his right. That warrior leapt back, only to slam himself into one of the plinths. As that warrior stumbled to the ground, Anakin dodged to his left, taking a step toward the central warrior. Because his earlier move had exposed his back to the left warrior, that Yuuzhan Vong had driven at him. Anakin reversed his grip on the lightsaber and stabbed it backward past his right hip, impaling the alien warrior on the blade.

The Yuuzhan Vong's armor held, preventing him from being opened up, but he did double over from the force of the blow. For his part, Anakin used some of the collision against the blade to drive himself forward. He rolled into a somersault, then spun to the right and brought his lightsaber around in a waist-high cut that caught the center Yuuzhan Vong across the thighs. Armor sizzled and cracked, but stopped the lightsaber from slashing through flesh and muscle. Instead he cut the legs out from under the Yuuzhan Vong, dumping him to the clearing floor.

Anakin lashed out with a foot, catching the fallen warrior in the side of the head. The warrior's head snapped to the right, but the Yuuzhan Vong still gathered his limbs beneath him and heaved himself to his feet. Anakin cut to the left, to kick the Yuuzhan Vong's amphistaff away, but the weapon coiled and struck at him. Then the Yuuzhan Vong scythed his leg through Anakin's ankles and dropped him to his back.

Anakin slashed at the Yuuzhan Vong's legs, but the warrior leapt above the cut, then came down with a foot heavily on Anakin's right wrist. Pain shot through it, and the boy was certain he'd heard something snap. His hand went numb, and his lightsaber flew from his grip.

The Yuuzhan Vong towered above him. The warrior's amphistaff slithered its way up the warrior's leg, then onto his right arm. It stiffened, and the warrior raised it above his head. Muttering words that sounded solemn and thankful, the warrior whipped the amphistaff down in a cut that would cleave Anakin open from crown to navel.

If it landed.

The snap-hiss of Luke Skywalker's green lightsaber interjected itself into the fight. The verdant blade caught the descending amphistaff before it could strike. The blade slid in along the amphistaff, evaporating water as it went, then slipped up and slashed through the Yuuzhan Vong's armpit. The warrior screamed, then spun away.

Off to the left, Jacen Solo leapt down from one of the plinths, landing on the Yuuzhan Vong warrior below. Jacen's feet hit the warrior square in the back, driving him face first into the ground. The Jedi slammed the butt end of his lightsaber against the base of the warrior's skull, then darted forward to engage the last Yuuzhan Vong. Jacen leapt above a low slash, then side-kicked the warrior in the gut. The Yuuzhan Vong flew back into a plinth, then slid down into a gap between two of them.

Jacen helped his brother up while Luke ran to Mara. Anakin reached out to use the Force to pull his extinguished lightsaber to him, then bent down and scooped it up with his left hand. "Jacen, how did you find us?"

Jacen shrugged and nodded toward Luke. "He knew when and where to be to find you two. He had a vision, and it led him to Dantooine. We might not have been able to pick the Yuuzhan Vong out with the Force, but plenty of the wildlife here in this forest scattered from them, so we headed for where life wasn't."

"Huh. I never thought of that."

Jacen tousled his brother's sopping hair. "Ah, you're just a kid."

"Don't give him a hard time, Jacen." Mara leaned heavily on her husband, and Anakin could tell Luke wanted to pick her up, but she'd have no part of it. "He got me this far. If he hadn't been taking care of me, I'd be dead."

Luke nodded solemnly at his youngest nephew. "I can't begin to thank you enough."

"Sure you can. Take us back to Coruscant."

"Can't, but we will get you to your mother."

Anakin looked down at his muddy, blood-soaked robes. "To Mom? I thought I was being thanked here."

"You are, and will be." Luke pointed toward the north. "Ship's not far from here."

Mara gave Luke a kiss on the cheek. "At least we'll be away from Dantooine."

"Actually, we won't."

Mara frowned. "But you got here in a ship, one capable of making the trip from Belkadan."

"You're right, we did." Luke nodded calmly. "It's just we can't leave Dantooine yet. Leia and some Dubrillion refugees landed here on the continent to the southeast. As we were coming in system, we saw a big Yuuzhan Vong ship sending troop carriers down, and it seems they found that continent as hospitable as Leia did."

Anakin winced. "Out of the firefight, into the carbon freeze."

"Pretty much."

The youngest Solo sighed. "So, if you had a vision that brought you here, do you have a vision that shows how things will turn out down to the southeast?"

"As Yoda said, the future is constantly in motion, so this vision might not be true." Luke's face became a steel mask. "It's just as well, because that vision did not have a happy ending."

CHAPTER
TWENTY-FIVE

Leia reached out and brushed hair from Anakin's forehead, then moved away from her sleeping son. They'd found clothes for him easily enough, so he lay there attired in bits and pieces of uniforms from several of the freighter crews. Leia imagined that the offers had come initially because of the traders' respect for who Anakin's father was, but as the story of his flight with Mara into the mountains to the north spread through the camp, many viewed the boy as a hero in his own right.

She took one last look at him, lying there, with a small glow lamp casting golden highlights into his dark hair. Some bruising discolored his face, and scratches marked his forehead and neck, but otherwise he looked remarkably hearty. She'd watched a 2-1B droid work on him cleaning and closing a variety of cuts he'd earned in his running battle with the Yuuzhan Vong. Bacta patches had been used on the cuts and abrasions. When the droid set his wrist fracture from the final fight, a light splint to help immobilize the wrist was all that Anakin needed. Leia knew Mara had been similarly cut and wounded during their escape and had been treated by droids for her injuries. Leia awaited word from Luke on Mara's condition.

Leia ducked her head beneath the edge of the tarp used to fashion a simple lean-to shelter for Anakin, then held it up as R2-D2 rolled in to keep an eye on the boy. She smiled at the droid, then let the tarp flop back down. The sun had not yet risen, but the winds from the north were picking up. She could see distant hints of clouds on the far horizon and assumed that by the next afternoon the showers that had plagued the northern continent would sweep down on them. *We go from being hungry and miserable to* wet, *hungry, and miserable.*

Elegos approached her and offered her a ration bar. "It would not do for you to faint from hunger."

"Well, that ration bar will certainly kill my hunger." Leia accepted it gratefully. "Anakin is sleeping. I don't think he had much more than a couple of hours while on the run. If they'd not had the Force to sustain them . . ."

"Your son must be very strong in the Force to have done what he did."

"Yes, I think so." Leia felt a cold shiver run down her spine. "He's so brave and was determined he'd not let his uncle down. He would do anything to make Luke proud of him."

The Caamasi's eyes slowly closed. "Perhaps you fear that with so much of the Force in him that, if frustrated, he might follow the path of his namesake."

Leia glanced down, not daring to voice the answer to that question.

Elegos kept his voice low and soothing. "I have wondered, in the past, why you chose to name him after your father?"

She sighed. "My father, Anakin Skywalker—not Darth Vader—turned against the Emperor and was the agent of his death. He atoned for the evil he had done—perhaps not all of it in the eyes of some, but he prevented future evil being wrought by the Emperor. Part of me wanted to name my son for him to redeem the name. At least, that is what I told myself."

"You have come to think differently on it now?"

Leia looked up at him. "You Caamasi are fortunate in that you can share memories between you. I have no clear memories of Anakin Skywalker—and my memories of Darth Vader are still the stuff of nightmares. I know that I contain part of Anakin in me, and I think it is the good parts of him that came through in Luke and me. But, I also know the darker parts of him are there, or could be there. In naming my youngest son for him, I was putting an innocence behind that name. All the things I saw in Anakin, I could imagine having come from his grandfather, through me."

"You sought to purge your fears of Darth Vader and what you inherited of him by looking at Anakin as being what your father could have been and perhaps once was?"

She nodded. "Does that make any sense?"

"It does, very much. Countless are the parents who, because they were disappointed in their own parents, vow to bring their children up *right*. Perhaps you are trying to prove to yourself that under different circumstances your father never would have become Darth Vader."

"You see a problem with that—"

"As do you." Elegos smiled at her carefully. "If you didn't, we wouldn't be having this conversation."

"If I ever figure out how you get into my brain and present me with problems I don't want to consider, I'll . . . I'll . . ."

"You'll have little need for me, and my work will be done."

Leia reached out and took Elegos's right arm in her hands, then walked beside him as they strode through the camp. "I'll always have need for friends like you."

"I'm honored."

"You should be more afraid. My friends tend to get into trouble."

Elegos gestured broadly with his free hand. "Like this?"

"Pretty much." Leia nodded at a few people, then looked up at the Caamasi. "I placed quite a burden on Anakin, didn't I, by giving him that name."

"He's strong enough to accept that burden, Leia. He has you and the Jedi to sustain him and keep him on the straight and narrow." Elegos patted her hands with his left hand. "Had he a bent for the dark side of the Force, he would have availed himself of it to save Mara Jade. He's young, yet he has courage and intelligence. This is a time that will demand both. When the Yuuzhan Vong come, the slaughter on both sides will be staggering."

Leia felt a slight shudder course through Elegos. "For a pacifist like you, this has to be horrible."

"It is horrible for everyone, those who realize it and those who do not." The Caamasi shook his head. "Were there a way to stave this off, I would try to avert it, but the Yuuzhan Vong seem content with probing and attacking. We don't know why they are here or what they want. We don't know if we can reason with them, and the fact that they seemed to play with Anakin and Mara does not bode well for our being able to reach mutual agreements on anything."

"I find that frustrating, too. I believe in negotiating when possible, but when an enemy refuses, we have little choice in how to deal with them." Leia frowned. "Where will you be during the assaults?"

"Your brother has consented to loan me Artoo, so I will be in the command shuttle, using the laser and blaster cannons."

She stopped and swung around to face him. "But, from what you've said, killing will create a memory so horrible you will never forget it."

The Caamasi's reply came cold and solemn. "There will be no forgetting what will happen here, not for me, not for anyone who survives. The only thing that would make it worse is knowing that I did nothing to stop the slaughter. I can and will take responsibility for dealing death—and perhaps will fill a role that means others will not find themselves in that unenviable position. If I cannot spare myself that discomfort, I can take solace in what I spare others from."

"You know that's how I feel."

"You've proved it many times, and now your children show this courage has bred true."

"I guess it has." She gave Elegos a smile. "So, when you're out there shooting, just aim a bit high so we don't get in your way."

Luke slowly seated himself on his wife's bunk aboard the *Courage*. When her eyes fluttered open, he raised a finger to his lips. "I didn't mean to wake you."

"It's okay." Her voice came a bit hoarsely and remained a whisper. "I've been sleeping too much lately."

"You've been under a lot of stress. The illness . . ."

She nodded slowly but not weakly, and that heartened Luke. Even when he'd found her close to complete collapse there in the mountains, she would not let him carry her and even made a weak attempt at demanding that she be allowed to copilot the blastboat. She refused to admit defeat or acknowledge any weakness.

Luke found this a great comfort, and it took him a moment or two to determine why. His aunt Beru had been utterly unlike Mara save in one aspect: She was a hardened survivor. Living on Tatooine required that of people. If you were inclined toward being soft or weak, the desert world dried you out, sanded you down to your bones, then buried you. Everyone he had known as he grew up had prided themselves in defying the planet every single day, and that inspired in him an appreciation of that survival sense.

Mara drew a small bottle from the shelf at the head of the bunk and drank some water. A droplet coursed down from the corner of her mouth. She tried to get it with a swipe of her hand, but missed.

Luke leaned forward and brushed it away with a finger. She caught his hand in hers, then raised his fingers to her lips. She kissed them, once, then clutched his hand against her breastbone. "I never doubted I would get out of those mountains. When I saw you . . . I thought poor Anakin . . ." Her grip tightened on his hand. "I'm so thankful you saved him."

"The least I could do for his saving you." Luke sighed. "I should have known better than to have you go to Dantooine. Ithor is farther back from the Rim. It would have been safer."

Mara sipped a bit more water. "Would it?"

"What do you mean?"

She scrunched the pillow up behind her and pulled herself into a semisitting position. "The Yuuzhan Vong were at Dubrillion and Belkadan. They are here at Dantooine. My guess is that they've hit other worlds, too. Either scouts or lots of troops. The whole of the Rim could be down."

"You're right. We don't know how far they've penetrated the galaxy. If they are as far as Ithor . . ." Luke shuddered. If the Yuuzhan Vong could reach Ithor, they would have carved a fairly wide swath through the galaxy and would be in a position to threaten many of the key Core worlds. Conquer them and the New Republic's economy would die. If that happened, the New Republic's constituent states would begin to look to each other for support, and the New Republic would fragment.

"If they are as far as Ithor, we're going to die right here, because there will be no help coming for us."

"We're not going to die here."

"Is that a vision?"

"A hope, actually." Luke sighed. "We've got a decent defensive perimeter set up here, with heavy weapons placed well. We can hold out for a while."

Her green eyes all but glowed. "For how long? The refugees were brought here because the ships didn't have enough supplies to last for the journey from Dantooine to other civilized worlds. Do we hold on until food gets critical? What if the Yuuzhan Vong attack and slaughter enough people that food isn't a problem anymore?"

"I don't know. No one is thinking like that right now."

Mara arched an eyebrow at him. "No one is, or you aren't? You think your sister isn't?"

"Maybe she is, but I have other things—" He smiled as he looked down at her. "Mara, you're my primary concern here. I love you, and your condition is not good. I spoke with Anakin, and he said you were getting weaker."

She nodded. "I was. Anakin suggested the disease responds to something having to do with the Yuuzhan Vong."

"You said you felt a connection between the disease and the beetles on Belkadan."

"Yes, I did. I feel a distant one here, and I know I've felt it before." She sighed. "That's not why I was getting weaker, though."

"No?" Luke frowned. "I don't understand."

"Neither did I until the Yuuzhan Vong found us and we

started running." Mara stroked the back of Luke's hand with her thumb. "After the events on Belkadan and Dubrillion, I *did* need to recover. You were right to send me away to do so, but we both made the mistake of thinking a little rest would become a cure. This disease feels as if it is slowly cutting me off from the Force. Only by drawing the Force to me am I able to combat it, and this is where we made our mistake."

"I'm not sure I follow."

"It's twisted, but you'll get it, my love." She smiled and kissed his hand again. "The Force, as you have defined it, is an energy field that surrounds us, penetrates us, and binds us with all things."

"Except, apparently, the Yuuzhan Vong."

"That exception aside, when we are able to access the Force, it makes us stronger. We are able to draw power from it."

The Jedi Master nodded. "On Belkadan, I drew on the Force very little except when I needed to rescue Jacen."

Mara smiled adoringly at him. "I do want to hear the story of that fight, Luke."

"When you are rested."

She shook her head. "No, that's the problem. I've had too much rest."

"Mara, you're having a hard time sitting up. You need more rest."

"No, I need to get back to who I am and how I interact with the Force." She snorted a quick laugh. "You remember me when we first met? You remember how I was?"

"Trying to kill me to comply with the Emperor's last command."

"Right. Luke, I'm a fighter. I've always been a fighter. The few times when I have been at leisure, I've been miserable. I want challenges, I crave them. As nice and peaceful as it was up north here, it lulled me, dulled me, took the edge off. Anakin made it so I had no needs, and Dantooine—before the Yuuzhan Vong—had nothing more dangerous than big thorns to worry about. I was wasting away, trying to conserve my strength, all the while turning away from the means I'd used in the past to tap the Force."

Mara gazed up into Luke's eyes, and he could feel their personal bond and connection strengthening. He got past the fatigue to the image of Mara that existed deep in the woman's psyche. This Mara, strong of limb and sharp of eye, wore armor, sported blasters, and looked like someone who could take a Death Star apart from the inside out.

"That's who I am, Luke. When Anakin and I had to run, I felt exhausted, physically, but I was stronger in the Force. I was able to repair some of the damage the disease had done. I realized that's the most insidious nature of the disease. Many people, when they become sick, retreat to their childhood and being helpless. They abandon who they have become and their place in the web that is the Force, then the disease severs those final connections and they die."

Luke watched for a moment, then frowned. "So you're telling me that no matter how tired you are, that letting you fight against the Yuuzhan Vong will make you stronger."

"As long as I'm fighting, I'm not dying."

He shivered. "I'm not sure I like the cure, but I like the disease less."

"You'll let me fight?"

"Despite my being a Jedi Master, I don't think I could stop you."

Mara laughed, and the rich sound of her voice poured like balm into Luke's ears. "Other men could have said that, but none of them would have meant it. I am so glad I found you and didn't kill you."

"Both of those things thrill me, too." Luke glanced at a bulkhead chronometer. "I don't know when they'll come, but you might want to sleep until then."

"I think I'd rather spend the time with my husband." Mara reached up and grabbed a handful of Luke's tunic, then pulled his face down to hers and kissed him. "Stay here with me. Tell me a story of Belkadan and a Jedi Master with two blades. Spending time with my husband is the best medicine on Dantooine, and I will gladly take as much as you can spare."

CHAPTER TWENTY-SIX

Corran didn't mind the sting of sand against his face as he stared out toward where the wind had begun to unbury the *Dalliance*. Stretching out with the Force, he could feel Ganner and Trista deep inside the ship. Though the distance muted their emotions, the fact that he detected anything more than just their presence meant they were probably locked in a charged conversation. Not surprising, since everyone's mood was charged since the fate of the missing students had become clear. Corran and Ganner had trekked out to the meteorological station and found the place a mess. Supplies had been scattered all over, and four sets of footprints led away from the station. There could be no other conclusion: Vil and Denna had been captured by Yuuzhan Vong warriors.

The scrape of boot on rock focused Corran's attention back locally. "Yes, Dr. Pace?"

"I hate it when you do that. You could at least look at me."

Corran glanced back over his shoulder. "Forgive me, but you are a very strong presence in the Force. Besides, your leather-soled boots make a particular sound. Your students wear synthetic soles that are virtually silent."

The woman pursed her lips, then nodded. "Neat trick that, but I think this mission of yours will take more than tricks. Are you sure you know what you're doing?"

Corran laughed for a moment, then shook his head. "One of your students, one of the ones captured, accused Jedi of being able to see into the future. Sometimes visions do come, but not for me, not now. I don't know if what we will do will succeed, but I know we can't do anything less."

Pace frowned. "I still don't like the whole thing."

"The whole thing?" Corran pointed toward several fiber-plast equipment crates at the mouth of the cave. "You took to packing up the Vong artifacts quickly enough. You're even abandoning equipment to do so."

"It was old anyway, and I have a budget surplus. I spend it or don't get as much next year." She folded her arms across her chest. "You know what I mean."

"Perhaps I do." Since the capture of the two students, Corran and Ganner had reconnoitered the alien village each day. As nearly as they had been able to determine, the Yuuzhan Vong were there taking samples of the local flora and fauna, as well as searching for something. They herded the slaves out and set up search grids. They poked and probed the sand for things, and Corran was fairly certain that what they wanted resided in the crates.

The students had determined that Bimmiel's magnetic field shifted from time to time, which meant if the Yuuzhan Vong were using old measurements to find the cave, they would be off a bit. *Of course, capturing Vil and Denna means they have a direct line to us.* Corran was actually surprised that the Yuuzhan Vong had not come for them yet.

In their scouting missions Corran and Ganner had managed to determine a number of things. First, they knew the two students were being held in the large shell. They were not in good shape, but their sense in the Force had not yet begun to diminish. This everyone took as a good sign.

The prisoners, on the other hand, had deteriorated. The Jedi witnessed no more murders, but the number of slaves shrank all the same. The growths became larger, and the pain the slaves were in was all that much more obvious. There seemed to be very little peace for them at night.

Corran had seen only the two warriors and began to assume there were, in fact, only two of them. He knew that was a dangerous assumption, but he clung to it because if there were more, there just was no way the rescue mission could succeed. He felt, deep down, that they would succeed, at least partially, and he let his trust in the Force reinforce his belief about the number of Yuuzhan Vong they would face.

Ganner had seized upon Corran's belief about the number of Yuuzhan Vong and used it to grind on him. The younger Jedi reminded him again and again that if they had just acted that night, none of the students would have been in danger and they could have all been away from Bimmiel a long time since. Corran countered that Yuuzhan Vong reinforcements could have arrived if the two stationed on the world didn't report regularly, making things worse, but he knew that was a sham argument. *If they were reporting to off-world sites, more Vong would already be here because of the discovery of humans.*

He looked at Dr. Pace and let his shoulders slump a bit. "We have been over all of this, I think, and I understand your protests over parts of the plan. Ganner and I will slip into the camp and liberate your students. Trista has learned enough about flying the freighter that she'll be able to handle getting it that far. It's bigger than a blastboat, but her experience piloting one of them should suffice. She laces the village with stuff you've been synthing up, Ganner and I get out of there, and we leave."

"Yes, we leave . . . We leave the slaves behind." Pace's eyes narrowed. "When we spray the area with the virus that will change the bacteria, we'll also be dumping an incredible amount of killscent. From your reports the slashrats actually have tunnels running under the village basin. When the killscent gets down there, they'll come up and will be everywhere. The slaves don't stand a chance."

A chill writhed up Corran's spine. "I know that, and I know we've asked you to trust us, to trust the sense Ganner and I have of the slaves. They're dying by little bits and pieces. I've never felt anything similar through the Force, but I know they're very sick and won't survive."

His head came up. "And you know we can't take them with us. We don't know what the growths are, how they are spread.

For all we know, it's an infectious disease, and the Yuuzhan Vong have set up this village as something we can rescue folks from. They intend us to bring plague carriers along with us. If we do, we will do an incredible amount of harm to the New Republic and its people."

"But what if Vil and Denna are infected?"

Corran sighed. "That's the crux of it, isn't it? I've been wrestling with it myself."

"And your decision?"

He glanced out at the distant ship and the two figures slowly walking back toward the cave. "If they are sick, we have no choice but to leave them."

"And if we can cure them?"

"You want to risk a planet on that chance?" Corran tapped his own chest. "I don't. I remember the Krytos virus. I know how devastating that can be. If they are infected, they don't make it off Bimmiel. If they aren't, we get them out and into evac suits on the freighter. The same goes for Ganner and me, just to safeguard you against the chance that we do develop a problem."

"And, if you do, you expect us to space all four of you?"

Corran turned and looked at her. "You know, Doctor, some choices just aren't easy. Spacing Ganner might break Trista's heart. I've got a wife and kids, and I think they'd not be too pleased at my dying; but when I have to choose between my death and the potential death of billions, I know which is the better choice. I serve the Force, and the Force is life itself. It doesn't make the decision easy, but it makes it easier."

Pace snorted, then shook her head. "You make it sound so simple."

"From one point of view, it is." Corran sighed. "I doubt, though, the Vong share that point of view, so this is going to be just plain hard and painful."

CHAPTER
TWENTY-SEVEN

Jaina Solo sat huddled and anonymous in the midst of the pilots gathered for Colonel Darklighter's briefing in the main cabin of Senator A'Kla's *Lambda*-class shuttle, *Impervious*. Despite the colonel's relative youth, he was one of the oldest people in the room. Jaina found it disturbing that many of the pilots tended to be closer to her age than not, and she had the feeling that one who had piloted an ugly was her younger brother's age.

In addition to the pilots from Rogue Squadron and the two squadrons of uglies, the pilots for the various freighters had joined the briefing. Elegos sat forward of them and off to the side, as if he were more an observer than a participant, despite the fact that his shuttle had been tasked with moving to a point position directly in line toward whichever direction from which the Yuuzhan Vong staged their attack.

Gavin nodded to Major Varth, and she keyed up a holograph of one of the coralskippers. "You've seen skips before and have engaged them in space combat. We have no idea what sort of role they will play in ground support of an attack, but their plasma bolts will undoubtedly kill folks who get in the way of them. Our job will be to engage the skips and keep them from their ground-support role. That's our primary mission and will belong to the Rogue and Savage Squadrons."

The Savage pilots nodded and slapped each other's backs.

The uglies had been divided into new squadrons here on Dantooine, with Savage being made up of uglies like clutches that had shields. The Rogues had referred to the squadron as Salvage Squadron at first, but the pilots proved game so the Rogues didn't rib them too much. *The fact is that we know they're likely to take a lot of casualties in the coming assault. Their ships aren't capable of handling the wear and tear ours are.*

The other squadron, designated Tough, consisted of the less powerful ships, including those armed with ion cannons or lacking shields. Gavin turned toward those pilots, all of whom had donned red scarves to give them a rakish air—and it worked, even for the Gamorrean aft gunner in an old shieldless Y-wing. "You will be given a ground-attack mission. As we pull the skips off, you can harry the ground troops. We have no idea what, if anything, they have as ground transport. Taking anything big out will be important, and you should use proton torpedoes or concussion missiles on them, but only with a very specific attack strategy."

Major Varth hit some keys on her datapad, and the static holograph shifted to an animation. The best-guess idea of a Yuuzhan Vong ground vehicle—shown as a giant beetlelike creature moving on thousands of little feet—moved along slowly as a trio of ships came in at it. The first two made strafing runs, coming in high and spraying flicker darts over the vehicle. The third fighter came in low and drilled one proton torpedo at the target. The Yuuzhan Vong vehicle used black holes to pick off the laser darts and let the proton torpedo through. The missile detonated, lifting the beetle and cracking it in half before dumping it back on the ground in pieces.

Gavin half smiled. "Again, we don't know what Vong ground craft will look like. We used a beetle because we know they use beetles. Regardless of what they look like, the idea is to overwhelm them with laser fire, then drive a torpedo into the craft."

The purple striping around Elegos's eyes tightened. "Colonel, forgive me, but is not this strategy based on wishful thinking? We have no idea how many dovin basals such ground vehicles would have. It could be we would be wasting torpedoes."

Gavin nodded wearily. "I agree, but the chance to kill a lot of Vong is worth that chance. Moreover, whatever heavy weaponry that thing is packing could hurt us, so we have to eliminate them."

Something clicked in the back of Jaina's brain. She raised a hand.

"Flight Officer Solo?"

"Forgive me, Colonel, but something you just said combined with what the senator said. The gravitic anomaly the dovin basal creates just sucks in the proton torpedo and crushes it down, preventing detonation or containing it."

"That is what we think happens. We think containing the energy may exhaust the dovin basal, which is the rough equivalent of overwhelming a shield."

"Right, that's what I thought." She smiled a bit. "What if we don't make it easy for the dovin basals to contain that energy?"

Gavin frowned. "I don't understand what you're saying."

"Okay, what I'm thinking is this: If we reprogram the proton torpedoes and concussion missiles so that they're getting targeting data from our ships on a constant basis, we could have them detonate prematurely when a gravitic anomaly is positioned to intercept them. The missiles go off, releasing all that energy. The black hole might suck a bunch of it in, but the rest could damage ground troops, or other vehicles that don't have black holes up on that side. The shock wave from the explosion would certainly knock troopers down, and the heat might ignite things."

Gavin ran a hand over his bearded jaw. "It does allow us to do some damage regardless. Pilots would have to hold their ships on target for a bit, though, which could make them targets themselves."

Major Inyri Forge raised a hand. "In ground-attack mode a torp isn't going to take that long to reach the target. A couple of seconds—no more."

One of the Tough pilots nodded. "We could also slave our missiles to targeting data coming from some of the freighters. We pop up, deliver the missiles, then scoot away or line up another shot. If we vector shots in over densely packed troops, we could do serious damage."

The leader of Rogue Squadron nodded. "As a plan modification, it's simple and works. Good. I'll get slicer droids coding up a sim for this strategy and see how it runs. You freight pilots are going to need to see if you can modify your sensor packages to provide the telemetry our missiles need, but that shouldn't be hard. You'll be shooting your guns by hand, though, since your sensors will be occupied—at least, at range. When the Vong get close enough that we won't be torping them, you really won't need sensor data, but you can have it."

Gavin chewed his lower lip for a moment. "Look, all of you, this is not going to be an easy fight. Normally we pilots get to cloak ourselves in tradition and the romance of single combat amid the stars. The kind of snubfighters we pilot killed the Death Stars and have downed lots of Imps and pirates. We often take pride and even solace in the fact that those we face in combat are our equals in skill. It's a fair fight.

"This won't even be close to a fair fight. Once we scrape fighter cover off the ground troops, we'll be slaughtering them as fast as we can. Scatter shots from the lasers may only burn paint from a fighter, but they'll broil a warrior in a second. It will not be pretty. What it is, though, is *necessary*."

Gavin nodded toward a viewport that looked out over the refugee camp and the fires lit to stave off night. "It's necessary because those people out there aren't warriors. Many of them might have blasters, but if they ever have to fire them, it's because we've failed. Safeguarding those people, adults and children alike, is more important than our survival. That doesn't mean that you should be stupid out there, but courage will sometimes demand you be a little less than coldly rational and sensible."

He snapped to attention and brought his hand up in a salute. "You know your duty. Get sim time, get sack time, and be ready. When they come, we have to stop them. Nothing more, nothing less will do."

Jacen stood behind one of the dirt-and-fiberplast-debris breastworks thrown up around the camp. His watch had ended a couple of hours earlier. He'd gotten something to eat and tried to lie down to sleep, but remained wide awake. He returned to the line and sent another man off to tuck children into bed. *If I'm going to be miserable, at least I can help others not be the same.*

The events of the past week had confused Jacen terribly. His vision had been incredibly real, yet when he went to follow it, he'd run into disaster. The image of his uncle moving into the Yuuzhan Vong camp, wielding twin light-sabers, still played through his head. He'd known Luke Sky-walker all his life, and had acknowledged him his Master, but until that point had never really seen Luke the way others had. Luke's greatest triumphs had been accomplished well before Jacen had been born, so he always knew Luke was a legend, but never had a way to see *why* he had been a legend.

The display he had put on had impressed Jacen, as had his uncle's weakness after the display. It seemed to age Luke ter-ribly to have used the Force so directly. Once on the *Courage,* the autopilot had been set, and Luke retreated to meditate and recover from the ordeal, leaving Jacen to tend to the cut on his own face. The youth lifted a hand and touched the scab, which was the one tangible reminder of how close he had come to becoming a Yuuzhan Vong slave.

Without it, I might not believe what had happened.

"Don't pick at the wound, Jacen. If it gets infected, you could end up with a nasty scar."

The young Jedi Knight turned and gave Danni a smile, de-spite how the expression tugged at the scab. "A scar would make me more dashing, don't you think?"

She cocked her head to the side and looked at him, then pursed her lips and shook her head. "You don't need it. You're perfectly handsome as it is—provided you get rid of the worry in your eyes."

Jacen blinked. "Not worry, just confusion. And it shouldn't be that evident, unless you're reading me through the Force."

"I have been practicing what Jaina has shown me, but I've mostly been focusing on light lifting and keeping my feelings to myself." She hugged her arms around her middle. "In becoming attuned to the Force, I'm suddenly aware of how sloppy folks are with their emotions. Some people are just buckets of emotions, sloshing all over the place."

Jacen reached out through the Force and could feel a tingle of fear over Danni. "You're keeping things to yourself pretty well, though fear shouldn't be one of them. Fear leads to hate—"

"I know, it's a step on the path to the dark side." She exhaled slowly, then moved up beside him on the rampart and stared out into the darkness. The firelight flashed gold from her hair. "They had me once, and I don't want to be their prisoner again. I couldn't stand it, I just couldn't."

"They don't make a good impression on their guests, do they?"

"No." She turned to look at him, half her face hidden in shadow. "I wish I could be brave like you. You joke about being a guest."

"It's joke or cry, Danni." Jacen leaned forward on the breastwork. "You know being brave really isn't that much of a trick. Most of the time courage is just ignorance of what's really going on. I didn't have time to be scared, and you didn't really, either, when we were escaping. You weren't, then, when it counted."

"But I am now. I just feel fear everywhere. It's all over."

Jacen slowly nodded. "There's a lot of fear in the camp, yes, and some out there." He pointed into the darkness. "You can probably feel it. It's a weird buzzing in the Force. Uncle Luke and I learned to associate it with Yuuzhan Vong slaves. The Yuuzhan Vong do something to their slaves. I'm assuming that whatever troops they send against us, the first wave will be slaves of some sort. They will be expendable and let the Yuuzhan Vong test their methods against us without killing too many Yuuzhan Vong warriors."

"Do you think we will win?"

He shrugged. "I don't see that we have a choice. I could say yes, but if I'm wrong, we'll not be around to discuss it."

Danni raised an eyebrow. "No hint of the future through the Force?"

"No, and I'm not sure I'd believe it if there was one." Jacen sighed heavily. "I don't know what to think. Two weeks ago I thought that the only way for me to reach my true potential as a Jedi was to retreat, become a hermit, work on my connection with the Force. Now I see that there is a need for me as a Jedi to help people. I can't tell you how good it felt to be able to save Mara and Anakin. Out there the Jedi might be held in contempt, but here the few of us are being looked upon as saviors. When my uncle wanders through the camp, you can feel pride and hope swell. There are kids using sticks and making a buzzing sound as they duel with mock lightsabers. It may just be people grasping at any hope in so dark a time, but being able to provide that hope makes me feel good."

"So you accept that a Jedi has responsibility beyond his relationship with the Force?"

"I'd not thought about it in exactly those terms, no, but I guess I'd have to answer yes." He shifted his shoulders uneasily. "Still, I wonder if I'd somehow had a stronger relationship with and understanding of the Force, I'd have been able to know where my vision went wrong. Uncle Luke says the future is constantly in motion, so the vision might have been correct right up to the point when it wasn't because of something someone else did. If it had gone right, we might not have been here and able to save Mara or Anakin, so I have no argument with how things turned out. Still . . ."

"Still, you want to have a better grasp on the Force. If it is the path you are to follow, you want to learn how the trail is blazed."

Jacen turned toward her and smiled. "I guess that's it, yes."

Danni nodded, then coiled a strand of blond hair around a finger. "Perhaps that path you seek is just like the future, constantly in motion. Perhaps this stretch demands you provide hope to these people, and another will let you go off on your own. When you come to a decision point, you can leave off one path and head out on another. Only your past experience can guide you."

"Yeah, and I don't have that much experience, do I?" Jacen shook his head. "It sounds as if you've thought a lot about the Force."

"Not the Force, just life. I've had to choose courses, too. We all do. I could have stayed on Commenor, gotten married, had children, but instead I applied to the ExGal Society and got posted to Belkadan. If I survive this ordeal, perhaps I will get the chance to revisit that sort of decision."

Jacen felt the hint of a flush on his cheeks. "You want to get married and have children?"

"If the right man comes along, it's possible, yes." She shrugged. "With all that's going on, I don't really know if I can trust my emotions. Gratitude, fear, curiosity—all these things are mixed up in me."

"But there is no one you are seeing?" Jacen felt the question hang in the air for a second, then crash down all leaden to the ground. He knew it was ridiculous for a woman five years older than he was to even give him a second glance, but . . . *She did say I was handsome . . . Still, she sees me as a boy, I'm sure . . .*

"Romance was pretty much a part of my life that I'd deferred until later. Perhaps later is now, I don't know." She gave him a smile. "Were you a bit older, or me a bit younger, and circumstances altogether different, I don't know. I mean, I have feelings for you, Jacen, but they're all mixed up with everything. You're so thoughtful, bringing me the holographs and mementos from Belkadan. You can't know how that made me feel . . ."

"With all that's going on, you don't trust your feelings?"

Danni nodded. "Liquids under pressure don't boil when they should, and emotions tend to act the opposite way. I think you are wonderful, and I treasure you as a friend. Anything else, well, as you said, the future is constantly in motion."

Jacen felt a twinge of hurt. Growing up at the academy, he'd certainly had his share of crushes on other students, but

Danni was the first woman he'd been attracted to outside of that setting. He agreed that having been pressed into close quarters with her in a rescue capsule had certainly gotten them acquainted with a degree of physical intimacy that wasn't usually associated with first meeting someone. He'd entertained his fantasies about her, but also realized they were as much tied up with the traditional romance of a hero saving a damsel in distress as they were anything else. *Reliving how my father met my mother . . .*

Her gaze searched his face. "I've hurt you, haven't I?"

"Jedi Knights do not know pain, Danni." Jacen gave her a brave smile. "In times like this, a friend truly *is* a treasure. Given what is going on here, and with my life and yours, being friends is probably the best thing possible for us."

She reached up and stroked his right cheek with her left hand. "That's a very mature answer, Jacen. You're very special indeed."

"Thanks, my friend." Jacen sighed and turned to focus on the darkness. "Friends tend to bring the best out in me."

Anakin stopped as the door on the cabin used by Mara and his uncle Luke slid open. Luke emerged and smiled at his nephew. "She's resting for the moment."

The boy nodded. "I won't disturb her." He pointed back over his shoulder down a passageway. "I'll just—"

"I'd like it if you would walk with me, Anakin."

Anakin caught a slightly distant tone in his uncle's voice and recognized it immediately. "Yes, Uncle Luke." He dropped into place a half step behind Luke, on his left. Anakin had learned that was the proper position for a right-handed apprentice; that way, if he were to draw and ignite his lightsaber in a sloppy way, he wouldn't accidentally bisect his Master.

Luke glanced at him and grinned. "I'm glad to see you up and around. The Yuuzhan Vong did their best to carve you up."

Anakin shrugged. He could still feel bacta patches affixed to some of the cuts; the superficial wounds were not serious enough to warrant a complete dunking for him. "A Jedi knows no pain, Master."

"But a Jedi knows gratitude." Luke stopped, then turned to his nephew and rested his hands on Anakin's shoulders. "You did a wonderful job taking care of Mara. She's told me all about it, and I am very proud of you. I never thought sending you with her would demand so much of you. I'm ashamed to say that *if* I knew what was going to happen, I might not have sent you. Now I am glad I did."

"I wasn't going to fail you, Uncle Luke. I wasn't going to fail Aunt Mara." Anakin shrugged and hooked his thumbs in his belt. "I just did what my mission required. I'm sorry I couldn't save the *Sabre* or the blasters and other things we had on it. If I'd thought—"

"No, Anakin, no reproof. What you did was the best that could be expected."

"You're being too generous."

Luke shook his head and gazed down at his nephew in a way that sent a thrill through Anakin. "When I had a vision of where you would be and where we would find you, I knew that a million different things could change that future. If you had faltered just a step, if you had paused or thought to quit, Jacen and I never would have been able to save you. You did exactly what you needed to; this time, as well as when you saved your father at Sernpidal. And your willingness to make that last stand for Mara . . ."

The Jedi Master lifted his chin. "In that moment you blazed so brightly within the Force . . . you were dazzling, and try their best, they never could have struck you down."

"Wow." Anakin blinked. "I mean, thank you, Master."

Luke laughed lightly. "As your Master I am grateful for your actions as a Jedi apprentice. And you have my personal gratitude for your saving my wife. Unfortunately, this is not the sort of situation where ceremonies are easily arranged."

The boy drew himself up as straight and as tall as he could. "Master, this apprentice merely asks that he be allowed to fight at your side."

Luke stroked Anakin's hair. "Don't think of that as a

reward, Anakin. Were it within my power, I would make it so you never again had to fight. Standing and killing, risking your own life—this is something I'd prefer none of us ever had to do. I will let you fight by my side because, truth be told, this situation demands it. I will also have you fight because I know, no matter what the situation, you have the heart and the intelligence to do whatever needs to be done to safeguard others."

Anakin felt a thrill shiver through him. "That sounds like a reward."

"Not from my point of view." Luke sighed. "I guess we'll just have to convince the Yuuzhan Vong that my point of view is the right one, so they'll realize there is no reward for their actions."

CHAPTER
TWENTY-EIGHT

Night had fallen thick and hard before the first warning was sounded. The troopers Admiral Kre'fey had sent down to help out with the situation had set up remote sensor pods that picked up the infrared energy the Yuuzhan Vong gave off. Once the first alarm came through, two TIE-wings from Tough Squadron went up for a quick recon of the area where the sensors had reported movement.

Gavin had watched the TIE-wings take off and head south. They became distant pinpoints of light to the naked eye, but situated in his cockpit, he was able to follow them on his primary monitor. He listened to their comm chatter and heard one pilot's voice strain as he saw a long column of Yuuzhan Vong coming in.

Out there, five to six kilometers distant, reddish ground fire reached up toward the fighters. They were able to avoid it fairly easily and still managed to report back what they saw. "Multiple contacts, command. Ground troops on foot, as well as two large vehicles and twelve smaller ones. Gravitic anomalies and plasma cannons on the big ones, plasma cannons on the smaller ones. Air contacts coming on now. We're scooting."

Gavin hit a button on his comm unit. "This is Rogue Leader to all Rogues. Light them up. The enemy is out there, and we're going to pulverize them." He keyed in his ignition sequence and waited for his power and weapons systems to go green. "Catch, monitor base tactical frequency and flash the button when there is an emergency."

The droid warbled a positive reply.

Gavin shunted power to his repulsorlift coils, then nudged the throttle forward. Once he was up and moving, he clicked the switch that locked the S-foils in combat position and ruddered the fighter around to 180 degrees. "One flight on me."

Multiple clicks came over the comm channel to acknowledge his command. Catch started painting multiple enemy contacts in the air ahead of them. *Looks like they have two squadrons of skips up. I have to like the odds and just have to hope we can make the best of them.*

He quadded up his lasers and dropped the aiming reticle on one of the skips harassing a returning Tough. Gavin hit the secondary trigger, spewing out a hail of red energy darts. "Tough, break port."

The ugly cut to Gavin's starboard, and the skip swerved to keep on the TIE-wing's tail. Gavin ruddered around to starboard and kept the skip in his sights. At the same time Nevil sprayed the skip with scatter shots, Gavin hit the primary trigger and sent one full-power burst of laser fire into the skip. The black hole being used to pick off the Quarren's shots did warp the flight path of the bolts Gavin had triggered, but managed only to draw them in toward the dovin basal creating the black hole.

The bolts hit and burned through the coralskipper's stony flesh. Something evaporated in a burst of steam, then the skip's aft began to drop. Seconds later the last of the laser bolts burst from the other side of the craft. For a half second the skip hung in the air, its nose pointing skyward, then Nevil's second flicker-shot barrage stippled the skip with glowing red points. One must have hit a dovin basal, killing it, because the skip then plummeted from the sky and crashed unseen into the ground below.

Ahead of Gavin the sky lit up like the Coruscant cityscape during a celebration of Liberation Day. Plasma bolts arced into the sky. Laser bolts, both red and green, as well as blue ion bolts, slanted down toward the ground. Flashes of color illuminated the two huge shadowy shapes moving through the night, but Gavin could not make out much in the way of detail. He almost asked Catch to switch him over to ground-attack mode on his sensors so he could get an idea of what the Yuuzhan Vong were bringing to assault the base, but incoming fighters demanded his attention.

And they'll get it. He spitted one on his aiming reticle and tightened up on the trigger. *My undivided attention.*

The nervous anxiety of the pilots woke Luke first, but the roar of the snubfighters taking off guaranteed to keep him awake. He pulled a tunic on, then looped his lightsaber belt over his shoulder before emerging from his tent. He watched the fighters head south and, just for a moment, wished he could be up there in one with them. *Once again, with Artoo behind me, rolling through a dogfight.*

He shivered, knowing that such remembrances were not quite the thing a Jedi Master should dwell on. An affinity for combat was a necessary evil, but one that could be tolerated only when a Jedi held himself back and used it only to defend people. Seeing the line between offensive action and defensive was, at the best of times, difficult, but as he watched sleepy people emerge from tents, rubbing their eyes and beginning to murmur, he knew where it lay in this case.

Mara appeared at his side. "Where do you want me?"

The urgency in her voice belied the weariness on her face.

"You want the honest truth?"

Mara hesitated for a moment, then nodded. "I trust your judgment, Luke."

"Good. I want you to find Leia. She's going to be running around herding the noncombatants. Right now I need you to be there and back her, so we don't get any grief from them. I know you want to be—"

Mara reached out and touched a finger to his lips. "I said I trusted your judgment. I trust you will have me where you need me, and if I am needed elsewhere, you will let me know."

Luke reached out and pulled Mara into a firm hug. "I love you very much, Mara. For this and for everything else."

"I know, Luke." Mara pulled her head back a bit, then rested her forehead on his, noses touching. "Each of us doing our parts will defeat the Yuuzhan Vong. Count on it."

"I do." Luke kissed her and held her as if it would be the last time, then reluctantly let her slip from his arms. "May the Force be with you."

"And you, my love." She winked at him and backed away toward the center of the camp. "When you need me, I'll be there."

He nodded, then jogged out toward the southern perimeter. He quickly found Colonel Bril'nilim, a Twi'lek in charge of the New Republic troopers, scanning the distance with a pair of macrobinoculars. Luke sensed frustration coming off the commando leader, so did nothing to disturb him.

The Twi'lek turned and offered him the vision device. "Perhaps you can see something more than I can."

Luke waved the macrobinoculars away. "The Yuuzhan Vong are out there, but that's obvious. The troops are likely slave forces they want to bear the brunt of the casualties. Where do you want me?"

Bril'nilim pointed over toward the southeast. "You, I'd like there, your nephews off to the southwest. Let me know anything you feel that is odd, and I can send scouts out."

"As ordered, Colonel." Luke turned and found his nephews hanging back a bit. "Did you hear?"

Jacen nodded. "Yes. Anakin and I go over there, you're over here. We report whatever is odd."

"Right. No going yourselves to investigate, understand?"

Colonel Bril'nilim's lekku twitched as he came around. "You better understand. No heroics. My troops will shoot things they don't understand, and a Jedi sneaking around will be one of them. Got it?"

"Yes, sir," the two young Jedi Knights said in unison.

Luke and the colonel exchanged smiles. "Good, get to it. I like having three Jedi on my line. I just hope none of us will have to see too much action."

* * *

"Tough Seven here. I could use some cover on my attack run."

Jaina clicked on her comm unit. "Rogue Eleven on you, T-sev."

"Thanks, Sticks."

The Jedi pilot rolled her X-wing up on the port stabilizer and came around on a heading that put her to starboard of the X-ceptor heading in at the ground formation. The TIE interceptor wings on the X-ceptor spat laser darts past its long X-wing nose, scything down rows of Yuuzhan Vong troopers. Though Jaina could not see much in the green light from the lasers, she could make out that none of the Yuuzhan Vong troopers broke or ran. *They also seem small to me, stockier than I thought the Yuuzhan Vong were from what Jacen described.*

A coralskipper came around and vectored in on the X-ceptor. Jaina shoved her stick forward and sprayed red laser splinters at the skip. It immediately sprouted a void that sucked in most of the laserfire. Jaina kept her ship coming on hard and loosed a solid quad burst in the midst of a spray, which caused the Yuuzhan Vong pilot to shy off. As he broke to her port, she rolled to port and leveled out in T-sev's aft. *I don't like being shielding, but I need to give him this shot.*

Fire blossomed from the X-ceptor's nose as a proton torpedo squirted out. Jaina bounced her ship up after the launch and gained a bit of altitude. Below her the torpedo streaked straight at the first moving mountain shadow, then it exploded into a brilliant silvery ball that lit up the night.

The X-wing's canopy flash suppressor engaged immediately, cutting out most of the glare but still allowing her to see what was going on at the point of the attack. The torpedo had detonated shy of the target by about one hundred meters, and a void had gobbled up a lot of the energy, but what little it didn't consume wrought havoc on the ground. The energy evaporated soldiers, eliminating whole companies in the blink of an eye. Others it scattered like toys beneath a vengeful child's feet. The shock wave toppled several of the smaller vehicles, which looked to Jaina like bony armored domes mounted on brush-bristle cilia. Several rolled onto their backs, with their little legs waving in the air, while others that had their cilia flash-fried ground to a halt.

Most impressive, however, had been the larger vehicle at which T-sev had aimed. Like the smaller creatures, it had a bony-plate armor. Along its spine, and at points on the flanks, hornlike growths jutted out. Plasma bolts shot from these horns, and while she couldn't tell if the horns could swivel, enough of them pointed in any one direction to be able to scour the skies of fighters.

She shuddered, as the whole thing looked to her like one giant, armored slug sprouting thorns.

Jaina rolled hard to starboard, then sideslipped back to port before triggering a burst at the thing, which she arbitrarily decided to call a range—short for mountain range. A void snapped her shots up, and the range launched plasma in her direction. She juked her way clear of most shots and heard the static of her shields absorbing damage from the others. Her sensors reported other gravitic anomalies, which she assumed were dovin basals trying to take her shields down, but her compensator sphere had been expanded to fend off that sort of assault.

She pulled up and throttled forward into the battle above the convoy. As she inverted her fighter to climb, she saw other ground detonations of proton torpedoes. It looked to her as if they had also gone off prematurely, which killed a lot of troopers and toppled the little creatures. She was glad to know her strategy would have some effect, but she feared it would not be enough.

"Sparky, what's the distance between the most forward and most distant ground explosions?"

The droid scrolled the answer up on her secondary monitor.

Jaina shivered. The distance made the Yuuzhan Vong column at least five kilometers long. *It doesn't matter how well we shoot. If we can't knock out the ranges, there is no way we will stop the Yuuzhan Vong from reaching the camp. And, when they do . . .*

* * *

Leia started as she felt a hand on her shoulder. She turned quickly and dropped a hand to the blaster she wore on her hip, but Mara bodied her back against the hull of the freighter in whose shadow they stood. Leia stared at her for a moment, then raised her free hand to her own throat. "You scared me."

"Sorry. Luke sent me to find you, stay with you."

"Are you sure? Shouldn't you be—"

"Resting?" Mara shook her head. "Never did like being helpless, so here I am. What are you doing out here?"

Leia jerked a thumb toward the camp's northeast perimeter. "People have been coming in to the center of the camp, but a couple of families from out here have not. I wanted to check on them . . . I was heading out, and then, I don't know, I got a feeling . . ."

Mara's head came up, and she peered off past the edge of the freighter. "Something wrong?"

"Nothing like that."

Mara nodded, then unclipped her lightsaber from her belt. "You got nothing at all, right?"

"What?"

Mara pointed at one of the tents. Movement was plainly visible in it, but as Leia reached out with the Force, she could sense no life in it. "That's impossible."

"Not quite." Mara darted forward, and her blue lightsaber extended itself in a sizzling line. She slashed at the guylines holding the tent up. It collapsed over three figures for a second, then they clawed their way free of the red fabric.

The trio of Yuuzhan Vong warriors stood there for a moment, looking tall but, because of what they wore, hardly like the lean figures others had described. A pale pseudoflesh covered them save for the claws that projected through it and where it hung like a hood back off their heads. They had also pulled on clothes. At their feet, revealed by the shredded folds of the tent, Leia saw three naked bodies, covered in blood.

In an instant she knew what had happened. Some of the Yuuzhan Vong had slipped into the camp, had killed refugees, and were using ooglith masquers to make themselves appear to be human. *If others have mixed with the real refugees, innocent people might be slaughtered.* The desire to run off and raise an alarm warred with her seeing the three warriors turn to face Mara and her lightsaber. *I have to protect the people, but I can't leave Mara. What am I going to do?*

CHAPTER
TWENTY-NINE

Huddled in the rocks within sight of the Yuuzhan Vong camp, Corran glanced over at Jens. The student tech sat with her back to a big rock, her knees drawn up, with a blocky remote balanced on them. She flicked a couple of switches on the device, and a small spherical probe started to hum as it rose from the ground. An antenna telescoped up, and a small suite of sensors deployed themselves from the bottom.

Corran nodded to her, and she sent the probe arcing around to the left, to come in at the camp from the north. The little black ball floated gently down into the camp. It circled several of the smallest shells, then darted directly toward the midsize ones. In front of the one that housed the two Yuuzhan Vong warriors, Jens used a strobe to flash the area, then started the sphere retreating to the north.

The two warriors boiled out of their shells and pointed at the probe. One dashed back into his shell, returning with weapons, armor, and the Yuuzhan Vong equivalent of sandshoes. He dressed himself while still watching the probe, giving the other one a chance to run into his shell and arm himself. When he returned, the two of them began to stalk off after the probe, which had disappeared into the dunes north of the lake bed.

Corran looked at Jens. "Keep them occupied. Once we enter the large shell, get Trista up and flying. She'll be here in five minutes. She laces the area with the killscent bombs, picks you up, and gets us out. If we are *not* out in that time, consider us dead and get going. No questions, right?"

Jens nodded. "Good luck."

"Thanks, you too."

He looked past her to Ganner. "Ready?"

The younger man nodded and vaulted himself up over a boulder. Corran cut around the stone that had hidden him and ran as best as his sandshoes would allow. Ganner reached the safe sand first and bent to hit the quick release on his bindings. He dropped the sandshoes there and sprinted toward the big shell. He brought his lightsaber to hand, but didn't ignite it.

Corran kicked himself free of his sandshoes, but scooped them up with his left hand. He ran after Ganner and reached the large shell only a couple of steps behind him. Corran tossed the sandshoes aside at the entrance, then pulled his own lightsaber. He left it unlit, but his right thumb hovered over the ignition button.

Ganner had paused inside the large shell's throat. The walls and floors—every surface, really—were smooth and varied in color from a dark ivory to a soft pink. Darker gray spots dappled the walls at various points, but Corran could discern no pattern to them. The walls also seemed faintly luminescent, but he allowed as how that might just be sunlight somehow pouring through the shell.

Ganner stalked forward and down a set of steps into the main chamber. Off it ran a number of tunnels that Corran assumed led to other smaller chambers, all of which made him wonder what sort of creature had grown the shell. While the flooring was very smooth, it wasn't particularly slippery. The only sound they heard came from their own breathing and the rasp of sand beneath their boot heels.

The grand chamber opened up as they came around a curve in the stairs. Ganner gasped and took a step back. Corran's eyes narrowed, but he made himself step past his aide and onto the main floor. He looked at the two students and really hoped they were dead.

The two of them hung from racks, bound ankle, thigh, and wrist. Their heads remained lower than their feet, and their limbs were locked rigidly. Both men had been stripped of clothing. Little maggot-white crablike creatures the size of a sabacc deck walked across their backs, pinching them with little claws, or digging needlelike appendages into their flesh. Little bloody rivulets striped the men's flesh and colored the floor.

Beneath them something that looked like more like a tongue than a slug slowly moved across the floor, cleansing it of the blood.

Corran reached out with the Force and got a sense of the students. They were in a lot of pain, but their sense within the Force was coming through strong and unadulterated. They might have been beaten up and tortured, but they were not yet dying.

Ganner stepped forward and waved a hand in Vil's direction. The pinchers flew off his back and smashed into the wall. They descended into a glistening, slimy pile at the base of the wall. Ganner ignited his lightsaber and pulled it back for a blow that would clip one of the rack arms off, partially freeing Vil.

Corran caught a spike of pain from Vil and held his hands up. "No, Ganner, wait."

"We don't have time to wait, Corran."

"The pain spiked in him after you cleared off the pinchers. Do the same for Denna. See if the same thing happens."

Ganner nodded, and the pinchers on the other student flew off. Pain spiked in Denna, and Corran caught the related tightening of the arm restraints. "I thought so. The rack keeps them in a constant level of pain."

"Why?"

"I don't know." Corran stared at Ganner with disbelief. "We're dealing with Vong logic here. I don't know what they are thinking or why they do what they do. We just have to find a way to get these guys out of these restraints."

Corran's comlink buzzed. "Horn, go ahead."

"Jens here. The Yuuzhan Vong are headed back your way. They stopped chasing the probe."

"Not good. Buzz them. Do something to attract their attention. We need some time."

"You won't have much. Trista is inbound."

"Sithspawn!" Corran's nostrils flared. "No time to play, no time to think."

Ganner raised his lightsaber again. "We cut them free."

"And if one cut won't do it? The restraints tighten and pop their arms out of their shoulder sockets or tear them clean off. No good."

"What do we do?"

Corran raked fingers back through his brown hair, then stepped up to Denna and stabbed his stiffened fingers deep into the man's armpit. Through the Force, he could feel a jolt of pain running through the man. He also saw the rack's restraints slacken slightly.

"That's it. They're being held in a constant level of pain. If the rack senses too much, it lets the pressure off. We have to put them in more pain, a lot of pain, to get the rack to release them."

The younger Jedi frowned. "How? Beat them up? Break some bones? Stab them with lightsabers?"

"It would do the trick, but it would kill them, obviously." Corran smiled grimly. "I will just have to make them think they're in pain."

Ganner's head came up, and he gave Corran a respectful nod. "Ah, yes. Get to it."

"Not that easy." Corran began to roll up his left sleeve. "It will take some work."

"What are you talking about?"

"Ever broken a limb?"

Ganner nodded. "My leg."

"You remember it hurt, right?"

"Yes."

"But you don't remember how *much* it hurt. The mind is like that. You forget the really sharp pains so you'll continue going on. Women forget the pain of childbirth or we'd all be only children." Corran sighed. "I can project pain into them, but I've got to feel it to get it right."

"How?" Ganner's question came very tentatively.

Corran moved between the two racks and stood facing Vil, with Denna behind him. "You face Denna. When the machines slacken fully, you've got to make one cut, get the restraint straps. You do him, I'll do Vil."

"Okay."

"Now the hard part." Corran extended his left forearm toward Ganner, with his hand open and palm up. "One of the other Force abilities I have is pretty rare. I can, under certain circumstances, absorb a certain amount of energy without much damage to myself. To get the pain I need, I want you to press your lightsaber against my forearm. Not too hard—I like the limb just fine. Just hold it out, maybe, and I'll move my arm up into it."

Ganner's jaw dropped. "You can't be serious."

"You want to save these two or not?"

"But—"

"But nothing. Are you ready?"

Ganner nodded and extended the lightsaber.

Corran could feel the buzz of it against his flesh as he slowly raised his arm. The blade's heat vaporized hairs, filling the area with the stink of singed protein. Corran knew that scent was nothing compared to what would follow. He swallowed, once, hard, then flattened his hand and raised his arm another centimeter.

Silver agony flashed right up his arm and into his brain. By reflex he started to use a Jedi technique to shunt the pain away, but then stopped himself. He concentrated, soaking in the energy of the blade. He looked out through slitted eyelids and saw his flesh reddening, then beginning to blister. Smoke rose from it, and the pain built. Then, as he saw the first hint of charring, he latched onto the Force and poured the torment out and into the students.

One second, two, three. Corran let the burning sharpness flow through him and into Vil and Denna. They twitched while he trembled. They shrieked while his flesh crackled. His clenched jaw ground his teeth together, and he tasted blood.

The racks slackened, dropping each student half a meter toward the floor. The restraining straps snapped taut, all glossy and black like wet leather. Corran ignited his own lightsaber and whipped the blade around, severing each strap, then he dropped to his knees and fell over Vil's prostrate form.

Gasping for air, Corran tried to employ the Jedi technique for shunting away pain, but he couldn't focus enough to do it. The world began to swim and darken at the edges. He was mindful enough to thumb his lightsaber off, then he wavered between complete collapse and the need to get up, get moving.

He heaved his torso upright and would have gone all the way over but Ganner caught the collar of his robe.

"Corran, are you—?"

"Functional? Yes." He let the worry in Ganner's voice appeal to his own sense of vanity, injecting steel into his spine. *It just wouldn't do for Ganner to see me as weak.* He struggled to get his left foot under him, and Ganner reached for his left arm to help him up, but Corran hissed a warning. "Don't touch the arm."

"How bad is it?"

"Pretty, ah, crusty, I guess." Corran was thankful his sleeve had slipped down over the arm, but his blackened fingers told him more than he needed to know. He staggered upright, then hugged his left arm to his chest. "How are they?"

"Out cold. We'll have to drag them—"

A sharp hiss and a whip crack cut Ganner off. Corran slowly straightened up and glanced at the stairway back to the lake bed. The two Yuuzhan Vong warriors stood on it, tall and daunting, their maroon armor and greenish leathery joints accentuating their alien nature. The lead warrior barked an order at the two Jedi and punctuated it with another whip crack of an amphistaff.

Corran forced a bit of a laugh. "Looks like they don't like the dragging idea, Ganner. Seems another plan will be required to get us out of here."

CHAPTER THIRTY

From out of nowhere the image of her husband flashed into Leia's head, and her question was answered. With a grim smile, she pulled her blaster and pumped two shots into the first of the Yuuzhan Vong. The red bolts hit him shoulder and chest, spinning him about. Thick pus sprayed from the ooglith masquer, drenching the second warrior. The third leapt toward Mara, his claws rending the air between them.

The second warrior flicked a hand at Leia even as she brought her blaster to bear on him. Something thin and sharp spun through the air and caught her in the right forearm. Pain shot up to her shoulder, and she lost her grip on the gun. As it fell toward the ground, she stooped to get it with her free hand, then looked up to see her attacker leaping toward her.

On her knees, Leia reflexively raised her left arm to fend off the Yuuzhan Vong, but the warrior never reached her. Bolpuhr, little more than a gray blur, tackled the Yuuzhan Vong in midair. The two of them hit the ground hard and rolled, with the Yuuzhan Vong finally succeeding in throwing the Noghri off him. Bolpuhr arced through the night and bounced once before rolling into the red tangle of tent and corpses.

The Yuuzhan Vong he'd tackled got up and took a step toward Leia, then faltered. He fell to his knees, with the ooglith masquer sloughing off slowly. The hilt of a Noghri dagger protruded from the Yuuzhan Vong's breastbone, and when the Yuuzhan Vong fell face forward, Leia caught the glint of the blade's blackened tip stabbing out of the alien warrior's back.

Beyond the dead warrior, Mara faced her foe with a fierce expression on her face. She'd reversed her grip on the blue lightsaber, letting the blade parallel her right forearm. She extended her left hand, then crouched, waiting and watching. The Yuuzhan Vong likewise crouched, his hands flexing. He hunched his shoulders and shifted his weight.

Mara took a half step forward and ducked her head toward him. The warrior leapt at her, but Mara had already pulled back from her feint. His claws flashed through where her head should have been. Mara pivoted on her right foot and brought her right arm around in a stroke that passed through where the warrior's belly was. The ooglith masquer melted away from the blade's searing touch, then the warrior's flesh smoked as the blade opened him from hip to hip.

Mara spun away from him, yet the Yuuzhan Vong still scratched her right thigh as he collapsed. Coming around full circle, she slashed the blade low and cleaved it cleanly through his neck. His body convulsed, and his head, which rolled a meter or two away, gnashed his teeth for the remaining seconds of life.

Mara ran to Leia. "How badly are you hurt?"

Leia shook her head, then started as the thing in her arm sprouted legs and tried to pry itself from her flesh. Mara reared back and tapped the razorbug with the tip of her lightsaber, killing it. Leia batted at the dead bug with her left hand and finally knocked it loose from her flesh. "Yuck!"

Mara tore the sleeve from her robe and quickly wrapped it around Leia's arm. "We'd better get that looked at."

"Later. There might be more Yuuzhan Vong with the refugees. We have to check—" Leia looked up. "Where's Bolpuhr?"

"I don't know." Mara stood and helped Leia to her feet. "He was back over here, wasn't he, near the tent?"

"Yes." Leia ran over to the ruins of the tent, then stopped and sank to her knees again. "Emperor's black bones, no."

The Noghri lay on his back, his sightless eyes staring up at the sky. The Yuuzhan Vong's claws had sliced deeply into Bolpuhr's neck and chest. The Noghri, who had been tireless and fearless in his duty, looked smaller in death, more child-like and fearfully innocent.

Leia shivered. *If the Yuuzhan Vong can kill Noghri with their bare hands* . . . She shook her head and closed Bolpuhr's eyes. "This is worse than anything we've faced before, isn't it, Mara?"

Her sister-in-law slowly shook her head. "If it is, chances are we won't have much longer to worry about it. Look, go to the refugees and see if you can sort out who the Yuuzhan Vong are. Maybe these were the only three to get in. I'll check tents in this area and hold the perimeter. I'll comm if there is trouble."

"I don't want to leave you here alone."

Mara gave her a brave wink. "I have the Force. I'm not alone. Move it. I don't want you here stealing more of my fun."

Luke Skywalker stared out into the darkness. Detonations from proton torpedoes and concussion missiles were drawing closer. He could feel the shock waves vibrate through him. In the backflashes he saw the huge vehicles moving closer, ever closer. Plasma bolts filled the air with an orange glow and, more often than he wanted to acknowledge, exploded something in the air. Fiery wreckage would tumble from the sky and scatter fire and debris across the ground, doing some damage, but generally only illuminating the horde coming at them.

Luke dried his left palm on his cloak, then unfastened the garment and whirled it off behind him. He gripped his lightsaber tightly in his right hand, again and again looking down to make sure the heel of his hand was over the activation plate. He reached out with the Force to gauge the distance to the front and could feel the line of Yuuzhan Vong slaves broadening as they approached the camp.

One of the troopers stationed nearby looked over at him

and smiled. "If you're nervous, I guess there is no problem with me being nervous."

Luke thought for a second and then nodded. In all the battles he'd fought, even Hoth, he'd been involved in one-on-one, man-and-machine fights. Flying an X-wing or piloting a snowspeeder demanded neither less nor more courage than fighting on the ground, but it was more impersonal. His shots broke other fighters or brought down Imperial walkers, and if his foes survived, that was okay. It was part of the game, part of what made such combat noble in the eyes of many.

But ground warfare was not noble. The object of the exercise was to kill as many of them as possible before they killed you. It was intimately personal because your target was another living being, not some machine encasing him. You succeeded when he dropped, and, yes, while an enemy might surrender, that was not viewed as anything nearly as noble as a pilot who was shot down and captured.

This is just going to be killing, pure and frighteningly simple. Luke could feel the frayed troops coming in, only five hundred meters distant. Beyond that line, fighters made strafing runs on the ground troops. Hails of red and green splinter shots flickered through the night, vaporizing soldiers. Luke caught flashes of pain from those who died, but not a whit of anxiety or fear from the survivors. *They're marching to their deaths uncaring or unable to care about what will happen to them.*

Off to the right Colonel Bril'nilim gave a signal, and the freighters began opening up. Elegos's shuttle rose and hovered in a forward position, with the fire from its laser cannons and blaster cannons pulsing out scarlet energy projectiles that warmed the night as they passed. The shipfire burned furrows through the Yuuzhan Vong ranks, thinning them, but not nearly enough. In the backlight of distant explosions or the burning of corpses, Luke could see the Yuuzhan Vong troops had come even closer.

When the Yuuzhan Vong soldiers reached the two-hundred-meter mark, the troopers started shooting. Their blaster fire came slowly, cautiously, fired without a hint of panic. Red bolts lanced out, striking silhouettes. Some of the Yuuzhan Vong troops spun before falling. Others just collapsed, and yet others sighed and sat, then flopped over as if exhausted and retiring for the day.

At a hundred meters the Yuuzhan Vong troops began to run forward, so the troopers' firing became more hurried. They still struck their targets, but gaps in the lines filled immediately as the wave of Yuuzhan Vong soldiers rushed ever closer. Smaller and stockier than the Yuuzhan Vong warriors Luke had fought, these troops looked reptilian, like Trandoshans but more compact. They did sprout a pair of calcifications from their foreheads, more domes than horns, and Luke suspected it was through these that the Yuuzhan Vong controlled them.

The large vehicles began pulsing plasma out toward the breastworks. Shots pounded into the ground, shaking it, pitching dirt and debris into the air. Shots that fell short plowed through the mass of Yuuzhan Vong troops. Those shots that were on target splashed against shuttle shields or the fortifications. In the latter case the shots blasted the fortifications apart, scattering troopers and, worse yet, opening gaps in the line that allowed the Yuuzhan Vong troops to pour into the compound.

Luke sprinted to the nearest gap and ignited his lightsaber. The green blade hissed and spat as he cut right and left, chopping down the reptilian troopers. The Yuuzhan Vong troops were armed with small amphistaffs, which froze themselves into a sharpened hook shape that clutched at arms and legs, cutting as the soldiers drew the amphistaffs back. The lightsaber couldn't slice through the amphistaffs, but the troops were too slow to prevent Luke from lopping off limbs or stabbing through chests.

Because he could feel the slave troops through the Force, killing them proved far too easy. He knew where they would be, what they wanted to do. A parry here and a stroke to the head, or a block, then a riposte to the heart. He wasn't fighting troops as much as he was battling for time. If killing each one took three seconds or five, he couldn't possibly stop them all.

Meter by meter he was being driven back by the sheer weight of the assault, and even with the Force to strengthen him, he couldn't kill them fast enough.

Unless I can think of something to do, it's over, it's all over.

Leia ran to the center of the camp and immediately appropriated a blaster carbine from one of the refugees standing guard. She found Danni and pulled the woman aside, then waved Lando over. "I need your help."

"You're bleeding," Lando said.

"It's nothing, for the moment anyway. I need you to use the Force. You can feel emotions, right?"

Danni nodded stiffly. "I've been trying to shut things out. They're all afraid here." She glanced down. "Like me."

"Look, there may be Yuuzhan Vong among them, using ooglith masquers to pretend to be people. We have to find them."

Danni blinked and raised a hand to cover her mouth. "Yuuzhan Vong here, hidden here?"

Leia grabbed the young woman's left shoulder. "Steady yourself, Danni. You can do this. You *must* do this."

Lando drew his blaster pistol and checked the power pack. "How will we find them?"

"If Danni can feel fear and hatred, she'll be able to spot those who are feeling nothing. Follow my lead, then move through the crowd." Leia looked at the four hundred assembled refugees and shook her head. "It's not going to be exacting work, but note those who aren't giving any fear off. We segregate them. Since we can't feel the Yuuzhan Vong in the Force, they're going to be the ones we want."

"I don't know." The young woman took a second, then swallowed hard and nodded. "I'll do my best."

Lando nodded. "Let's go."

Leia steeled herself, then triggered a series of blaster shots into the air. People reflexively ducked down, and a wave of terror pounded her. Leia looked out over the crowd and set her face in a grim mask. "The Yuuzhan Vong are incoming, and stopping them is going to be harder than we thought. If you have anything you want to say to others here, your last words, you'd better do it now and be quick about it."

A roiling storm of fear broke over the refugees, with wails and sobs punctuating it like soft thunder. Leia nodded at Danni and Lando, then the three of them began to move through the crowd, gridding it off, searching for those who found nothing to fear in Leia's announcement.

Jacen's green blade slashed right and left as he and Anakin attacked the flank of the Yuuzhan Vong thrust driving Luke back. Jacen didn't care about finesse or skill; he just set about butchering soldiers. What he was doing, he knew, had nothing to do with being a Jedi. Yes, he could feel it when the sparks of life winked out, but the Yuuzhan Vong slave troops felt less like living creatures to him than droids made of flesh and blood. *They are alive in the same way plants are. They might once have been individuals, but now they are just puppets, lethal puppets.*

Jacen lashed out to his right with the lightsaber, burning a gap in a soldier's spine. The soldier collapsed at Anakin's feet. The younger Jedi leapt back, then scythed his blade low, though the legs of a Yuuzhan Vong trooper. That one went down and tripped up two others. Anakin dispatched them with quick thrusts to the backs of their necks, then flicked his left hand in Jacen's direction.

Beyond Jacen a trooper flew back, as if he'd been hit in the chest with a metric ton of transparisteel. The telekinetic blast cleared a path to Luke's side. Jacen slipped into it, keeping the gap open, then Anakin joined him. In a line the trio of Jedi fended off the soldiers, cutting them down and pressing them back toward the gap.

As their stand halted the thrust at that gap, Elegos's shuttle ruddered around and laced an inferno of laser and blaster fire into the column of Yuuzhan Vong soldiery. Jacen raised a hand to shield his eyes as row after row of little reptoids vanished in a brilliant blaze of light. Those Yuuzhan Vong soldiers untouched by the shuttle's lasers came on, but the Jedi dispatched them easily enough.

Elegos's action gained the Jedi some breathing room. Luke flicked his comlink on. "Thank you for the save, Senator."

"My fire was not effective against the larger vehicles, so I employed it where useful." The Caamasi's voice filled with gravity. "We are fortunate that the troops cannot shield themselves with voids."

Anakin laughed. "Are you joking? One good push and one would back into the void of the one behind him, and so on and so on. Pretty soon they'd be all gone."

Jacen frowned at his brother's suggestion and would have made a comment, but Luke snapped his fingers. "That's it!"

"What is it?"

"No time to explain, Jacen." Luke looked up at the shuttle. "Senator, I need a ride."

The shuttle's landing ramp descended, and Elegos brought the ship down to hover about five meters above the ground. Luke leapt up and quickly ran into the shuttle. It pulled up and headed out away from the compound.

Anakin blinked. "What did I say?"

Jacen shook his head and tightened his grip on his lightsaber. "I don't know, but I hope it works." He nodded toward the ramparts. "Until we see if it does or not, we've got work to do."

CHAPTER THIRTY-ONE

Before either Corran or Ganner could offer a new plan for escape, an explosion outside shook the giant shell building. The cloying odor of killscent wafted in and down the stairs. All around him Corran could feel slashrats gathering, coursing through the sand, looking for any morsel of food. Panic rose among the slaves, but, one by one, their weakening sense in the Force ended.

Corran slipped past Ganner and ignited his lightsaber. "Okay, Ganner, here's the new plan. You're the telekinesis champ here, so you float the students to the rear of this shell, carve yourself an exit with your lightsaber, and get them out."

"You can't possibly think, in your state, that you can beat these two."

"Immaterial, isn't it? As they say on Tatooine, when being hunted by a krayt dragon, you don't have to be faster than it is, you just have to be faster than the slowest guy in the group you're with. I'm the slow guy here, and you're getting them out."

Corran raised his left hand and extended two fingers toward the Yuuzhan Vong. He forced himself to ignore the pain and composed his face in an expression that suggested facing two Yuuzhan Vong was slightly less inconvenient than getting his beard trimmed. He bent his wrist to motion them forward, inviting them down to meet him in single combat.

The lead Yuuzhan Vong let his amphistaff coil itself around

his waist. He stepped to the side and waved his subordinate forward. The other Yuuzhan Vong, whom Corran thought of as the younger, bounced down several steps, then set himself in a pose of great martial grandeur. His amphistaff slithered down into his hand and stiffened itself.

"Ganner, I still hear you breathing back there. *Go!* Now, go! Get them aboard and get the ship out of here." Corran glanced back and gave Ganner as hard a stare as he could. "You're the only one who can save them, and I'm the only one who can buy you the time you need to do it. Go!"

The younger Jedi Knight nodded once, then gestured, and the two students rose from the floor as if on invisible stretchers. Ganner started walking backward into one of the many tunnels, with the two of them floating behind him. The younger Yuuzhan Vong came down two more steps and raised his amphistaff like a spear, ready to throw.

The elder Yuuzhan Vong hissed something, stopping his subordinate.

Corran twirled his silver lightsaber blade around in a humming circle, then moved to interpose himself between the Yuuzhan Vong and Ganner's line of retreat. "I hope you two think this is a good day to die."

The younger Yuuzhan Vong slowly stalked down the steps and spun his amphistaff in his right hand. He held his left hand out toward Corran, with his gauntleted fingers splayed out. The Yuuzhan Vong moved with the casual grace of a predator. He took one step toward Corran's left, clearly as the first part of a gambit to make Corran circle around and present his back to the elder Yuuzhan Vong.

Corran countered by stepping to his left and bringing his left hand onto the hilt of the lightsaber. The blade's hilt had been constructed long ago from the throttle assembly of a speeder bike, so it had ample length to accommodate the second hand. Corran brought his hands down toward his waist and pointed the blade at the younger Yuuzhan Vong's throat.

The Yuuzhan Vong came in with a sweeping slash at Corran's left leg. Corran blocked the cut low. The tip of his lightsaber sliced through the shell floor with ease, leaving a blackened scar between the two of them. *At least now I know Ganner can cut his way out of this place.* Corran stepped back and aimed his lightsaber at the Yuuzhan Vong again.

The Yuuzhan Vong tried the same attack a second time. Corran parried a bit higher, then pivoted on his right foot. His left foot came around in a roundhouse kick that caught the Vong in the chest. The younger warrior fell back and went down, then rolled from beneath Corran's overhand strike. That blow left another scar in the shell, but by the time Corran had pulled his blade free, the Vong had gotten up again and set himself for an attack.

Corran squared off with him, presenting his left flank for attack. He held the lightsaber's hilt up near his right ear, with the blade pointing straight forward. He leveled it at the Vong's eyes, then gave the alien a nod. "You want me, come get me."

The Yuuzhan Vong took a step forward, and Corran cranked his right wrist around. The throttle assembly twisted, swapping a diamond for an emerald in the lightsaber's interior assembly. The energy beam narrowed and went from silver to purple, then more than doubled in length. The blade's tip stabbed deep through the younger Vong's left eye socket.

The Yuuzhan Vong jerked and bounced as his limbs snapped straight. He fell back, slipping from the blade's tip, with smoke rising from his skull. He clattered to the shell floor, his limp limbs rebounding from the hard surface, then he twitched once and lay still.

And Ganner ridiculed me for having an old-style, dual-phase lightsaber. Corran returned the blade to its normal length and nodded to the elder Yuuzhan Vong. "He was too eager. I knew I could use that trick once, and only with him." The Jedi sincerely doubted the alien warrior understood what he'd said, but clearly the tone of his voice had conveyed some sort of message.

The elder Yuuzhan Vong moved down the steps with a fluid gait that was not hurried. He did not waste the effort to twirl his amphistaff, but instead held it in two hands, high right, low left, ready to fend off any long-bladed strike at his eyes. The leathery joints on his armor creaked as he moved, slowly circling. Hungry eyes watched Corran and seemed to take note of the fluid dripping from his left wrist when the Jedi let the arm hang at his side.

The elder Yuuzhan Vong stopped and set himself. He pulled both hands up above his head. The amphistaff straightened itself into a spear, with its head flattening out into a thin blade. Corran crouched low, making himself a small target, with his lightsaber held in both hands. The sizzling silver beam splashed bright highlights over the Vong's armor.

They waited.

Corran could not sense the Yuuzhan Vong through the Force, and the magnificence of the Vong warrior challenged his physical senses as well. All the other activity outside the shell vanished as Corran focused on his enemy. Despite all their differences—their nature, their origins—the two of them were shaped in the same mold. The Yuuzhan Vong had killed people Corran claimed as his own, and vice versa. Both of them were trained warriors now facing a skilled foe. Only one of them would walk away at best.

Corran suspected he would not be the one. Images of his wife and children surfaced in his brain. He made himself remember them laughing and smiling. He refused to allow images of them grieving to enter his mind. *If I am going to be lost to them and they to me, I want good memories, not bad.*

He wondered if the Yuuzhan Vong warrior was thinking the same thing, and then the Vong attacked. He slashed low and to the right. Corran parried, then lunged with his hissing blade. The Vong slipped to the right, trailing smoke from where the blade caught the armor over his right hip, then he slashed back with his amphistaff. The tip caught Corran on the right thigh, slicing through clothes and flesh, spraying blood up onto the walls.

Corran whirled, shunting the pain aside, then darted in and slashed twice at the Yuuzhan Vong's right flank. The Vong brought the amphistaff across in a vertical block and then, with a twist of his left wrist, powered the lightsaber blade up and around. Corran cocked his wrists, bringing the blade back so it almost touched the crown of his head, then lashed forward with it. The lightsaber sparked off the armor on the Vong's right shoulder.

The Yuuzhan Vong spun away from a cut at his neck, then continued the spin and slashed with a backhanded cut at Corran's knees. The Jedi leapt above it, then sliced down at the Vong's left elbow as it flashed past. The silver blade pierced the leathery joint and scored flesh, winning a hiss and a small black rivulet of blood from the Vong.

The two combatants backed off for a second, each eyeing the other. Corran could feel the warmth spreading from his leg. The Yuuzhan Vong's blood dripped down beneath the armor, forcing him to remove his gauntlet and dry his left hand against his chest. Each fighter nodded to the other, out of respect. *And out of fear, just a hint of it.*

They set themselves. The Yuuzhan Vong again raised his amphistaff above his head. Corran lowered the tip of his blade, letting it point at one of the Vong's knees. He drew in a deep breath, then shifted his shoulders. *This is it.*

War cries echoed within the chamber as each fighter sprinted across the floor at his foe. Corran ducked his head, letting the amphistaff flash past over his right shoulder. His lightsaber slipped into the space between the Yuuzhan Vong's knees, then Corran brought both hands up. The silver blade split the armored joint at the Vong's right hip. Corran sawed the blade forward and back once, lifting as he went, then spun away to the left.

Inexplicably his spin went out of control, and he crashed to the ground. He felt a moment of pain in his back, near his spine, then his legs went numb. His lightsaber skittered from his hand, scoring a small circle in the shell. Corran landed hard on his back, but avoided smashing his head into the ground.

Fear and urgency pounded him. He tried to sit up, but couldn't. Past his feet he saw the Yuuzhan Vong's amphistaff coiled near its master, hissing, flashing fangs, and he knew in an instant what had happened to him. He reached his right

hand beneath his back and felt the torn cloth, the nasty bite
mark. His hand came away slick with blood. *Venom, too, I
have no doubt. The numbness is spreading.*

The Yuuzhan Vong stirred, posting his body up on his
hands. He gathered his left knee beneath him and tried to
straighten up. He pushed off with his hands and almost made
it upright, but his right leg swung awkwardly around. The
weight of it pulled the Vong off balance and crashed him
down to the ground again. The Vong's helmet popped off and
danced across the floor.

His leg is all but severed and he's still coming? Corran
dragged himself over toward his lightsaber and got his right
hand on it. *If only these things didn't cauterize the cuts they
make, he'd bleed to death.*

The Yuuzhan Vong rolled onto his belly and grabbed his
amphistaff. He started to crawl toward Corran. The Jedi
Knight slashed at him with the silver lightsaber, gouging
chunks from the shell. His strikes chewed the floor into
rubble, spraying up sand from below, but the Vong seemed
undaunted by Corran's weak attacks.

He knows the venom will get me. Corran already felt the
numbness spreading up his back. It was becoming harder for
him to breathe. He tried to use the Force to limit the damage,
restrict blood flow, but the best techniques for that would
drop him into a trance. *And the Vong will kill me.*

Corran pushed himself back and back, leaving a bloody
red smear on the floor. He slashed again and again at the
Yuuzhan Vong, but the warrior kept coming, slowly, certainly, waiting for Corran's arm to tire, his fingers to lose all
sensation. *And he won't have long to wait.*

Corran's breathing became labored. His chest heaved with
every effort. He knew he was done and again called to himself images of his family. Happy images. Images that made
him proud. He saw them through various times and situations, flashing finally on his most recent and strongest memories of them.

He reached out through the Force in one last desperate
gamble. He half closed his eyes and let his smile slacken. The

Yuuzhan Vong, with the help of his amphistaff, had risen to his good left leg. The warrior stared down at him, his bare face all scrunched up, uneven teeth and uneven features giving Corran a nightmare image to carry with him into eternity.

Then a frenzied explosion of slashrats burst up through the holes Corran had gouged in the shell's floor. One of the toothy rodents sank its teeth into the Vong's left forearm, crushing it as if it were an eggshell. Two others bit into the nearly severed right leg and tugged, dragging the Yuuzhan Vong out of Corran's sight.

If the Vong screamed—and Corran decided he never would have—the sounds of snarling slashrats fighting over his body drowned it out completely.

With a smile on his face, Corran pushed himself back as best he could from the killballs that were feasting on the Yuuzhan Vong warriors. With his last memory of his son, he had recalled how Valin had made the garnants attack Ganner, so he had reached out with the Force to summon the slashrats for a Yuuzhan Vong meal. The snarling, growling packs of slashrats showed how effective that strategy had been.

Corran laughed to himself and laid his head down. *Of course, now I'm dessert.* He exhaled slowly and closed his eyes before the creeping numbness would rob him of the ability to do even so simple a task. For a moment he wondered if he would fade from existence upon death, as had other Jedi, robbing the slashrats of their meal. *No matter. The others are safe and away. My work here is done.*

Before the numbness consumed him completely, he felt himself floating. He would have smiled if he could have. *So this is it. This is what it is like to die a Jedi and fade into nothingness.* Though he gave no external sign, his spirit felt buoyed, and Corran Horn passed into black oblivion a happy man.

CHAPTER
THIRTY-TWO

A whistle from Catch prompted Gavin to check his secondary monitor. The shuttle *Impervious* was moving forward, into the battle over the ground army. While the shuttle had powerful shields and weapons, it was much safer and more effective hanging back with the other ships, pouring fire into the ground troopers.

Gavin keyed his comm unit. "*Impervious,* this is Rogue Lead. What are you doing?"

Senator A'Kla's voice came back through the comm channel all serene. "Master Skywalker has a task for us, Colonel. Here he is."

"Gavin, I need two of you to make a run on the large lead vehicle down there. I need four torps, all coming in at the same flank. We'll give you the telemetry." The Jedi's voice betrayed a hint of excitement. "Can you do it?"

"As ordered, Jedi One." Gavin punched a button, bringing his squadron's tactical frequency into the channel. "Sticks, on me. A Jedi wants us to shoot a spread at the big lead vehicle out there."

"I copy, Lead, coming in on your vector now."

"Capture the telemetry data from *Impervious* and use it to shoot."

"As ordered, Lead." Jaina's voice rose a bit. "Going to drill a range."

Gavin smiled to himself. *You and me both, Sticks.* "Two and Twelve, keep the last skips off us."

Double clicks from comm units confirmed that their wingmen had heard the order and would comply with it. Gavin kicked his X-wing up onto the port S-foils, then dove and leveled out a hundred meters over the battlefield. Lines of plasma bolts stretched out toward him, but they came slowly enough that he was able to dance his fighter between them.

He dropped the aiming reticle over the slow-moving vehicle, then flipped a switch that turned control of the torpedoes' flight data to the *Impervious*. He kept his fighter pointed on target, then hit the trigger. Two proton torpedoes jetted away on azure fire, and another two came from his port. All four headed in on target.

Catch reported a gravitic anomaly, somewhat larger than most, had positioned itself to intercept the missiles. Gavin narrowed his eyes, waiting for the blast. *I hope you know what you're doing, Luke.*

Leia stalked through the refugees, occasionally glancing up to see Danni and Lando as they wove their way through groups. Once Leia discerned the people who were actually exuding terror, she told them to move toward the perimeter of the holding area. The knot of refugees slowly shrank, and Leia could feel tension beginning to intensify in the area. *Those who are left behind know we're searching for something, and they hope it isn't them.*

Lando had gotten a step ahead of Danni when the young woman gasped. She pointed at an older woman and a man of an age to be her adult son. Lando spun, bringing his blaster up, but the old woman's fingers sprouted claws. She raked her right hand up across Lando's chest, shredding his blue tunic and spinning him into a group of screaming refugees.

As the old woman came up to her full height, the ooglith masquer stretched into a parody of what she had been. Leia brought her blaster carbine around and clipped off two shots. One missed high, but the second burned through the Yuuzhan Vong's throat. His hands clutched at the wound as he went down, with black fluid and white pus flowing out between his fingers.

The Yuuzhan Vong who had masqueraded as her son dove to the right and came up from a somersault with Lando's blaster in one hand and a small child clutched to his chest with the other arm. The Yuuzhan Vong croaked at her as he pressed the blaster pistol to the blond little girl's head.

"Harm me. This dies."

The malevolence in the words could not be missed, but the lack of it coming through the Force seemed incongruous to Leia. She raised her own blaster carbine and sighted in on the Yuuzhan Vong's head. "You won't kill *just one,* so I'll take that risk."

The Yuuzhan Vong took a moment to parse Leia's words, then brought the pistol around to point it at her. Before he could pull the trigger, however, the power pack slid from the weapon and slowly tumbled to the ground. The alien's taut human mask stretched oddly as the face beneath it contorted into a surprised grimace. Leia triggered a shot that passed over the child's head and incinerated a hole through the Yuuzhan Vong's forehead.

The warrior pitched over backward, cushioning his hostage with his own body. It did take a moment for the child's terrified mother to pry her from the Yuuzhan Vong's arms, by which time the child realized she was supposed to be afraid. The little girl started crying, but the cries were muffled as her mother hugged the child tightly to her.

Leia's comlink buzzed. "Go ahead."

"Mara here. I found tracks for a half-dozen Yuuzhan Vong."

"We got two here, so there must be one more . . ."

"I got him."

"Are you hurt?"

"Some scratches. He just went to pieces, though." Levity lightened Mara's voice. "I'll stay out here and see what else I can scare up."

Leia ran over to where Danni was helping Lando sit up. The Yuuzhan Vong's claws had scratched him deeply, but

Lando seemed more concerned about the state of his shirt than he was the wounds. He held his bloodied hands out in front of him as if looking for something on which to wipe them off. He considered using his cloak for a moment, then rejected that plan.

Leia waved over two volunteers. "Get Lando to an aid station."

"I'll be fine, Leia."

"You'll be fine after we stop your leaking."

Lando nodded toward the dead Yuuzhan Vong. "Neat trick slipping the clip like that. I knew you had that in mind when you invited him to shoot toward you instead of the kid."

"Not me, Lando. Danni did the trick." Leia smiled at the young scientist. "That was very brave."

"Was it? I guess, maybe." Danni shivered. "Being that close to a Yuuzhan Vong again, I just didn't know what to do. What Jaina taught me, I tried to calm myself down, but it didn't work. I thought . . . I guess it worked, the trick."

"You saved my life, Danni. A small victory for us, and a small defeat for them." Leia sighed and looked out toward the south. *Let's hope the others can scale our victories up so we can get out of here alive.*

In *Impervious*'s cockpit, Luke pointed toward the large vehicle. "Get us closer."

"Yes, Master Skywalker."

"How's the missile telemetry coming through, Artoo?"

The little droid tootled confidently, spinning his head around to look at Luke.

A beep sounded from the droid, and Elegos glanced at a secondary monitor. "I have four torpedo launches. All are hot."

"Good."

Luke sank back into the chair and closed his eyes. He took a deep breath and reached out through the Force. He let his sense of things ride above the frayed ones' jagged profile and vectored in toward the vehicle. He got no solid sense of it directly, though a few frayed ones did appear to be housed inside. Instead he used that emptiness as a way point to search out a void, and as it formed, the black hole blossomed fully in the Force.

The void that the vehicle's dovin basals created to intercept the missiles was a gravitic anomaly that had substance in the real world. Tiny threads of the Force leaked into it as insects and birds, bats and bugs were pulled into it. Luke used their vanishing life traces and the very currents in the air that the void created to define the void. He traced its edges, knew exactly where it was, and knew how powerful it was.

He opened himself to the Force more fully than he had in years. He sought more power than he had when freeing his nephew. The Force flooded into him, at once molten-metal hot, yet as soothing as a cool rain. It swirled through him, filling every cell of his body, freeing him from fatigue, sharpening his mind.

Luke reached out with that power and latched onto the void that the Yuuzhan Vong vehicle had created. He pushed a bit, then tugged, in nanoseconds getting a feel for the power the dovin basals were able to exert to control the void. He almost smiled, since that amount of power was nothing compared to the Force, but he stopped himself short of pride in that fact.

"Artoo, juke the missiles."

R2-D2 keened sharply and fed the proton torpedoes a new set of data. The torpedoes twisted in flight and arced toward the sky, flying up and over the void. Then they turned again and fell toward the ground, aimed at the vehicle's spine.

Immediately the dovin basals started to shift the void to cover this new attack vector. Luke fed the Force into his hold on the void, thwarting them. Their pressure increased, and still Luke held it unmoving. The torpedoes got closer and closer. The dovin basals pulled harder, and when their effort reached a new peak, Luke let the void slip over toward intercepting the proton torpedoes.

The dovin basals devoted their efforts to sliding the void into place, which required both some lateral movement and shortening the arc over which the void would travel. As they brought it close to the vehicle, Luke pushed with the Force.

Since the dovin basals were already tugging the void back toward the vehicle, they were not prepared to have the travel accelerated.

The void crashed into the vehicle, striking it in midspine. The long vehicle bent backward as both ends became sucked into the black hole. It flowed like thick liquid, all the sharp horns and bony plates becoming fluid as they curved up over the void's event horizon. In less than an eye blink the vehicle had been consumed by the void, leaving a huge gap in the Yuuzhan Vong formation.

Then the proton torpedoes detonated. One after another the four missiles slammed into the ground and exploded. Their blasts scattered Yuuzhan Vong warriors and lit the night. They gouged a huge canyon across the Yuuzhan Vong line of advance, and the shock waves were such that the ground rippled even into the refugee compound. Soldiers fell on both sides of the battlefield, and ramparts collapsed.

"What now, Master Skywalker?"

Luke stared at the Caamasi for a moment, trying to reply, but a wave of exhaustion crested over him and eroded his ability to think. He shook his head, then slumped back in the chair. The Force energy he had used to help the Yuuzhan Vong destroy themselves had drained out of him completely, leaving him limp and barely able to keep his eyes open.

"Master Skywalker?"

"Do . . . what you . . . think best, Senator," Luke managed to say before the world closed in on him tight and black.

Anakin picked himself up off the ground and blinked away the flash of torpedo detonations that had ruined his night vision. He found his lightsaber and brought it to hand, then called out for his brother. "Jacen! Jacen!"

He turned to his left as he heard a reply, then lashed at the crowd of reptoids swarming over his brother. He cut one or two away, then a ripple of Force energy pulsed upward, scattering the others. Some rolled to their feet and struck wildly at him, but Anakin parried their assaults easily and replied with cuts that dropped them.

Bleeding from the nose and mouth, with his left eye slowly swelling shut, Jacen regained his feet. He extended his right hand, drawing his lightsaber to it, and in a second, thumbed the green blade to life. "That thing, that vehicle, must have been a warmaster, a command and control center. The slaves have gone mad."

All around them the reptoids swarmed over the ramparts. Many had dropped their weapons and howled, tearing at the nearest target with their claws and teeth. They did not limit their assaults to Bril'nilim's troopers, but attacked each other. It seemed less a military force than a swarm of insects pouring into the camp.

The two young Jedi moved into the flow of the reptoids. Anakin slashed right and left, cutting down Yuuzhan Vong soldiers as he went. With Jacen, he angled over to the right, clearing a path to several of Bril'nilim's troopers who had become trapped. With them in tow, they fought their way deeper into the refugee camp. Ahead of them from where the refugees had gathered, blaster fire sounded. Anakin could see errant bolts flying off in all directions, which suggested to him some confusion among the volunteers defending the refugees.

Above them the *Impervious* swooped and poured gouts of fire into the massed soldiery. Smaller blaster bolts thinned the ranks between the Jedi and the refugees. Jacen and Anakin darted forward, using their lightsabers to redirect blaster bolts away from the troopers coming with them and at reptoids. They broke into the refugee compound and fended off more reptoids, but those that had gotten through had already wrought havoc.

Blaster-burnt reptoid bodies lay everywhere, splashed with the blood of their victims. Children lay broken, and men and women stared sightlessly up at the bellies of the freighters beneath which they'd huddled. Moans and screams filled the area, sparked by the whine of blaster bolts or the sight of another reptoid face.

Leia ran to her sons, and Anakin saw she'd been wounded. "Mom, you're hurt."

"Not that badly. Elegos says the second half of the Yuuzhan Vong host is still coming. Luke can't deal with the other vehicle. The torpedoes bought us some time, though." She pointed at the freighters. "We have to get everyone aboard and out of here as fast as we can. We have to leave Dantooine."

Jacen frowned. "But there wasn't enough food for a run to another system before, and we've been here for days . . ."

Anakin looked around. "Not as many mouths to feed anymore."

His older brother hesitated for a moment. "Oh."

"It doesn't matter, boys." Leia clapped them on the shoulders. "Get started rounding people up. Get them to move. We've precious little time before we all die."

CHAPTER
THIRTY-THREE

Jaina Solo rolled her X-wing to port and leveled out for a ground-attack strafing run. Sparky switched her targeting controls over to ground-attack mode, which superimposed a targeting grid over her view of the ground. On the secondary monitor the sensors calculated the number of life signs found in each square of the grid and then colored those squares. The brightest colors meant they had the highest concentrations of life. The heads-up display likewise added these colors to the grid it displayed, but in muted tones so the pilot could still see the ground.

Jaina ruddered her X-wing around and hit the flicker trigger for the lasers. Hundreds of laser splinters shot through the night, lancing down toward the Yuuzhan Vong soldiers climbing up out of the pit the proton torpedoes had created. Some of the splinters hit nothing, others ricocheted into the air after touching armor, but most stabbed through reptoids, killing them instantly.

She pulled up, trying to climb her X-wing above the sensation of life-forms dying, but their pain and despair clung to her like mud to a boot. She detested having to slaughter so many individuals, but she also knew she had no choice. These reptoids were coming on in good order, and from the chaos that marked the refugee camp, either she killed the reptoids on the ground or they'd kill the refugees. *And my mother and brothers and Danni . . .*

Gavin's voice crackled as it came through the comm unit. "Rogues, we have a new assignment. The freighters are lifting off. We have them outbound." His voice faltered for a moment. "Each one of you picks up a freighter. Assignments coming now."

Jaina saw that she'd been attached t̶ ̶t̶h̶ ̶l̶ which she didn't mind, but it was the six̶ voy. "Sparky, give me a rundown on whi̶ operational!"

The droid came back with a grim rep̶ lighter and Captain Nevil were all that wer̶ Two flight had been reduced to Major F̶ had fared better, with Major Varth, Jaina, a̶ Anni Capstan, still alive, but the squadro̶ been cut in half. Savage Squadron was d̶ and the Toughs . . . *They're all gone . . . We̶ the skips, but at a great cost.*

Jaina keyed her comm. "Do we have ̶ nates, Colonel?"

"Solution in progress, Sticks."

She shook her head. The reason they ha̶ tooine was because they had too many peop̶ distance in hyperspace. They had no sup̶ *found supplies or . . .* She glanced at the back̶ around the camp beneath the freighters liftin̶

A lump rose in her throat. *I hope none̶* reached out with the Force to try to find̶ brothers or uncle, but she focused herself inst̶ her ship in on the shuttle's port wing and pulling for stars. *I have a mission to perform here before I worry about my family.*

"Sparky, have you received those coordinates?"

The little droid tootled as it downloaded the navigational information. Jaina's X-wing and shuttle cleared the Dantooine atmosphere before any of the other ships and moved into a high orbit around the world. The other ships followed them, lining up perfectly in an orbit that would take them from pole to pole around Dantooine.

Sparky whistled and fed the solution to Jaina's secondary monitor.

"Agamar! Just where we wanted to head anyway. And the outbound vector is coming up just on the other side of the pole . . ."

The droid shrilled, and Jaina looked out her viewport. Coming up over the edge of Dantooine's disk, sitting in the outbound vector for Agamar, was a Yuuzhan Vong cruiser. Jaina couldn't be certain that it was the one they'd already damaged, but some of the spines were broken. Worse yet, as the secondary monitor showed, the cruiser was again employing its dovin basals to create a gravitic anomaly strong enough to prevent any ship from making the jump to hyperspace.

"This is Rogue Eleven. We have a Yuuzhan Vong cruiser acting as an Interdictor again. We're going nowhere."

In the shuttle's cockpit, Leia stood between the seats her brother and Elegos occupied. "Jaina's right, that will stop us from traveling away from here."

In the distance red-gold plasma bolts started flying lazily toward the convoy. All the shots passed high. The intent of the gunners seemed clearly to be to herd the ships back down to Dantooine. *Where the ground troops can finish us.*

Luke winced and pulled himself up in the seat. "I don't know how much I can do, Leia."

She patted Luke on the shoulder. "You may not have to do it alone, Luke." Leia keyed the comm unit. "Colonel Darklighter, what do the Rogues have left in the way of proton torpedoes?"

"We have one left, Highness. We'll drop it in on the cruiser if you want. We can take our fighters in and strafe. Perhaps that will be enough to pull the interdiction field off."

Leia shook her head as Elegos pointed to new sensor traces coming up. "Negative, Rogue Leader. We have new coralskipper traces on sensor. The cruiser is launching fighters. Looks like they really *do* want us back down there."

"We'll convince them otherwise."

She shivered. "It feels to me as if Dubrillion and this fight here have all been an exercise. The Yuuzhan Vong have been learning. This Interdictor tactic is something they didn't do in the first attack on Dubrillion. They want to herd us back down there to test us again. If we try to run, we die up here. If we don't, we die down there. Either way we're dead."

Luke shook his head. "That's not certain."

Leia frowned. "How can you say that?" She gasped, then covered her mouth with a hand. "You have a vision in the Force?"

"Glimmerings."

The sensor console beeped. Elegos glanced at it, then cocked his head to the left. "Something coming out of hyperspace. Something big."

The reversion to realspace for the *Ralroost* occurred several seconds sooner than Admiral Kre'fey had intended. In the instant the white tunnel through which his ship had been traveling began to fall apart he knew at least one Yuuzhan Vong cruiser had made itself into an Interdictor. The only reason for this could be to prevent the escape of the ships that had been grounded there. *Which means I've arrived right in time.*

He glanced over at his weapons-control officer. "Tell the *Corusca Fire* to let go with everything they have. Fire for effect what we have, as well."

The black Bothan weapons-control officer snarled orders into a comm unit. Golden streaks of turbolaser fire flashed out at the Yuuzhan Vong cruiser. Blue bolts of ion cannon beams lanced down. A tremor ran through the *Ralroost* as the twenty proton torpedo launchers on board spat out their deadly missiles.

The *Corusca Fire,* which was an old *Victory*-class Star Destroyer, likewise launched all the concussion missiles it had available. Eighty rockets spiraled in at the Yuuzhan Vong cruiser, with each target evenly spaced around the enemy ship so no one void could capture more than one missile.

The gravitic anomaly that had dragged the New Republic

ships prematurely from hyperspace evaporated as the dovin basals broke off to stop the incoming missiles and laser fire. Whether because the assault just overwhelmed the available dovin basals, or the creatures had exhausted themselves creating the interdiction field, they failed to intercept all the lasers and missiles. Proton torpedoes pulverized yorik coral hull panels. Turbolasers melted plasma spines and scored long furrows in the ship's hull. More than one spine broke off and floated free in space.

The Yuuzhan Vong cruiser fired back with its plasma cannons. Red-gold gouts of energy slammed into the *Ralroost*'s shields, nibbling away at them. The golden energy coating faded, and drained away 20 percent of the shields' power as it did so, but the shields still held.

But if we have to slug it out with them, they won't hold for long. The idea of those plasma blasts getting through to melt his ship's hull sent a trickle of fear through Kre'fey's guts. *If there is no other way, however, to get the freighters out of here . . .*

The sensor officer glanced at the admiral. "Sir, the Yuuzhan Vong cruiser is pulling back. Its skips are diving for atmosphere."

A round of cheers greeted the news, but Kre'fey cut it off with a slash of his hand. "Communications, get me the *Impervious*."

"On-line, Admiral."

"This is Admiral Kre'fey. Senator, are you still in charge of my shuttle?"

"I am, Admiral. Would you like it back now?"

"I would, yes. Please bring it aboard and have your fighters recover through my dorsal recovery bay. The freighters can form up on us, and we will escort you away from here." Kre'fey smiled. "Provided your fact-finding mission is over."

"For now it is, Admiral." The Caamasi sighed. "And the senate is not going to like this report at all."

"That hardly surprises me, Senator." The Bothan admiral's violet eyes narrowed. "And it's all the more reason we make for Coruscant as fast as we can."

CHAPTER THIRTY-FOUR

Gavin Darklighter refused to give in to the aches and pains in his body. Normally he would have put them down to fatigue, but he'd been able to get plenty of rest on the journey from Dantooine to Agamar and then on to Coruscant. The fact was that he felt as rested as he ever had during his time with the squadron, yet he also knew he was engaged in one of the most difficult battles he'd ever faced with it.

And everything he had learned on the trip in to Coruscant had convinced him it was a battle that Rogue Squadron and the New Republic could not afford to lose.

Gavin, Leia Organa Solo, Admiral Traest Kre'fey, and Senator A'Kla had been summoned to a meeting of Chief of State Borsk Fey'lya's advisory council to report on what they had found. It seemed clear to Gavin that from the smug look on Fey'lya's face, and the superior airs his confederates were projecting, that they either had no clue about what was going on in the Rim—which simply wasn't possible—or were choosing not to let it deflect them from whatever schemes and plans they had in mind.

He feared the latter situation was true, and saw the New Republic's death as the logical consequence of it.

The chamber boasted a solid wall of transparisteel that provided a hypnotic tableau of Coruscant at night. Lights winking on and off, speeders sailing through the night, and the curious patterns of lights in various buildings all seemed present to distract whomever the council wanted to interrogate. The seats offered to the visitors were positioned to maximize this effect. Gavin found himself succumbing to it, but exerted the effort required to refocus himself on the New Republic's leaders.

The Caamasi senator stood in the center of the arc described by the council's table and spread his arms. "You now have heard the substance of what I will report to the senate. There is no doubt that these Yuuzhan Vong have come to this galaxy with conquest on their agenda. The assaults on Dubrillion and Dantooine were not only relentless, but clearly designed as learning exercises."

Niuk Niuv, the senator from Sullust, clucked deep in his throat for a moment. "If this is true, a lesson was taught them at Dantooine, wasn't it? You drove a cruiser off and escaped, did you not?"

Elegos nodded slowly. "We did that, yes. It seems, however, you are ignoring the evidence of Belkadan, that they have come and set up factories to produce war matériel. You ignore their operation on Bimmiel, which we know about only because the students there were evacuated to Agamar and arrived when we did."

Pwoe, the Quarren, curled and uncurled his mouth tentacles. "Three systems, four if we count Sernpidal, and five if we include Helska 4, the place where the first incursion was destroyed, but the latter two are useless to them."

"And useless to us." The Caamasi let his hand slowly drift down to his side. "You also greatly discount the sacrifices we paid to save as many people as we did. Rogue Squadron has lost two-thirds of the pilots it had two months ago. Over fifty other pilots and troopers lost their lives. The Yuuzhan Vong killed countless people on Dubrillion, and the refugees on Dantooine suffered 50 percent casualties."

Borsk Fey'lya shook his head and smoothed the cream-colored fur at the back of his neck. "We do nothing of the sort. We acknowledge the sacrifices of Colonel Darklighter's command. We have directed a unit commendation for the

Dantooine and Dubrillion actions be added to the unit history."

Gavin glanced at Admiral Kre'fey and caught the all-but-imperceptible nod that was his signal. Raising his head slowly, twisting his ring unconsciously, Gavin stared straight into Fey'lya's eyes. *Almost two decades ago you drove my Bothan lover, Asyr Sei'lar, to distraction, and that distraction got her killed. It's an old debt you owe me, and that debt gets paid back now, in full.*

"If you value our effort, Chief Fey'lya, then I have to wonder why you are working so hard to deceive me, to deceive the rest of the New Republic's military."

Fey'lya blinked, and the fur on the back of his neck rose. "You will be forgiven that insubordinate outburst, Colonel. You are clearly overwrought."

Gavin stood slowly, letting his body uncurl into its full height. His contracted his hands into fists and let the muscles of his arms strain the seams of his jacket. He wanted them to see he was physically powerful, not just someone who sat in a seat and pulled a trigger. *I want them to know I am something they could never be.*

He kept his voice even, despite the anger and disgust boiling inside of him. "Chief Fey'lya, in here we know the truth. The only reason the *Corusca Fire* was at Agamar is because Captain Rimsen is from Agamar and he diverted from his assigned patrol. He was suspicious of the fact the patrol route had been changed to prevent him from heading to Dubrillion and past Belkadan. In speaking to his family on Agamar, he learned of Leia's visit there. He returned home to assess the situation and was able to travel with Admiral Kre'fey to save us. If he had not been there, none of us would be here."

"You have misinterpreted—"

Gavin cut him off with the sharp chop of a hand through the air. "I'm not finished."

"Your career most assuredly can be, Colonel." Fey'lya's ears flattened back against his skull. "Are you resigning, effective immediately?"

Admiral Kre'fey snapped off a quick comment in Bothan that brought Fey'lya's head around as if he'd been punched. The chief of state clawed curls of wood from the table. He snarled a comment in return.

Admiral Kre'fey came smoothly to his feet. "Oh, I dare, cousin, speak to you in that manner because you have grossly overstepped your bounds in this. Did you expect we would not know of Bimmiel? Did you expect we did not know of the sightings of Yuuzhan Vong on Garqi? How many other worlds that the Yuuzhan Vong have attacked did you expect us to remain ignorant of?"

The Sullustan looked aghast. "How could you know—?"

The admiral slowly shook his head. "There are a million ways to know. Commodities found on these worlds are being bid up in the futures markets. Communications companies that service these worlds are reporting outages and reduced earnings from these sectors. Recruiting numbers for our military from these worlds are down sharply. While you might have been able to shut off the flow of real news to various outlets, doubtless to prevent a panic, you have forgotten that information that doesn't get through is just as valuable as that which does."

The members of the advisory council looked shocked. They murmured among themselves, then turned to Borsk Fey'lya. To his credit, the Bothan snorted as if what he had been told was inconsequential. "Even if these worlds are involved with the Yuuzhan Vong invasion—and you have no proof they are—the prosecution of the war against the Yuuzhan Vong is a matter for us to determine."

Gavin shook his head. "Not when it is *our* lives on the line."

"Again, Colonel Darklighter, are you quoting from a resignation letter?" Fey'lya sneered at him. "You Rogues quit the New Republic once before and we survived."

Gavin's eyes narrowed. "Perhaps I am resigning, Chief Fey'lya."

Traest Kre'fey stepped forward between Gavin and Elegos. "Beware accepting his resignation, cousin, because if he goes, so do I. So will the New Republic's military."

"You're talking mutiny."

"I'm talking the only thing that makes sense. You, you're all politicians. Your focus is on acquiring power. Why? So you can make lives better for some people. This is a laudable goal, but your efforts collapse when a true crisis arises. An earthquake shakes a continent and kills thousands. You take the blame even though it was not your fault. Why? Because you had too few regulations about how the buildings were to be maintained, or your rescue operations were too slow, your food supplies were too low, your payments to the uninsured are lower than they imagined they would get. There are hundreds and thousands of reasons you take the blame, and with each bit of blame you lose some power."

Kre'fey tapped himself on his chest. "My mandate is to keep people safe, and the Yuuzhan Vong are a direct threat to their safety. Let us assume, to be charitable, that you did not believe Princess Leia when she explained the problem of the Yuuzhan Vong to you. Let us assume you thought they truly *were* finished. Your lack of response to that threat could be explained as naive, perhaps, but a lack of response now would be *criminal*.

"So, would I take the New Republic's military and draw it off into, say, the Unknown Regions and carve out my own little empire? Yes. I would prepare it as a haven for those who flee the New Republic as it falls to the Yuuzhan Vong."

Pwoe's nostrils flared. "If you feel this way, Admiral, would you not be better off staging a revolt and unseating us?"

"No, because I am not a politician. I can't fight a war and administer worlds." He shook his head. "I cannot say I would not back someone else in toppling an ineffective government, however."

Kre'fey twisted to his left and waved a hand at Leia.

She sat forward and let a feral grin blossom on her face.

Fey'lya stood and folded his arms across his chest. "So, this is it, then, Leia? You so hate being out of power that you have seduced Admiral Kre'fey into backing you in a revolt? Do you wish to establish a Jedi hegemony to rule the New Republic? Will your children inherit your position after you?"

Leia laughed quickly and politely, then came up out of her chair with a fluid grace that reminded Gavin of a teopari stretching languidly. "Is that what you want, Chief Fey'lya? Do you want to be humiliated? Do you want to be remembered as the one who led the New Republic to such ruin that *I* had to rescue it again?"

Her voice came low enough that even Gavin had to strain to hear her. As her words poured into his ears, Fey'lya's facial expression changed. It went from a look of triumph to one of sour disappointment, then resignation. He leaned forward, posting himself up on his arms.

"How is it that you wish to play this, then?"

Leia smiled carefully. "First, you will cede control of military operations to the military. There will be no political micromanagement of the war. What they want, they get."

"Of course."

"Second, you will coordinate relief supplies and matériel to handle the incoming refugees. Agamar is already overstressed, and people will be fleeing further Coreward as the Yuuzhan Vong advance."

Fey'lya glanced at Pwoe. "You can handle all that."

"Lastly, you will allow Senator A'Kla to make his report to the full senate, with complete coverage of it to go out over the media."

Fey'lya barked a sharp laugh. "So he can put the blame for this squarely on my shoulders? Never."

Kre'fey glanced at Gavin. "In my empire, would you like a world for each of your children, or will they need whole systems to rule?"

Fey'lya's violet eyes flashed with fire. "We will work up the text of the report together, yes?"

Elegos nodded. "I find that acceptable."

"Good." Leia stepped forward and offered Fey'lya her hand. "I'd forgotten what it was like to work with you."

"Be assured, I had *not*."

Fey'lya shook Leia's hand, but the guarded expression on her face confirmed that she was thinking what Gavin could feel in his bones: Fey'lya's compliance now was not guaranteed to continue in the future. *In the short term we get what we need, but that won't always be so. If he can take advantage, he will.*

Leia bowed her head to the council. "Thank you for your cooperation. It is for the best, and that, after all, is what we all desire, isn't it?"

"Most assuredly, Leia." Borsk Fey'lya gave them all a predatory grin. "We shall put the New Republic above all petty, personal concerns. For the best."

Gavin wanted nothing more than to head home to his wife, but he knew he was going to be poor company. Too many people had died, and when he was in a mourning mood, it tended to remind his sister that her husband had died fighting the Yevetha. She had come with her children to live with Gavin at that point, just to get back on her feet, but she'd remained since. From time to time she'd get to thinking of herself and her kids as a burden on Gavin, and that was something he just couldn't deal with at the moment.

He made his way back to Rogue Squadron headquarters and stalked through darkened hallways. He really didn't mind the building being deserted; it *was* very early in the morning. Admiral Kre'fey agreed that no alert would go out until noon the next day, allowing the warriors who would be on the front lines a lazy morning before they committed their lives to the bloody grind of war.

The only real bright spot in the whole disaster of the retreat from Dubrillion had been Jaina Solo's joining the squadron. Gavin had asked Leia if her daughter might stay on with the unit, and permission had been granted cautiously. When he saw the joy on Jaina's face at the decision, Gavin suspected Leia had agreed just because she didn't want to have to deal with Jaina if she'd said no. Jaina immediately moved into the squadron barracks, taking up a room with Anni Capstan, her wingman, and settling in as if she'd belonged there all along.

And flying the way she does, there's little doubt she will remain with us for a long time.

It surprised Gavin to find a trooper with a blaster rifle standing in front of his office door. The trooper was little more than a kid—*barely older than I was when I joined the squadron.* "Is there a problem here, Private?"

The youth swallowed hard. "Sir, I tried to stop them, sir, but they said it would be okay to enter your office. They said you wouldn't mind."

Gavin blinked with astonishment. "Did they? And did they say who they were?"

The trooper shook his head. "Just some old guys, sir."

"And you let them in there? Why didn't you stop them?"

The soldier winced. "I tried, but they took my blaster away from me." He turned the weapon enough to let Gavin see that it had no power pack.

The colonel nodded. "And your comlink?"

"They took that, too. They told me to wait here for you, otherwise I'd be guilty of abandoning a post, sir."

"Yes, do that, wait right there." Gavin steered the youth to the side and opened the door to his office. He knew walking in there was foolish, but he dismissed the possibility that his visitors were assassins. The Yuuzhan Vong didn't seem to operate that way. *Besides, dying now might just be easier than fighting a war.*

The two visitors looked up from where they had seated themselves in the easy chairs. On the table before them sat three tumblers, two of which had been filled from the decanter of Corellian whiskey Gavin kept hidden in the bottom drawer of his desk. The two men smiled at him, and he began to laugh.

The trooper glanced into the room. "Are you all right, sir?"

"Yes, Private, you're dismissed."

"Here," one of the visitors said, and lofted the soldier the clip and comlink that had been appropriated from him.

Gavin closed the door behind the trooper, then shook his head. "He described you as 'two old guys.' "

"No respect among the young anymore, is there, Tycho?"

"None, Wedge, none at all. Probably the fault of the command staff."

Gavin poured himself a glass of whiskey. "What are you two doing here?"

"We heard from various sources that you're going to be going to war." Wedge Antilles raised his glass. "We're too old to fly, but not to help out. You need us, you've got us."

"You may want to reconsider that offer. This isn't going to be pretty at all."

Tycho Celchu shook his head. "War never is, Gavin. Let's just hope, together, we can make it very short."

CHAPTER
THIRTY-FIVE

Jacen Solo turned from where he had been leaning on the balcony railing and faced his little brother. "Couldn't sleep?"

Anakin shook his head as he emerged on the Solos' balcony. "Nightmares."

"Of?"

"Dantooine." Anakin rubbed sleep sand from his eyes. "I keep having this dream where I'm cutting down reptoids right and left, but it's never enough. They still overrun the refugee camp. When we get there—'cuz you're in the dream, too—we find a lot of dead people. Chewie and Dad and Mom are among them."

Jacen sighed. "That's a nasty one."

"What do you think it means?"

The older brother shook his head and turned to lean on the balcony railing. "After my experience on Belkadan, I've given up trying to figure out what dreams mean. Yours could mean anything. You're still dealing with Chewie's death. By the same token, since Mara wasn't among the dead, could be you're congratulating yourself over having saved her. I don't know."

Anakin joined his brother at the railing and stared out at the lights moving through the Coruscant cityscape. It was hard to believe a month had passed since he had left for Dantooine with Mara. "Mine is clearly a dream. Yours could have been a vision. Uncle Luke thinks it was."

"Right, but the future changed, so I got drowned and tortured." He half smiled at his brother. "And since we left Belkadan to come save you, it was probably you that set the future in motion that got me."

"So I could be dead and you'd be happy?"

"Not what I said, Anakin." Jacen caught a quick flash of sadness from his younger brother. "And Dad wouldn't be happy if you were dead, either."

Anakin snorted. "Have you seen him yet?"

"No, you?"

"No. Threepio thinks he's 'inspecting' cantinas here. Inspecting the bottom of glasses, more like."

Jacen sighed. "I'm not sure I don't envy him."

"What?"

"I'm having nightmares, too, Anakin. Nightmares of Dantooine."

"Like mine?"

"Sort of." Jacen scratched at the back of his neck with his right hand. "I'm there, like you, killing and killing and killing. I'm a gatekeeper. The reptoids really need to get to the other side of the gate, and I'm only letting them through in pieces."

"That's what you had to do."

"Did I?" Jacen ducked back as an inebriated swoop jockey buzzed them. "What we did wasn't noble, it was just butchery. While the control vehicle had them under its sway, they marched forward like droids and we just took them apart. Then, when Uncle Luke destroyed the control vehicle, they went berserk. They were beasts and we just slaughtered them."

Anakin grabbed hold of Jacen's left wrist. "But you had no choice. If you didn't kill them, they would have killed lots more refugees."

"Yes, I know that. I acknowledge it. I take responsibility for it, but I still have to ask myself what does doing that have to do with becoming a Jedi Knight?" He squeezed his eyes tightly shut. "How did that bring me closer to understanding the Force? How am I now a better Jedi Knight than I was before?"

Anakin's hand slipped from Jacen's wrist. "But the job of a Jedi is to safeguard people. There's no more noble a reason to do anything. You risked your life to save others."

"Did I? Do you honestly believe any of those reptoids could have seriously hurt us? Over half of Colonel Bril'nilim's soldiers survived that assault. They aren't Jedi. We didn't need to be using lightsabers there, Anakin. We could have been using vibroblades or simple clubs."

He turned and opened his arms. "And was saving those refugees all that special? We stopped them from dying, but to what end? Does this make them better people than those who died? Are they more noble? Will they learn from this experience and make the universe a better place?"

"I don't know, Jacen. That's the future—"

"Which is always in motion."

"Right. What I do know is that we kept some of them alive. That's enough for me."

Jacen nodded slowly. "I know it is, Anakin. I wish it was enough for me, too."

"I don't understand."

"I know." Jacen lowered his voice to a whisper as anguish poured off Anakin. "Look, Anakin, you did wonderfully on Dantooine. You learned a lot. You took good care of Mara. You kept her alive under very difficult circumstances. You really *are* a hero because of all that and everything you did to fend off the reptoids. I'm not trying to take anything away from you or what you did. I want you to understand that."

"Okay." Anakin folded his arms across his chest. "What about you?"

"That's just it. I don't know." He pressed his fingertips to his temples. "I thought that going off on my own would be the key to getting closer to the Force; but then I saw the slaves and had to act. The Force sends me a vision and I act on it, only to have things go wrong. But, from that wrong came the right of saving you and Mara on Dantooine, and being there to help hold off the reptoids. It's as if I'm walking around in a circle, circling around the goal I want. Sometimes it seems as if I need to be alone, and others I'm thrust into the heroic mold that has shaped and consumed Uncle Luke. I know there are other approaches, but I don't know if they are right for me."

Anakin frowned for a moment. "Sounds like you're trying to plot a course without knowing what your final destination is."

"Huh?"

The younger Solo boy made a circle in the air with his right index finger. "You said you were circling your goal, but you never defined it. You never said what it was. Me, I want to be a Jedi Knight, just like Uncle Luke and others before him. I don't know what you want, and I don't think you do, either."

Jacen nodded. "That's how I feel, but I think it's because I want to be something *more*. I don't know what it is, but I guess I think there's something more to the Jedi order than we've been able to recover. I know it's out there, but I don't know what it is."

"Then it could be that going off and thinking about it isn't going to get you closer to your goal."

Jacen cocked an eyebrow at Anakin. "How is it that you're so philosophical all of a sudden?"

The younger boy blushed. "On Dantooine, when Mara made me stop using the Force like a crutch, I had a lot of time to think about things. I realized I was using the Force too much. Uncle Luke uses it like an adviser or sometimes a power source. Others use it like a vibroblade, some like an opinion poll, and yet others like a whole variety of tools. I thought a lot about all that, and I guess I chose to follow in Uncle Luke's footsteps.

"That's not an easy path."

"Easy isn't for Jedi." Anakin smiled. "Of course, trying to find your own path is much more difficult. Maybe what you have to do is to walk a bit on the other paths and see how you can weave bits and pieces of them together."

Anakin's comment found echoes in Luke's admonishment that Jacen was still young and lacking in experience. *Perhaps I do need to explore more of the Jedi ways* and *get to know myself better.* He realized that while he was more judicious in his use of the Force than Anakin, he didn't really know how he would function without it. *Can I truly discover how to integrate myself with the Force if I do not know who I am without it?*

Jacen reached out and tousled his brother's hair. "Look, one thing, no matter what I think about what we did at Dantooine, I was proud to have you at my side. I don't know what I'll be in the future, Anakin, but I know you'll be a great Jedi Knight. I have confidence that you will succeed, no matter what life throws at you."

Anakin sharpened his eyes. "Are you really Jacen, or some Yuuzhan Vong in an ooglith masquer?"

Jacen threw an arm around his little brother's shoulders. "For now, I'm Jacen Solo." *What I will be in the future, however, is anyone's guess.*

CHAPTER THIRTY-SIX

"So there I was, feeling like I was floating, and I was thinking to myself, 'So, this is what it's like to die a Jedi and fade from existence like my grandfather.' " A sheepishly grinning Corran Horn toweled bacta off himself. "Then I noticed that despite the numbness I still had a touch of pain from my hand. I also realized I was being bumped around a bit, which didn't strike me as appropriate for a disembodied spirit, but I couldn't open my eyes, so I hung in for the ride."

Luke shook his head. "Which is when you discovered that Ganner had returned and was lifting you above the slashrats and out of the shell."

Corran nodded. "Yes. Against my orders he had Trista bring the *Dalliance* around, they lased the top off the big shell, and hanging from the landing ramp, Ganner pulled me up. If he hadn't . . ."

Corran's wife, Mirax, tossed Corran a robe from the hospital room's small wardrobe. "If he hadn't, he'd be running from me. It's also a good thing they stuck you in the bacta tank on the *Dalliance*. That venom would have killed you otherwise."

"Sure, but imagine their surprise if it hadn't worked." Corran gave a last rub of his hair with the towel. "They put me in, then only find torn up clothes."

Mirax arched an eyebrow at her husband. "And that is funny, *how*?"

"I would have been amused."

"The dead, apparently, find almost anything entertaining."

Luke nodded toward Mirax. "We need to know if what Dr. Pace alleged about Jedi appropriating artifacts is true. I appreciate your looking into that for me."

"Gladly, Master Skywalker." Mirax frowned. "The items I've brought you have solid pre-Empire provenance. The current anti-Jedi sentiment has depressed the collector prices on that material, while the market for Imperial trinkets is spiking. No accounting for taste, of course, or sense, but if the collectors weren't meant to be skinned, they wouldn't act like nerfs."

"Do let me know what you learn in this regard." Luke had no doubt that some Jedi were overzealous in their pursuit of things that could link the current order with the one that the Emperor had all but destroyed. *But to be stealing mementos from people . . .* "While finding items that expand our knowledge of the Jedi is important, doing it at the expense of people and the image of the Jedi is too high a price to pay."

Corran shrugged the evergreen robe on and cinched it with a black tie around his waist. "I think the attitude is that we're the Jedi and these relics belong to us, regardless of who found them. I don't agree with it, but I do understand it."

"I understand it, as well, Corran, and I'm torn. I think having the items to study is valuable, but I'm also not certain if we have the resources and expertise necessary to make the most of them." Luke stroked a hand over his jaw. "Dr. Pace and her students have the background and knowledge to be able to put a lot of this material in perspective. I think we need the help of scholars, which means we need to make certain Jedi don't see them as despoilers and thieves of our artifacts."

Mirax laughed. "Does it strike either of you as ironic, then, that the mission to Bimmiel ended up being one that stole Yuuzhan Vong artifacts out from under the Yuuzhan Vong's noses?"

"That observation had occurred to me, yes, Mirax." Luke pressed his fingertips together. "The little warning sign they left outside the ExGal facility included a skull and broken machinery, which makes me believe they consider both warnings of death."

Corran climbed up on the hospital bed and pulled a couple of pillows behind his back. "I don't understand the technophobia, either. They clearly can produce items through biological means that do everything our machines can. The only difference is that their machines are living."

"That's a significant difference, though, Corran. Perhaps, in their past, there was a war waged with droids on one side and the Yuuzhan Vong on the other. It might have almost wiped them out, so they have a pathological hatred of machines." The Jedi Master pulled a chair away from the small room's single round table and sat. "Who knows? In any event, they might actually view us as evil, since we rely on machines so much."

"If that's their attitude, they just would have loved seeing Jens going over the Yuuzhan Vong body with a digitizer and scanning microscope." Corran narrowed his eyes. "That's not the most disturbing aspect of them, however, to my mind. We have the whole slave issue. The slaves we saw were probably picked up on the Rim and once came from the New Republic. I don't recall seeing any of the reptoids you described their using on Dantooine."

"Yet you had the six Yuuzhan Vong who infiltrated the compound and tried to murder the refugees." Mirax leaned back against the transparisteel viewport through which sunlight poured. "I don't understand why they would do that if these other troops were designated to assault the compound."

Corran shrugged. "Well, could be they were like Ganner and decided to disobey orders to seek their own glory."

Luke arched an eyebrow at Corran. "You think that's why Ganner came back for you?"

"Part of his reason, yes."

"And you don't like being in his debt at all, do you?"

Corran's expression soured. "It's not as bad as being in Booster's debt, but it does rankle a bit."

"You'll get over it." Mirax gathered her long black hair at the back of her neck and twisted it into a knot. "Do you think the Yuuzhan Vong were out for personal glory, or something else?"

"Given how poorly they fought, there is no question they were inexperienced." Luke sighed. "Yet, even at that, they killed a Noghri, which isn't easy. Forensic examination of their bodies has shown very little in the way of scarring, tattooing, and broken bones that both the Bimmiel body and some of the other specimens we've had do. Either they struck out on their own, or they were given the infiltration assignment as a means for advancement, I would guess."

Corran flexed his left hand. "There is another thing I'm not sure I understand. The racks that they had the students in—and the one you've described as holding Jacen—they were designed to inflict pain. Not too much, not too little, just pain. We both saw Yuuzhan Vong slay slaves rather ruthlessly and, in my case, for sport and, yet, something more. The scarring, tattoos, and broken bones—just having come out of my last bit of bacta tank therapy may give me a bad perspective on things, but pain and recreation don't go hand in hand for me."

"The killing of slaves might not seem like recreation to the Yuuzhan Vong, just something some of them take to very well." Luke opened his arms. "We all know there are some Jedi who like using the Force more than others. As for the broken bones and the other things, you've the friend who is a Gand findsman. You know what he went through to achieve that rank among his people. Perhaps the injuries, tattoos, and scars are rank signs among the Yuuzhan Vong."

Mirax raised a hand. "Being that I make my living trading in artifacts of cultural significance, it's my sense that most of those signs remain external. The scarring and tattoos make sense, but broken bones? Especially when they destroy symmetry? It doesn't seem right to me."

Luke shrugged. "It doesn't need to seem right to us, just to the Yuuzhan Vong. Pain and scarring and the rest may serve some higher purpose in their culture. The fact that they have these rack creatures that inflict pain so exactly points that out. I don't know if you noticed it on Bimmiel, but on Belkadan, the rack holding Jacen would have easily accommodated any of the Yuuzhan Vong warriors I saw."

"Now that you mention it."

The Jedi Master continued. "I think it is very important to note that their attacks on Dubrillion and Dantooine definitely pointed toward action meant to test us and train soldiers. They're clearly intelligent and seem driven. Leia told me that Lando's assessment of the first wave of Yuuzhan Vong and the second is that the second are definitely more highly trained and skilled. This could be reflective of learning from the first series of attacks or a hint of what might come through in a third wave."

Corran sighed. "I didn't like the second wave. The idea of a third, or even a continuation of the second—I'm not looking forward to it at all."

"It doesn't please me, either, but to imagine they're just going to go away after this round of attacks is as foolish as the senate's belief that the Yuuzhan Vong would not come back after the first."

"I know, Luke, I know." Corran hugged his arms around himself. "And I'll be there, doing what you need done. Nice to know we'll have the New Republic backing us up this time."

"I agree, Corran." Luke exhaled slowly. "For the good of the galaxy, I hope that will be enough."

EPILOGUE

That looking upon his naked visage made the subordinates below tremble greatly, pleased Shedao Shai. The Yuuzhan Vong commander had opted to enter the grashal on Bimmiel without a helmet or the armored face mask that his exalted rank permitted him to wear. His baton of rank lay coiled around his right forearm. Narrower and much shorter than an amphistaff, the tsaisi belonged to the same species as its longer cousin, but remained more delicate. Its lethal employment required more skill, hence the rarity of its being granted.

Shedao Shai stood at the top of the stairway leading down into the grashal. What he saw would have sickened him, but he would give no sign of weakness to those below him. *To those beneath me.* On the floor they had larval gricha eating up sand and excreting shell material to patch over the breeches that had permitted the sandbiters to enter the shell and devour two Yuuzhan Vong warriors.

Two warriors from my family. Shedao Shai began a slow, deliberate descent of the steps, letting the heel spurs on his feet click with each footfall. He kept his pace measured and watched to see who among those below kept at their tasks or chose to look up at him as he descended. Those who did not look were feigning disinterest, which meant they hid their ambition; whereas those who watched from the first instance were fawning morons, thinking their advancement would come through means other than valor and success in combat.

Those who steal glances as they work, these are the ones who are naturally curious, but respectful and attentive to duty. He noted which they were, then selected from among them one who had chosen to oversee the ngdin as it slowly effaced any trace of the interlopers who had desecrated the grashal. He waited until his chosen one looked up, then summoned him with a single wave of a crooked finger.

The warrior scooped up the ngdin, holding the slimy creature in both hands despite the way the cilia on which it moved could deliver numbing stings to the hands. He set it down again on the grashal floor, letting it attack a scarlet smear, then dropped to one knee before his master and pounded right fist to his left shoulder.

Shedao Shai looked down at him. "You are permitted to gaze upon me, Krag Val."

"Were I worthy of that honor, Commander Shai, my tasks here would already have been completed."

Very good. The Yuuzhan Vong warrior half lidded his eyes, then nodded slowly. "I would have you tell me what happened here."

"As I am able, Commander." The warrior stood and turned to gesture at the racks. "I believe two of the humans on this world were being kept in the Embrace of Pain. Two individuals—at a minimum, two—came to free them. The cuts on the Embrace, the floor, and on the relics of your kinsmen lead me to believe these two were of the *jeedai*. In the battling I believe Neira Shai was slain first. His skull has carbon scoring inside an eye socket. Dranae Shai hurt his foe badly, but scoring on the bones of his hip joint suggests he was greatly hurt in return. I found no evidence of a killing stroke to his remains."

Krag Val's voice shrank. "Of the remains we have recovered, that is."

Fury began to build in Shedao Shai, but he kept it in check. What Krag Val reported was much the substance of the preliminary report he had been given while in transit from

Dantooine. His battles there and at Dubrillion had begun to give him a measure of his enemies. He had thought them resourceful and even courageous in cases. *I almost thought them worthy foes.* But what he learned of their conduct on Bimmiel confirmed for him that they were beyond redemption.

"This *jeedai* who left his blood here, what of his remains?"

Krag kept his eyes to the floor and clasped his hands behind his back. He bent forward, defenseless, allowing his master to strike him if he so desired. "Of him we have no remains. There is blood evidence that he may have been lifted from here and taken away."

Shedao Shai's hands curled into fists studded with horns at the knuckles. "You tell me they recovered the body of their fallen and yet left ours to be carrion for vermin?"

"This I fear, Commander."

Shedao Shai snarled, raising his right fist toward his own misshapen face. *This is the fault of Nom Anor, that gods-cursed whelp of a machine.* Nom Anor had infiltrated the New Republic and had sent back much information about the enemies the Yuuzhan Vong would face here, but he had not included all he should have. Moreover, he had made a bid for power, allowing his political faction to launch a strike at Dubrillion and Belkadan. *Had his people won those battles, he would have dictated the course of our invasion. His failures dictated my first moves, since we could not allow the shame of his defeat to linger to sully our victory. I finished his work, but now my kinsmen have paid for his deficiencies with their lives.*

The Yuuzhan Vong commander kept his voice even, despite the words coming through clenched teeth. "And of Mongei Shai?"

Krag Val sank to both knees and prostrated himself at the base of the stairs. "There is evidence, Commander, that a group of humans found the cave where he had been waiting. They . . . I fear to say it, Master . . ."

Tremors ran through Shedao Shai's body, but he kept them out of his voice. "Their crimes are not yours, Krag Val."

"They disturbed his rest, Master. They used . . . They left behind their mechanical abominations, there, where they found him."

The Yuuzhan Vong commander turned his face away from those below. The image of his grandfather's remains being pawed by these soft humans, of his being disturbed, of all evidence of his passing being destroyed—it was too much. It soured Shedao Shai's breath and thickened his saliva. Mongei Shai had, fifty years ago, been part of a team to venture forth from their worldships to this new galaxy. He had not returned with the others, remaining behind on Bimmiel to report to them via villips until the range proved too great. His sacrifice had brought honor to Domain Shai, and Shedao had hoped his cousins could heap more glory upon the family by recovering the remains.

They failed and the enemy has taken his relics. They taunt us with their audacity.

Shedao Shai again looked at his subordinates, then pressed a foot against Krag Val's head, pinning it to the floor. "Why did Neira and Dranae fail to find Mongei's remains first?"

"The old coordinates were based on this world's magnetic field. It has shifted. Their searches progressed incrementally. Fourteen revolutions from their deaths they would have found the right formation. Their conduct was above reproach."

"And without imagination." Shedao Shai gestured back toward the minshal village to the west. "The vermin destroyed the slaves?"

"It appears so, Master."

"And their remains were not recovered by the *jeedai*?"

"No, Master."

Shedao Shai removed his foot from Krag Val's head, then stepped down to the floor of the grashal. He crouched above the ngdin twitching its way along the bloody streak the *jeedai* had left on the floor. He watched it sucking up the blood, then looked past the creature at Krag Val.

"At the world they call Dantooine they did not recover their dead. These people have no sense of what is proper or honorable. That they removed this *jeedai* tells me something valuable."

Krag Val, his head still held low, glanced at Shedao Shai. "What does it tell you, Master?"

"It tells me this *jeedai* is yet alive." Shedao Shai plucked the plump ngdin from the floor and held it up. On its belly countless cilia glistened within bloodstained mucus. Shedao Shai leaned forward and bit deeply into the ngdin, tasting the blood, feeling the stings. He tore flesh from the creature and swallowed, paying no mind to the cool sensation of fluid running down over his chin.

"This *jeedai* lives, and I will again taste his blood as he dies."